THE TYRANT'S TOMB

RICK RIORDAN

PUFFIN

PUFFIN BOOKS

UK | USA | Canada | Ireland | Australia
India | New Zealand | South Africa

Puffin Books is part of the Penguin Random House group of companies
whose addresses can be found at global.penguinrandomhouse.com.

www.penguin.co.uk   www.puffin.co.uk   www.ladybird.co.uk

First published in the USA by Disney • Hyperion, an imprint of
Disney Book Group, and in Great Britain by Puffin Books 2019
This edition published 2020

003

This book is set in Danton, Gauthier FY/Fontspring;
Goudy Old Style, Goudy, Sabon/Monotype
Designed by Joann Hill

Printed and bound in Great Britain by Clays Ltd, Elcograf S.p.A.
A CIP catalogue record for this book is available from the British Library

ISBN: 978–0–141–36405–6

All correspondence to:
Puffin Books, Penguin Random House Children's
One Embassy Gardens, 8 Viaduct Gardens, London SW11 7BW

In memory of Diane Martinez,
who changed many lives for the better

The Dark Prophecy

The words that memory wrought are set to fire,
Ere new moon rises o'er the Devil's Mount.
The changeling lord shall face a challenge dire,
Till bodies fill the Tiber beyond count.

Yet southward must the sun now trace its course,
Through mazes dark to lands of scorching death
To find the master of the swift white horse
And wrest from him the crossword speaker's breath.

To westward palace must the Lester go;
Demeter's daughter finds her ancient roots.
The cloven guide alone the way does know,
To walk the path in thine own enemy's boots.

When three are known and Tiber reached alive,
'Tis only then Apollo starts to jive.

1

There is no food here
Meg ate all the Swedish Fish
Please get off my hearse

I BELIEVE IN RETURNING DEAD BODIES.

It seems like a simple courtesy, doesn't it? A warrior dies, you should do what you can to get their body back to their people for funerary rites. Maybe I'm old-fashioned. (I *am* over four thousand years old.) But I find it rude not to properly dispose of corpses.

Achilles during the Trojan War, for instance. *Total* pig. He chariot-dragged the body of the Trojan champion Hector around the walls of the city for days. Finally I convinced Zeus to pressure the big bully into returning Hector's body to his parents so he could have a decent burial. I mean, *come on*. Have a little respect for the people you slaughter.

Then there was Oliver Cromwell's corpse. I wasn't a fan of the man, but please. First, the English bury him with honours. Then they decide they hate him, so they dig him up and 'execute' his body. Then his head falls off the pike where it's been impaled for decades and gets passed around from collector to collector for almost three centuries like a disgusting souvenir snow globe. Finally, in

1960, I whispered in the ears of some influential people, *Enough, already. I am the god Apollo, and I order you to bury that thing. You're grossing me out.*

When it came to Jason Grace, my fallen friend and half-brother, I wasn't going to leave anything to chance. I would personally escort his coffin to Camp Jupiter and see him off with full honours.

That turned out to be a good call. What with the ghouls attacking us and everything.

Sunset turned San Francisco Bay into a cauldron of molten copper as our private plane landed at Oakland Airport. I say *our* private plane; the chartered trip was actually a parting gift from our friend Piper McLean and her movie-star father. (Everyone should have at least one friend with a movie-star parent.)

Waiting for us beside the runway was another surprise the McLeans must have arranged: a gleaming black hearse.

Meg McCaffrey and I stretched our legs on the tarmac while the ground crew sombrely removed Jason's coffin from the Cessna's storage bay. The polished mahogany box seemed to glow in the evening light. Its brass fixtures glinted red. I hated how beautiful it was. Death shouldn't be beautiful.

The crew loaded it into the hearse, then transferred our luggage to the back seat. We didn't have much: Meg's backpack and mine, my bow and quiver and ukulele, and a couple of sketchbooks and a poster-board diorama we'd inherited from Jason.

I signed some paperwork, accepted the flight crew's

condolences, then shook hands with a nice undertaker who handed me the keys to the hearse and walked away.

I stared at the keys, then at Meg McCaffrey, who was chewing the head off a Swedish Fish. The plane had been stocked with half a dozen tins of the squishy red candy. Not any more. Meg had single-handedly brought the Swedish Fish ecosystem to the brink of collapse.

'I'm supposed to drive?' I wondered. 'Is this a rental hearse? I'm pretty sure my New York junior driver's licence doesn't cover this.'

Meg shrugged. During our flight, she'd insisted on sprawling on the Cessna's sofa, so her dark pageboy haircut was flattened against the side of her head. One rhinestone-studded point of her cat-eye glasses poked through her hair like a disco shark fin.

The rest of her outfit was equally disreputable: floppy red high-tops, threadbare yellow leggings, and the well-loved knee-length green frock she'd got from Percy Jackson's mother. By *well-loved*, I mean the frock had been through so many battles, been washed and mended so many times, it looked less like a piece of clothing and more like a deflated hot-air balloon. Around Meg's waist was the pièce de résistance: her multi-pocketed gardening belt, because children of Demeter never leave home without one.

'I don't have a driver's licence,' she said, as if I needed a reminder that my life was presently being controlled by a twelve-year-old. 'I call shotgun.'

'Calling shotgun' didn't seem appropriate for a hearse. Nevertheless, Meg skipped to the passenger's side and climbed in. I got behind the wheel. Soon we were out of the airport and cruising north on I-880 in our rented black grief-mobile.

Ah, the Bay Area . . . I'd spent some happy times here. The vast misshapen geographic bowl was jam-packed with interesting people and places. I loved the green-and-golden hills, the fog-swept coastline, the glowing lacework of bridges, and the crazy zigzag of neighbourhoods shouldered up against one another like subway passengers at rush hour.

Back in the 1950s, I played with Dizzy Gillespie at Bop City in the Fillmore. During the Summer of Love, I hosted an impromptu jam session in Golden Gate Park with the Grateful Dead. (Lovely bunch of guys, but did they *really* need those fifteen-minute-long solos?) In the 1980s, I hung out in Oakland with Stan Burrell – otherwise known as MC Hammer – as he pioneered pop rap. I can't claim credit for Stan's music, but I *did* advise him on his fashion choices. Those gold lamé parachute pants? My idea. You're welcome, fashionistas.

Most of the Bay Area brought back good memories. But as I drove, I couldn't help glancing to the northwest – towards Marin County and the dark peak of Mount Tamalpais. We gods knew the place as Mount Othrys, seat of the Titans. Even though our ancient enemies had been cast down, their palace destroyed, I could still feel the evil pull of the place – like a magnet trying to extract the iron from my now-mortal blood.

I did my best to shake the feeling. We had other problems to deal with. Besides, we were going to Camp Jupiter – friendly territory on this side of the bay. I had Meg for backup. I was driving a hearse. What could possibly go wrong?

The Nimitz Freeway snaked through the East Bay flatlands, past warehouses and docklands, strip malls and rows of dilapidated bungalows. To our right rose downtown Oakland, its small cluster of high-rises facing off against its cooler neighbour San Francisco across the bay as if to proclaim: *We are Oakland! We exist, too!*

Meg reclined in her seat, propped her red high-tops up on the dashboard and cracked open her window.

'I like this place,' she decided.

'We just got here,' I said. 'What is it you like? The abandoned warehouses? That sign for Bo's Chicken 'N' Waffles?'

'Nature.'

'Concrete counts as nature?'

'There's trees, too. Plants flowering. Moisture in the air. The eucalyptus smells good. It's not like . . .'

She didn't need to finish her sentence. Our time in Southern California had been marked by scorching temperatures, extreme drought and raging wildfires – all thanks to the magical Burning Maze controlled by Caligula and his hate-crazed sorceress bestie, Medea. The Bay Area wasn't experiencing any of those problems. Not at the moment, anyway.

We'd killed Medea. We'd extinguished the Burning Maze. We'd freed the Erythraean Sibyl and brought relief to the mortals and withering nature spirits of Southern California.

But Caligula was still very much alive. He and his co-emperors in the Triumvirate were still intent on controlling all means of prophecy, taking over the world and writing the future in their own sadistic image. Right now, Caligula's fleet of evil luxury yachts was making its way towards San Francisco to attack Camp Jupiter. I could only imagine what sort of hellish destruction the emperor would rain down on Oakland and Bo's Chicken 'N' Waffles.

Even if we somehow managed to defeat the Triumvirate, there was still that greatest Oracle, Delphi, under the control of my old nemesis Python. How I could defeat him in my present form as a sixteen-year-old weakling, I had no idea.

But, hey. Except for that, everything was fine. The eucalyptus smelled nice.

Traffic slowed at the I-580 interchange. Apparently, California drivers didn't follow that custom of yielding to hearses out of respect. Perhaps they figured at least one of our passengers was already dead, so we weren't in a hurry.

Meg toyed with her window control, raising and lowering the glass. *Reeee. Reeee. Reeee.*

'You know how to get to Camp Jupiter?' she asked.

'Of course.'

''Cause you said that about Camp Half-Blood.'

'We got there! Eventually.'

'Frozen and half dead.'

'Look, the entrance to camp is right over there.' I waved vaguely at the Oakland Hills. 'There's a secret passage in the Caldecott Tunnel or something.'

'Or something?'

'Well, I haven't actually ever *driven* to Camp Jupiter,' I admitted. 'Usually I descend from the heavens in my glorious sun chariot. But I know the Caldecott Tunnel is the main entrance. There's probably a sign. Perhaps a *demigods only* lane.'

Meg peered at me over the top of her glasses. 'You're the dumbest god ever.' She raised her window with a final *reeee SHLOOMP!* – a sound that reminded me uncomfortably of a guillotine blade.

We turned northeast onto Highway 24. The congestion eased as the hills loomed closer. The elevated lanes soared past neighbourhoods of winding streets and tall conifers, white stucco houses clinging to the sides of grassy ravines.

A road sign promised CALDECOTT TUNNEL ENTRANCE, 2 MI. That should have comforted me. Soon, we'd pass through the borders of Camp Jupiter into a heavily guarded, magically camouflaged valley where an entire Roman legion could shield me from my worries, at least for a while.

Why, then, were the hairs on the back of my neck quivering like sea worms?

Something was wrong. It dawned on me that the uneasiness I'd felt since we landed might not be the distant threat of Caligula or the old Titan base on Mount Tamalpais, but something more immediate . . . something malevolent, and getting closer.

I glanced in the rear-view mirror. Through the back window's gauzy curtains, I saw nothing but traffic. But then, in the polished surface of Jason's coffin lid, I caught the reflection of movement from a dark shape outside – as if a human-size object had just flown past the hearse.

'Oh, Meg?' I tried to keep my voice even. 'Do you see anything unusual behind us?'

'Unusual like what?'

THUMP.

The hearse lurched as if we'd been hitched to a trailer full of scrap metal. Above my head, two foot-shaped impressions appeared in the upholstered ceiling.

'Something just landed on the roof,' Meg deduced.

'Thank you, Sherlock McCaffrey! Can you get it off?'

'Me? How?'

That was an annoyingly fair question. Meg could turn the rings on her middle fingers into wicked gold swords, but if she summoned them in close quarters, like the interior of the hearse, she a) wouldn't have room to wield them, and b) might end up impaling me and/or herself.

CREAK. CREAK. The footprint impressions deepened as the thing adjusted its weight like a surfer on a board. It must have been immensely heavy to sink into the metal roof.

A whimper bubbled in my throat. My hands trembled on the steering wheel. I yearned for my bow and quiver in the back seat, but I couldn't have used them. DWSPW, driving while shooting projectile weapons, is a big no-no, kids.

'Maybe you can open the window,' I said to Meg. 'Lean out and tell it to go away.'

'Um, no.' (Gods, she was stubborn.) 'What if you try to shake it off?'

Before I could explain that this was a terrible idea while travelling at fifty miles an hour on a highway, I heard a sound like a pop-top aluminium can opening – the crisp, pneumatic hiss of air through metal. A claw punctured the ceiling – a grimy white talon the size of a drill bit. Then another. And another. And another, until the upholstery was studded with ten pointy white spikes – just the right number for two very large hands.

'Meg?' I yelped. 'Could you –?'

I don't know how I might have finished that sentence. *Protect me? Kill that thing? Check in the back to see if I have any spare undies?*

I was rudely interrupted by the creature ripping open our roof like we were a birthday present.

Staring down at me through the ragged hole was a withered, ghoulish humanoid, its blue-black hide glistening like the skin of a housefly, its eyes filmy white orbs, its bared teeth dripping saliva. Around its torso fluttered a loincloth of greasy black feathers. The smell coming off it was more putrid than any dumpster – and, believe me, I'd fallen into a few.

'FOOD!' it howled.

'Kill it!' I yelled at Meg.

'Swerve!' she countered.

One of the many annoying things about being incarcerated in my puny mortal body: I was Meg McCaffrey's servant. I was bound to obey her direct commands. So when she yelled, 'Swerve,' I yanked the steering wheel hard to the right. The hearse handled beautifully. It careened across three lanes of traffic, barrelled straight through the guardrail and plummeted into the canyon below.

2

Dude, this isn't cool
Dude just tried to eat my dude
That's my dead dude, dude

I LIKE FLYING CARS. I prefer it when the car is actually capable of flight, however.

As the hearse achieved zero gravity, I had a few microseconds to appreciate the scenery below – a lovely little lake edged with eucalyptus trees and walking trails, and a small beach on the far shore, where a cluster of evening picnickers relaxed on blankets.

Oh, good, some small part of my brain thought. *Maybe we'll at least land in the water.*

Then we dropped – not towards the lake, but towards the trees.

A sound like Luciano Pavarotti's high C in *Don Giovanni* issued from my throat. My hands glued themselves to the wheel.

As we plunged into the eucalypti, the ghoul disappeared from our roof – almost as if the tree branches had purposefully swatted it away. Other branches seemed to bend around the hearse, slowing our fall, dropping us from one leafy cough-drop-scented bough to another until we hit the ground on all four wheels with a jarring *thud*. Too late to do any good, the airbags deployed, shoving my head against the backrest.

Yellow amoebas danced in my eyes. The taste of blood stung my throat. I clawed for the door handle, squeezed my way out between the airbag and the seat, and tumbled onto a bed of cool soft grass.

'Blergh,' I said.

I heard Meg retching somewhere nearby. At least that meant she was still alive. About ten feet to my left, water lapped at the shore of the lake. Directly above me, near the top of the largest eucalyptus tree, our ghoulish blue-black friend was snarling and writhing, trapped in a cage of branches.

I struggled to sit up. My nose throbbed. My sinuses felt like they were packed with menthol rub. 'Meg?'

She staggered into view around the front of the hearse. Ring-shaped bruises were forming around her eyes – no doubt courtesy of the passenger-side airbag. Her glasses were intact but askew. 'You suck at swerving.'

'Oh my gods!' I protested. 'You *ordered* me to –' My brain faltered. 'Wait. How are we alive? Was that *you* who bent the tree branches?'

'Duh.' She flicked her hands, and her twin golden *sica* blades flashed into existence. Meg used them like ski poles to steady herself. 'They won't hold that monster much longer. Get ready.'

'What?' I yelped. 'Wait. No. Not ready!'

I pulled myself to my feet with the driver's-side door.

Across the lake, the picnickers had risen from their blankets. I suppose a hearse falling from the sky had got their attention. My vision was blurry, but something seemed odd about the group . . . Was one of them wearing armour? Did another have goat legs?

Even if they were friendly, they were much too far away to help.

I limped to the back door and yanked it open. Jason's coffin appeared safe and secure in the rear bay. I grabbed my bow and quiver. My ukulele had vanished somewhere under the back seat. I would have to do without it.

Above, the creature howled, thrashing in its branch cage.

Meg stumbled. Her forehead was beaded with sweat. Then the ghoul broke free and hurtled downward, landing only a few yards away. I hoped the creature's legs might break on impact, but no such luck. It took a few steps, its feet punching wet craters in the grass, before it straightened and snarled, its pointy white teeth like tiny mirror-image picket fences.

'KILL AND EAT!' it screamed.

What a lovely singing voice. The ghoul could've fronted any number of Norwegian death-metal groups.

'Wait!' My voice was shrill. 'I – I know you.' I wagged my finger, as if that might crank-start my memory. Clutched in my other hand, my bow shook. The arrows rattled in my quiver. 'H-hold on, it'll come to me!'

The ghoul hesitated. I've always believed that most sentient creatures like to be recognized. Whether we are gods, people or slavering ghouls in vulture-feather loincloths, we enjoy others knowing who we are, speaking our names, appreciating that we exist.

Of course, I was just trying to buy time. I hoped Meg would catch her breath, charge the creature and slice it into putrid-ghoul pappardelle. At the moment, though, it didn't seem that she was capable of using her swords for anything but crutches. I supposed controlling gigantic trees could be tiring, but honestly, couldn't she have waited to run out of steam until *after* she killed Vulture Diaper?

Wait. Vulture Diaper . . . I took another look at the ghoul: its strange mottled blue-and-black hide, its milky eyes, its oversize mouth and tiny nostril slits. It smelled of rancid meat. It wore the feathers of a carrion eater . . .

'I *do* know you,' I realized. 'You're a *eurynomos*.'

I dare you to try saying *You're a eurynomos* when your tongue is leaden, your body is shaking from terror, and you've just been punched in the face by a hearse's airbag.

The ghoul's lips curled. Silvery strands of saliva dripped from its chin. 'YES! FOOD SAID MY NAME!'

'B-but you're a corpse-eater!' I protested. 'You're supposed to be in the Underworld, working for Hades!'

The ghoul tilted its head as if trying to remember the words *Underworld* and *Hades*. It didn't seem to like them as much as *kill* and *eat*.

'HADES GAVE ME OLD DEAD!' it shouted. 'THE MASTER GIVES ME FRESH!'

'The master?'

'THE MASTER!'

I really wished Vulture Diaper wouldn't scream. It didn't have any visible ears, so perhaps it had poor volume control. Or maybe it just wanted to spray that gross saliva over as large a radius as possible.

'If you mean Caligula,' I ventured, 'I'm sure he's made you all sorts of promises, but I can tell you, Caligula is *not* –'

'HA! STUPID FOOD! CALIGULA IS NOT THE MASTER!'

'Not the master?'

'NOT THE MASTER!'

'MEG!' I shouted. Ugh. Now *I* was doing it.

'Yeah?' Meg wheezed. She looked fierce and warlike as she granny-walked towards me with her sword-crutches. 'Gimme. Minute.'

It was clear she would not be taking the lead in this particular fight. If I let Vulture Diaper anywhere near her, it would kill her, and I found that idea ninety-five percent unacceptable.

'Well, eurynomos,' I said, 'whoever your master is, you're not killing and eating anyone today!'

I whipped an arrow from my quiver. I nocked it in my bow and took aim, as I had done literally millions of times before – but it wasn't quite as impressive with my hands shaking and my knees wobbling.

Why do mortals tremble when they're scared, anyway? It seems so counterproductive. If *I* had created humans, I would have given them steely determination and super-human strength during moments of terror.

The ghoul hissed, spraying more spit.

'SOON THE MASTER'S ARMIES WILL RISE AGAIN!' it bellowed. 'WE WILL FINISH THE JOB! I WILL SHRED FOOD TO THE BONE, AND FOOD WILL JOIN US!'

Food will join us? My stomach experienced a sudden loss of cabin pressure. I remembered why Hades loved these eurynomoi so much. The slightest cut from their claws caused a wasting disease in mortals. And when those mortals died, they rose again as what the Greeks called *vrykolakai* – or, in TV parlance, zombies.

That wasn't the worst of it. If a eurynomos managed to devour the flesh from a corpse, right down to the bones, that skeleton would reanimate as the fiercest, toughest kind of undead warrior. Many of them served as Hades's elite palace guards, which was a job I did *not* want to apply for.

'Meg?' I kept my arrow trained on the ghoul's chest. 'Back away. Do not let this thing scratch you.'

'But –'

'Please,' I begged. 'For once, trust me.'

Vulture Diaper growled. 'FOOD TALKS TOO MUCH! HUNGRY!'

It charged me.

I shot.

The arrow found its mark – the middle of the ghoul's chest – but it bounced off like a rubber mallet against metal. The Celestial bronze point must have hurt, at least. The ghoul yelped and stopped in its tracks, a steaming, puckered wound on its sternum. But the monster was still very much alive. Perhaps if I managed twenty or thirty shots at that exact same spot, I could do some real damage.

With trembling hands, I nocked another arrow. 'Th-that was just a warning!' I bluffed. 'The next one will kill!'

Vulture Diaper made a gurgling noise deep in its throat.

I hoped it was a delayed death rattle. Then I realized it was only laughing. 'WANT ME TO EAT DIFFERENT FOOD FIRST? SAVE YOU FOR DESSERT?'

It uncurled its claws, gesturing towards the hearse.

I didn't understand. I refused to understand. Did it want to eat the airbags? The upholstery?

Meg got it before I did. She screamed in rage.

The creature was an eater of the dead. We were driving a hearse.

'NO!' Meg shouted. 'Leave him alone!'

She lumbered forward, raising her swords, but she was in no shape to face the ghoul. I shouldered her aside, putting myself between her and the eurynomos, and fired my arrows again and again.

They sparked off the monster's blue-black hide, leaving steaming, annoyingly non-lethal wounds. Vulture Diaper staggered towards me, snarling in pain, its body twitching from the impact of each hit.

It was five feet away.

Two feet away, its claws splayed to shred my face.

Somewhere behind me, a female voice shouted, 'HEY!'

The sound distracted Vulture Diaper just long enough for me to fall courageously on my butt. I scrambled away from the ghoul's claws.

Vulture Diaper blinked, confused by its new audience. About ten feet away, a ragtag assortment of fauns and dryads, perhaps a dozen in total, were all attempting to hide behind one gangly pink-haired young woman in Roman legionnaire armour.

The girl fumbled with some sort of projectile weapon.

Oh, dear. A *manubalista*. A Roman heavy crossbow. Those things were *awful*. Slow. Powerful. Notoriously unreliable. The bolt was set. She cranked the handle, her hands shaking as badly as mine.

Meanwhile, to my left, Meg groaned in the grass, trying to get back on her feet. 'You *pushed* me,' she complained, by which I'm sure she meant, *Thank you, Apollo, for saving my life*.

The pink-haired girl raised her manubalista. With her long, wobbly legs, she reminded me of a baby giraffe. 'G-get away from them,' she ordered the ghoul.

Vulture Diaper treated her to its trademark hissing and spitting. 'MORE FOOD! YOU WILL ALL JOIN THE KING'S DEAD!'

'Dude.' One of the fauns nervously scratched his belly under his PEOPLE'S REPUBLIC OF BERKELEY T-shirt. 'That's not cool.'

'Not cool,' several of his friends echoed.

'YOU CANNOT OPPOSE ME, ROMAN!' the ghoul snarled. 'I HAVE ALREADY TASTED THE FLESH OF YOUR COMRADES! AT THE BLOOD MOON, YOU WILL JOIN THEM –'

THWUNK.

An Imperial gold crossbow bolt materialized in the centre of Vulture Diaper's chest. The ghoul's milky eyes widened in surprise. The Roman legionnaire looked just as stunned.

'Dude, you hit it,' said one of the fauns, as if this offended his sensibilities.

The ghoul crumbled into dust and vulture feathers. The bolt clunked to the ground.

Meg limped to my side. 'See? *That's* how you're supposed to kill it.'

'Oh, shut up,' I grumbled.

We faced our unlikely saviour.

The pink-haired girl frowned at the pile of dust, her chin quivering as if she might cry. She muttered, 'I *hate* those things.'

'Y-you've fought them before?' I asked.

She looked at me like this was an insultingly stupid question.

One of the fauns nudged her. 'Lavinia, dude, ask who these guys are.'

'Um, right.' Lavinia cleared her throat. 'Who are you?'

I struggled to my feet, trying to regain some composure. 'I am Apollo. This is Meg. Thank you for saving us.'

Lavinia stared. 'Apollo, as in –'

'It's a long story. We're transporting the body of our friend, Jason Grace, to Camp Jupiter for burial. Can you help us?'

Lavinia's mouth hung open. 'Jason Grace . . . is dead?'

Before I could answer, from somewhere across Highway 24 came a wail of rage and anguish.

'Um, hey,' said one of the fauns, 'don't those ghoul things usually hunt in pairs?'

Lavinia gulped. 'Yeah. Let's get you guys to camp. Then we can talk about –' she gestured uneasily at the hearse – 'who is dead, and why.'

3

I cannot chew gum
And run with a coffin at
The same time. Sue me.

HOW MANY NATURE SPIRITS does it take to carry a coffin?

The answer is unknowable, since all the dryads and fauns except one scattered into the trees as soon as they realized work was involved. The last faun would have deserted us, too, but Lavinia grabbed his wrist.

'Oh, no, you don't, Don.'

Behind his round rainbow-tinted glasses, Don the faun's eyes looked panicky. His goatee twitched – a facial tic that made me nostalgic for Grover the satyr.

(In case you're wondering, fauns and satyrs are virtually the same. Fauns are simply the Roman version, and they're not quite as good at . . . well, anything, really.)

'Hey, I'd love to help,' Don said. 'It's just I remembered this appointment –'

'Fauns don't make appointments,' Lavinia said.

'I double-parked my car –'

'You don't have a car.'

'I need to feed my dog –'

'Don!' Lavinia snapped. 'You *owe* me.'

'Okay, okay.' Don tugged his wrist free and rubbed it, his expression aggrieved. 'Look, just because I said Poison Oak *might* be at the picnic doesn't mean, you know, I *promised* she would be.'

Lavinia's face turned terracotta red. 'That's not what I meant! I've covered for you, like, a thousand times. Now you need to help me with *this*.'

She gestured vaguely at me, the hearse, the world in general. I wondered if Lavinia was new to Camp Jupiter. She seemed uncomfortable in her legionnaire armour. She kept shrugging her shoulders, bending her knees, tugging at the silver Star of David pendant that hung from her long, slender neck. Her soft brown eyes and tuft of pink hair only accentuated my first impression of her – a baby giraffe that had wobbled away from her mother for the first time and was now examining the savannah as if thinking, *Why am I here?*

Meg stumbled up next to me. She grabbed my quiver for balance, garrotting me with its strap in the process. 'Who's Poison Oak?'

'Meg,' I chided, 'that's none of our business. But if I had to guess, I'd say Poison Oak is a dryad whom Lavinia here is interested in, just like you were interested in Joshua back at Palm Springs.'

Meg barked, 'I was *not* interested –'

Lavinia chorused, 'I am *not* interested –'

Both girls fell silent, scowling at each other.

'Besides,' Meg said, 'isn't Poison Oak . . . like, poisonous?'

Lavinia splayed her fingers to the sky as if thinking, *Not that question again.* 'Poison Oak is gorgeous! Which is not to say I'd definitely go out with her –'

Don snorted. 'Whatever, dude.'

Lavinia glared crossbow bolts at the faun. 'But I'd *think* about it – if there was chemistry or whatever. Which is why I was willing to sneak away from my patrol for this *picnic*, where Don assured me –'

'Whoa, hey!' Don laughed nervously. 'Aren't we supposed to be getting these guys to camp? How about that hearse? Does it still run?'

I take back what I said about fauns not being good at anything. Don was quite adept at changing the subject.

Upon closer inspection, I saw how badly damaged the hearse was. Aside from numerous eucalyptus-scented dents and scratches, the front end had crumpled going through the guardrail. It now resembled Flaco Jiménez's accordion after I took a baseball bat to it. (Sorry, Flaco, but you played so well I got jealous, and the accordion had to die.)

'We can carry the coffin,' Lavinia suggested. 'The four of us.'

Another angry screech cut through the evening air. It sounded closer this time – somewhere just north of the highway.

'We'll never make it,' I said, 'not climbing all the way back up to the Caldecott Tunnel.'

'There's another way,' Lavinia said. 'Secret entrance to camp. A lot closer.'

'I like close,' Meg said.

'Thing is,' said Lavinia, 'I'm supposed to be on guard

duty right now. My shift is about to end. I'm not sure how long my partner can cover for me. So when we get to the camp, let me do the talking about where and how we met.'

Don shuddered. 'If anyone finds out Lavinia skipped sentry duty again –'

'Again?' I asked.

'Shut up, Don,' Lavinia said.

On one hand, Lavinia's troubles seemed trivial compared to, say, dying and getting eaten by a ghoul. On the other hand, I knew that Roman-legion punishments could be harsh. They often involved whips, chains and rabid live animals, much like an Ozzy Osbourne concert circa 1980.

'You must really like this Poison Oak,' I decided.

Lavinia grunted. She scooped up her manubalista bolt and shook it at me threateningly. 'I help you, you help me. That's the deal.'

Meg spoke for me: 'Deal. How fast can we run with a coffin?'

Not very fast, as it turned out.

After grabbing the rest of our things from the hearse, Meg and I took the back end of Jason's coffin. Lavinia and Don took the front. We did a clumsy pallbearer jog along the shoreline, me glancing nervously at the treetops, hoping no more ghouls would rain from the sky.

Lavinia promised us that the secret entrance was just across the lake. The problem was, it was *across the lake*, which meant that, not being able to pall-bear on water, we had to lug Jason's casket roughly a quarter of a mile around the shore.

'Oh, come on,' Lavinia said when I complained. 'We ran over here from the beach to help you guys. The least you can do is run back with us.'

'Yes,' I said, 'but this coffin is heavy.'

'I'm with him,' Don agreed.

Lavinia snorted. 'You guys should try marching twenty miles in full legionnaire gear.'

'No, thanks,' I muttered.

Meg said nothing. Despite her drained complexion and laboured breathing, she shouldered her side of the coffin without complaint – probably just to make me feel bad.

Finally we reached the picnic beach. A sign at the trailhead read:

LAKE TEMESCAL

SWIM AT YOUR OWN RISK

Typical of mortals: they warn you about drowning, but not about flesh-devouring ghouls.

Lavinia marched us to a small stone building that offered restrooms and a changing area. On the exterior back wall, half hidden behind blackberry bushes, stood a nondescript metal door, which Lavinia kicked open. Inside, a concrete shaft sloped down into the darkness.

'I suppose the mortals don't know about this,' I guessed.

Don giggled. 'Nah, dude, they think it's a generator room or something. Even most of the legionnaires don't know about it. Only the cool ones like Lavinia.'

'You're not getting out of helping, Don,' said Lavinia. 'Let's set down the coffin for a second.'

I said a silent prayer of thanks. My shoulders ached. My back was slick with sweat. I was reminded of the time Hera made me lug a solid-gold throne around her Olympian living room until she found exactly the right spot for it. Ugh, that goddess.

Lavinia pulled a pack of bubblegum from the pocket of her jeans. She stuffed three pieces in her mouth, then offered some to me and Meg.

'No, thanks,' I said.

'Sure,' said Meg.

'Sure!' said Don.

Lavinia jerked the bubblegum pack out of his reach. 'Don, you know bubblegum doesn't agree with you. Last time, you were hugging the toilet for days.'

Don pouted. 'But it *tastes* good.'

Lavinia peered into the tunnel, her jaw working furiously at the gum. 'It's too narrow to carry the coffin with four people. I'll lead the way. Don, you and Apollo –' she frowned as if she still couldn't believe that was my name – 'each take one end.'

'Just the two of us?' I protested.

'What he said!' Don agreed.

'Just carry it like a sofa,' said Lavinia, as if that was supposed to mean something to me. 'And you – what's your name? Peg?'

'Meg,' said Meg.

'Is there anything you don't need to bring?' asked Lavinia. 'Like . . . that poster-board thing under your arm – is that a school project?'

Meg must have been incredibly tired, because she didn't

scowl or hit Lavinia or cause geraniums to grow out of her ears. She just turned sideways, shielding Jason's diorama with her body. 'No. This is important.'

'Okay.' Lavinia scratched her eyebrow, which, like her hair, was frosted pink. 'Just stay at the back, I guess. Guard our retreat. This door can't be locked, which means –'

As if on cue, from the far side of the lake came the loudest howl yet, filled with rage, as if the ghoul had discovered the dust and vulture diaper of its fallen comrade.

'Let's go!' Lavinia said.

I began to revise my impression of our pink-haired friend. For a skittish baby giraffe, she could be *very* bossy.

We descended single-file into the passage, me carrying the back of the coffin, Don the front.

Lavinia's gum scented the stale air, so the tunnel smelled like mouldy candy floss. Every time Lavinia or Meg popped a bubble, I flinched. My fingers quickly began to ache from the weight of the casket.

'How much further?' I asked.

'We're barely inside the tunnel,' Lavinia said.

'So . . . not far, then?'

'Maybe a quarter of a mile.'

I tried for a grunt of manly endurance. It came out as more of a snivel.

'Guys,' Meg said behind me, 'we need to move faster.'

'You see something?' Don asked.

'Not yet,' Meg said. 'Just a feeling.'

Feelings. I hated those.

Our weapons provided the only light. The gold fittings of the manubalista slung across Lavinia's back cast a ghostly halo around her pink hair. The glow of Meg's swords threw our elongated shadows across either wall, so we seemed to be walking in the midst of a spectral crowd. Whenever Don looked over his shoulder, his rainbow-tinted lenses seemed to float in the dark like patches of oil on water.

My hands and forearms burned from strain, but Don didn't seem to be having any trouble. I was determined not to weep for mercy before the faun did.

The path widened and levelled out. I chose to take that as a good sign, though neither Meg nor Lavinia offered to help carry the casket.

Finally, my hands couldn't take any more. 'Stop.'

Don and I managed to set down Jason's coffin a moment before I would've dropped it. Deep red gouges marred my fingers. Blisters were beginning to form on my palms. I felt like I'd just played a nine-hour set of duelling jazz guitar with Pat Metheny, using a six-hundred-pound iron Fender Stratocaster.

'Ow,' I muttered, because I was once the god of poetry and have great descriptive powers.

'We can't rest long,' Lavinia warned. 'My sentry shift must have ended by now. My partner's probably wondering where I am.'

I almost wanted to laugh. I'd forgotten we were supposed to be worried about Lavinia playing hooky along with all our other problems. 'Will your partner report you?'

Lavinia stared into the dark. 'Not unless she has to. She's my centurion, but she's cool.'

'Your *centurion* gave you permission to sneak off?' I asked.

'Not exactly.' Lavinia tugged at her Star of David pendant. 'She just kinda turned a blind eye, you know? She gets it.'

Don chuckled. 'You mean having a crush on someone?'

'No!' Lavinia said. 'Like, just *standing* on guard duty for five hours straight. Ugh. I can't do it! Especially after all that's happened recently.'

I considered the way Lavinia fiddled with her necklace, viciously chewed her bubblegum, wobbled constantly about on her gangly legs. Most demigods have some form of attention deficit/hyperactivity disorder. They are hardwired to be in constant movement, jumping from battle to battle. But Lavinia definitely put the *H* in *ADHD*.

'When you say "all that's happened recently . . ."' I prompted, but before I could finish the question, Don's posture stiffened. His nose and goatee quivered. I'd spent enough time in the Labyrinth with Grover Underwood to know what that meant.

'What do you smell?' I demanded.

'Not sure . . .' He sniffed. 'It's close. And funky.'

'Oh.' I blushed. 'I did shower this morning, but when I exert myself, this mortal body sweats –'

'It's not that. Listen!'

Meg faced the direction we'd come from. She raised her swords and waited. Lavinia unslung her manubalista and peered into the shadows ahead of us.

Finally, over the pounding of my own heartbeat, I heard the clink of metal and the echo of footsteps on stone. Someone was running towards us.

'They're coming,' Meg said.

'No, wait,' said Lavinia. 'It's her!'

I got the feeling Meg and Lavinia were talking about two different things, and I wasn't sure I liked either one.

'Her who?' I demanded.

'Them where?' Don squeaked.

Lavinia raised her hand and shouted, 'I'm here!'

'Shhhh!' Meg said, still facing the way we'd come. 'Lavinia, what are you *doing*?'

Then, from the direction of Camp Jupiter, a young woman jogged into our circle of light.

She was about Lavinia's age, maybe fourteen or fifteen, with dark skin and amber eyes. Curly brown hair fell around her shoulders. Her legionnaire greaves and breastplate glinted over jeans and a purple T-shirt. Affixed to her breastplate was the insignia of a centurion, and strapped to her side was a *spatha* – a cavalry sword. Ah, yes . . . I recognized her from the crew of the *Argo II*.

'Hazel Levesque,' I said. 'Thank the gods.'

Hazel stopped in her tracks, no doubt wondering who I was, how I knew her, and why I was grinning like a fool. She glanced at Don, then Meg, then the coffin. 'Lavinia, what's going on?'

'Guys,' Meg interrupted. 'We have company.'

She did not mean Hazel. Behind us, at the edge of the light from Meg's swords, a dark form prowled, its blue-black skin glistening, its teeth dripping saliva. Then another, identical ghoul emerged from the gloom behind it.

Just our luck. The eurynomoi were having a *kill one*, *get two free* special.

4

Ukulele song?
No need to remove my guts
A simple 'no' works

'OH,' DON SAID IN A SMALL VOICE. 'That's what smells.'

'I thought you said they travel in pairs,' I complained.

'Or threes,' the faun whimpered. 'Sometimes in threes.'

The eurynomoi snarled, crouching just out of reach of Meg's blades. Behind me, Lavinia hand-cranked her manubalista – *click, click, click* – but the weapon was so slow to prime that she wouldn't be ready to fire until sometime next Thursday. Hazel's spatha rasped as she slid the blade from its scabbard. That, too, wasn't a great weapon for fighting at close quarters.

Meg seemed unsure whether she should charge, stand her ground or drop from exhaustion. Bless her stubborn little heart, she still had Jason's diorama wedged under her arm, which would not help her in battle.

I fumbled for a weapon and came up with my ukulele. Why not? It was only slightly more ridiculous than a spatha or a manubalista.

My nose might have been busted from the hearse's airbag, but my sense of smell was sadly unaffected. The combination of ghoul stench with the scent of bubblegum made my nostrils burn and my eyes water.

'FOOD,' said the first ghoul.

'FOOD!' agreed the second.

They sounded delighted, as if we were favourite meals they hadn't been served in ages.

Hazel spoke, calm and steady. 'Guys, we fought these things in the battle. Don't let them scratch you.'

The way she said *the battle* made it sound like there could only be one horrible event to which she might be referring. I flashed back to what Leo Valdez had told us in Los Angeles – that Camp Jupiter had suffered major damage, lost good people in their last fight. I was beginning to appreciate how bad it must have been.

'No scratches,' I agreed. 'Meg, hold them at bay. I'm going to try a song.'

My idea was simple: strum a sleepy tune, lull the creatures into a stupor, then kill them in a leisurely, civilized fashion.

I underestimated the eurynomoi's hatred of ukuleles. As soon as I announced my intentions, they howled and charged.

I shuffled backwards, sitting down hard on Jason's coffin. Don shrieked and cowered. Lavinia kept cranking her manubalista. Hazel yelled, 'Make a hole!' Which in the moment made no sense to me.

Meg burst into action, slicing an arm off one ghoul, swiping at the legs of the other, but her movements were sluggish and, with the diorama under one arm, she could only use a single sword effectively. If the ghouls had been interested in killing her, she would've been overwhelmed.

Instead, they shoved past her, intent on stopping me before I could strum a chord.

Everyone is a music critic.

'FOOD!' screamed the one-armed ghoul, lunging at me with its five remaining claws.

I tried to suck in my gut. I really did.

But, oh, cursed flab! If I had been in my godly form, the ghoul's claws never would have connected. My hammered-bronze abs would have scoffed at the monster's attempt to reach them. Alas, Lester's body failed me yet again.

The eurynomos raked its hand across my midsection, just below my ukulele. The tip of its middle finger – barely, just barely – found flesh. Its claw sliced through my shirt and across my belly like a dull razor.

I tumbled sideways off Jason's coffin, warm blood trickling into the waistline of my trousers.

Hazel Levesque yelled in defiance. She vaulted over the coffin and drove her spatha straight through the eurynomos's clavicle, creating the world's first ghoul-on-a-stick.

The eurynomos screamed and lurched backwards, ripping the spatha from Hazel's grip. The wound smoked where the Imperial gold blade had entered. Then – there is no delicate way to put it – the ghoul burst into steaming, crumbling chunks of ash. The spatha clanged to the stone floor.

The second ghoul had stopped to face Meg, as one does when one has been slashed across the thighs by an annoying twelve-year-old, but when its comrade cried out it spun to face us. This gave Meg an opening, but, instead of striking, she pushed past the monster and ran straight to my side, her blades retracting back into her rings.

'You okay?' she demanded. 'Oh, NO. You're bleeding. You *said* don't get scratched. You *got* scratched!'

I wasn't sure whether to be touched by her concern or annoyed by her tone. 'I didn't *plan* it, Meg.'

'Guys!' yelled Lavinia.

The ghoul stepped forward, positioning itself between Hazel and her fallen spatha. Don continued to cower like a champ. Lavinia's manubalista remained only half primed. Meg and I were now wedged side by side next to Jason's coffin.

That left Hazel, empty-handed, as the only obstacle between the eurynomos and a five-course meal.

The creature hissed, 'You cannot win.'

Its voice changed. Its tone became deeper, its volume modulated. 'You will join your comrades in my tomb.'

Between my throbbing head and my aching gut, I had trouble following the words, but Hazel seemed to understand.

'Who are you?' she demanded. 'How about you stop hiding behind your creatures and show yourself!'

The eurynomos blinked. Its eyes turned from milky white to a glowing purple, like iodine flames. 'Hazel Levesque. You of all people should understand the fragile boundary between life and death. But don't be afraid. I will save a special place for you at my side, along with your beloved Frank. You will make glorious skeletons.'

Hazel clenched her fists. When she glanced back at us, her expression was almost as intimidating as the ghoul's. 'Back up,' she warned us. 'As far as you can.'

Meg half dragged me to the front end of the coffin. My

gut felt like it had been stitched with a molten-hot zip. Lavinia grabbed Don by his T-shirt collar and pulled him to a safer cowering spot.

The ghoul chuckled. 'How will you defeat me, Hazel? With this?' It kicked the spatha further away behind him. 'I have summoned more undead. They will be here soon.'

Despite my pain, I struggled to get up. I couldn't leave Hazel by herself. But Lavinia put a hand on my shoulder.

'Wait,' she murmured. 'Hazel's got this.'

That seemed ridiculously optimistic, but, to my shame, I stayed put. More warm blood soaked into my underwear. At least I hoped it was blood.

The eurynomos wiped drool from its mouth with one clawed finger. 'Unless you intend to run and abandon that lovely coffin, you might as well surrender. We are strong underground, daughter of Pluto. Too strong for you.'

'Oh?' Hazel's voice remained steady, almost conversational. 'Strong underground. That's good to know.'

The tunnel shook. Cracks appeared in the walls, jagged fissures branching up the stone. Beneath the ghoul's feet, a column of white quartz erupted, skewering the monster against the ceiling and reducing it to a cloud of vulture-feather confetti.

Hazel faced us as if nothing remarkable had happened. 'Don, Lavinia, get this . . .' She looked uneasily at the coffin. 'Get this out of here. You –' she pointed at Meg – 'help your friend, please. We have healers at camp who can deal with that ghoul scratch.'

'Wait!' I said. 'Wh-what just happened? Its voice –'

'I've seen that happen before with a ghoul,' Hazel said

grimly. 'I'll explain later. Right now, get going. I'll follow in a sec.'

I started to protest, but Hazel stopped me with a shake of her head. 'I'm just going to pick up my sword and make sure no more of those things can follow us. Go!'

Rubble trickled from new cracks in the ceiling. Perhaps leaving wasn't such a bad idea.

Leaning on Meg, I managed to stagger further down the tunnel. Lavinia and Don lugged Jason's coffin. I was in so much pain I didn't even have the energy to yell at Lavinia to carry it like a couch.

We'd gone perhaps fifty feet when the tunnel behind us rumbled even more strongly than before. I looked back just in time to get hit in the face by a billowing cloud of debris.

'Hazel?' Lavinia called into the swirling dust.

A heartbeat later, Hazel Levesque emerged, coated from head to toe in glittering powdered quartz. Her sword glowed in her hand.

'I'm fine,' she announced. 'But nobody's going to be sneaking out that way any more. Now –' she pointed at the coffin – 'somebody want to tell me who's in there?'

I really didn't.

Not after I'd seen how Hazel skewered her enemies.

Still . . . I owed it to Jason. Hazel had been his friend.

I steeled my nerves, opened my mouth to speak, and was beaten to the punchline by Hazel herself.

'It's Jason,' she said, as if the information had been whispered in her ear. 'Oh, gods.'

She ran to the coffin. She fell to her knees and threw her arms across the lid. She let out a single devastated sob. Then she lowered her head and shivered in silence. Strands of her hair sketched through the quartz dust on the polished wood surface, leaving squiggly lines like the readings of a seismograph.

Without looking up, she murmured, 'I had nightmares. A boat. A man on a horse. A . . . a spear. How did it happen?'

I did my best to explain. I told her about my fall into the mortal world, my adventures with Meg, our fight aboard Caligula's yacht, and how Jason had died saving us. Recounting the story brought back all the pain and terror. I remembered the sharp ozone smell of the wind spirits swirling around Meg and Jason, the bite of zip-tie handcuffs around my wrists, Caligula's pitiless, delighted boast: *You don't walk away from me alive!*

It was all so awful, I momentarily forgot about the agonizing cut across my belly.

Lavinia stared at the floor. Meg did her best to staunch my bleeding with one of the extra dresses from her backpack. Don watched the ceiling, where a new crack was zigzagging over our heads.

'Hate to interrupt,' said the faun, 'but maybe we should continue this outside?'

Hazel pressed her fingers against the coffin lid. 'I'm so angry with you. Doing this to Piper. To us. Not letting us be there for you. What were you thinking?'

It took me a moment to realize she wasn't talking to us. She was speaking to Jason.

Slowly, she stood. Her mouth trembled. She straightened,

as if summoning internal columns of quartz to brace her skeletal system.

'Let me carry one side,' she said. 'Let's bring him home.'

We trudged along in silence, the sorriest pallbearers ever. All of us were covered in dust and monster ash. At the front of the coffin, Lavinia squirmed in her armour, occasionally glancing over at Hazel, who walked with her eyes straight ahead. She didn't even seem to notice the random vulture feather fluttering from her shirtsleeve.

Meg and Don carried the back of the casket. Meg's eyes were bruising up nicely from the car crash, making her look like a large, badly dressed raccoon. Don kept twitching, tilting his head to the left as if he wanted to hear what his shoulder was saying.

I stumbled after them, Meg's spare dress pressed against my gut. The bleeding seemed to have stopped, but the cut still burned and needled. I hoped Hazel was right about her healers being able to fix me. I did not relish the idea of becoming an extra for *The Walking Dead*.

Hazel's calmness made me uneasy. I would almost have preferred it if she'd screamed and thrown things at me. Her misery was like the cold gravity of a mountain. You could stand next to that mountain and close your eyes, and, even if you couldn't see it or hear it, you *knew* it was there – unspeakably heavy and powerful, a geological force so ancient it made even immortal gods feel like gnats. I feared what would happen if Hazel's emotions turned volcanically active.

At last we emerged into the open air. We stood on a rock promontory about halfway up a hillside, with the valley of New Rome spread out below. In the twilight, the hills had turned violet. The cool breeze smelled of wood smoke and lilacs.

'Wow,' said Meg, taking in the view.

Just as I remembered, the Little Tiber wended its way across the valley floor, making a glittering curlicue that emptied into a blue lake where the camp's belly button might have been. On the north shore of that lake rose New Rome itself, a smaller version of the original imperial city.

From what Leo had said about the recent battle, I'd expected to see the place levelled. At this distance, though, in the waning light, everything looked normal – the gleaming white buildings with red-tiled roofs, the domed Senate House, the Circus Maximus and the Colosseum.

The lake's south shore was the site of Temple Hill, with its chaotic assortment of shrines and monuments. On the summit, overshadowing everything else, was my father's impressively ego-tastic Temple of Jupiter Optimus Maximus. If possible, his Roman incarnation, Jupiter, was even more insufferable than his original Greek personality of Zeus. (And, yes, we gods have multiple personalities, because you mortals keep changing your minds about what we're like. It's exasperating.)

In the past, I'd always hated looking at Temple Hill, because my shrine wasn't the largest. Obviously, it *should* have been the largest. Now I hated looking at the place for a different reason. All I could think of was the diorama Meg was carrying, and the sketchbooks in her backpack – the designs for Temple Hill as Jason Grace had reimagined it. Compared to Jason's poster-board display, with its handwritten notes and glued-on Monopoly tokens, the real Temple Hill seemed an unworthy tribute to the gods. It could never mean as much as Jason's goodness, his fervent desire to honour *every* god and leave no one out.

I forced myself to look away.

Directly below, about half a mile from our ledge, stood Camp Jupiter itself. With its picketed walls, watchtowers and trenches, its neat rows of barracks lining two principal streets, it could have been any Roman legion camp, anywhere in the old empire, at any time during Rome's many centuries of rule. Romans were so consistent about how they built their forts – whether they meant to stay there for a night or a decade – that, if you knew one camp, you knew them all. You could wake up in the dead of night, stumble around in total darkness, and know exactly where everything was. Of course, when I visited Roman camps, I usually spent all my time in the commander's tent, lounging and eating grapes like I used to do with Commodus . . . Oh, gods, why was I torturing myself with such thoughts?

'Okay.' Hazel's voice shook me out of my reverie. 'When we get to camp, here's the story: Lavinia, you went to Temescal on my orders, because you saw the hearse go over the railing. I stayed on duty until the next shift arrived, then I rushed down to help you, because I thought you might be in danger. We fought the ghouls, saved these guys, et cetera. Got it?'

'So, about that . . .' Don interrupted, 'I'm sure you guys can manage from here, right? Seeing as you might get in trouble or whatever. I'll just be slipping off –'

Lavinia gave him a hard stare.

'Or I can stick around,' he said hastily. 'You know, happy to help.'

Hazel shifted her grip on the coffin's handle. 'Remember, we're an honour guard. No matter how bedraggled we look, we have a duty. We're bringing home a fallen comrade. Understood?'

'Yes, Centurion,' Lavinia said sheepishly. 'And, Hazel? Thanks.'

Hazel winced, as if regretting her soft heart. 'Once we get to the *principia* –' her eyes settled on me – 'our visiting god can explain to the leadership what happened to Jason Grace.'

5

Hi, everybody,
Here's a little tune I call
'All the Ways I Suck'

THE LEGION SENTRIES SPOTTED US from a long way off, as legion sentries are supposed to do.

By the time our small band arrived at the fort's main gates, a crowd had gathered. Demigods lined either side of the street and watched in curious silence as we carried Jason's coffin through the camp. No one questioned us. No one tried to stop us. The weight of all those eyes was oppressive.

Hazel led us straight down the Via Praetoria.

Some legionnaires stood on the porches of their barracks – their half-polished armour temporarily forgotten, guitars set aside, card games unfinished. Glowing purple *Lares*, the house gods of the legion, milled about, drifting through walls or people with little regard for personal space. Giant eagles whirled overhead, eyeing us like potentially tasty rodents.

I began to realize how *sparse* the crowd was. The camp seemed . . . not deserted, exactly, but only half full. A few young heroes walked on crutches. Others had arms in casts. Perhaps some of them were just in their barracks, or in the sick bay, or on an extended march, but I didn't like the haunted, grief-stricken expressions of the legionnaires who watched us.

I remembered the gloating words of the eurynomos at Lake Temescal: *I HAVE ALREADY TASTED THE FLESH OF YOUR COMRADES! AT THE BLOOD MOON, YOU WILL JOIN THEM*.

I wasn't sure what a blood moon was. Lunar things were more my sister's department. But I didn't like the sound of it. I'd had quite enough of blood. From the looks of the legionnaires, so had they.

Then I thought about something else the ghoul had said: *YOU WILL ALL JOIN THE KING'S DEAD*. I thought about the words of the prophecy we'd received in the Burning Maze, and a troubling realization started to form in my head. I did my best to suppress it. I'd already had my full day's quota of terror.

We passed the storefronts of merchants who were allowed to operate inside the fort's walls – only the most essential services, like a chariot dealership, an armoury, a gladiator supply store and a coffee bar. In front of the coffee place stood a two-headed barista, glowering at us with both faces, his green apron stained with latte foam.

Finally we reached the main intersection, where two roads came to a T in front of the principia. On the steps of the gleaming white headquarters building, the legion's praetors waited for us.

I almost didn't recognize Frank Zhang. The first time I'd seen him, back when I was a god and he was a legion newbie, Frank had been a baby-faced, heavy-set boy with dark flat-top hair and an adorable fixation on archery. He'd had this idea that I might be his father. He prayed to me all the time. Honestly, he was so cute I would've been happy to adopt him but, alas, he was one of Mars's.

The second time I saw Frank, during his voyage on the *Argo II*, he'd had a growth spurt or a magical testosterone injection or something. He'd grown taller, stronger, more imposing – though still in an adorable, cuddly, grizzly-bear sort of way.

Now, as I'd often noticed happening with young men still coming into their own, Frank's weight had begun to catch up with his growth spurt. He was once again a big, girthy guy with baby cheeks you just wanted to pinch, only now he was larger and more muscular. He'd apparently fallen out of bed and scrambled to meet us, despite it being just early evening. His hair stuck up on top like a breaking wave. One of his jean cuffs was tucked into his sock. His top was a yellow silk nightshirt decorated with eagles and bears – a fashion statement he was doing his best to cover with his purple praetor's cloak.

One thing that hadn't changed was his bearing – that slightly awkward stance, that faint perplexed frown, as if he were constantly thinking, *Am I really supposed to be here?*

That feeling was understandable. Frank had climbed the ranks from *probatio* to centurion to praetor in record time. Not since Julius Caesar had a Roman officer risen so rapidly and brightly. That wasn't a comparison I would have shared with Frank, though, given what had happened to my man Julius.

My gaze drifted to the young woman at Frank's side: Praetor Reyna Avila Ramírez-Arellano . . . and I remembered.

A bowling ball of panic formed in my heart and rolled into my lower intestines. It was a good thing I wasn't carrying Jason's coffin or I would have dropped it.

How can I explain this to you?

Have you ever had an experience so painful or embarrassing you *literally* forgot it happened? Your mind dissociates, scuttles away from the incident yelling *Nope, nope, nope*, and refuses to acknowledge the memory ever again?

That was me with Reyna Avila Ramírez-Arellano.

Oh, yes, I knew who she was. I was familiar with her name and reputation. I was fully aware we were destined to run into her at Camp Jupiter. The prophecy we'd deciphered in the Burning Maze had told me as much.

But my fuzzy mortal brain had completely refused to make the most important connection: that this Reyna was *that* Reyna, the one whose face I had been shown long ago by a certain annoying goddess of love.

That's her! my brain screamed at me, as I stood before her in my flabby and acne-spotted glory, clutching a bloody dress to my gut. *Oh, wow, she's beautiful!*

Now *you recognize her?* I mentally screamed back. *Now you want to talk about her? Can't you please forget again?*

But, like, remember what Venus said? my brain insisted. *You're supposed to stay away from Reyna or –*

Yes, I remember! Shut up!

You have conversations like this with your brain, don't you? It's completely normal, right?

Reyna was indeed beautiful and imposing. Her Imperial gold armour was cloaked in a mantle of purple. Military medals twinkled on her chest. Her dark ponytail swept over her shoulder like a horsewhip, and her obsidian eyes were every bit as piercing as those of the eagles that circled above us.

I managed to wrest my eyes from her. My face burned with humiliation. I could still hear the other gods laughing after Venus made her proclamation to me, her dire warnings if I should ever dare –

PING! Lavinia's manubalista chose that moment to crank itself another half-notch, mercifully diverting everyone's attention to her.

'Uh, s-so,' she stammered, 'we were on duty when I saw this hearse go flying over the guardrail –'

Reyna raised her hand for silence.

'Centurion Levesque.' Reyna's tone was guarded and weary, as if we weren't the first battered procession to tote a coffin into camp. 'Your report, please.'

Hazel glanced at the other pallbearers. Together, they gently lowered the casket.

'Praetors,' Hazel said, 'we rescued these travellers at the borders of camp. This is Meg.'

'Hi,' said Meg. 'Is there a bathroom? I need to pee.'

Hazel looked flustered. 'Er, in a sec, Meg. And this . . .' She hesitated, as if she couldn't believe what she was about to say. 'This is Apollo.'

The crowd murmured uneasily. I caught snatches of their conversations:

'Did she say –?'

'Not actually –'

'Dude, obviously not –'

'Named after –?'

'*In his dreams —*'

'Settle down,' Frank Zhang ordered, pulling his purple mantle tighter around his pyjama top. He studied me, perhaps looking for any sign that I was in fact Apollo, the god he'd always admired. He blinked as if the concept had short-circuited his brain.

'Hazel, can you . . . explain that?' he pleaded. 'And, erm, the coffin?'

Hazel locked her golden eyes on me, giving me a silent command: *Tell them.*

I didn't know how to start.

I was not a great orator like Julius or Cicero. I wasn't a weaver of tall tales like Hermes. (Boy, that guy can tell some whoppers.) How could I explain the many months of horrifying experiences that had led to Meg and me standing here, with the body of our heroic friend?

I looked down at my ukulele.

I thought of Piper McLean aboard Caligula's yachts – how she'd burst into singing 'Life of Illusion' in the midst of a gang of hardened mercenaries. She had rendered them helpless, entranced by her serenade about melancholy and regret.

I wasn't a charmspeaker like Piper. But I *was* a musician, and surely Jason deserved a tribute.

After what had happened with the eurynomoi, I felt skittish about my ukulele, so I began to sing *a cappella*.

For the first few bars, my voice quavered. I had no idea what I was doing. The words simply billowed up from deep inside me like the clouds of debris from Hazel's collapsed tunnel.

I sang of my fall from Olympus – how I had landed in New York and become bound to Meg McCaffrey. I sang of our time at Camp Half-Blood, where we'd discovered the Triumvirate's plot to control the great Oracles and thus the future of the world. I sang of Meg's childhood, her terrible years of mental abuse in the household of Nero, and how we'd finally driven that emperor from the Grove of Dodona. I sang of our battle against Commodus at the Waystation in Indianapolis, of our harrowing journey into Caligula's Burning Maze to free the Sibyl of Erythraea.

After each verse, I sang a refrain about Jason: his final stand on Caligula's yacht, courageously facing death so that we could survive and continue our quest. Everything we had been through led to Jason's sacrifice. Everything that might come next, if we were lucky enough to defeat the Triumvirate and Python at Delphi, would be possible because of *him*.

The song wasn't really about me at all. (I know. I could hardly believe it, either.) It was 'The Fall of Jason Grace'. In the last verses, I sang of Jason's dream for Temple Hill, his plan to add shrines until every god and goddess, no matter how obscure, was properly honoured.

I took the diorama from Meg, lifted it to show the assembled demigods, then set it on Jason's coffin like a soldier's flag.

I'm not sure how long I sang. When I finished the last line, the sky was fully dark. My throat felt as hot and dry as a spent bullet cartridge.

The giant eagles had gathered on the nearby rooftops. They stared at me with something like respect.

The legionnaires' faces were streaked with tears. Some sniffled and wiped their noses. Others embraced and wept silently.

I realized they weren't just grieving for Jason. The song had unleashed their collective sorrow about the recent battle, their losses, which – given the sparseness of the crowd – must have been extreme. Jason's song became their song. By honouring him, we honoured all the fallen.

On the steps of the principia, the praetors stirred from their private anguish. Reyna took a long, shaky breath. She exchanged a look with Frank, who was having difficulty controlling the tremble of his lower lip. The two leaders seemed to come to silent agreement.

'We will have a state funeral,' Reyna announced.

'And we'll realize Jason's dream,' Frank added. 'Those temples and – everything Ja–' His voice caught on Jason's name. He needed a count of five to compose himself. 'Everything he envisioned. We'll build it all in one weekend.'

I could feel the mood of the crowd change, as palpably as a weather front, their grief hardening into steely determination.

Some nodded and murmured assent. A few shouted, *Ave!* Hail! The rest of the crowd picked up the chant. Javelins pounded against shields.

No one baulked at the idea of rebuilding Temple Hill in a weekend. A task like that would've been impossible even for the most skilled engineering corps. But this was a Roman legion.

'Apollo and Meg will be guests of Camp Jupiter,' Reyna said. 'We will find them a place to stay –'

'And a bathroom?' Meg pleaded, dancing with her knees crossed.

Reyna managed a faint smile. 'Of course. Together, we'll mourn and honour our dead. Afterwards, we will discuss our plan of war.'

The legionnaires cheered and banged their shields.

I opened my mouth to say something eloquent, to thank Reyna and Frank for their hospitality.

But all my remaining energy had been expended on my song. My gut wound burned. My head twirled on my neck like a carousel.

I fell face-first and bit the dirt.

6

Sailing north to war
With my Shirley Temple and
Three cherries. Fear me.

OH, THE DREAMS.

Dear reader, if you are tired of hearing about my awful
prophetic nightmares, I don't blame you. Just think how *I*
felt experiencing them first-hand. It was like having the
Pythia of Delphi butt-dial me all night long, mumbling
lines of prophecy I hadn't asked for and didn't want to hear.

I saw a line of luxury yachts cutting through moonlit
waves off the California coast – fifty boats in a tight chevron
formation, strings of lights gleaming along their bows,
purple pennants snapping in the wind on illuminated comm
towers. The decks were crawling with all manner of monsters
– Cyclopes, wild centaurs, big-eared *pandai* and chest-
headed *blemmyae*. On the aft deck of each yacht, a mob of
the creatures seemed to be constructing something like a
shed or . . . or some sort of siege weapon.

My dream zoomed in on the bridge of the lead ship. The
crew hustled about, checking monitors and adjusting
instruments. Lounging behind them, in matching
gold-upholstered La-Z-Boy recliners, were two of my least
favourite people in the world.

On the left sat the emperor Commodus. His pastel-blue beach shorts showed off his perfect tanned calves and pedicured bare feet. His grey Indianapolis Colts hoodie was unzipped over his bare chest and perfectly sculpted abs. He had a lot of nerve wearing Colts gear, since we'd humiliated him in the team's home stadium only a few weeks before. (Of course we'd humiliated ourselves, too, but I wanted to forget that part.)

His face was almost as I remembered: annoyingly handsome, with a haughty chiselled profile and ringlets of golden hair framing his brow. The skin around his eyes, however, looked as if it had been sandblasted. His pupils were cloudy. The last time we'd met, I had blinded him with a burst of godly radiance, and it was obvious he still hadn't healed. That was the only thing that pleased me about seeing him again.

On the other recliner sat Gaius Julius Caesar Augustus Germanicus, otherwise known as Caligula.

Rage tinted my dream blood-pink. How could he lounge there, so relaxed in his ridiculous captain's outfit – those white slacks and boat shoes, that navy jacket over a striped collarless shirt, that officer's hat tilted at a rakish angle on his walnut curls – when only a few days before, he had killed Jason Grace? How dare he sip a refreshing iced beverage garnished with three maraschino cherries (*Three! Monstrous!*) and smile with such self-satisfaction?

Caligula looked human enough, but I knew better than to credit him with any sort of compassion. I wanted to strangle him. Alas, I could do nothing except watch and fume.

'Pilot,' Caligula called out lazily. 'What's our speed?'

'Five knots, sir,' said one of the uniformed mortals. 'Should I increase?'

'No, no.' Caligula plucked out one of the maraschino cherries and popped it in his mouth. He chewed and grinned, showing bright red teeth. 'In fact, let's slow to four knots. The journey is half the fun!'

'Yessir!'

Commodus scowled. He swirled the ice in his own drink, which was clear and bubbly with red syrup pooled at the bottom. He only had two maraschino cherries, no doubt because Caligula would never allow Commodus to equal him in anything.

'I don't understand why we're moving so slowly,' Commodus grumbled. 'At top speed, we could have been there by now.'

Caligula chuckled. 'My friend, it's all about timing. We have to allow our deceased ally his best window of attack.'

Commodus shuddered. 'I *hate* our deceased ally. Are you sure he can be controlled –'

'We've discussed this.' Caligula's singsong tone was light and airy and pleasantly homicidal, as if to say: *The next time you question me, I will control you with some cyanide in your beverage*. 'You should trust me, Commodus. Remember who aided you in your hour of need.'

'I've thanked you a dozen times already,' Commodus said. 'Besides, it wasn't my fault. How was I supposed to know Apollo still had some light left in him?' He blinked painfully. 'He got the better of you – and your horse, too.'

A cloud passed over Caligula's face. 'Yes, well, soon, we'll make things right. Between your troops and mine, we have more than enough power to overwhelm the battered Twelfth Legion. And if they prove too stubborn to surrender, we always have Plan B.' He called over his shoulder, 'Oh, Boost?'

A pandos hurried in from the aft deck, his enormous shaggy ears flopping around him like throw rugs. In his hands was a large sheet of paper, folded into sections like a map or set of instructions. 'Y-yes, Princeps?'

'Progress report.'

'Ah.' Boost's dark furry face twitched. 'Good! Good, master! Another week?'

'A week,' Caligula said.

'Well, sir, these instructions . . .' Boost turned the paper upside down and frowned at it. 'We are still locating all the "slot 'A's" on "assembly piece sevens". And they did not send us enough lug nuts. And the batteries required are not standard size, so –'

'A week,' Caligula repeated, his tone still pleasant. 'Yet the blood moon will rise in . . .'

The pandos winced. 'Five days?'

'So you can have your work done in five days? Excellent! Carry on.'

Boost gulped, then scuttled away as fast as his furry feet could carry him.

Caligula smiled at his fellow emperor. 'You see, Commodus? Soon Camp Jupiter will be ours. With luck, the Sibylline Books will be in our hands as well. Then we'll have some proper bargaining power. When it's time to face

Python and carve up our portions of the world, you'll remember who helped you . . . and who did not.'

'Oh, I'll remember. Stupid Nero.' Commodus poked the ice cubes in his drink. 'Which one is this again, the Shirley Temple?'

'No, that's the Roy Rogers,' Caligula said. 'Mine is the Shirley Temple.'

'And you're sure this is what modern warriors drink when they go into battle?'

'Absolutely,' Caligula said. 'Now enjoy the ride, my friend. You have five whole days to work on your tan and get your vision back. Then we'll have some lovely carnage in the Bay Area!'

The scene vanished, and I fell into cold darkness.

I found myself in a dimly lit stone chamber filled with shuffling, stinking, groaning undead. Some were as withered as Egyptian mummies. Others looked almost alive except for the ghastly wounds that had killed them. At the far end of the room, between two rough-hewn columns, sat . . . a presence, wreathed in a magenta haze. It raised its skeletal visage, fixing me with its burning purple eyes – the same eyes that had stared out at me from the possessed ghoul in the tunnel – and began to laugh.

My gut wound ignited like a line of gunpowder.

I woke, screaming in agony. I found myself shaking and sweating in a strange room.

'You too?' Meg asked.

She stood next to my bed, leaning out of an open window and digging in a windowbox. Her gardening belt's pockets sagged with bulbs, seed packets and tools. In one muddy hand, she held a trowel. Children of Demeter. You can't take them anywhere without them playing in the dirt.

'Wh-what's going on?' I tried to sit up, which was a mistake.

My gut wound really was a fiery line of agony. I looked down and found my bare midsection wrapped in bandages that smelled of healing herbs and ointments. If the camp's healers had already treated me, why was I still in so much pain?

'Where are we?' I croaked.

'Coffee shop.'

Even by Meg's standards, that statement seemed ridiculous.

Our room had no coffee bar, no espresso machine, no barista, no yummy pastries. It was a simple whitewashed cube with a camp bed against either wall, an open window between them and a trapdoor in the far corner, which led me to believe we were on an upper storey. We might have been in a prison cell, except there were no bars on the window, and a prison bed would have been more comfortable. (Yes, I am sure. I did some research on Folsom Prison with Johnny Cash. Long story.)

'The coffee shop is downstairs,' Meg clarified. 'This is Bombilo's spare room.'

I remembered the two-headed, green-aproned barista who had scowled at us on the Via Praetoria. I wondered why he would've been kind enough to give us lodging, and why, of all places, the legion had decided to put us here. 'Why, exactly –?'

'Lemurian spice,' Meg said. 'Bombilo had the nearest supply. The healers needed it for your wound.'

She shrugged, like, *Healers, what can you do?* Then she went back to planting iris bulbs.

I sniffed at my bandages. One of the scents I detected was indeed Lemurian spice. Effective stuff against the undead, though the Lemurian Festival wasn't until June, and it was barely April . . . Ah, no wonder we'd ended up in the coffee shop. Every year, retailers seemed to start Lemurian season earlier and earlier – Lemurian-spice lattes, Lemurian-spice muffins – as if we couldn't wait to celebrate the season of exorcising evil spirits with pastries that tasted faintly of lima beans and grave dust. Yum.

What else did I smell in that healing balm . . . crocus, myrrh, unicorn-horn shavings? Oh, these Roman healers were good. Then why didn't I feel better?

'They didn't want to move you too many times,' Meg said. 'So we just kind of stayed here. It's okay. Bathroom downstairs. And free coffee.'

'You don't drink coffee.'

'I do now.'

I shuddered. 'A caffeinated Meg. Just what I need. How long have I been out?'

'Day and a half.'

'*What?!*'

'You needed sleep. Also, you're less annoying unconscious.'

I didn't have the energy for a proper retort. I rubbed the gunk out of my eyes, then I forced myself to sit up, fighting down the pain and nausea.

Meg studied me with concern, which must have meant I looked even worse than I felt.

'How bad?' she asked.

'I'm okay,' I lied. 'What did you mean earlier, when you said, "You too"?'

Her expression closed up like a hurricane shutter. 'Nightmares. I woke up screaming a couple of times. You slept through it, but . . .' She picked a clod of dirt off her trowel. 'This place reminds me of . . . you know.'

I regretted I hadn't thought about that sooner. After Meg's experience growing up in Nero's Imperial Household, surrounded by Latin-speaking servants and guards in Roman armour, purple banners, all the regalia of the old empire – of course Camp Jupiter must have triggered unwelcome memories.

'I'm sorry,' I said. 'Did you dream . . . anything I should know about?'

'The usual.' Her tone made it clear she didn't want to elaborate. 'What about you?'

I thought about my dream of the two emperors sailing leisurely in our direction, drinking cherry-garnished mocktails while their troops rushed to assemble secret weapons they'd ordered from IKEA.

Our deceased ally. Plan B. Five days.

I saw those burning purple eyes in a chamber filled with the undead. The *king's* dead.

'The usual,' I agreed. 'Help me up?'

It hurt to stand, but if I'd been lying in that bed for a ˌnd a half, I wanted to move before my muscles turned ˌˌa. Also, I was beginning to realize I was hungry and ˌˌ, in the immortal words of Meg McCaffrey, I ˌˌ Human bodies are annoying that way.

I braced myself against the windowsill and peered outside. Below, demigods bustled along the Via Praetoria – carrying supplies, reporting for duty assignments, hurrying between the barracks and the mess hall. The pall of shock and grief seemed to have faded. Now everyone looked busy and determined. Craning my head and looking south, I could see Temple Hill abuzz with activity. Siege engines had been converted to cranes and earthmovers. Scaffolding had been erected in a dozen locations. The sounds of hammering and stone-cutting echoed across the valley. From my vantage point, I could identify at least ten new small shrines and two large temples that hadn't been there when we arrived, with more in the works.

'Wow,' I murmured. 'Those Romans don't mess around.'

'Tonight's the funeral for Jason,' Meg informed me. 'They're trying to finish work before then.'

Judging from the angle of the sun, I guessed it was about two in the afternoon. Given their pace so far, I figured that would give the legion ample time to finish Temple Hill and maybe construct a sports stadium or two before dinner.

Jason would have been proud. I wished he could have been here to see what he had inspired.

My vision fluttered and darkened. I thought I might be passing out again. Then I realized something large and dark *had* in fact fluttered right by my face, straight from the open window.

I turned and found a raven sitting on my bed. It ruffled its oily feathers, regarding me with a beady black eye. *SQUAWK!*

'Meg,' I said, 'are you seeing this?'

'Yeah.' She didn't even look up from her iris bulbs. 'Hey, Frank. What's up?'

The bird shape-shifted, its form swelling into that of a bulky human, its feathers melting into clothes, until Frank Zhang sat before us, his hair now properly washed and combed, his silk nightshirt changed for a purple Camp Jupiter tee.

'Hey, Meg,' he said, as if it were completely normal to change species during a conversation. 'Everything's on schedule. I was just checking to see if Apollo was awake, which . . . obviously, he is.' He gave me an awkward wave. 'I mean, you are. Since, er, I'm sitting on your bed. I should get up.'

He rose, tugged at his shirt, then didn't seem to know what to do with his hands. At one time, I would have been used to such nervous behaviour from mortals I encountered, but now it took me a moment to realize Frank was still in awe of me. Perhaps, being a shape-shifter, Frank was more willing than most to believe that, despite my unimpressive mortal appearance, I was still the same old god of archery inside.

You see? I told you Frank was adorable.

'Anyway,' he continued, 'Meg and I have been talking, the last day or so, while you were passed out – I mean, recovering – sleeping, you know. It's fine. You needed sleep. Hope you feel better.'

Despite how terrible I felt, I couldn't help but smile. 'You've been very kind to us, Praetor Zhang. Thank you.'

'Erm, sure. It's, you know, an honour, seeing as you're . . . or you were –'

'Ugh, Frank.' Meg turned from her windowbox. 'It's just Lester. Don't treat him like a big deal.'

'Now, Meg,' I said, 'if Frank wants to treat me like a big deal –'

'Frank, just tell him.'

The praetor glanced back and forth between us, as if making sure the Meg and Apollo Show was over for now. 'So, Meg explained the prophecy you got in the Burning Maze. *Apollo faces death in Tarquin's tomb unless the doorway to the soundless god is opened by Bellona's daughter*, right?'

I shivered. I didn't want to be reminded of those words, especially given my dreams, and the implication that I would soon face death. Been there. Done that. Got the belly wound.

'Yes,' I said warily. 'I don't suppose you've figured out what those lines mean and have already undertaken the necessary quests?'

'Um, not exactly,' Frank said. 'But the prophecy did answer a few questions about . . . well, about what's been happening around here. It gave Ella and Tyson enough information to work with. They think they might have a lead.'

'Ella and Tyson . . .' I said, sifting through my foggy mortal brain. 'The harpy and the Cyclops who have been working to reconstruct the Sibylline Books.'

'Those are the ones,' Frank agreed. 'If you're feeling up to it, I thought we could take a walk into New Rome.'

7

Nice stroll into town
Happy birthday to Lester
Here's some gift-wrapped pain

I DID NOT FEEL UP TO IT.

My gut hurt terribly. My legs could barely support my weight. Even after using the toilet, washing, dressing and grabbing a Lemurian-spice latte and a muffin from our grumpy host, Bombilo, I didn't see how I could walk the mile or so to New Rome.

I had no desire to find out more about the prophecy from the Burning Maze. I didn't want to face more impossible challenges, especially after my dream about that thing in the tomb. I didn't even want to be human. But, alas, I had no choice.

What do mortals say – *Suck it up?* I sucked it way, way up.

Meg stayed at camp. She had an appointment in an hour to feed the unicorns with Lavinia, and Meg was afraid if she went anywhere she might miss it. Given Lavinia's reputation for going AWOL, I supposed Meg's concern was valid.

Frank led me through the main gates. The sentries snapped to attention. They had to hold that pose for quite a while, since I was moving at the speed of cough syrup. I caught them studying me apprehensively – perhaps because they were worried I might launch into another heartbreaking song, or perhaps because they still couldn't believe this shambling heap of adolescence had once been the god Apollo.

The afternoon was California perfect: turquoise sky, golden grass rippling on the hillsides, eucalyptus and cedar rustling in the warm breeze. This should have dispelled any thoughts of dark tunnels and ghouls, yet I couldn't seem to get the smell of grave dust out of my nostrils. Drinking a Lemurian-spice latte did not help.

Frank walked at my speed, staying close enough for me to lean on him if I felt shaky, but not insisting on helping.

'So,' he said at last, 'what's with you and Reyna?'

I stumbled, sending fresh jabs of pain through my abdomen. 'What? Nothing. What?'

Frank brushed a raven feather off his cloak. I wondered how that worked, exactly – being left with bits and pieces after shape-shifting. Did he ever discard a spare feather and realize later, *Whoops, that was my pinky finger*? I'd heard rumours that Frank could even turn into a swarm of bees. Even I, a former god who used to transform himself all the time, had no idea how he managed that.

'It's just that . . . when you saw Reyna,' he said, 'you froze, like . . . I dunno, you realized you owed her money or something.'

I had to restrain a bitter laugh. If only my problem regarding Reyna were as simple as that.

The incident had come back to me with glass-shard

clarity: Venus scolding me, warning me, upbraiding me as only she could. *You will not stick your ugly, unworthy godly face anywhere near her, or I swear on the Styx . . .*

And of course she'd done this in the throne room, in the presence of all the other Olympians, as they howled with cruel amusement and shouted, *Ooh!* Even my father had joined in. Oh, yes. He loved every minute of it.

I shuddered.

'There is nothing *with* Reyna and me,' I said quite honestly. 'I don't think we've ever exchanged more than a few words.'

Frank studied my expression. Obviously, he realized I was holding something back, but he didn't push. 'Okay. Well, you'll see her tonight at the funeral. She's trying to get some sleep right now.'

I almost asked why Reyna would be asleep in the middle of the afternoon. Then I remembered that Frank had been wearing a pyjama shirt when we'd encountered him at dinnertime . . . Had that really been the day before yesterday?

'You're taking shifts,' I realized. 'So one of you is always on duty?'

'It's the only way,' he agreed. 'We're still on high alert. Everyone is edgy. There's so much to do since the battle . . .'

He said the word *battle* the same way Hazel had, as if it was a singular, terrible turning point in history.

Like all the divinations Meg and I had retrieved during our adventures, the Dark Prophecy's nightmarish prediction about Camp Jupiter remained burned into my mind:

The words that memory wrought are set to fire,
Ere new moon rises o'er the Devil's Mount.
The changeling lord shall face a challenge dire,
Till bodies fill the Tiber beyond count.

After hearing that, Leo Valdez had raced cross-country on his bronze dragon, hoping to warn the camp. According to Leo, he had arrived just in time, but the toll had still been horrendous.

Frank must have read my pained expression.

'It would've been worse if it hadn't been for you,' he said, which only made me feel guiltier. 'If you hadn't sent Leo here to warn us. One day, out of nowhere, he just flew right in.'

'That must have been quite a shock,' I said. 'Since you thought Leo was dead.'

Frank's dark eyes glittered like they still belonged to a raven. 'Yeah. We were so mad at him for making us worry, we lined up and took turns hitting him.'

'We did that at Camp Half-Blood, too,' I said. 'Greek minds think alike.'

'Mmm.' Frank's gaze drifted towards the horizon. 'We had about twenty-four hours to prepare. It helped. But it wasn't enough. They came from over there.'

He pointed north to the Berkeley Hills. 'They swarmed. Only way to describe it. I'd fought undead before, but this . . .' He shook his head. 'Hazel called them zombies. My grandmother would have called them *jiangshi*. The Romans have a lot of words for them: *immortuos, lamia, nuntius*.'

'*Messenger*,' I said, translating the last word. It had always seemed an odd term to me. A messenger from whom? Not Hades. He hated it when corpses wandered around the mortal world. It made him look like a sloppy warden.

'The Greeks call them vrykolakai,' I said. 'Usually, it's rare to see even one.'

'There were hundreds,' Frank said. 'Along with dozens of those other ghoul things, the eurynomoi, acting as herders. We cut them down. They just kept coming. You'd think having a fire-breathing dragon would've been a game-changer, but Festus could only do so much. The undead aren't as flammable as you might think.'

Hades had explained that to me once, in one of his famously awkward 'too much information' attempts at small talk. Flames didn't deter the undead. They just wandered right through, no matter how extra crispy they became. That's why he didn't use the Phlegethon, the River of Fire, as the boundary of his kingdom. Running water, however, especially the dark magical waters of the River Styx, was a different story . . .

I studied the glittering current of the Little Tiber. Suddenly a line of the Dark Prophecy made sense to me. '*Bodies fill the Tiber beyond count*. You stopped them at the river.'

Frank nodded. 'They don't like freshwater. That's where we turned the battle. But that line about "bodies beyond count"? It doesn't mean what you think.'

'Then what –?'

'HALT!' yelled a voice right in front of me.

I'd been so lost in Frank's story that I hadn't realized how close we were getting to the city. I hadn't even noticed the statue at the side of the road until it screamed at me.

Terminus, the god of boundaries, looked just as I remembered him. From the waist up, he was a finely sculpted man with a large nose, curly hair and a disgruntled expression (which may have been because no one had ever carved him a pair of arms). From the waist down, he was a block of white marble. I used to tease him that he should try skinny jeans, as they'd be very slimming. From the way he glowered at me now, I guessed he remembered those insults.

'Well, well,' he said. 'Who do we have here?'

I sighed. 'Terminus, can we not?'

'No!' he barked. 'No, we can*not* not. I need to see identification.'

Frank cleared his throat. 'Uh, Terminus . . .' He tapped the praetor's laurels on his breastplate.

'Yes, Praetor Frank Zhang. You are good to go. But your *friend* here –'

'Terminus,' I protested, 'you know very well who I am.'

'Identification!'

A cold slimy feeling spread outward from my Lemurian-spice-bandaged gut. 'Oh, you can't mean –'

'ID.'

I wanted to protest this unnecessary cruelty. Alas, there is no arguing with bureaucrats, traffic cops or boundary gods. Struggling would just make the pain last longer.

Slumped in defeat, I pulled out my wallet. I produced the junior driver's licence Zeus had provided me with when I fell to earth. Name: Lester Papadopoulos. Age: Sixteen. State: New York. Photo: one hundred percent eye acid.

'Hand it over,' Terminus demanded.

'You don't –' I caught myself before I could say *have hands*. Terminus was stubbornly delusional about his phantom appendages. I held up the driver's licence for him to see. Frank leaned in, curious, then caught me glaring and backed away.

'Very well, *Lester*,' Terminus crowed. 'It's unusual to have a mortal visitor in our city – an *extremely* mortal visitor – but I suppose we can allow it. Here to shop for a new toga? Or perhaps some skinny jeans?'

I swallowed back my bitterness. Is there anyone more vindictive than a minor god who finally gets to lord it over a major god?

'May we pass?' I asked.

'Any weapons to declare?'

In better times, I would have answered, *Only my killer personality*. Alas, I was beyond even finding that ironic. The question did make me wonder what had happened to my ukulele, bow and quiver, however. Perhaps they were tucked under my bed? If the Romans had somehow lost my quiver, along with the talking prophetic Arrow of Dodona, I would have to buy them a thank-you gift.

'No weapons,' I muttered.

'Very well,' Terminus decided. 'You may pass. And happy impending birthday, Lester.'

'I . . . what?'

'Move along! Next!'

There was no one behind us, but Terminus shooed us into the city, yelling at the non-existent crowd of visitors to stop pushing and form a single line.

'Is your birthday coming up?' Frank asked as we continued. 'Congratulations!'

'It shouldn't be.' I stared at my licence. 'April eighth, it says here. That can't be right. I was born on the seventh day of the seventh month. Of course, the months were different back then. Let's see, the month of Gamelion? But that was in the wintertime –'

'How do gods celebrate, anyway?' Frank mused. 'Are you seventeen now? Or four thousand and seventeen? Do you eat cake?'

He sounded hopeful about that last part, as if imagining a monstrous gold-frosted confection with seventeen Roman candles on the top.

I tried to calculate my correct day of birth. The effort made my head pound. Even when I'd had a godly memory, I hated keeping track of dates: the old lunar calendar, the Julian calendar, the Gregorian calendar, leap years, daylight saving time. Ugh. Couldn't we just call every day *Apolloday* and be done with it?

Yet Zeus had definitely assigned me a new birthdate: 8 April. Why? Seven was my sacred number. The date 8/4 had no sevens. The sum wasn't even divisible by seven. Why would Zeus mark my birthday as four days from now?

I stopped in my tracks, as if my own legs had turned into a marble pedestal. In my dream, Caligula had insisted that his pandai finish their work by the time the blood moon rose in five days. If what I observed had happened last night . . . that meant there were only four days left from today, which would make doomsday 8 April, Lester's birthday.

'What is it?' Frank asked. 'Why is your face grey?'

'I – I think my father left me a warning,' I said. 'Or perhaps a threat? And Terminus just pointed it out to me.'

'How can your birthday be a threat?'

'I'm mortal now. Birthdays are *always* a threat.' I fought down a wave of anxiety. I wanted to turn and run, but there was nowhere to go – only forward into New Rome, to gather more unwelcome information about my impending doom.

'Lead on, Frank Zhang,' I said half-heartedly, slipping my licence back in my wallet. 'Perhaps Tyson and Ella will have some answers.'

New Rome . . . the likeliest city on earth to find Olympian gods lurking in disguise. (Followed closely by New York, then Cozumel during spring break. Don't judge us.)

When I was a god, I would often hover invisibly over the red-tiled rooftops, or walk the streets in mortal form, enjoying the sights, sounds and smells of our imperial heyday.

It was not the same as Ancient Rome, of course. They'd made quite a few improvements. No slavery, for one thing. Better personal hygiene, for another. Gone was the Subura – the jam-packed slum quarter with its firetrap apartments.

Nor was New Rome a sad theme-park imitation, like a mock Eiffel Tower in the middle of Las Vegas. It was a living city where modern and ancient mixed freely. Walking through the Forum, I heard conversations in a dozen languages, Latin among them. A band of musicians held a jam session with lyres, guitars and a washboard. Children played in the fountains while adults sat nearby under trellises shaded with vines. Lares drifted here and there, becoming more visible in the long afternoon shadows. All manner of people mingled and chatted – one-headed, two-headed, even dog-headed *cynocephali* who grinned and panted and barked to make their points.

This was a smaller, kinder, much-improved Rome – the Rome we always thought mortals were capable of but never achieved. And, yes, of course we gods came here for nostalgia, to relive those wonderful centuries when mortals worshipped us freely across the empire, perfuming the air with burnt sacrifices.

That may sound pathetic to you – like an oldies concert cruise, pandering to over-the-hill fans of washed-up bands. But what can I say? Nostalgia is one ailment immortality can't cure.

As we approached the Senate House, I began to see vestiges of the recent battle. Cracks in the dome glistened with silver adhesive. The walls of some buildings had been hastily replastered. As with the camp, the city streets seemed less crowded than I remembered, and every so often – when a cynocephalus barked, or a blacksmith's hammer clanged against a piece of armour – the people nearby flinched at the noise, as if wondering whether they should seek shelter.

This was a traumatized city, trying very hard to get back to normal. And, based on what I'd seen in my dreams, New Rome was about to be re-traumatized in just a few days.

'How many people did you lose?' I asked Frank.

I was afraid to hear numbers, but I felt compelled to ask.

Frank glanced around us, checking if anyone else was within earshot. We were heading up one of New Rome's many winding cobblestone streets into the residential neighbourhoods.

'Hard to say,' he told me. 'From the legion itself, at least twenty-five. That's how many are missing from the roster. Our maximum strength is . . . *was* two hundred and fifty. Not that we actually have that many in camp at any given time, but still. The battle literally decimated us.'

I felt as if a Lar had passed through me. Decimation, the ancient punishment for bad legions, was a grim business: every tenth soldier was killed whether they were guilty or innocent.

'I'm so sorry, Frank. I should have . . .'

I didn't know how to finish that sentence. I should have what? I was no longer a god. I could no longer snap my fingers and cause zombies to explode from a thousand miles away. I had never adequately appreciated such simple pleasures.

Frank pulled his cloak tighter around his shoulders. 'It was hardest on the civilians. A lot of retired legionnaires from New Rome came out to help. They've always acted as our reserves. Anyway, that line of prophecy you mentioned: *Bodies fill the Tiber beyond count?* That didn't mean there were many bodies after the battle. It meant we couldn't count our dead, because they disappeared.'

My gut wound began to seethe. 'Disappeared how?'

'Some were dragged away when the undead retreated. We tried to get them all, but . . .' He turned up his palms. 'A few got swallowed by the ground. Even Hazel couldn't explain it. Most went underwater during the fight in the Little Tiber. The naiads tried to search and recover them for us. No luck.'

He didn't vocalize the truly horrible thing about this news, but I imagined he was thinking it. Their dead had not simply disappeared. They would be back – as enemies.

Frank kept his gaze on the cobblestones. 'I try not to dwell on it. I'm supposed to lead, stay confident, you know? But like today, when we saw Terminus . . . There's usually a little girl, Julia, who helps him out. She's about seven. Adorable kid.'

'She wasn't there today.'

'No,' Frank agreed. 'She's with a foster family. Her father and mother both died in the fight.'

It was too much. I put my hand against the nearest wall. Another innocent little girl made to suffer, like Meg McCaffrey, when Nero killed her father . . . Like Georgina, when she was taken from her mothers in Indianapolis. These three monstrous Roman emperors had shattered so many lives. I *had* to put a stop to it.

Frank took my arm gently. 'One foot in front of the other. That's the only way to do it.'

I had come here to support the Romans. Instead this Roman was supporting me.

We made our way past cafés and storefronts. I tried to focus on anything positive. The vines were in bud. The fountains still had running water. The buildings in this neighbourhood were all intact.

'At least – at least the city didn't burn,' I ventured.

Frank frowned like he didn't see the cause for optimism. 'What do you mean?'

'That other line of prophecy: *The words that memory wrought are set to fire.* That refers to Ella and Tyson's work on the Sibylline Books, doesn't it? The Books must be safe, since you prevented the city from burning.'

'Oh.' Frank made a sound somewhere between a cough and a laugh. 'Yeah, funny thing about that . . .'

He stopped in front of a quaint-looking bookshop. Painted on the green awning was the simple word LIBRI. Racks of used hardbacks were set out on the sidewalk for browsing. Inside the window, a large orange cat sunned itself atop a stack of dictionaries.

'Prophecy lines don't always mean what you think they do.' Frank rapped on the door: three sharp taps, two slow ones, then two fast ones.

Immediately, the door flew inward. Standing in the entrance was a bare-chested, grinning Cyclops.

'Come in!' said Tyson. 'I am getting a tattoo!'

8

Tattoos! Get yours now!
Free, wherever books are sold
Also, a large cat

MY ADVICE: Never enter a place where a Cyclops gets his tattoos. The odour is memorable, like a boiling vat of ink and leather purses. Cyclops skin is much tougher than human skin, requiring superheated needles to inject the ink, hence the odious burning smell.

How did I know this? I had a long, bad history with Cyclopes.

Millennia ago, I'd killed four of my father's favourites because they had made the lightning bolt that killed my son Asclepius. (And because I couldn't kill the actual murderer who was, ahem, Zeus.) That's how I got banished to earth as a mortal the first time. The stench of burning Cyclops brought back the memory of that wonderful rampage.

Then there were the countless other times I'd run into Cyclopes over the years: fighting alongside them during the First Titan War (always with a clothespeg over my nose), trying to teach them how to craft a proper bow when they had no depth perception, surprising one on the toilet in the Labyrinth during my travels with Meg and Grover. I will never get *that* image out of my head.

Mind you, I had no problem with Tyson himself. Percy Jackson had declared him a brother. After the last war against Kronos, Zeus had rewarded Tyson with the title of general and a very nice stick.

As far as Cyclopes went, Tyson was tolerable. He took up no more space than a large human. He'd never forged a lightning bolt that had killed anyone I liked. His gentle big brown eye and his broad smile made him look almost as cuddly as Frank. Best of all, he had devoted himself to helping Ella the harpy reconstruct the lost Sibylline Books.

Reconstructing lost prophecy books is always a good way to win a prophecy god's heart.

Nevertheless, when Tyson turned to lead us into the bookshop, I had to suppress a yelp of horror. It looked like he was having the complete works of Charles Dickens engraved on his back. From his neck to halfway down his back scrolled line after line of miniature bruised purple script, interrupted only by streaks of old white scar tissue.

Next to me, Frank whispered, 'Don't.'

I realized I was on the verge of tears. I was having sympathy pains from the idea of so much tattooing, and from whatever abuse the poor Cyclops had suffered to get such scars. I wanted to sob, *You poor thing!* or even give the bare-chested Cyclops a hug (which would have been a first for me). Frank was warning me not to make a big deal out of Tyson's back.

I wiped my eyes and tried to compose myself.

In the middle of the store, Tyson stopped and faced us. He grinned, spreading his arms with pride. 'See? Books!'

He was not lying. From the till/information desk at the centre of the room, freestanding shelves radiated in all directions, crammed with tomes of every size and shape. Two ladders led to a railed balcony, also with wall-to-wall books. Overstuffed reading chairs filled every available corner. Huge windows offered views of the city aqueduct and the hills beyond. The sunlight streamed in like warm honey, making the shop feel comfortable and drowsy.

It would've been the perfect place to plop down and leaf through a relaxing novel, except for that pesky smell of boiling oil and leather. There was no visible tattoo-parlour equipment, but against the back wall, under a sign that read SPECIAL COLLECTIONS, a set of thick velvet curtains seemed to provide access to a back room.

'Very nice,' I said, trying not to make it sound like a question.

'Books!' Tyson repeated. 'Because it's a bookshop!'

'Of course.' I nodded agreeably. 'Is this, um, your store?'

Tyson pouted. 'No. Sort of. The owner died. In the battle. It was sad.'

'Ah.' I wasn't sure what to say to that. 'At any rate, it's good to see you again, Tyson. You probably don't recognize me in this form, but –'

'You are Apollo!' He laughed. 'You look funny now.'

Frank covered his mouth and coughed, no doubt to hide a smile. 'Tyson, is Ella around? I wanted Apollo to hear what you guys discovered.'

'Ella is in the back room. She was giving me a tattoo!' He leaned towards me and lowered his voice. 'Ella is pretty.

But shh. She doesn't like me saying that all the time. She gets embarrassed. Then I get embarrassed.'

'I won't tell,' I promised. 'Lead on, General Tyson.'

'General.' Tyson laughed some more. 'Yes. That's me. I bashed some heads in the war!'

He galloped away like he was riding a hobbyhorse, straight through the velvet curtains.

Part of me wanted to turn, leave and take Frank for another cup of coffee. I dreaded what we might find on the other side of those curtains.

Then something at my feet said, *Mrow.*

The cat had found me. The enormous orange tabby, which must have eaten all the other bookshop cats to achieve its current size, pushed its head against my leg.

'It's touching me,' I complained.

'That's Aristophanes.' Frank smiled. 'He's harmless. Besides, you know how Romans feel about cats.'

'Yes, yes, don't remind me.' I had never been a fan of felines. They were self-centred, smug, and thought they owned the world. In other words . . . All right, I'll say it. I didn't like the competition.

For Romans, however, cats were a symbol of freedom and independence. They were allowed to wander anywhere they wished, even inside temples. Several times over the centuries, I'd found my altar smelling like a tomcat's new marking post.

Mrow, Aristophanes said again. His sleepy eyes, pale green as lime pulp, seemed to say, *You're mine now, and I may pee on you later.*

'I have to go,' I told the cat. 'Frank Zhang, let's find our harpy.'

As I suspected, the special-collections room had been set up as a tattoo parlour.

Rolling bookshelves had been pushed aside, heaped with leather-bound volumes, wooden scroll cases and clay cuneiform tablets. Dominating the centre of the room, a black leather reclining chair with foldable arms gleamed under an LED magnifying lamp. At its side stood a workstation with four humming electric steel-needle guns connected to ink hoses. I myself had never got a tattoo. When I was a god, if I wanted some ink on my skin, I could simply will it into being. But this set-up reminded me of something Hephaestus might try – a lunatic experiment in godly dentistry, perhaps.

In the back corner, a ladder led to a second-level balcony similar to the one in the main room. Two sleeping areas had been created up there: one a harpy's nest of straw, cloth and shredded paper; the other a sort of cardboard fort made of old appliance boxes. I decided not to enquire.

Pacing behind the tattoo chair was Ella herself, mumbling as if having an internal argument.

Aristophanes, who had followed us inside, began shadowing the harpy, trying to butt his head against Ella's leathery bird legs. Every so often, one of her rust-coloured feathers fluttered away and Aristophanes pounced on it. Ella ignored the cat completely. They seemed like a match made in Elysium.

'Fire . . .' Ella muttered. 'Fire with . . . something, something . . . something bridge. Twice something, something . . . Hmm.'

She seemed agitated, though I gathered that was her natural state. From what little I knew, Percy, Hazel and Frank had discovered Ella living in Portland, Oregon's main library, subsisting on food scraps and nesting in discarded novels. Somehow, at some point, the harpy had chanced across copies of the Sibylline Books, three volumes that had been thought lost forever in a fire towards the end of the Roman Empire. (Discovering a copy would've been like finding an unknown Bessie Smith recording, or a pristine *Batman* No. 1 from 1940, except more . . . er, *prophecy-ish*.)

With her photographic but disjointed memory, Ella was now the sole source of those old prophecies. Percy, Hazel and Frank had brought her to Camp Jupiter, where she could live in safety and hopefully recreate the lost books with the help of Tyson, her doting boyfriend. (Cyclops-friend? Interspecies significant other?)

Past that, Ella was an enigma wrapped in red feathers wrapped in a linen shift.

'No, no, no.' She ran one hand through her luxuriant swirls of red hair, ruffling it so vigorously I was afraid she might give her scalp lacerations. 'Not enough words. "Words, words, words." *Hamlet*, act two, scene two.'

She looked in good health for a former street harpy. Her humanlike face was angular but not emaciated. Her arm feathers were carefully preened. Her weight seemed about right for an avian, so she must have been getting plenty of birdseed or tacos or whatever harpies preferred to eat. Her taloned feet had shredded a well-defined path where she paced across the carpet.

'Ella, look!' Tyson announced. 'Friends!'

Ella frowned, her eyes sliding off Frank and me as if we were minor annoyances – pictures hung askew on a wall.

'No,' she decided. Her long fingernails clacked together. 'Tyson needs more tattoos.'

'Okay!' Tyson grinned as if this were fantastic news. He bounded over to the reclining chair.

'Wait,' I pleaded. It was bad enough to *smell* the tattoos. If I saw them being made, I was sure I would puke all over Aristophanes. 'Ella, before you start, could you please explain what's going on?'

'"What's Going On",' Ella said. 'Marvin Gaye, 1971.'

'Yes, I know,' I said. 'I helped write that song.'

'No.' Ella shook her head. 'Written by Renaldo Benson, Al Cleveland and Marvin Gaye; inspired by an incident of police brutality.'

Frank smirked at me. 'You can't argue with the harpy.'

'No,' Ella agreed. 'You can't.'

She scuttled over and studied me more carefully, sniffing at my bandaged belly, poking my chest. Her feathers glistened like rust in the rain. 'Apollo,' she said. 'You're all wrong, though. Wrong body. *Invasion of the Body Snatchers*, directed by Don Siegel, 1956.'

I did not like being compared to a black-and-white horror film, but I'd just been told not to argue with the harpy.

Meanwhile, Tyson adjusted the tattoo chair into a flat bed. He lay on his stomach, the recently inked purple lines of script rippling across his scarred, muscular back.

'Ready!' he announced.

The obvious finally dawned on me.

'*The words that memory wrought are set to fire,*' I recalled. 'You're rewriting the Sibylline Books on Tyson with hot needles. That's what the prophecy meant.'

'Yep.' Ella poked my love handles as if assessing them for a writing surface. 'Hmm. Nope. Too flabby.'

'Thanks,' I grumbled.

Frank shifted his weight, suddenly looking self-conscious about his own writing surfaces. 'Ella says it's the only way she can record the words in the right order,' he explained. 'On living skin.'

I shouldn't have been surprised. In the last few months, I'd sorted out prophecies by listening to the insane voices of trees, hallucinating in a dark cave, and racing across a fiery crossword puzzle. By comparison, assembling a manuscript on a Cyclops's back sounded downright civilized.

'But . . . how far have you got?' I asked.

'The first lumbar,' Ella said.

She showed no sign that she was joking.

Facedown on his torture bed, Tyson paddled his feet excitedly. 'READY! Oh, boy! Tattoos tickle!'

'Ella,' I tried again, 'what I mean is: have you found anything *useful* for us concerning – oh, I don't know – threats in the next four days? Frank said you had a lead?'

'Yep, found the tomb.' She poked my love handles again. 'Death, death, death. Lots of death.'

9

Dearly beloved,
We are gathered here because
Hera stinks. Amen.

IF THERE IS ANYTHING WORSE than hearing
Death, death, death, it's hearing those words while having
your flab poked.

'Can you be more specific?'

I actually wanted to ask: *Can you make all this go away,*
and can you also stop poking me? But I doubted I would get
either wish.

'Cross references,' Ella said.

'Sorry?'

'Tarquin's tomb,' she said. 'The Burning Maze words.
Frank told me: *Apollo faces death in Tarquin's tomb unless the*
doorway to the soundless god is opened by Bellona's daughter.'

'I know the prophecy,' I said. 'I sort of wish people would
stop repeating it. What exactly –?'

'Cross-referenced *Tarquin* and *Bellona* and *soundless god*
with Tyson's index.'

I turned to Frank, who seemed to be the only other
comprehensible person in the room. 'Tyson has an index?'

Frank shrugged. 'He wouldn't be much of a reference
book without an index.'

'On the back of my thigh!' Tyson called, still happily kicking his feet, waiting to be engraved with red-hot needles. 'Want to see?'

'No! Gods, no. So you cross-referenced –'

'Yep, yep,' said Ella. 'No results for *Bellona* or the *soundless god*. Hmm.' She tapped the sides of her head. 'Need more words for those. But *Tarquin's tomb*. Yep. Found a line.'

She scuttled to the tattoo chair, Aristophanes trotting close behind, swatting at her wings. Ella tapped Tyson's shoulder blade. 'Here.'

Tyson giggled.

'A *wildcat near the spinning lights*,' Ella read aloud. '*The tomb of Tarquin with horses bright. To open his door, two-fifty-four.*'

Mrow, said Aristophanes.

'No, Aristophanes,' Ella said, her tone softening, 'you are not a wildcat.'

The beast purred like a chainsaw.

I waited for more prophecy. Most of the Sibylline Books read like *The Joy of Cooking*, with sacrificial recipes to placate the gods in the event of certain catastrophes. Plague of locusts ruining your crops? Try the Ceres soufflé with loaves of honey bread roasted over her altar for three days. Earthquake destroying the city? When Neptune comes home tonight, surprise him with three black bulls basted in holy oil and burned in a fire pit with sprigs of rosemary!

But Ella seemed to be done reading.

'Frank,' I said, 'did that make any sense to you?'

He frowned. 'I thought *you* would understand it.'

When would people realize that just because I was the god of prophecy it didn't mean I understood prophecies? I was also the god of poetry. Did I understand the metaphors in T. S. Eliot's *The Waste Land*? No.

'Ella,' I said, 'could those lines describe a location?'

'Yep, yep. Close by, probably. But only to go in. Look around. Find out the right things and leave. Not to kill Tarquinius Superbus. Nope. He's much too dead to kill. For that, hmm . . . Need more words.'

Frank Zhang picked at the mural-crown badge on his chest. 'Tarquinius Superbus. The last king of Rome. He was considered a myth even back in Imperial Roman times. His tomb was never discovered. Why would he be . . . ?' He gestured around us.

'In our neck of the woods?' I finished. 'Probably the same reason why Mount Olympus is hovering above New York, or Camp Jupiter is in the Bay Area.'

'Okay, that's fair,' Frank admitted. 'Still, if the tomb of a Roman king was near Camp Jupiter, why would we just be learning about it now? Why the attack of the undead?'

I didn't have a ready answer. I'd been so fixated on Caligula and Commodus, I hadn't given much thought to Tarquinius Superbus. As evil as he might have been, Tarquin had been a minor-league player compared to the emperors. Nor did I understand why a semi-legendary, barbaric, apparently undead Roman king would have joined forces with the Triumvirate.

Some distant memory tickled at the base of my skull . . .

It couldn't be a coincidence that Tarquin would make himself known just as Ella and Tyson were reconstructing the Sibylline Books.

I remembered my dream of the purple-eyed entity, the deep voice that had possessed the eurynomos in the tunnel: *You of all people should understand the fragile boundary between life and death.*

The cut across my stomach throbbed. Just once, for variety, I wished I could encounter a tomb where the occupants were actually dead.

'So, Ella,' I said, 'you suggest we find this tomb.'

'Yep. Go in the tomb. *Tomb Raider* for PC, PlayStation and Sega Saturn, 1996. *Tombs of Atuan*, Ursula Le Guin, Atheneum Press, 1971.'

I barely noticed the extraneous information this time. If I stayed here much longer, I'd probably start speaking in Ella-ese, too, spouting random Wikipedia references after every sentence. I really needed to leave before that happened.

'But we only go in to look around,' I said. 'To find out –'

'The right things. Yep, yep.'

'And then?'

'Come back alive. "Stayin' Alive", the Bee Gees, second single, *Saturday Night Fever* motion-picture soundtrack, 1977.'

'Right. And . . . you're sure there's no more information in the Cyclops index that might actually be, oh, helpful?'

'Hmm.' Ella stared at Frank, then trotted over and sniffed his face. 'Firewood. Something. No. That's for later.'

Frank couldn't have looked more like a cornered animal

if he'd actually turned into one. 'Um, Ella? We don't talk about the firewood.'

That reminded me of another reason I liked Frank Zhang. He, too, was a member of the *I Hate Hera* club. In Frank's case, Hera had inexplicably tied his life force to a small piece of wood, which I'd heard Frank now carried around with him at all times. If the wood burned up, so did Frank. Such a typical controlling Hera thing to do: *I love you and you're my special hero, and also here's a stick – when it burns you die HA-HA-HA-HA-HA.* I disliked that woman.

Ella ruffled her feathers, providing Aristophanes with lots of new targets to play with. 'Fire with . . . something, something bridge. Twice something, something . . . Hmm, nope. That's later. Need more words. Tyson needs a tattoo.'

'Yay!' said Tyson. 'Can you also do a picture of Rainbow? He's my friend! He's a fish pony!'

'A rainbow is white light,' Ella said. 'Refracted through water droplets.'

'Also a fish pony!' Tyson said.

'Hmph,' said Ella.

I got the feeling I had just witnessed the closest the harpy and Cyclops ever came to having an argument.

'You two can go.' Ella brushed us away. 'Come back tomorrow. Maybe three days. "Eight Days a Week", the Beatles. First UK release, 1964. Not sure yet.'

I was about to protest that we had only four days before Caligula's yachts arrived and Camp Jupiter suffered another onslaught of destruction, but Frank stopped me with a touch on the arm. 'We should go. Let her work. It's almost time for evening muster anyway.'

After the mention of firewood, I got the feeling he would have used any faun-level excuse to get out of that bookshop.

My last glimpse of the special-collections room was Ella holding her tattoo gun, etching steaming words on Tyson's back while the Cyclops giggled, 'IT TICKLES!' and Aristophanes used the harpy's rough leather legs as scratching posts.

Some images, like Cyclops tattoos, are permanent once burned onto your brain.

Frank hustled us back to camp as fast as my wounded gut would tolerate.

I wanted to ask him about Ella's comments, but Frank wasn't in a talkative mood. Every so often his hand strayed to the side of his belt, where a cloth pouch hung tucked behind his scabbard. I hadn't noticed it before, but I assumed this was where he stored his Hera-Cursed Life-Ending Souvenir™.

Or perhaps Frank was sombre because he knew what awaited us at evening muster.

The legion had assembled for the funeral procession.

At the head of the column stood Hannibal, the legion's elephant, decked in Kevlar and black flowers. Harnessed behind him was a wagon with Jason's coffin, draped in purple and gold. Four of the cohorts had fallen into line behind the coffin, with purple Lares shifting in and out of their ranks. The Fifth Cohort, Jason's original unit, served as honour guards and torch bearers on either side of the wagon. Standing with them, between Hazel and Lavinia, was Meg McCaffrey. She frowned when she saw me and mouthed, *You're late*.

Frank jogged over to join Reyna, who was waiting at Hannibal's shoulder.

The senior praetor looked drained and weary, as if she'd spent the last few hours weeping in private and then pulled herself back together as best she could. Next to her stood the legion's standard bearer, holding aloft the eagle of the Twelfth.

Being close to the eagle made my hairs stand on end. The golden icon reeked of Jupiter's power. The air around it crackled with energy.

'Apollo.' Reyna's tone was formal, her eyes like empty wells. 'Are you prepared?'

'For . . . ?' The question died in my throat.

Everyone was staring at me expectantly. Did they want another song?

No. Of course. The legion had no high priest, no pontifex maximus. Their former augur, my descendant Octavian, had died in the battle against Gaia. (Which I had a hard time feeling sad about, but that's another story.) Jason would've been the logical next choice to officiate, but he was our guest of honour. That meant that I, as a former god, was the ranking spiritual authority. I would be expected to lead the funeral rites.

Romans were all about proper etiquette. I couldn't excuse myself without that being taken as a bad omen. Besides, I owed Jason my best, even if that was a sad Lester Papadopoulos version of my best.

I tried to remember the correct Roman invocation.

Dearly beloved . . . ? No.
Why is this night different . . . ? No.
Aha.

'Come, my friends,' I said. 'Let us escort our brother to his final feast.'

I suppose I did all right. No one looked scandalized. I turned and led the way out of the fort, the entire legion following in eerie silence.

Along the road to Temple Hill, I had a few moments of panic. What if I led the procession in the wrong direction? What if we ended up in the parking lot of an Oakland supermarket?

The golden eagle of the Twelfth loomed over my shoulder, charging the air with ozone. I imagined Jupiter speaking through its crackle and hum, like a voice over shortwave radio: *YOUR FAULT. YOUR PUNISHMENT.*

Back in January, when I'd fallen to earth, those words had seemed horribly unfair. Now, as I led Jason Grace to his final resting place, I *believed* them. So much of what had happened *was* my fault. So much of it could never be made right.

Jason had exacted a promise from me: *When you're a god again, remember. Remember what it's like to be human.*

I meant to keep that promise, if I survived long enough. But in the meantime there were more pressing ways I needed to honour Jason: by protecting Camp Jupiter, defeating the Triumvirate and, according to Ella, descending into the tomb of an undead king.

Ella's words rattled around in my head: *A wildcat near*

the spinning lights. The tomb of Tarquin with horses bright. To open his door, two-fifty-four.

Even for a prophecy, the lines seemed like gibberish.

The Sibyl of Cumae had always been vague and verbose. She refused to take editorial direction. She'd written nine entire volumes of Sibylline Books – honestly, who needs *nine books* to finish a series? I'd secretly felt vindicated when she'd been unable to sell them to the Romans until she whittled them down to a trilogy. The other six volumes had gone straight into the fire when . . .

I froze.

Behind me, the procession creaked and shuffled to a halt.

'Apollo?' Reyna whispered.

I shouldn't stop. I was officiating Jason's funeral. I couldn't fall down, roll into a ball and cry. That would be a definite no-no. But, Jupiter's gym shorts, why did my brain insist on remembering important facts at such inconvenient times?

Of course Tarquin was connected to the Sibylline Books. Of course he would choose now to show himself, and send an army of undead against Camp Jupiter. And the Sibyl of Cumae herself . . . Was it possible –?

'Apollo,' Reyna said again, more insistently.

'I'm fine,' I lied.

One problem at a time. Jason Grace deserved my full attention. I forced down my turbulent thoughts and kept walking.

When I reached Temple Hill, it was obvious where to

go. At the base of Jupiter's temple stood an elaborate wooden pyre. At each corner, an honour guard waited with a blazing torch. Jason's coffin would burn in the shadow of our father's temple. That seemed bitterly appropriate.

The legion's cohorts fanned out in a semicircle around the pyre, the Lares in their ranks glowing like birthday candles. The Fifth Cohort unloaded Jason's coffin and bore it to the platform. Hannibal and his funeral cart were led away.

Behind the legion, at the periphery of the torchlight, *aura* wind spirits swirled about, setting up folding tables and black tablecloths. Others flew in with drink pitchers, stacks of plates and baskets of food. No Roman funeral would be complete without a final meal for the departed. Only after the food was shared by the mourners would the Romans consider Jason's spirit safely on its way to the Underworld – immune from indignities like becoming a restless ghost or a zombie.

While the legionnaires got settled, Reyna and Frank joined me at the pyre.

'You had me worried,' Reyna said. 'Is your wound still bothering you?'

'It's getting better,' I said, though I might have been trying to assure myself more than her. Also, why did she have to look so beautiful in the firelight?

'We'll have the healers look at it again,' Frank promised. 'Why did you stop in the road?'

'Just . . . remembered something. Tell you later. I don't suppose you guys had any luck notifying Jason's family? Thalia?'

They exchanged frustrated looks.

'We tried, of course,' Reyna said. 'Thalia's the only earthly family he had. But with the communications problems . . .'

I nodded, unsurprised. One of the more annoying things the Triumvirate had done was shut down all forms of magical communication used by demigods. Iris-messages failed. Letters sent by wind spirits never arrived. Even mortal technology – which demigods tried to avoid anyway because it attracted monsters – now wouldn't work for them at all. How the emperors had managed this, I had no idea.

'I wish we could wait for Thalia,' I said, watching as the last of the Fifth Cohort pallbearers climbed down from the pyre.

'Me too,' Reyna agreed. 'But –'

'I know,' I said.

Roman funeral rites were meant to be performed as soon as possible. Cremation was necessary to send Jason's spirit along. It would allow the community to grieve and heal . . . or at least turn our attention to the next threat.

'Let's begin,' I said.

Reyna and Frank rejoined the front line.

I began to speak, the Latin ritual verses pouring out of me. I chanted from instinct, barely aware of the words' meanings. I had already praised Jason with my song. That had been deeply personal. This was just a necessary formality.

In some corner of my mind, I wondered if this was how mortals felt when they used to pray to me. Perhaps their devotions had been nothing but muscle memory, reciting by rote while their minds drifted elsewhere, uninterested in my glory. I found the idea strangely . . . understandable. Now that I was a mortal, why should I not practise non-violent resistance against the gods, too?

I finished my benediction.

I gestured for the aurae to distribute the feast, to place the first serving on Jason's coffin so he could symbolically share a last meal with his brethren in the mortal world. Once that happened, and the pyre was lit, Jason's soul would cross the Styx – so Roman tradition said.

Before the torches could be set to the wood, a plaintive howl echoed in the distance. Then another, much closer. An uneasy ripple passed through the assembled demigods. Their expressions weren't alarmed, exactly, but definitely surprised, as if they hadn't planned on extra guests. Hannibal grunted and stamped.

At the edges of our gathering, grey wolves emerged from the gloom – dozens of huge beasts, keening for the death of Jason, a member of their pack.

Directly behind the pyre, on the raised steps of Jupiter's temple, the largest wolf appeared, her silvery hide glowing in the torchlight.

I felt the legion holding its collective breath. No one knelt. When facing Lupa, the wolf goddess, guardian spirit of Rome, you don't kneel or show any sign of weakness. Instead we stood respectfully, holding our ground, as the pack bayed around us.

At last, Lupa fixed me with her lamp-yellow eyes. With a curl of her lip, she gave me a simple order: *Come.*

Then she turned and paced into the darkness of the temple.

Reyna approached me.

'Looks like the wolf goddess wants to have a private word.' She frowned with concern. 'We'll get the feast started. You go ahead. Hopefully Lupa isn't angry. Or hungry.'

10

Sing it with me: Who's
Afraid of the Big Good Wolf?
Me. That would be me.

LUPA WAS BOTH ANGRY AND HUNGRY.

I didn't claim to be fluent in Wolf, but I'd spent enough time around my sister's pack to understand the basics. Feelings were the easiest to read. Lupa, like all her kind, spoke in a combination of glances, snarls, ear twitches, postures and pheromones. It was quite an elegant language, though not well suited to rhyming couplets. Believe me, I'd tried. Nothing rhymes with *grr-rrr-row-rrr*.

Lupa was trembling with fury over Jason's death. The ketones on her breath indicated she had not eaten in days. The anger made her hungry. The hunger made her angry. And her twitching nostrils told her that I was the nearest, most convenient sack of mortal meat.

Nevertheless, I followed her into Jupiter's massive temple. I had little choice.

Ringing the open-air pavilion, columns the size of redwoods supported a domed, gilded ceiling. The floor was a colourful mosaic of Latin inscriptions: prophecies, memorials, dire warnings to praise Jupiter or face his lightning. In the centre, behind a marble altar, rose a massive golden statue of Dad himself: Jupiter Optimus Maximus, draped in a purple silk toga big enough to be a ship's sail. He looked stern, wise and paternal, though he was only one of those in real life.

Seeing him tower above me, lightning bolt raised, I had to fight the urge to cower and plead. I knew it was only a statue, but if you've ever been traumatized by someone, you'll understand. It doesn't take much to trigger those old fears: a look, a sound, a familiar situation. Or a fifty-foot-tall golden statue of your abuser – that does the trick.

Lupa stood before the altar. Mist shrouded her fur as if she were off-gassing quicksilver.

It is your time, she told me.

Or something like that. Her gestures conveyed expectation and urgency. She wanted me to do something. Her scent told me she wasn't sure I was capable of it.

I swallowed dryly, which in itself was Wolf for *I'm scared*. No doubt Lupa already smelled my fear. It wasn't possible to lie in Lupa's language. Threaten, bully, cajole . . . yes. But not outright lie.

'My time,' I said. 'For what, exactly?'

She nipped the air in annoyance. *To be Apollo. The pack needs you.*

I wanted to scream, *I've been trying to be Apollo! It's not that easy!*

But I restrained my body language from broadcasting that message.

Talking face-to-face with any god is dangerous business. I was out of practice. True, I'd seen Britomartis back in Indianapolis, but she didn't count. She liked torturing me too much to want to kill me. With Lupa, though . . . I had to be careful.

Even when I was a god myself, I'd never been able to get a good read on the Wolf Mother. She didn't hang out with the Olympians. She never came to the family Saturnalia dinners. Not once had she attended our monthly book group, even when we discussed *Dances with Wolves*.

'Fine,' I relented. 'I know what you mean. The last lines from the Dark Prophecy. I've reached the Tiber alive, et cetera, et cetera. Now I am supposed to "jive". I assume that entails more than dancing and snapping my fingers?'

Lupa's stomach growled. The more I talked, the tastier I smelled.

The pack is weak, she signalled with a glance towards the funeral pyre. *Too many have died. When the enemy surrounds this place, you must show strength. You must summon help.*

I tried to suppress another wolfish display of irritation. Lupa was a goddess. This was her city, her camp. She had a pack of supernatural wolves at her command. Why couldn't *she* help?

But, of course, I knew the answer. Wolves are not frontline fighters. They are hunters who attack only when they have overwhelming numbers. Lupa expected her Romans to solve their own problems. To be self-sufficient or die. She would advise. She would teach and guide and warn. But she would not fight their battles. *Our* battles.

Which made me wonder why she was telling me to summon help. And *what* help?

My expression and body language must have conveyed the question.

She flicked her ears. *North. Scout the tomb. Find answers. That is the first step.*

Outside, at the base of the temple, the funeral pyre crackled and roared. Smoke drifted through the open rotunda, buffeting the statue of Jupiter. I hoped, somewhere up on Mount Olympus, Dad's divine sinuses were suffering.

'Tarquinius Superbus,' I said. 'He's the one who sent the undead. He'll attack again at the blood moon.'

Lupa's nostrils twitched in confirmation. *His stench is on you. Be careful in his tomb. The emperors were foolish to call him forth.*

Emperor was a difficult concept to express in Wolf. The term for it could mean *alpha wolf, pack leader* or *submit to me now before I rip out your jugular.* I was fairly sure I interpreted Lupa's meaning correctly. Her pheromones read *danger, disgust, apprehension, outrage, more danger.*

I put a hand over my bandaged abdomen. I was getting better . . . wasn't I? I'd been slathered with enough Lemurian spice and unicorn-horn shavings to kill a zombie mastodon. But I didn't like Lupa's worried look, or the idea of anyone's stench being on me, especially not an undead king's.

'Once I explore this tomb,' I said, 'and get out alive . . . what then?'

The way will be clearer. To defeat the great silence. Then summon help. Without this, the pack will die.

I was less sure I comprehended those lines. 'Defeat the silence. You mean the soundless god? The doorway that Reyna is supposed to open?'

Her response was frustratingly ambivalent. It could have meant *Yes and no,* or *Sort of,* or *Why are you so dense?*

I stared up at Large Golden Dad.

Zeus had thrown me into the middle of all this trouble. He'd stripped me of my power, then kicked me to the earth to free the Oracles, defeat the emperors and – Oh, wait! I got a bonus undead king and a silent god, too! I hoped the soot from the funeral pyre was really annoying Jupiter. I wanted to climb up his legs and finger-write across his chest *WASH ME!*

I closed my eyes. This probably wasn't the wisest thing to do when facing a giant wolf, but I had too many half-formed ideas swirling around in my head. I thought about the Sibylline Books, the various prescriptions they contained for warding off disasters. I considered what Lupa might mean by *the great silence.* And summoning help.

My eyes snapped open. 'Help. As in godly help. You mean if I survive the tomb and – and defeat the soundless whatever-it-is, I might be able to summon *godly* help?'

Lupa made a rumbling sound deep in her chest. *Finally, he understands. This will be the beginning. The first step to rejoining your own pack.*

My heart *ka-thumped* like it was falling down a flight of stairs. Lupa's message seemed too good to be true. I could contact my fellow Olympians, despite Zeus's standing orders that they shun me while I was human. I might even be able to invoke their aid to save Camp Jupiter. Suddenly I really *did* feel better. My gut didn't hurt. My nerves tingled with a sensation I hadn't felt for so long I almost didn't recognize it: hope.

Beware. Lupa brought me back to reality with a low snarl. *The way is hard. You will face more sacrifices. Death. Blood.*

'No.' I met her eyes – a dangerous sign of challenge that surprised me as much as it did her. 'No, I will succeed. I won't allow any more losses. There has to be a way.'

I managed maybe three seconds of eye contact before looking away.

Lupa sniffed – a dismissive noise like, *Of course I won*, but I thought I detected a hint of grudging approval, too. It dawned on me that Lupa appreciated my bluster and determination, even if she didn't believe I was capable of doing what I said. Maybe *especially* because she didn't believe it.

Rejoin the feast, she ordered. *Tell them you have my blessing. Continue to act strong. It is how we start.*

I studied the old prophecies set in the floor mosaic. I had lost friends to the Triumvirate. I had suffered. But I realized that Lupa had suffered, too. Her Roman children had been decimated. She carried the pain of all their deaths. Yet she had to act strong, even as her pack faced possible extinction.

You couldn't lie in Wolf. But you could bluff. Sometimes you *had* to bluff to keep a grieving pack together. What do mortals say? *Fake it till you make it?* That is a very wolfish philosophy.

'Thank you.' I looked up, but Lupa was gone. Nothing remained except silver mist, blending with the smoke from Jason's pyre.

I gave Reyna and Frank the simplest version: I had received the wolf goddess's blessing. I promised to tell them more the next day, once I'd had time to make sense of it. Meanwhile, I trusted that word would spread among the legion about Lupa giving me guidance. That would be enough for now. These demigods needed all the reassurance they could get.

As the pyre burned, Frank and Hazel stood hand in hand, keeping vigil as Jason made his final voyage. I sat on a funeral picnic blanket with Meg, who ate everything in sight and went on and on about her excellent afternoon tending unicorns with Lavinia. Meg boasted that Lavinia had even let her clean out the stables.

'She pulled a Tom Sawyer on you,' I observed.

Meg frowned, her mouth full of hamburger. 'Whad'ya mean?'

'Nothing. You were saying, about unicorn poop?'

I tried to eat my dinner, but despite how hungry I was, the food tasted like dust.

When the pyre's last embers died and the wind spirits cleared away the remnants of the feast, we followed the legionnaires back to camp.

Up in Bombilo's spare room, I lay on my bed and studied the cracks in the ceiling. I imagined they were lines of tattooed script across a Cyclops's back. If I stared at them long enough, maybe they would start to make sense, or at least I could find the index.

Meg threw a shoe at me. 'You gotta rest. Tomorrow's the senate meeting.'

I brushed her red high-top off my chest. 'You're not asleep, either.'

'Yeah, but you'll have to speak. They'll wanna hear your plan.'

'My *plan*?'

'You know, like an oration. Inspire them and stuff. Convince them what to do. They'll vote on it and everything.'

'One afternoon in the unicorn stables, and you're an expert on Roman senatorial proceedings.'

'Lavinia told me.' Meg sounded positively smug about it. She lay on her bed, tossing her other high-top in the air and catching it again. How she managed this without her glasses on, I had no idea.

Minus the rhinestone cat-eye frames, her face looked older, her eyes darker and more serious. I would have even called her mature, had she not come back from her day at the stables wearing a glittery green T-shirt that read VNICORNES IMPERANT!

'What if I don't have a plan?' I asked.

I expected Meg to throw her other shoe at me. Instead she said, 'You do.'

'I do?'

'Yep. You might not have it all put together yet, but you will by tomorrow.'

I couldn't tell if she was giving me an order, or expressing faith in me, or just vastly underestimating the dangers we faced.

Continue to act strong, Lupa had told me. *It is how we start.*

'Okay,' I said tentatively. 'Well, for starters, I was thinking that we could –'

'Not now! Tomorrow. I don't want spoilers.'

Ah. *There* was the Meg I knew and tolerated.

'What is it with you and spoilers?' I asked.

'I hate them.'

'I'm trying to strategize with y—'

'Nope.'

'Talking through my ideas —'

'Nope.' She tossed aside her shoe, put a pillow over her head and commanded in a muffled voice: 'Go to sleep!'

Against a direct order, I had no chance. Weariness washed over me, and my eyelids crashed shut.

11

Dirt and bubblegum
Lavinia brought enough
For the whole senate

HOW DO YOU TELL A DREAM from a nightmare?

If it involves a book burning, it's probably a nightmare.

I found myself in the Roman senate room – not the grand, famous chamber of the republic or the empire, but the *old* senate room of the Roman kingdom. The mud-brick walls were painted slapdash white and red. Straw covered the filthy floor. Fires from iron braziers billowed soot and smoke, darkening the plaster ceiling.

No fine marble here. No exotic silk or imperial purple grandeur. This was Rome in its oldest, rawest form: all hunger and viciousness. The royal guards wore cured leather armour over sweaty tunics. Their black iron spears were crudely hammered, their helmets stitched of wolf hide. Enslaved women knelt at the foot of the throne, which was a rough-hewn slab of rock covered with furs. Lining either side of the room were crude wooden benches – for the senators, who sat more like prisoners or spectators than powerful politicians. In this era, senators had only one true power: to vote for a new king when the old one died.

Otherwise, they were expected to applaud or shut up as required.

On the throne sat Lucius Tarquinius Superbus – seventh king of Rome, murderer, schemer, slave-driver and all-round swell guy. His face was like wet porcelain cut with a steak knife – a wide glistening mouth pulled into a lopsided scowl; cheekbones too pronounced; a nose broken and healed in an ugly zigzag; heavy-lidded, suspicious eyes; and long, stringy hair that looked like drizzled clay.

Just a few years before, when he ascended the throne, Tarquin had been praised for his manly good looks and his physical strength. He'd dazzled the senators with flattery and gifts, then plopped himself down on his father-in-law's throne and persuaded the senate to confirm him as the new king.

When the old king rushed in to protest that he was, you know, still very much alive, Tarquin picked him up like a sack of turnips, carried him outside and threw him into the street, where the old king's daughter, Tarquin's wife, ran over her unfortunate dad with her chariot, splattering the wheels with his blood.

A lovely start to a lovely reign.

Now Tarquin wore his years heavily. He'd grown hunched and thick, as if all the building projects he'd forced on his people had actually been heaped on his own shoulders. He wore the hide of a wolf for a cloak. His robes were such a dark mottled pink that it was impossible to tell if they'd once been red and then spattered with bleach, or had once been white and spattered with blood.

Aside from the guards, the only person standing in the

room was an old woman facing the throne. Her rose-coloured hooded cloak, her hulking frame and her stooped back made her look like a mocking reflection of the king himself: the *Saturday Night Live* version of Tarquin. In the crook of one arm she held a stack of six leather-bound volumes, each the size of a folded shirt and just as floppy.

The king scowled at her. 'You're back. Why?'

'To offer you the same deal as before.'

The woman's voice was husky, as if she'd been shouting. When she pulled down her hood, her stringy grey hair and haggard face made her look even more like Tarquin's twin sister. But she was not. She was the Cumaean Sibyl.

Seeing her again, my heart twisted. She had once been a lovely young woman – bright, strong-willed, passionate about her prophetic work. She had wanted to change the world. Then things between us soured . . . and I had changed *her* instead.

Her appearance was only the beginning of the curse I had set on her. It would get much, much worse as the centuries progressed. How had I put this out of my mind? How could I have been so cruel? The guilt for what I'd done burned worse than any ghoul scratch.

Tarquin shifted on his throne. He tried for a laugh, but the sound came out more like a bark of alarm. 'You must be insane, woman. Your original price would have bankrupted my kingdom, and that was when you had *nine* books. You burned three of them, and now you come back to offer me only six, for the same exorbitant sum?'

The woman held out the books, one hand on top as if preparing to say an oath. 'Knowledge is expensive, King of

Rome. The less there is, the more it is worth. Be glad I am not charging you double.'

'Oh, I see! I should be *grateful*, then.' The king looked at his captive audience of senators for support. That was their cue to laugh and jeer at the woman. None did. They looked more afraid of the Sibyl than of the king.

'I expect no gratitude from the likes of you,' the Sibyl rasped. 'But you should act in your own self-interest, and in the interest of your kingdom. I offer knowledge of the future . . . how to avert disaster, how to summon the help of the gods, how to make Rome a great empire. All that knowledge is here. At least . . . six volumes of it remain.'

'Ridiculous!' snapped the king. 'I should have you executed for your disrespect!'

'If only that were possible.' The Sibyl's voice was as bitter and calm as an arctic morning. 'Do you refuse my offer, then?'

'I am high priest as well as king!' cried Tarquin. 'Only *I* decide how to appease the gods! I don't need –'

The Sibyl took the top three books off the stack and casually threw them into the nearest brazier. The volumes blazed immediately, as if they'd been written in kerosene on sheets of rice paper. In a single great roar, they were gone.

The guards gripped their spears. The senators muttered and shifted on their seats. Perhaps they could feel what *I* could feel – a cosmic sigh of anguish, the exhale of destiny as so many volumes of prophetic knowledge vanished from the world, casting a shadow across the future, plunging generations into darkness.

How could the Sibyl do it? Why?

Perhaps it was her way of taking revenge on me. I'd criticized her for writing so many volumes, for not letting me oversee her work. But by the time she wrote the Sibylline Books, I had been angry with her for different reasons. My curse had already been set. Our relationship was beyond repair. By burning her own books, she was spitting on my criticism, on the prophetic gift I had given her, and on the too-high price she had paid to be my Sibyl.

Or perhaps she was motivated by something other than bitterness. Perhaps she had a reason for challenging Tarquin as she did and exacting such a high penalty for his stubbornness.

'Last chance,' she told the king. 'I offer you three books of prophecy for the same price as before.'

'For the same –' The king choked on his rage.

I could see how much he wanted to refuse. He wanted to scream obscenities at the Sibyl and order his guards to impale her on the spot.

But his senators were shifting and whispering uneasily. His guards' faces were pale with fear. His enslaved women were doing their best to hide behind the dais.

Romans were a superstitious people.

Tarquin knew this.

As high priest, he was responsible for protecting his subjects by interceding with the gods. Under no circumstances was he supposed to make the gods angry. This old woman was offering him prophetic knowledge to help his kingdom. The crowd in the throne room could sense her power, her closeness to the divine.

If Tarquin allowed her to burn those last books, if he

threw away her offer . . . it might not be the Sibyl whom his guards decided to impale.

'Well?' the Sibyl prompted, holding her three remaining volumes close to the flames.

Tarquin swallowed back his anger. Through clenched teeth, he forced out the words: 'I agree to your terms.'

'Good,' said the Sibyl, no visible relief or disappointment on her face. 'Let payment be brought to the Pomerian Line. Once I have it, you will have the Books.'

The Sibyl disappeared in a flash of blue light. My dream dissolved with her.

'Put on your sheet.' Meg threw a toga in my face, which was not the nicest way to be woken up.

I blinked, still groggy, the smell of smoke, mouldy straw and sweaty Romans lingering in my nostrils. 'A toga? But I'm not a senator.'

'You're honorary, because you used to be a god or whatever.' Meg pouted. 'I don't get to wear a sheet.'

I had a horrible mental image of Meg in a traffic-light-coloured toga, gardening seeds spilling from the folds of the cloth. She would just have to make do with her glittery unicorn T-shirt.

Bombilo gave me his usual *Good morning* glare when I came downstairs to appropriate the café bathroom. I washed, then changed my bandages with a kit the healers had thoughtfully left in our room. The ghoul scratch looked no worse, but it was still puckered and angry red. It still burned. That was normal, right? I tried to convince myself it was. As they say, doctor gods make the worst patient gods.

I got dressed, trying to remember how to fold a toga, and mulled over the things I'd learned from my dream. Number one: I was a terrible person who ruined lives. Number two: there was not a single bad thing I'd done in the last four thousand years that was *not* going to come back and bite me in the *clunis*, and I was beginning to think I deserved it.

The Cumaean Sibyl. Oh, Apollo, what had you been *thinking*?

Alas, I knew what I'd been thinking – that she was a pretty young woman I wanted to get with, despite the fact that she was my Sibyl. Then she'd outsmarted me and, being the bad loser that I was, I had cursed her.

No wonder I was now paying the price: tracking down the evil Roman king to whom she'd once sold her Sibylline Books. If Tarquin was still clinging to some horrible undead existence, could the Cumaean Sibyl be alive as well? I shuddered to think what she might be like after all these centuries, and how much her hatred for me would have grown.

First things first: I had to tell the senate my marvellous plan to make things right and save us all. Did I have a marvellous plan? Shockingly, maybe. Or at least the beginnings of a marvellous plan. The marvellous index of one.

On our way out, Meg and I grabbed Lemurian-spice lattes and a couple of blueberry muffins – because Meg clearly needed more sugar and caffeine – then we joined the loose procession of demigods heading for the city.

By the time we got to the Senate House, everyone was taking their seats. Flanking the rostrum, Praetors Reyna and Frank were arrayed in their finest gold and purple. The first row of benches was occupied by the camp's ten senators – each in a white toga trimmed in purple – along with the most senior veterans, those with accessibility needs, and Ella and Tyson. Ella fidgeted, doing her best to avoid brushing shoulders with the senator on her left. Tyson grinned at the Lar on his right, wriggling his fingers inside the ghost's vaporous ribcage.

Behind them, the semicircle of tiered seats was packed to overflowing with legionnaires, Lares, retired veterans, and other citizens of New Rome. I hadn't seen a lecture hall this crowded since Charles Dickens's 1867 Second American Tour. (Great show. I still have the autographed T-shirt framed in my bedroom in the Palace of the Sun.)

I thought I should sit at the front, being an honorary wearer of bed linen, but there was simply no room. Then I spotted Lavinia (thank you, pink hair) waving at us from the back row. She patted the bench next to her, indicating that she'd saved us seats. A thoughtful gesture. Or maybe she wanted something.

Once Meg and I had settled on either side of her, Lavinia gave Meg the super-secret Unicorn Sisterhood fist bump, then turned and ribbed me with her sharp elbow. 'So, you're really Apollo, after all! You must know my mom.'

'I – what?'

Her eyebrows were extra distracting today. The dark roots had started to grow out under the pink dye, which made them seem to hover slightly off centre, as if they were about to float off her face.

'My mom?' she repeated, popping her bubblegum. 'Terpsichore?'

THE TYRANT'S TOMB   111

'The – the Muse of Dance. Are you asking me if she's your mother, or if I know her?'

'Of course she's my mother.'

'Of course I know her.'

'Well, then!' Lavinia drummed a riff on her knees, as if to prove she had a dancer's rhythm despite being so gangly. 'I wanna hear the dirt!'

'The dirt?'

'I've never met her.'

'Oh. Um . . .' Over the centuries, I'd had many conversations with demigods who wanted to know more about their absentee godly parents. Those talks rarely went well. I tried to conjure up a picture of Terpsichore, but my memories of Olympus were getting fuzzier by the day. I vaguely recalled the Muse frolicking around one of the parks on Mount Olympus, casting rose petals in her wake as she twirled and pirouetted. Truth be told, Terpsichore had never been my favourite of the Nine Muses. She tended to take the spotlight off me, where it rightly belonged.

'She had your colour hair,' I ventured.

'Pink?'

'No, I mean . . . dark. Lots of nervous energy, I suppose, like you. She was never happy unless she was moving, but . . .'

My voice died. What could I say that wouldn't sound mean? Terpsichore was graceful and poised and didn't look like a wobbly giraffe? Was Lavinia sure there hadn't been some mistake about her parentage? Because I couldn't believe they were related.

'But what?' she pressed.

'Nothing. Hard to remember.'

Down at the rostrum, Reyna was calling the meeting to order. 'Everyone, if you'll please take your seats! We need to get started. Dakota, can you scoot in a little to make room for – Thanks.'

Lavinia regarded me sceptically. 'That's the lamest dirt ever. If you can't tell me about my mom, at least tell me what's going on with you and Ms Praetor down there.'

I squirmed. The bench suddenly felt a great deal harder under my clunis. 'There's nothing to tell.'

'Oh, please. The way you've been sneaking glances at Reyna since you got here? I noticed it. Meg noticed.'

'I noticed,' Meg confirmed.

'Even Frank Zhang noticed.' Lavinia turned up her palms as if she'd just provided the ultimate proof of complete obviousness.

Reyna began to address the crowd: 'Senators, guests, we have called this emergency meeting to discuss –'

'Honestly,' I whispered to Lavinia, 'it's awkward. You wouldn't understand.'

She snorted. 'Awkward is telling your rabbi that Daniella Bernstein is going to be your date for your bat mitzvah party. Or telling your dad that the only dancing you want to do is tap, so you're not going to carry on the Asimov family tradition. I know all about awkward.'

Reyna continued, 'In light of Jason Grace's ultimate sacrifice, and our own recent battle against the undead, we have to take very seriously the threat –'

'Wait,' I whispered to Lavinia, her words sinking in. 'Your dad is Sergei Asimov? The dancer? The –' I stopped myself before I could say *The smoking-hot Russian ballet star*, but, judging from Lavinia's eye roll, she knew what I was thinking.

'Yeah, yeah,' she said. 'Stop trying to change the subject. Are you going to dish on –?'

'Lavinia Asimov!' Reyna called from the rostrum. 'Did you have something to say?'

All eyes turned towards us. A few legionnaires smirked, as if this was not the first time Lavinia had been called out during a senate meeting.

Lavinia glanced from side to side, then pointed to herself as if unsure which of the many Lavinia Asimovs Reyna might be addressing. 'No, ma'am. I'm good.'

Reyna did not look amused at being called *ma'am*. 'I notice you're chewing gum as well. Did you bring enough for the whole senate?'

'Er, I mean . . .' Lavinia pulled multiple packs of gum from her pockets. She scanned the crowd, making a quick guesstimate. 'Maybe?'

Reyna glanced heavenward, as if asking the gods, *Why do I have to be the only adult in the room?*

'I'll assume,' the praetor said, 'that you were just trying to draw attention to the guest seated next to you, who has important information to share. Lester Papadopoulos, rise and address the senate!'

12

I now have a plan
To make a plan concerning
The plan for my plan

NORMALLY, WHEN I'M ABOUT TO PERFORM,
I wait backstage. Once I'm announced and the crowd is
frenzied with anticipation, I burst through the curtains, the
spotlights hit me, and TA-DA! I am A GOD!

Reyna's introduction did not inspire wild applause.
Lester Papadopoulos, rise and address the senate was about as
exciting as *We will now have a PowerPoint about adverbs*.

As soon as I started making my way to the aisle, Lavinia
tripped me. I glared back at her. She gave me an innocent
face, like her foot just happened to be there. Given the size
of her legs, maybe it had been.

Everyone watched as I fumbled my way through the
crowd, trying not to trip on my toga.

'Excuse me. Sorry. Excuse me.'

By the time I made it to the rostrum, the audience was
whipped into a frenzy of boredom and impatience. No
doubt they would've all been checking their phones –
except demigods couldn't use smartphones without risking
monster attack, so they had no alternative but to stare at
me. I had wowed them two days ago with a fantastic musical

tribute to Jason Grace, but what had I done for them lately? Only the Lares looked content to wait. They could endure sitting on hard benches forever.

From the back row, Meg waved at me. Her expression was less like, *Hi, you'll do great*, and more like, *Get on with it*. I turned my gaze to Tyson, who was grinning at me from the front row. When you find yourself focusing on the Cyclops in the crowd for moral support, you know you're going to bomb.

'So . . . hi.'

Great start. I hoped another burst of inspiration might lead to a follow-up song. Nothing happened. I'd left my ukulele in my room, sure that if I'd tried to bring it into the city Terminus would have confiscated it as a weapon.

'I have some bad news,' I said. 'And some bad news. Which do you want to hear first?'

The crowd exchanged apprehensive looks.

Lavinia yelled, 'Start with the bad news. That's always best.'

'Hey,' Frank chastised her. 'Like, decorum, you know?'

Having restored solemnity to the senate meeting, Frank gestured for me to proceed.

'The emperors Commodus and Caligula have combined forces,' I said. I described what I'd seen in my dream. 'They're sailing towards us right now with a fleet of fifty yachts, all equipped with some kind of terrible new weapon. They'll be here by the blood moon. Which, as I understand it, is in three days, April the eighth, which also happens to be Lester Papadopoulos's birthday.'

'Happy birthday!' Tyson said.

'Thanks. Also, I'm not sure what a blood moon is.'

A hand shot up in the second row.

'Go ahead, Ida,' Reyna said, then added for my benefit, 'Centurion of the Second Cohort, legacy of Luna.'

'Seriously?' I didn't mean to sound incredulous, but Luna, a Titan, had been in charge of the moon before my sister Artemis took over the job. As far as I knew, Luna had faded away millennia ago. Then again, I'd thought there was nothing left of Helios the sun Titan until I found out that Medea was collecting shreds of his consciousness to heat the Burning Maze. Those Titans were like my acne. They just kept popping up.

The centurion stood, scowling. 'Yes, seriously. A blood moon is a full moon that looks red because there's a full lunar eclipse. It's a bad time to fight the undead. They're especially powerful on those nights.'

'Actually . . .' Ella stood, picking at her finger talons. 'Actually, the colour is caused by the dispersal of reflected light from the sunrise and sunset of earth. A true blood moon refers to four lunar eclipses in a row. The next one is on April the eighth, yep. *Farmer's Almanac*. Moon Phase Calendar supplemental.'

She plopped down again, leaving the audience in stunned silence. Nothing is quite so disconcerting as having science explained to you by a supernatural creature.

'Thank you, Ida and Ella,' Reyna said. 'Lester, did you have more to add?'

Her tone suggested that it would be totally okay if I didn't, since I'd already shared enough information to cause a camp-wide panic.

'I'm afraid so,' I said. 'The emperors have allied themselves with Tarquin the Proud.'

The Lares in the room guttered and flickered.

'Impossible!' cried one.

'Horrible!' cried another.

'We'll all die!' screamed a third, apparently forgetting that he was already dead.

'Guys, chill,' Frank said. 'Let Apollo talk.'

His leadership style was less formal than Reyna's, but he seemed to command just as much respect. The audience settled, waiting for me to continue.

'Tarquin is now some sort of undead creature,' I said. 'His tomb is nearby. He was responsible for the attack you repulsed on the new moon –'

'Which is also a really cruddy time to fight the undead,' Ida volunteered.

'And he'll attack again on the blood moon, in concert with the emperors' assault.'

I did my best to explain what I'd seen in my dreams, and what Frank and I had discussed with Ella. I did not mention the reference to Frank's unholy piece of firewood – partly because I didn't understand it, partly because Frank was giving me the pleading teddy-bear eyes.

'Since Tarquin was the one who originally purchased the Sibylline Books,' I summed up, 'it makes a twisted kind of sense that he would reappear now, when Camp Jupiter is trying to reconstruct those prophecies. Tarquin would be . . . *invoked* by what Ella is doing.'

'Enraged,' Ella suggested. 'Infuriated. Homicidal.'

Looking at the harpy, I thought of the Cumaean Sibyl,

and the terrible curse I'd laid upon her. I wondered how Ella might suffer, just because we'd coerced her into entering the prophecy business. Lupa had warned me: *You will face more sacrifices. Death. Blood.*

I forced that idea aside. 'Anyway, Tarquin was monstrous enough when he was alive. The Romans despised him so much they did away with the monarchy forever. Even centuries later, the emperors never dared to call themselves kings. Tarquin died in exile. His tomb was never located.'

'And now it's here,' Reyna said.

It wasn't a question. She accepted that an Ancient Roman tomb could pop up in Northern California, where it had no business being. The gods moved. The demigod camps moved. It was just our luck that an evil undead lair would move in next door. We really needed stricter mythological zoning laws.

In the first row, next to Hazel, a senator rose to speak. He had dark curly hair, off-centre blue eyes and a cherry-red moustache stain on his upper lip. 'So, to sum up: in three days, we're facing an invasion from two evil emperors, their armies, and fifty ships with weapons we don't understand, along with another wave of undead like the one that nearly destroyed us last time, when we were a lot stronger. If that's the bad news, what's the bad news?'

'I assume we're getting to that, Dakota.' Reyna turned to me. 'Right, Lester?'

'The other bad news,' I said, 'is that I have a plan, but it's going to be hard, maybe impossible, and parts of the plan aren't exactly . . . plan-worthy, yet.'

Dakota rubbed his hands. 'Well, I'm excited. Let's hear it!'

He sat back down, pulled a flask from his toga and took a swig. I guessed that he was a child of Bacchus, and, judging from the smell that wafted across the senate floor, his chosen beverage was fruit punch.

I took a deep breath. 'So. The Sibylline Books are basically like emergency recipes, right? Sacrifices. Ritual prayers. Some are designed to appease angry gods. Some are designed to call for divine aid against your enemies. I believe . . . I'm pretty sure . . . if we're able to find the correct recipe for our predicament, and do what it says, I may be able to summon help from Mount Olympus.'

No one laughed or called me crazy. Gods didn't intervene in demigod affairs often, but it did happen on rare occasions. The idea wasn't completely unbelievable. On the other hand, no one looked terribly assured that I could pull it off.

A different senator raised his hand. 'Uh, Senator Larry here, Third Cohort, son of Mercury. So, when you say *help*, do you mean like . . . battalions of gods charging down here in their chariots, or more like the gods just giving us their blessing, like, *Hey, good luck with that, legion!?*'

My old defensiveness kicked in. I wanted to argue that we gods would never leave our desperate followers hanging like that. But, of course, we did. All the time.

'That's a good question, Senator Larry,' I admitted. 'It would probably be somewhere between those extremes. But I'm confident it would be real help, capable of turning the tide. It may be the only way to save New Rome. And I have to believe Zeus – I mean, Jupiter – set my supposed birthday as April the eighth for a reason. It's meant to be a turning point, the day I finally . . .'

My voice cracked. I didn't share the other side of that thought: that 8 April might either be the day I began to prove myself worthy of rejoining the gods, or my last birthday ever, the day I went up in flames once and for all.

More murmuring from the crowd. Lots of grave expressions. But I detected no panic. Even the Lares didn't scream, *We're all going to die!* The assembled demigods were Romans, after all. They were used to facing dire predicaments, long odds and strong enemies.

'Okay.' Hazel Levesque spoke for the first time. 'So how do we find this correct recipe? Where do we start?'

I appreciated her confident tone. She might have been asking if she could help with something completely doable – like carrying groceries, or impaling ghouls with quartz spikes.

'The first step,' I said, 'is to find and explore Tarquin's tomb –'

'And kill him!' yelled one of the Lares.

'No, Marcus Apulius!' scolded one of his peers. 'Tarquin is as dead as we are!'

'Well, what, then?' grumbled Marcus Apulius. 'Ask him nicely to leave us alone? This is Tarquin the Proud we're talking about! He's a maniac!'

'The first step,' I said, 'is only to *explore* the tomb and, ah, find out the right things, as Ella said.'

'Yep,' the harpy agreed. 'Ella said that.'

'I have to assume,' I continued, 'that if we succeed in this, and come out alive, we will know more about how to proceed. Right now, all I can say with certainty is that the next step will involve finding a soundless god, whatever that means.'

Frank sat forward in his praetor's chair. 'But don't you know all the gods, Apollo? I mean, you *are* one. Or *were* one. Is there a god of silence?'

I sighed. 'Frank, I can barely keep my own *family* of gods straight. There are hundreds of minor gods. I don't remember any silent gods. Of course, if there *is* one, I doubt we would've hung out, me being the god of music.'

Frank looked crestfallen, which made me feel bad. I hadn't meant to take out my frustrations on one of the few people who still called me Apollo unironically.

'Let's tackle one thing at a time,' Reyna suggested. 'First, the tomb of Tarquin. We have a lead on its location, right, Ella?'

'Yep, yep.' The harpy closed her eyes and recited, 'A *wildcat near the spinning lights. The tomb of Tarquin with horses bright. To open his door, two-fifty-four.*'

'That is a prophecy!' Tyson said. 'I have it on my back!' The Cyclops stood and ripped off his shirt so fast he must have been waiting for any excuse. 'See?'

The spectators all leaned forward, though it would've been impossible to read the tattoos from any distance.

'I also have a fish pony by my kidney,' he announced proudly. 'Isn't it cute?'

Hazel averted her eyes as if she might pass out with embarrassment. 'Tyson, could you . . . ? I'm sure it's a lovely fish pony, but . . . shirt back on, please? I don't suppose anyone knows what those lines *mean*?'

The Romans observed a moment of silence for the death of clarity that all prophecies symbolized.

Lavinia snorted. 'Seriously? Nobody gets it?'

'Lavinia,' Reyna said, her voice strained, 'are you suggesting you –'

'Know where the tomb is?' Lavinia spread her hands. 'Well, I mean, A *wildcat near the spinning lights. The tomb of Tarquin with horses bright*. There's a Wildcat Drive in Tilden Park, right over the hills.' She pointed north. 'And *horses bright, spinning lights*? That would be the Tilden Park carousel, wouldn't it?'

'Ohhhh.' Several Lares nodded in recognition, as if they spent all their free time riding the local merry-go-rounds.

Frank shifted in his chair. 'You think the tomb of an evil Roman king is under a carousel?'

'Hey, I didn't write the prophecy,' Lavinia said. 'Besides, it makes as much sense as anything else we've faced.'

Nobody disputed that. Demigods eat weirdness for breakfast, lunch and dinner.

'All right, then,' Reyna said. 'We have a goal. We need a quest. A *short* quest, since time is very limited. We must designate a team of heroes and have them approved by the senate.'

'Us.' Meg stood. 'Gotta be Lester and me.'

I gulped. 'She's right,' I said, which counted as my heroic act for the day. 'This is part of my greater quest to regain my place among the gods. I've brought this trouble to your doorstep. I need to make it right. Please, don't anyone try to talk me out of it.'

I waited desperately, in vain, for someone to try to talk me out of it.

Hazel Levesque rose. 'I'll go, too. A centurion is required to lead a quest. If this place is underground, well, that's kind of my speciality.'

Her tone also said, *I have a score to settle*.

Which was fine, except I remembered how Hazel had collapsed that tunnel we'd taken into camp. I had a sudden terrifying vision of being crushed under a merry-go-round.

'That's three questers, then,' Reyna said. 'The correct number for a quest. Now –'

'Two and a half,' Meg interrupted.

Reyna frowned. 'Sorry?'

'Lester's my servant. We're kind of a team. He shouldn't count as a full quester.'

'Oh, come on!' I protested.

'So we can take one more,' Meg offered.

Frank sat up. 'I'd be happy to –'

'If you didn't have praetor duties to attend to,' Reyna finished, giving him a look like, *You are not leaving me alone, dude*. 'While the questers are out, the rest of us have to prepare the valley's defences. There's a lot to do.'

'Right.' Frank slumped. 'So, is there anyone else –?'

POP!

The sound was so loud, half the Lares disintegrated in alarm. Several senators ducked under their seats.

In the back row, Lavinia had a flattened pink gum

bubble smeared across her face. She quickly peeled it away and stuck it back in her mouth.

'Lavinia,' Reyna said. 'Perfect. Thanks for volunteering.'

'I – But –'

'I call for a senate vote!' Reyna said. 'Do we send Hazel, Lester, Meg and Lavinia on a quest to find the tomb of Tarquin?'

The measure passed unanimously.

We were given full senate approval to find a tomb under a carousel and confront the worst king in Roman history, who also happened to be an undead zombie lord.

My day just kept getting better.

13

Romance disaster
I'm poison for guys and gals
You wanna hang out?

'LIKE CHEWING GUM IS A CRIME.' Lavinia tossed a piece of her sandwich off the roof, where it was immediately snatched up by a seagull.

For our picnic lunch, she had brought me, Hazel and Meg to her favourite thinking place: the rooftop of New Rome University's bell tower, which Lavinia had discovered access to on her own. People were not exactly encouraged to be up here, but it was not strictly forbidden, either, which seemed to be the space Lavinia most liked inhabiting.

She explained that she enjoyed sitting here because it was directly above the Garden of Faunus, Reyna's favourite thinking spot. Reyna was not in the garden at present, but whenever she was, Lavinia could look down at the praetor, a hundred feet below, and gloat, *Ha-ha, my thinking spot is higher than your thinking spot.*

Now, as I sat on the precariously slanted red clay tiles, a half-eaten piece of focaccia on my lap, I could see the entire city and valley spread out below us – everything we stood to lose in the coming invasion. Beyond stretched the flatlands of Oakland, and the San Francisco Bay, which in just a few days would be dotted with Caligula's luxury battle yachts.

'Honestly.' Lavinia threw another piece of her grilled cheese to the seagulls. 'If the legionnaires went for a stupid *hike* once in a while, they'd know about Wildcat Drive.'

I nodded, though I suspected that most legionnaires, who spent a good deal of their time marching in heavy armour, probably wouldn't consider hiking much fun. Lavinia, however, seemed to know every back road, trail and secret tunnel within twenty miles of Camp Jupiter – I suppose because you never knew when you'd need to sneak out for a date with some pretty Hemlock or Deadly Nightshade.

On my other side, Hazel ignored her veggie wrap and grumbled to herself, 'Can't believe Frank . . . Trying to volunteer . . . Bad enough after his crazy stunts in the battle . . .'

Nearby, having already ploughed through her lunch, Meg aided her digestion by doing cartwheels. Every time she landed, catching her balance on the loose tiles, my heart free-climbed a little further up my throat.

'Meg, could you *please* not do that?' I asked.

'It's fun.' She fixed her eyes on the horizon and announced, 'I want a unicorn.' Then she cartwheeled again.

Lavinia muttered to no one in particular, 'You popped a bubble – you'll be perfect for this quest!'

'Why do I have to like a guy with a death wish?' Hazel mused.

'Meg,' I pleaded, 'you're going to fall.'

'Even a small unicorn,' Meg said. 'Not fair they have so many here and I don't have *any*.'

We continued this four-part disharmony until a giant eagle swooped out of the sky, snatched the rest of the grilled cheese from Lavinia's hand, and soared away, leaving behind a flock of irritated seagulls.

'Typical.' Lavinia wiped her fingers on her trousers. 'Can't even have a sandwich.'

I shoved the rest of my focaccia into my mouth, just in case the eagle came back for seconds.

'Well,' Hazel sighed, 'at least we got the afternoon off to make plans.' She gave half of her veggie wrap to Lavinia.

Lavinia blinked, apparently unsure how to respond to the kind gesture. 'I – uh, thanks. But, I mean, what is there to plan? We go to the carousel, find the tomb, try not to die.'

I swallowed the last of my food, hoping it might push my heart back down to its proper location. 'Perhaps we could concentrate on the *not-dying* part. For instance, why wait until tonight? Wouldn't it be safer to go when it's daylight?'

'It's always dark underground,' Hazel said. 'Besides, during the daytime, lots of kids will be at the carousel. I don't want any of them getting hurt. At night, the place will be deserted.'

Meg plopped down next to us. Her hair now looked like a distressed elderberry shrub. 'So, Hazel, can you do other cool underground stuff? Some people were saying you can summon diamonds and rubies.'

Hazel frowned. 'Some people?'

'Like Lavinia,' Meg said.

'Oh my gods!' Lavinia said. 'Thanks a lot, Meg!'

Hazel peered into the sky, as if wishing a giant eagle would come and snatch her away. 'I can summon precious metals, yes. Riches of the earth. That's a Pluto thing. But you can't spend the stuff I summon, Meg.'

I leaned back against the roof tiles. 'Because it's cursed? I seem to recall something about a curse – and not because Lavinia told me anything,' I added hastily.

Hazel picked at her veggie wrap. 'It's not so much a *curse* any more. In the old days, I couldn't control it. Diamonds, gold coins, stuff like that would just pop up from the ground whenever I got nervous.'

'Cool,' Meg said.

'No, it really wasn't,' Hazel assured her. 'If somebody picked up the treasures and tried to spend them . . . horrible things would happen.'

'Oh,' Meg said. 'What about now?'

'Since I met Frank . . .' Hazel hesitated. 'A long time ago, Pluto told me that a descendant of Poseidon would wash away my curse. It's complicated, but Frank *is* a descendant of Poseidon on his mom's side. Once we started dating . . . He's just a *good person*, you know? I'm not saying I needed a fella to solve my problems –'

'A *fella?*' Meg asked.

Hazel's right eye twitched. 'Sorry. I grew up in the 1930s. Sometimes my vocab slips. I'm not saying I needed a *guy* to solve my problems. It's just that Frank had his own curse to deal with, so he understood me. We helped each other through some dark times – talking together, learning to be happy again. He makes me feel –'

'Loved?' I suggested.

Lavinia met my eyes and mouthed, *Adorable*.

Hazel tucked her feet underneath her. 'I don't know why I'm telling you all this. But yes. Now I can control my powers a lot better. Jewels don't pop up randomly when I get upset. Still, they're not meant to be spent. I think . . . I have this gut feeling that Pluto wouldn't like that. I don't want to find out what would happen if somebody tried.'

Meg pouted. 'So you can't give me even a small diamond? Like, just to keep for fun?'

'Meg,' I chided.

'Or a ruby?'

'Meg.'

'Whatever.' Meg frowned at her unicorn shirt, no doubt thinking how cool it would look decorated with several million dollars' worth of precious stones. 'I just wanna fight stuff.'

'You'll probably get your wish,' Hazel said. 'But remember, tonight, the idea is to explore and gather intel. We'll need to be stealthy.'

'Yes, Meg,' I said. 'Because, if you'll recall, *Apollo faces death in Tarquin's tomb*. If I must face death, I would rather do so while hiding in the shadows, and then sneak away from it without it ever knowing I was there.'

Meg looked exasperated, as if I'd suggested an unfair rule in freeze tag. 'Okay. I guess I can stealth.'

'Good,' Hazel said. 'And, Lavinia, no chewing gum.'

'Give me some credit. I have very sneaky moves.' She wriggled her feet. 'Daughter of Terpsichore and all that.'

'Hmm,' Hazel said. 'Okay, then. Everybody gather your supplies and get some rest. We'll meet on the Field of Mars at sundown.'

Resting should have been an easy assignment.

Meg went off to explore the camp (read: see the unicorns again), which left me by myself in the café's upstairs room. I lay on my bed, enjoying the quiet, staring at Meg's newly planted irises, which were now in full bloom in the window-box. Still, I couldn't sleep.

My stomach wound throbbed. My head buzzed.

I thought of Hazel Levesque and how she'd credited Frank with washing away her curse. Everyone deserved someone who could wash away their curses by making them feel loved. But that was not my fate. Even my greatest romances had *caused* more curses than they lifted.

Daphne. Hyacinthus.

And later, yes, the Cumaean Sibyl.

I remembered the day we had sat together on a beach, the Mediterranean stretching out before us like a sheet of blue glass. Behind us, on the hillside where the Sibyl had her cave, olive trees baked and cicadas droned in the summer heat of southern Italy. In the distance, Mount Vesuvius rose, hazy and purple.

Conjuring an image of the Sibyl herself was more difficult – not the hunched and grizzled old woman from Tarquin's throne room, but the beautiful young woman she'd been on that beach, centuries before, when Cumae was still a Greek colony.

I had loved everything about her – the way her hair caught the sunlight, the mischievous gleam in her eyes, the easy way she smiled. She didn't seem to care that I was a god, despite having given up everything to be my Oracle: her family, her future, even her name. Once pledged to me, she was known simply as the Sibyl, the voice of Apollo.

But that wasn't enough for me. I was smitten. I convinced myself it was love – the one true romance that would wash away all my past missteps. I wanted the Sibyl to be my partner throughout eternity. As the afternoon went on, I coaxed and pleaded.

'You could be so much more than my priestess,' I urged her. 'Marry me!'

She laughed. 'You can't be serious.'

'I am! Ask for anything in return, and it's yours.'

She twisted a strand of her auburn locks. 'All I've ever wanted is to be the Sibyl, to guide the people of this land to a better future. You've already given me that. So, ha-ha. The joke's on you.'

'But – but you've only got one lifetime!' I said. 'If you were immortal, you could guide humans to a better future forever, at my side!'

She looked at me askance. 'Apollo, please. You'd be tired of me by the end of the week.'

'Never!'

'So, you're saying –' she scooped up two heaped handfuls

of sand – 'if I wished for as many years of life as there are grains of this sand, you would grant me that.'

'It is done!' I pronounced. Instantly, I felt a portion of my own power flowing into her life force. 'And now, my love –'

'Whoa, whoa!' She scattered the sand, clambering to her feet and backing away as if I were suddenly radioactive. 'That was a hypothetical, lover boy! I didn't agree –'

'What's done is done!' I rose. 'A wish cannot be taken back. Now you must honour your side of the bargain.'

Her eyes danced with panic. 'I – I can't. I won't!'

I laughed, thinking she was merely nervous. I spread my arms. 'Don't be afraid.'

'Of *course* I'm afraid!' She backed away further. 'Nothing good ever happens to your lovers! I just wanted to be your Sibyl, and now you've made things weird!'

My smile crumbled. I felt my ardour cooling, turning stormy. 'Don't anger me, Sibyl. I am offering you the universe. I've given you near-immortal life. You cannot refuse payment.'

'*Payment?*' She balled her hands into fists. 'You dare think of me as a *transaction?*'

I frowned. This afternoon really wasn't going the way I'd planned. 'I didn't mean – Obviously, I wasn't –'

'Well, *Lord* Apollo,' she growled, 'if this is a transaction, then I defer payment until your side of the bargain is complete. You said it yourself: *near*-immortal life. I'll live until the grains of sand run out, yes? Come back to me at the end of that time. Then, if you still want me, I'm yours.'

I dropped my arms. Suddenly, all the things I'd loved about the Sibyl became things I hated: her headstrong attitude, her lack of awe, her infuriating, unattainable beauty. Especially her beauty.

'Very well.' My voice turned colder than any sun god's should be. 'You want to argue over the fine print of our *contract*? I promised you life, not youth. You can have your centuries of existence. You will remain my Sibyl. I cannot take those things away, once given. But you will grow old. You will wither. You will not be *able* to die.'

'I would prefer that!' Her words were defiant, but her voice trembled with fear.

'Fine!' I snapped.

'Fine!' she yelled back.

I vanished in a column of flame, having succeeded in making things very weird indeed.

Over the centuries, the Sibyl had withered, just as I'd threatened. Her physical form lasted longer than any ordinary mortal's, but the pain I had caused her, the lingering agony . . . Even if I'd had regrets about my hasty curse, I couldn't have taken it back any more than she could take back her wish. Finally, around the end of the Roman Empire, I'd heard rumours that the Sibyl's body had crumbled away entirely, yet still she could not die. Her attendants kept her life force, the faintest whisper of her voice, in a glass jar.

I assumed that the jar had been lost sometime after that. That the Sibyl's grains of sand had finally run out. But what if I was wrong? If she were still alive, I doubted she was using her faint whisper of a voice to be a pro-Apollo social media influencer.

I deserved her hatred. I saw that now.

Oh, Jason Grace . . . I promised you I would remember what it was to be human. But why did human shame have to hurt so much? Why wasn't there an off button?

And, thinking of the Sibyl, I couldn't help considering that *other* young woman with a curse: Reyna Avila Ramírez-Arellano.

I'd been completely blindsided the day I strolled into the Olympian throne room, fashionably late for our meeting as usual, and found Venus studying the luminous image of a young lady floating above her palm. The goddess's expression had been weary and troubled . . . something I didn't often see.

'Who's that?' I asked foolishly. 'She's beautiful.'

That's all the trigger Venus needed to unleash her fury. She told me Reyna's fate: no demigod would ever be able to heal her heart. But that did NOT mean I was the answer to Reyna's problem. Quite the contrary. In front of the entire assembly of gods, Venus announced that I was unworthy. I was a disaster. I had ruined every relationship I was in, and I should keep my godly face away from Reyna, or Venus would curse me with even worse romantic luck than I already had.

The mocking laughter of the other gods still rang in my ears.

Had it not been for that encounter, I might never have known Reyna existed. I certainly had no designs on her. But we always want what we cannot have. Once Venus declared Reyna off-limits, I became fascinated with her.

Why had Venus been so emphatic? What did Reyna's fate mean?

Now I thought I understood. As Lester Papadopoulos, I no longer had a *godly face*. I was neither mortal, nor god, nor demigod. Had Venus somehow known this would happen someday? Had she shown me Reyna and warned me off knowing full well that it would make me obsessed?

Venus was a wily goddess. She played games within games. If it was my fate to be Reyna's true love, to wash away her curse as Frank had done for Hazel, would Venus allow it?

But at the same time, I *was* a romantic disaster. I had ruined every one of my relationships, brought nothing but destruction and misery to the young men and women I'd loved. How could I believe I would be any good for the praetor?

I lay on my bed, these thoughts tossing around in my mind, until late afternoon. Finally, I gave up on the idea of rest. I gathered my supplies – my quiver and bow, my ukulele and my backpack – and I headed out. I needed guidance, and I could think of only one way to get it.

14

Reluctant arrow
Grant me this boon: permission
To skedaddleth

I HAD THE FIELD OF MARS ALL TO MYSELF.

Since no war games were scheduled that evening, I could frolic through the wasteland to my heart's content, admiring the wreckage of chariots, broken battlements, smouldering pits and trenches filled with sharpened spikes. Another romantic sunset stroll wasted because I had no one to share it with.

I climbed an old siege tower and sat facing the northern hills. With a deep breath, I reached into my quiver and pulled out the Arrow of Dodona. I'd gone several days without talking to my annoying far-sighted projectile weapon, which I considered a victory, but now, gods help me, I could think of no one else to turn to.

'I need help,' I told it.

The arrow remained silent, perhaps stunned by my admission. Or perhaps I'd pulled out the wrong arrow and I was talking to an inanimate object.

Finally, the shaft rattled in my hand. Its voice resonated in my mind like a thespian tuning fork: *THY WORDS ARE*

TRUE. BUT IN WHAT SENSE MEANEST THOU?

Its tone sounded less derisive than usual. That scared me.

'I . . . I am supposed to show strength,' I said. 'According to Lupa, I'm supposed to save the day somehow, or the pack – New Rome – will die. But how do I *do* that?'

I told the arrow all that had happened in the last few days: my encounter with the eurynomoi, my dreams about the emperors and Tarquin, my conversation with Lupa, our quest from the Roman senate. To my surprise, it felt good to pour out my troubles. Considering the arrow didn't have ears, it was a good listener. It never looked bored, shocked or disgusted, because it had no face.

'I crossed the Tiber alive,' I summed up, 'just like the prophecy said. Now, how do I "start to jive"? Does this mortal body have a reset switch?'

The arrow buzzed: *I SHALL THINK UPON THIS.*

'That's it? No advice? No snarky comments?'

GIVE ME TIME TO CONSIDER, O IMPATIENT LESTER.

'But I don't *have* time! We're leaving for Tarquin's tomb, like –' I glanced to the west, where the sun was beginning to sink behind the hills – 'basically now!'

THE JOURNEY INTO THE TOMB WILL NOT BE THY FINAL CHALLENGE. UNLESS THOU SUCKEST MOST WOEFULLY.

'Is that supposed to make me feel better?'

FIGHT NOT THE KING, said the arrow. *HEAREST THOU WHAT THOU NEEDEST, AND SKEDADDLETH.*

'Did you just use the term *skedaddleth*?'

I TRY TO SPEAK PLAINLY TO THEE, TO GRANT THEE A BOON, AND STILL THOU COMPLAINEST.

'I appreciate a good boon as much as the next person. But, if I'm going to contribute to this quest and not just cower in the corner, I need to know how –' my voice cracked – 'how to be *me* again.'

The vibration of the arrow felt almost like a cat purring, trying to soothe an ill human. *ART THOU SURE THAT IS THY WISH?*

'What do you mean?' I demanded. 'That's the whole point! Everything I'm doing is so –'

'Are you talking to that arrow?' said a voice below me.

At the base of the siege tower stood Frank Zhang. Next to him was Hannibal the Elephant, impatiently pawing the mud.

I'd been so distracted, I'd let an elephant get the drop on me.

'Hi,' I squeaked, my voice still ragged with emotion. 'I was just . . . This arrow gives prophetic advice. It talks. In my head.'

Bless him, Frank managed to maintain a poker face. 'Okay. I can leave if –'

'No, no.' I slipped the arrow back in my quiver. 'It needs time to process. What brings you out here?'

'Walking the elephant.' Frank pointed to Hannibal, in case I might be wondering which elephant. 'He gets stir-crazy when we don't have war games. Bobby used to be our elephant handler, but . . .'

Frank shrugged helplessly. I got his meaning: Bobby had

been another casualty of the battle. Killed . . . or maybe worse.

Hannibal grunted deep in his chest. He wrapped his trunk around a broken battering ram, picked it up and started pounding it into the ground like a pestle.

I remembered my elephant friend Livia back at the Waystation in Indianapolis. She, too, had been grief-stricken, having lost her mate to Commodus's brutal games. If we survived this upcoming battle, perhaps I should try to introduce Livia and Hannibal. They'd make a cute couple.

I mentally slapped myself. What was I thinking? I had enough to worry about without playing matchmaker to pachyderms.

I climbed down from my perch, careful to protect my bandaged gut.

Frank studied me, perhaps worried by how stiffly I was moving.

'You ready for your quest?' he asked.

'Is the answer to that question ever *yes*?'

'Good point.'

'And what will you do while we're gone?'

Frank ran a hand across his buzz cut. 'Everything we can. Shore up the valley's defences. Keep Ella and Tyson working on the Sibylline Books. Send eagles to scout the coast. Keep the legion drilling so they don't have time to worry about what's coming. Mostly, though? It's about being with the troops, assuring them that everything is going to be okay.'

Lying to them, in other words, I thought, though that was bitter and uncharitable.

Hannibal stuck his battering ram upright in a sinkhole. He patted the old tree trunk as if to say, *There you go, little fella. Now you can start growing again.*

Even the elephant was hopelessly optimistic.

'I don't know how you do it,' I admitted. 'Staying positive after all that's happened.'

Frank kicked a piece of stone. 'What's the alternative?'

'A nervous breakdown?' I suggested. 'Running away? But I'm new to this *being mortal* business.'

'Yeah, well. I can't say those ideas haven't crossed my mind, but you can't really do that when you're a praetor.' He frowned. 'Though I'm worried about Reyna. She's been carrying the burden a lot longer than I have. *Years* longer. The strain of that . . . I dunno. I just wish I could help her more.'

I recalled Venus's warning: *You will not stick your ugly, unworthy godly face anywhere near her.* I wasn't sure which idea was more terrifying: that I might make Reyna's life worse, or that I might be responsible for making her life better.

Frank apparently misinterpreted my look of concern. 'Hey, you'll be fine. Hazel will keep you safe. She's one powerful demigod.'

I nodded, trying to swallow the bitter taste in my mouth. I was tired of others keeping me safe. The whole point of consulting the arrow had been to figure out how I could get back to the business of keeping *others* safe. That used to be so easy with my godlike powers.

Was it, though? another part of my brain asked. *Did you keep the Sibyl safe? Or Hyacinthus or Daphne? Or your own son Asclepius? Should I go on?*

Shut up, me, I thought back.

'Hazel seems more worried about *you*,' I ventured. 'She mentioned some crazy stunts in the last battle?'

Frank squirmed as if trying to shake an ice cube out of his shirt. 'It wasn't like that. I just did what I had to.'

'And your piece of tinder?' I pointed to the pouch hanging from his belt. 'You're not worried about what Ella said . . . ? Something about fires and bridges?'

Frank gave me a dry little smile. 'What, me worry?'

He reached into the pouch and casually pulled out his life stick: a chunk of charred wood the size of a TV remote control. He flipped it and caught it, which almost gave me a panic attack. He might as well have pulled out his beating heart and started juggling it.

Even Hannibal looked uncomfortable. The elephant shifted from foot to foot, shaking his massive head.

'Shouldn't that stick be locked in the principia's vault?' I asked. 'Or coated in magical flame retardant at least?'

'The pouch is flameproof,' Frank said. 'Compliments of Leo. Hazel carried it for me for a while. We talked about other ways to keep it safe. But, honestly, I've kind of learned to accept the danger. I prefer having the firewood with me. You know how it is with prophecies. The harder you try to avoid them, the harder you fail.'

I couldn't argue with that. Still, there was a fine line between accepting one's fate and tempting it. 'I'm guessing Hazel thinks you're too reckless.'

'That's an ongoing conversation.' He slipped the firewood back in its pouch. 'I promise you, I *don't* have a death wish. It's just . . . I can't let fear hold me back. Every time I lead the legion into battle, I have to put everything on the line, commit to the battle one hundred percent. We all do. It's the only way to win.'

'That's a very Mars thing to say,' I noted. 'Despite my many disagreements with Mars, I mean that as a compliment.'

Frank nodded. 'You know, I was standing right about here when Mars appeared on the battlefield last year, told me I was his son. Seems like so long ago.' He gave me a quick scan. 'I can't believe I used to think –'

'That I was your father? But we look so much alike.'

He laughed. 'Just take care of yourself, okay? I don't think I could handle a world with no Apollo in it.'

His tone was so genuine it made me tear up. I'd started to accept that no one wanted Apollo back – not my fellow gods, not the demigods, perhaps not even my talking arrow. Yet Frank Zhang still believed in me.

Before I could do anything embarrassing – like hug him, or cry, or start believing I was a worthwhile individual – I spotted my three quest partners trudging towards us.

Lavinia wore a purple camp T-shirt and ratty jeans over a silver leotard. Her sneakers sported glittery pink laces that matched her hair and no doubt helped her with her stealthy moves. Her manubalista clunked against her shoulder.

Hazel looked slightly more ninja-esque in her black jeans and black zip-up cardigan, her oversize cavalry sword strapped to her belt. I recalled that she favoured the spatha because she sometimes fought while riding the immortal steed Arion. Alas, I doubted Hazel would summon Arion for our quest today. A magical horse wouldn't be much use for sneaking around an underground tomb.

As for Meg, she looked like Meg. Her red high-tops and yellow leggings clashed epically with her new unicorn T-shirt, which she seemed determined to wear until it fell to pieces. She had applied plasters across her cheekbones, like warriors or footballers might do. Perhaps she thought they made her look 'commando', despite the fact that the plasters were decorated with pictures of Dora the Explorer.

'What are those for?' I demanded.

'They keep the light out of my eyes.'

'It'll be night-time soon. We're going underground.'

'They make me look scary.'

'Not even remotely.'

'Shut up,' she ordered, so of course I had to.

Hazel touched Frank's elbow. 'Can I talk to you for a sec?'

It wasn't really a question. She led him out of earshot, followed by Hannibal, who apparently decided their private conversation required an elephant.

'Oi.' Lavinia turned to Meg and me. 'We may be here a while. When those two start mother-henning . . . I swear, if they could encase each other in Styrofoam peanuts, they would.'

She sounded part judgemental, part wistful, as if she wished she had an overprotective girlfriend who would encase *her* in Styrofoam peanuts. I could very much relate.

Hazel and Frank had an anxious exchange. I couldn't hear their words, but I imagined the conversation went something like:

I'm worried about you.

No, I'm worried about you.

But I'm more *worried.*

No, I'm more *worried.*

Meanwhile, Hannibal stomped and grunted like he was enjoying himself.

Finally, Hazel rested her fingers on Frank's arm, as if she were afraid he might dissolve into smoke. Then she marched back to us.

'All right,' she announced, her expression dour. 'Let's go find this tomb before I change my mind.'

15

Nightmare carousel
Totally let your kids ride
I'm sure they'll be fine

'NICE NIGHT FOR A HIKE,' LAVINIA SAID.

The sad thing was, I think she meant it.

By that point, we'd been trekking through the Berkeley Hills for over an hour. Despite the cool weather, I was dripping with sweat and gasping for breath. Why did hilltops have to be uphill? Lavinia wasn't satisfied with sticking to the valleys, either. Oh, no. She wanted to conquer every summit for no apparent reason. Like fools, we followed her.

We had crossed the borders of Camp Jupiter without a problem. Terminus hadn't even popped up to check our passports. So far we had not been accosted by ghouls or panhandling fauns.

The scenery was pleasant enough. The trail wound through sweet-smelling sage and bay trees. To our left, silver luminescent fog blanketed the San Francisco Bay. Before us, the hills formed an archipelago of darkness in the ocean of city lights. Regional parks and nature reserves kept the area mostly wild, Lavinia explained.

'Just be on the lookout for mountain lions,' she said. 'They're all over these hills.'

'We're going to face the undead,' I said, 'and you're warning us about mountain lions?'

Lavinia shot me a look like, *Dude*.

She was right, of course. With my luck, I would probably come all this way, fighting monsters and evil emperors, only to get killed by an overgrown house cat.

'How much further?' I asked.

'Not this again,' Lavinia said. 'You aren't even carrying a coffin this time. We're about halfway there.'

'Halfway. And we couldn't have taken a car, or a giant eagle, or an elephant?'

Hazel patted me on the shoulder. 'Relax, Apollo. Sneaking up on foot draws less attention. Besides, this is an easy quest. Most of mine have been like, *Go to Alaska and fight literally everything along the way*, or, *Sail halfway across the world and be seasick for months*. This is just, *Go over that hill and check on a merry-go-round*.'

'A *zombie-infested* merry-go-round,' I corrected. 'And we've been over several hills.'

Hazel glanced at Meg. 'Does he always complain this much?'

'He used to be a lot whinier.'

Hazel whistled softly.

'I know,' Meg agreed. 'Big baby.'

'I beg your pardon!' I said.

'Shh,' Lavinia said, before blowing and popping a giant pink bubble. 'Stealth, remember?'

We continued along the trail for another hour or so. As we passed a silver lake nestled between the hills, I couldn't help thinking it was just the sort of place my sister would love. Oh, how I wished she would appear with her Hunters!

Despite our differences, Artemis understood me. Well, okay, she tolerated me. Most of the time. All right, some of the time. I longed to see her beautiful, annoying face again. That's how lonely and pathetic I had become.

Meg walked a few yards ahead of me, flanking Lavinia so they could share bubblegum and talk unicorns. Hazel walked beside me, though I got the feeling she was mostly trying to make sure I didn't collapse.

'You don't look so good,' she noted.

'What gave it away? The cold sweat? The rapid breathing?'

In the darkness, Hazel's gold eyes reminded me of an owl's: supremely alert, ready to fly or pounce as needed. 'How's the gut wound?'

'Better,' I said, though I was having more and more trouble convincing myself.

Hazel redid her ponytail, but it was a losing battle. Her hair was so long, curly and luxuriant it kept escaping its scrunchie. 'Just no more cuts, all right? Is there anything else you can tell me about Tarquin? Weaknesses? Blind spots? Pet peeves?'

'Don't they teach you Roman history as part of legion training?'

'Well, yes. But I may have tuned out during the lectures. I went to Catholic school back in New Orleans in the 1930s. I have a lot of experience in tuning out teachers.'

'Mmm. I can relate. Socrates. Very smart. But his discussion groups . . . not exactly riveting entertainment.'

'So, Tarquin.'

'Right. He was power-mad. Arrogant. Violent. Would kill anyone who got in his way.'

'Like the emperors.'

'But without any of their refinement. Tarquin was also obsessed with building projects. He started the Temple of Jupiter. Also, Rome's main sewer.'

'Claim to fame.'

'His subjects finally got so weary of taxes and forced labour that they rebelled.'

'They didn't like digging a sewer? I can't imagine why.'

It occurred to me that Hazel wasn't so much interested in information as she was in distracting me from my worries. I appreciated that, but I had trouble returning her smile. I kept thinking about Tarquin's voice speaking through the ghoul in the tunnel. He had known Hazel's name. He had promised her a special place among his undead horde.

'Tarquin is sly,' I said. 'Like any true psychopath, he has always been good at manipulating people. As for weaknesses, I don't know. His relentlessness, maybe. Even after he got kicked out of Rome, he never stopped trying to win back the crown. He kept gathering new allies, attacking the city over and over again, even when it was clear he didn't have the strength to win.'

'Apparently he still hasn't given up.' Hazel pushed a eucalyptus branch out of our way. 'Well, we'll stick to the plan: get in quietly, investigate, leave. At least Frank is safe back at camp.'

'Because you value his life more than ours?'

'No. Well . . .'

'You can leave it at *no*.'

Hazel shrugged. 'It's just that Frank seems to be *looking* for danger these days. I don't suppose he told you what he did at the Battle of the New Moon?'

'He said the battle turned at the Little Tiber. Zombies don't like running water.'

'*Frank* turned the tide of battle, almost single-handedly. Demigods were falling all around him. He just kept fighting – shape-shifting into a giant snake, then a dragon, then a hippopotamus.' She shuddered. 'He makes a *terrifying* hippo. By the time Reyna and I managed to bring up reinforcements, the enemy was already in retreat. Frank had no fear. I just . . .' Her voice tightened. 'I don't want to lose him. Especially after what happened to Jason.'

I tried to reconcile Hazel's story of Frank Zhang, fearless-hippo killing-machine, with the easygoing, big cuddly praetor who slept in a yellow silk pyjama shirt decorated with eagles and bears. I remembered the casual way he'd flipped his stick of firewood. He'd assured me he hadn't had a death wish. Then again, neither had Jason Grace.

'I don't intend to lose anyone else,' I told Hazel.

I stopped short of making a promise.

The goddess of the River Styx had excoriated me for my broken oaths. She'd warned that everyone around me would pay for my crimes. Lupa, too, had foreseen more blood and sacrifice. How could I promise Hazel that any of us would be safe?

Lavinia and Meg halted so abruptly I almost ran into them.

'See?' Lavinia pointed through a break in the trees. 'We're almost there.'

In the valley below, an empty parking lot and picnic area occupied a clearing in the redwoods. At the far end of the meadow, silent and still, stood a carousel, all its lights blazing.

'Why is it lit up?' I wondered.

'Maybe somebody's home,' said Hazel.

'I like merry-go-rounds,' said Meg, and she started down the path.

The carousel was topped by a tan-coloured dome like a giant pith helmet. Behind a barricade of teal and yellow metal railings, the ride blazed with hundreds of lights. The painted animals threw long distorted shadows across the grass. The horses looked frozen in panic, their eyes wild, their forelegs kicking. A zebra's head was raised as if in agony. A giant rooster flared its red comb and stretched its talons. There was even a hippocampus like Tyson's friend Rainbow, but this fish pony had a snarling face. What sort of parents would let their children ride such nightmarish creatures? Maybe Zeus, I thought.

We approached cautiously, but nothing challenged us, neither living nor dead. The place seemed empty, just inexplicably lit up.

Meg's glowing swords made the grass shimmer at her feet. Lavinia held her manubalista, primed and ready. With her pink hair and gangly limbs, she stood the best chance of sneaking up on the carousel animals and blending in with them, but I decided not to share that observation, as it would no doubt get me shot. Hazel left her sword in its sheath. Even empty-handed, she radiated a more intimidating demeanour than any of us.

I wondered if I should pull out my bow. Then I looked down and realized I had instinctively readied my combat ukulele. Okay. I could provide a jolly tune if we found ourselves in battle. Did that count as heroism?

'Something's not right,' Lavinia murmured.

'You think?' Meg crouched. She put down one of her swords and touched the grass with her fingertips. Her hand sent a ripple across the lawn like a stone thrown in water.

'Something's wrong with the soil here,' she announced. 'The roots don't want to grow too deep.'

Hazel arched her eyebrows. 'You can talk to plants.'

'It's not really talking,' Meg said. 'But yeah. Even the trees don't like this place. They're trying to grow away from that carousel as fast as they can.'

'Which, since they're trees,' I said, 'is not very fast.'

Hazel studied our surroundings. 'Let's see what I can find out.'

She knelt at the edge of the carousel's base and pressed her palm against the concrete. There were no visible ripples, no rumbling or shaking, but after a count of three Hazel snatched her hand away. She staggered backwards, almost falling over Lavinia.

'Gods.' Hazel's whole body trembled. 'There's . . . there's a *massive* complex of tunnels under here.'

My mouth went dry. 'Part of the Labyrinth?'

'No. I don't think so. It feels self-contained. The structure is ancient, but – but it also hasn't been here very long. I know that doesn't make sense.'

'It does,' I said, 'if the tomb relocated.'

'Or regrew,' Meg offered. 'Like a tree clipping. Or a fungal spore.'

'Gross,' said Lavinia.

Hazel hugged her elbows. 'The place is full of death. I mean, I'm a child of Pluto. I've been to the Underworld. But this is worse somehow.'

'I don't love that,' Lavinia muttered.

I looked down at my ukulele, wishing I'd brought a bigger instrument to hide behind. A double bass, perhaps. 'How do we get in?'

I hoped the answer would be, *Gosh darn it, we can't.*

'There.' Hazel pointed to a section of concrete that looked no different from the rest.

We followed her over. She ran her fingers across the dark surface, leaving glowing silver grooves that outlined a rectangular slab the size of a coffin. Oh, why did I have to make that particular analogy?

Her hand hovered over the middle of the rectangle. 'I think I'm supposed to write something here. A combination, maybe?'

'*To open his door,*' Lavinia recalled, '*two-fifty-four.*'

'Wait!' I fought down a wave of panic. 'There are lots of ways to write "two-fifty-four".'

Hazel nodded. 'Roman numerals, then?'

'Yes. But two-five-four would be written differently in Roman numerals than two hundred and fifty-four, which is different from two and fifty-four.'

'Which is it, then?' Meg asked.

I tried to think. 'Tarquin would have a reason to choose that number. He'd make it about himself.'

Lavinia popped a small, stealthy pink bubble. 'Like using your birthday for your password?'

'Exactly,' I said. 'But he wouldn't use his birthday. Not for his tomb. Perhaps his date of death? Except that can't be right. No one's sure when he died, since he was in exile and buried in secret, but it had to have been around 495 BCE, not 254.'

'Wrong date system,' Meg said.

We all stared at her.

'What?' she demanded. 'I got raised in an evil emperor's palace. We dated everything from the founding of Rome. AUC. *Ab urbe condita*, right?'

'My gods,' I said. 'Good catch, Meg. 254 AUC would be . . . let's see . . . 500 BCE. That's pretty close to 495.'

Hazel's fingers still hesitated over the concrete. 'Close enough to risk it?'

'Yes,' I said, trying to channel my inner Frank Zhang confidence. 'Write it as a date: two hundred and fifty-four. C-C-L-I-V.'

Hazel did. The numbers glowed silver. The entire stone slab dissipated into smoke, revealing steps leading down into darkness.

'Okay, then,' Hazel said. 'I have a feeling the next part is going to be harder. Follow me. Step only where I step. And *don't* make any noise.'

16

Meet the new Tarquin
Same as the old Tarquin, but
With a lot less flesh

SO . . . NO JOLLY TUNES on the ukulele, then.

Fine.

I silently followed Hazel down the steps into the merry-go-tomb.

As we descended, I wondered why Tarquin had chosen to reside under a carousel. He had watched his wife run over her own father in a chariot. Perhaps he liked the idea of an endless ring of horses and monsters circling above his resting place, keeping guard with their fierce faces, even if they were ridden mostly by mortal toddlers. (Who, I suppose, were fierce in their own way.) Tarquin had a brutal sense of humour. He enjoyed tearing families apart, turning their joy into anguish. He was not above using children as human shields. No doubt he found it amusing to place his tomb under a brightly coloured kiddie ride.

My ankles wobbled in terror. I reminded myself there was a reason I was climbing into this murderer's lair. I couldn't remember what that reason was at the moment, but there had to be one.

The steps ended in a long corridor, its limestone walls

decorated with rows of plaster death masks. At first, this did not strike me as odd. Most wealthy Romans kept a collection of death masks to honour their ancestors. Then I noticed the masks' expressions. Like the carousel animals above, the plaster faces were frozen in panic, agony, rage, terror. These were not tributes. They were trophies.

I glanced back at Meg and Lavinia. Meg stood at the base of the stairs, blocking any possible retreat. The glittery unicorn on her T-shirt grinned at me hideously.

Lavinia met my eyes as if to say, *Yes, those masks are messed up. Now, keep moving.*

We followed Hazel down the corridor, every clink and rustle of our weapons echoing against the barrel ceiling. I was sure the Berkeley Seismology Lab, several miles away, would pick up my heartbeat on their seismographs and send out earthquake early warnings.

The tunnel split several times, but Hazel always seemed to know which direction to take. Occasionally she'd stop, look back at us, and point urgently to some part of the floor, reminding us not to stray from her path. I didn't know what would happen if I took a wrong step, but I had no desire to have my death mask added to Tarquin's collection.

After what seemed like hours, I began to hear water dripping somewhere in front of us. The tunnel opened into a circular room like a large cistern, the floor nothing but a narrow stone path across a deep dark pool. Hooked on the far wall were half a dozen wicker boxes like lobster traps, each with a circular opening at the bottom just the right size for . . . Oh, gods. Each box was the right size to be fitted over a person's head.

A tiny whimper escaped my mouth.

Hazel glanced back and mouthed, *What?*

A half-remembered story floated up from the sludge of my brain: how Tarquin had executed one of his enemies by drowning him in a sacred pool – binding the man's hands, placing a wicker cage over his head, then slowly adding rocks to the cage until the man could no longer keep his head above water.

Apparently, Tarquin still enjoyed that particular form of entertainment.

I shook my head. *You don't want to know.*

Hazel, being wise, took my word for it. She led us onward.

Just before the next chamber, Hazel held up a hand in warning. We halted. Following her gaze, I could make out two skeleton guards at the far side of the room, flanking an elaborately carved stone archway. The guards faced each other, wearing full war helmets, which was probably why they hadn't spotted us yet. If we made the slightest sound, if they glanced this way for any reason, we would be seen.

About seventy feet separated us from their position. The floor of their chamber was littered with old human bones. No way could we sneak up on them. These were skeleton warriors, the special forces of the undead world. I had zero desire to fight them. I shivered, wondering who they had been before the eurynomoi stripped them to the bone.

I met Hazel's eyes, then pointed back the way we'd come. *Retreat?*

She shook her head. *Wait.*

Hazel shut her eyes in concentration. A bead of sweat trickled down the side of her face.

The two guards snapped to attention. They turned away from us, facing the archway, then marched through, side by side, into the darkness.

Lavinia's gum almost fell out of her mouth. 'How?' she whispered.

Hazel put her finger to her lips, then motioned for us to follow.

The chamber was now empty except for the bones scattered across the floor. Perhaps the skeleton warriors came here to pick up spare parts. Along the opposite wall, above the archway, ran a balcony accessed by a staircase on either side. Its railing was a latticework of contorted human skeletons, which did not freak me out at all. Two doorways led off from the balcony. Except for the main archway through which our skeleton friends had marched, those seemed to be the only exits from the chamber.

Hazel led us up the left-hand staircase. Then, for reasons known only to herself, she crossed the balcony and took the doorway on the right. We followed her through.

At the end of a short corridor, about twenty feet ahead, firelight illuminated another balcony with a skeletal railing, the mirror image of the one we'd just left. I couldn't see much of the chamber beyond it, but the space was clearly occupied. A deep voice echoed from within – a voice I recognized.

Meg flicked her wrists, retracting her swords into rings – not because we were out of danger, but because she understood that even a little extra glow might give away our position. Lavinia tugged an oil cloth from her back pocket and draped it over her manubalista. Hazel gave me a look of warning that was completely unnecessary.

I knew what lay just ahead. Tarquin the Proud was holding court.

I crouched behind the balcony's skeletal latticework and peered into the throne room below, desperately hoping none of the undead would look up and see us. Or smell us. Oh, human body odour, why did you have to be so pungent after several hours of hiking?

Against the far wall, between two massive stone pillars, sat a sarcophagus chiselled with bas-relief images of monsters and wild animals, much like the creatures on the Tilden Park carousel. Lounging across the sarcophagus lid was the thing that had once been Tarquinius Superbus. His robes had not been laundered in several thousand years. They hung off him in mouldering shreds. His body had withered to a blackened skeleton. Patches of moss clung to his jawbone and cranium, giving him a grotesque beard and hairdo. Tendrils of glowing purple gas slithered through his ribcage and circled his joints, coiling up his neck and into his skull, lighting his eye sockets fiery violet.

Whatever that purple light was, it seemed to be holding Tarquin together. It probably wasn't his soul. I doubted Tarquin had ever had one of those. More likely it was his sheer ambition and hatred, a stubborn refusal to give up no matter how long he'd been dead.

The king seemed to be in the middle of scolding the two skeleton guards Hazel had manipulated.

'Did I call you?' demanded the king. 'No, I did not. So why are you here?'

The skeletons looked at each other as if wondering the same thing.

'Get back to your posts!' Tarquin shouted.

The guards marched back the way they had come.

This left three eurynomoi and half a dozen zombies milling around in the room, though I got the feeling there might be more directly beneath our balcony. Even worse, the zombies – vrykolakai, whatever you wanted to call them – were former Roman legionnaires. Most were still dressed for battle in dented armour and torn clothing, their skin puffy, their lips blue, gaping wounds in their chests and limbs.

The pain in my gut became almost intolerable. The words from the Burning Maze prophecy were stuck on replay in my mind: *Apollo faces death. Apollo faces death.*

Next to me, Lavinia trembled, her eyes tearing up. Her gaze was fixed on one of the dead legionnaires: a young man with long brown hair, the left side of his face badly burned. A former friend, I guessed. Hazel gripped Lavinia's shoulder – perhaps to comfort her, perhaps to remind her to be silent. Meg knelt at my other side, her glasses glinting. I desperately wished I had a permanent marker to black out her rhinestones.

She seemed to be counting enemies, calculating how fast she could take them all down. I had great faith in Meg's sword skills, at least when she wasn't exhausted from bending eucalyptus trees, but I also knew these enemies were too many, too powerful.

I touched her knee for attention. I shook my head and tapped my ear, reminding her that we were here to spy, not to fight.

She stuck out her tongue.

We were simpatico like that.

Below, Tarquin grumbled something about not being able to find good help. 'Anyone seen Caelius? Where is he? CAELIUS!'

A moment later, a eurynomos shuffled in from a side tunnel. He knelt before the king and screamed, 'EAT FLESH! SOOOON!'

Tarquin hissed. 'Caelius, we've discussed this. Keep your wits!'

Caelius slapped himself in the face. 'Yes, my king.' His voice now had a measured British accent. 'Terribly sorry. The fleet is on schedule. It should arrive in three days, just in time for the blood moon's rising.'

'Very well. And our own troops?'

'EAT FLESH!' Caelius slapped himself again. 'Apologies, sire. Yes, everything is ready. The Romans suspect nothing. As they turn outward to face the emperors, we will strike!'

'Good. It is imperative we take the city first. When the emperors arrive, I want to be already in control! They can burn the rest of the Bay Area if they wish, but the city is mine.'

Meg clenched her fists until they turned the colour of the bone latticework. After our experiences with the heat-distressed dryads of Southern California, she had got a little touchy whenever evil megalomaniacs threatened to torch the environment.

I gave her my most serious *Stay cool* glare, but she wouldn't look at me.

Down below, Tarquin was saying, 'And the silent one?'

'He is well-guarded, sire,' Caelius promised.

'Hmm,' Tarquin mused. 'Double the flock, nevertheless. We must be sure.'

'But, my king, surely the Romans cannot know about Sutro –'

'Silence!' Tarquin ordered.

Caelius whimpered. 'Yes, my king. FLESH! Sorry, my king. EAT FLESH!'

Tarquin raised his glowing purple skull towards our balcony. I prayed that he hadn't noticed us. Lavinia stopped chewing her gum. Hazel looked deep in concentration, perhaps willing the undead king to look away.

After a count of ten, Tarquin chuckled. 'Well, Caelius, it looks like you'll get to eat flesh sooner than I thought.'

'Master?'

'We have interlopers.' Tarquin raised his voice: 'Come down, you four! And meet your new king!'

17

Meg, don't you dare – MEG!
Or you could just get us killed
Yeah, sure, that works, too

I HOPED THERE WERE FOUR OTHER interlopers hidden somewhere on this balcony. Surely Tarquin was talking to them and not us.

Hazel jabbed her thumb towards the exit, the universal sign for *LET'S VAMOOSE!* Lavinia began crawling that way on her hands and knees. I was about to follow when Meg ruined everything.

She stood up tall (well, as tall as Meg can be), summoned her swords and leaped over the railing.

'MEEEEEEEEEGAH!' I shouted, half war cry, half *What in Hades are you doing?*

Without any conscious decision, I was on my feet, my bow in hand, an arrow nocked and loosed, then another and another. Hazel muttered a curse no proper lady from the 1930s should've known, drew her cavalry sword and jumped into the fray so Meg would not have to stand alone. Lavinia rose, struggling to uncover her manubalista, but the oil cloth seemed to be stuck on the crossbeam.

More undead swarmed at Meg from under the balcony. Her twin swords whirled and flashed, cutting off limbs and heads, reducing zombies to dust. Hazel decapitated Caelius, then turned to face another two eurynomoi.

The deceased former legionnaire with the burned face would have stabbed Hazel in the back, but Lavinia loosed her crossbow just in time. The Imperial gold bolt hit the zombie between the shoulder blades, causing him to implode in a pile of armour and clothes.

'Sorry, Bobby!' Lavinia said with a sob.

I made a mental note never to tell Hannibal how his former trainer had met his end.

I kept firing until only the Arrow of Dodona remained in my quiver. In retrospect, I realized I'd fired a dozen arrows in about thirty seconds, each a kill shot. My fingers literally steamed. I hadn't unleashed a volley like that since I was a god.

This should have delighted me, but any feeling of satisfaction was cut short by Tarquin's laughter. As Hazel and Meg cut down the last of his minions, he rose from his sarcophagus couch and gave us a round of applause. Nothing sounds more sinister than the ironic slow-clap of two skeletal hands.

'Lovely!' he said. 'Oh, that was very nice! You'll all make valuable members of my team!'

Meg charged.

The king didn't touch her but, with a flick of his hand, some invisible force sent Meg flying backwards into the far wall. Her swords clattered to the floor.

A guttural sound escaped my throat. I leaped over the railing, landing on one of my own spent arrow shafts (which are every bit as treacherous as banana peels). I slipped and fell hard on my hip. Not my most heroic entrance. Meanwhile, Hazel ran at Tarquin. She was hurled aside with another blast of unseen force.

Tarquin's hearty chuckle filled the chamber. From the corridors on either side of his sarcophagus, the sounds of shuffling feet and clanking armour echoed, getting closer and closer. Up on the balcony, Lavinia furiously cranked her manubalista. If I could buy her another twenty minutes or so, she might be able to take a second shot.

'Well, Apollo,' said Tarquin, purple coils of mist slithering from his eye sockets and into his mouth. Yuck. 'Neither of us have aged well, have we?'

My heart pounded. I groped around for usable arrows but found only more broken shafts. I was half tempted to shoot the Arrow of Dodona, but I couldn't risk giving Tarquin a weapon with prophetic knowledge. Can talking arrows be tortured? I didn't want to find out.

Meg struggled to her feet. She looked unhurt but grumpy, as she tended to whenever she got thrown into walls. I imagined she was thinking the same thing as me: this situation was too familiar, too much like Caligula's yacht when Meg and Jason had been imprisoned by *venti*. I couldn't let another scenario like that play out. I was tired of evil monarchs tossing us around like rag dolls.

Hazel was covered head to toe in zombie dust. That couldn't have been good for her respiratory system. In the back of my mind, I wondered if we could get Justicia the Roman law goddess to file a class-action suit on our behalf against Tarquin for hazardous tomb conditions.

'Everyone,' Hazel said, 'back up.'

It was the same thing she'd told us in the tunnel to camp, right before turning the eurynomos into ceiling art.

Tarquin just laughed. 'Ah, Hazel Levesque, your clever tricks with rocks won't work here. This is my seat of power! My reinforcements will arrive any moment. It will be easier if you don't resist your deaths. I'm told it's less painful that way.'

Above me, Lavinia continued to crank her hand-cannon.

Meg picked up her swords. 'Fight or run, guys?'

The way she glared at Tarquin, I was pretty sure I knew her preference.

'Oh, child,' Tarquin said. 'You can try to run, but soon enough you'll be fighting at my side with those wonderful blades of yours. As for Apollo . . . he's not going anywhere.'

He curled his fingers. He was nowhere close to me, but my gut wound convulsed, sending hot skewers into my ribcage and groin. I screamed. My eyes welled with tears.

'Stop it!' Lavinia shrieked. She dropped from the balcony and landed at my side. 'What are you doing to him?'

Meg charged again at the undead king, perhaps hoping to catch him off guard. Without even looking at her, Tarquin tossed her aside with another blast of force. Hazel stood as stiff as a limestone column, her eyes fixed on the wall behind the king. Tiny cracks had begun to spiderweb across the stone.

'Why, Lavinia,' the king said, 'I'm calling Apollo home!'

He grinned, which was the only facial expression he was capable of, having no face. 'Poor Lester would've been compelled to seek me out eventually, once the poison took hold of his brain. But getting him here so soon – this is a special treat!'

He clenched his bony fist tighter. My pain tripled. I groaned and blubbered. My vision swam in red Vaseline. How was it possible to feel so much pain and not die?

'Leave him alone!' yelled Meg.

From the tunnels on either side of Tarquin's sarcophagus, more zombies began to spill into the room.

'Run.' I gasped. 'Get out of here.'

I now understood the lines from the Burning Maze: I would face death in Tarquin's tomb, or a fate *worse* than death. But I would not allow my friends to perish, too.

Stubbornly, annoyingly, they refused to leave.

'Apollo is *my* servant now, Meg McCaffrey,' Tarquin said. 'You really shouldn't mourn him. He's terrible to the people he loves. You can ask the Sibyl.'

The king regarded me as I writhed like an insect pinned to a corkboard. 'I hope the Sibyl lasts long enough to see you humbled. That may be what finally breaks her. And when those bumbling emperors arrive, they will see the true terror of a Roman king!'

Hazel howled. The back wall collapsed, bringing down half the ceiling. Tarquin and his troops disappeared under an avalanche of rocks the size of assault vehicles.

My pain subsided to mere agony levels. Lavinia and Meg hauled me to my feet. Angry purple lines of infection now twisted up my arms. That probably wasn't good.

Hazel hobbled over. Her corneas had turned an unhealthy shade of grey. 'We need to move.'

Lavinia glanced at the pile of rubble. 'But isn't he –?'

'Not dead,' Hazel said with bitter disappointment. 'I can feel him squirming under there, trying to . . .' She shivered. 'It doesn't matter. More undead will be coming. Let's go!'

Easier said than done.

Hazel limped along, breathing heavily as she led us back through a different set of tunnels. Meg guarded our retreat, slicing down the occasional zombie that stumbled across our path. Lavinia had to support most of my weight, but she was deceptively strong, just as she was deceptively nimble. She seemed to have no trouble hauling my sorry carcass through the tomb.

I was only semiconscious of my surroundings. My bow clanged against my ukulele, making a jarring open chord in perfect sync with my rattled brain.

What had just happened?

After that beautiful moment of godlike prowess with my bow, I'd suffered an ugly, perhaps terminal setback with my gut wound. I now had to admit I was *not* getting better. Tarquin had spoken of a poison slowly making its way to my brain. Despite the best efforts of the camp's healers, I was turning, becoming one of the king's creatures. By facing him, I had apparently accelerated the process.

This should have terrified me. The fact that I could think about it with such detachment was itself concerning. The medical part of my mind decided I must be going into shock. Or possibly just, you know, dying.

Hazel stopped at the intersection of two corridors. 'I – I'm not sure.'

'What do you mean?' Meg asked.

Hazel's corneas were still the colour of wet clay. 'I can't get a read. There should be an exit here. We're close to the surface, but . . . I'm sorry, guys.'

Meg retracted her blades. 'That's okay. Keep watch.'

'What are you doing?' Lavinia asked.

Meg touched the nearest wall. The ceiling shifted and cracked. I had a fleeting image of us getting buried like Tarquin under several tons of rock – which, in my present state of mind, seemed like an amusing way to die. Instead, dozens of thickening tree roots wriggled their way through the cracks, pushing apart the stones. Even as a former god accustomed to magic, I found it mesmerizing. The roots spiralled and wove themselves together, shoving aside the earth, letting in the dim glow of moonlight, until we found ourselves at the base of a gently sloping chute (a root chute?) with handholds and footholds for climbing.

Meg sniffed the air above. 'Smells safe. Let's go.'

While Hazel stood guard, Meg and Lavinia joined forces to get me up the chute. Meg pulled. Lavinia pushed. It was all very undignified, but the thought of Lavinia's half-primed manubalista jostling around somewhere below my delicate posterior gave me an incentive to keep moving.

We emerged at the base of a redwood in the middle of the forest. The carousel was nowhere in sight. Meg gave Hazel a hand up, then touched the trunk of the tree. The root chute spiralled shut, submerging under the grass.

Hazel swayed on her feet. 'Where are we?'

'This way,' Lavinia announced.

She shouldered my weight again, despite my protestations

that I was fine. Really, I was only dying a little bit. We staggered down a trail among the looming redwoods. I couldn't see the stars or discern any landmarks. I had no idea in which direction we were heading, but Lavinia seemed undeterred.

'How do you know where we are?' I asked.

'Told you,' she said. 'I like to explore.'

She must really like Poison Oak, I thought for the umpteenth time. Then I wondered if Lavinia simply felt more at home in the wild than she did at camp. She and my sister would get along fine.

'Are any of you hurt?' I asked. 'Did the ghouls scratch you?'

The girls all shook their heads.

'What about you?' Meg scowled and pointed at my gut. 'I thought you were getting better.'

'I guess I was too optimistic.' I wanted to scold her for jumping into combat and nearly getting us all killed, but I didn't have the energy. Also, the way she was looking at me, I got the feeling that her grumpy facade might collapse into tears faster than Tarquin's ceilings had crumbled.

Hazel eyed me warily. 'You should have healed. I don't understand.'

'Lavinia, can I have some gum?' I asked.

'Seriously?' She dug in her pocket and handed me a piece.

'You're a corrupting influence.' With leaden fingers, I managed to unwrap the gum and stick it in my mouth. The flavour was sickly sweet. It *tasted* pink. Still, it was better than the sour ghoul poison welling up in my throat. I chewed, glad of something to focus on beside the memory of Tarquin's skeletal fingers curling and sending scythes of fire through my intestines. And what he had said about the Sibyl . . . ? No. I couldn't process that right now.

After a few hundred yards of torturous hiking, we reached a small stream.

'We're close,' Lavinia said.

Hazel glanced behind us. 'I'm sensing maybe a dozen behind us, closing fast.'

I saw and heard nothing, but I took Hazel's word for it. 'Go. You'll move faster without me.'

'Not happening,' Meg said.

'Here, take Apollo.' Lavinia offered me to Meg like I was a sack of groceries. 'You guys cross this stream, go up that hill. You'll see Camp Jupiter.'

Meg straightened her grimy glasses. 'What about you?'

'I'll draw them away.' Lavinia patted her manubalista.

'That's a terrible idea,' I said.

'It's what I do,' Lavinia said.

I wasn't sure if she meant *drawing away enemies* or *executing terrible ideas*.

'She's right,' Hazel decided. 'Be careful, legionnaire. We'll see you at camp.'

Lavinia nodded and darted into the woods.

'Are you sure that was wise?' I asked Hazel.

'No,' she admitted. 'But whatever Lavinia does, she always seems to come back unscathed. Now let's get you home.'

18

Cooking with Pranjal
Chickweed and unicorn horn
Slow-basted zombie

HOME. SUCH A WONDERFUL WORD.

I had no idea what it meant, but it sounded nice.

Somewhere along the trail back to camp, my mind must have detached from my body. I don't remember passing out. I don't remember reaching the valley. But at some point my consciousness drifted away like an escaped helium balloon.

I dreamed of homes. Had I ever really had one?

Delos was my birthplace, but only because my pregnant mother, Leto, took refuge there to escape Hera's wrath. The island served as an emergency sanctuary for my sister and me, too, but it never felt like *home* any more than the back seat of a taxi would feel like home to a child born on the way to a hospital.

Mount Olympus? I had a palace there. I visited for the holidays. But it always felt more like the place my dad lived with my stepmom.

The Palace of the Sun? That was Helios's old crib. I'd just redecorated.

Even Delphi, home of my greatest Oracle, had originally

been the lair of Python. Try as you might, you can *never* get the smell of old snakeskin out of a volcanic cavern.

Sad to say, in my four-thousand-plus years, the times I'd felt most at home had all happened during the past few months: at Camp Half-Blood, sharing a cabin with my demigod children; at the Waystation with Emma, Jo, Georgina, Leo and Calypso, all of us sitting around the kitchen table chopping vegetables from the garden for dinner; at the Cistern in Palm Springs with Meg, Grover, Mellie, Coach Hedge and a prickly assortment of cactus dryads; and now at Camp Jupiter, where the anxious, grief-stricken Romans, despite their many problems, despite the fact that I brought misery and disaster wherever I went, had welcomed me with respect, a room above their coffee shop and some lovely bed linen to wear.

These places were homes. Whether I deserved to be part of them or not – that was a different question.

I wanted to linger in those good memories. I suspected I might be dying – perhaps in a coma on the forest floor as ghoul poison spread through my veins. I wanted my last thoughts to be happy ones. My brain had different ideas.

I found myself in the cavern of Delphi.

Nearby, dragging himself through the darkness, wreathed in orange and yellow smoke, was the all-too-familiar shape of Python, like the world's largest and most rancid Komodo dragon. His smell was oppressively sour – a physical pressure that constricted my lungs and made my sinuses scream. His eyes cut through the sulphuric vapour like headlamps.

'You think it matters.' Python's booming voice rattled

my teeth. 'These little victories. You think they lead to something?'

I couldn't speak. My mouth still tasted like bubblegum. I was grateful for the sickly sweetness – a reminder that a world existed outside this cave of horrors.

Python lumbered closer. I wanted to grab my bow, but my arms were paralysed.

'It was for nothing,' he said. 'The deaths you caused – the deaths you *will* cause – they don't matter. If you win every battle, you will still lose the war. As usual, you don't understand the true stakes. Face me, and you will die.'

He opened his vast maw, slavering reptilian lips pulled over glistening teeth.

'GAH!' My eyes flew open. My limbs flailed.

'Oh, good,' said a voice. 'You're awake.'

I was lying on the floor inside some sort of wooden structure, like . . . ah, a stable. The smells of hay and horse manure filled my nostrils. A hessian blanket prickled against my back. Peering down at me were two unfamiliar faces. One belonged to a handsome young man with silky black hair cresting over his wide sepia forehead.

The other face belonged to a unicorn. Its muzzle glistened with mucus. Its startled blue eyes, wide and unblinking, fixed on me as if I might be a tasty bag of oats. Stuck on the tip of its horn was a rotary cheese grater.

'GAH!' I said again.

'Calm down, dummy,' Meg said, somewhere to my left. 'You're with friends.'

I couldn't see her. My peripheral vision was still blurry and pink.

I pointed weakly at the unicorn. 'Cheese grater.'

'Yes,' said the lovely young man. 'It's the easiest way to get a dose of horn shavings directly into the wound. Buster doesn't mind. Do you, Buster?'

Buster the unicorn continued to stare at me. I wondered if he was even alive, or just a prop unicorn they had wheeled in.

'My name's Pranjal,' said the young man. 'Head healer for the legion. I worked on you when you first got here, but we didn't really meet then, since, well, you were unconscious. I'm a son of Asclepius. I guess that makes you my grandpa.'

I moaned. 'Please don't call me Grandpa. I feel terrible enough already. Are – are the others all right? Lavinia? Hazel?'

Meg hovered into view. Her glasses were clean, her hair was washed and her clothes were changed, so I must have been out for quite a while. 'We're all fine. Lavinia got back right after we did. But you almost died.' She sounded annoyed, as if my death would have inconvenienced her greatly. 'You should've told me how bad that cut was.'

'I thought . . . I assumed it would heal.'

Pranjal knitted his eyebrows. 'Yes, well, it *should* have. You got excellent care, if I do say so myself. We know about ghoul infections. They're usually curable, if we catch them within twenty-four hours.'

'But *you*,' Meg said, scowling at me. 'You aren't responding to treatment.'

'That's not *my* fault!'

'It could be your godly side,' Pranjal mused. 'I've never had a patient who was a former immortal. That might make you resistant to demigod healing, or more susceptible to undead scratches. I just don't know.'

I levered myself up on my elbows. I was bare-chested. My wound had been re-bandaged, so I couldn't tell how bad it looked underneath, but the pain had subsided to a dull ache. Tendrils of purple infection still snaked from my belly, up my chest and down my arms, but their colour had faded to a faint lavender.

'Whatever you did obviously helped,' I said.

'We'll see.' Pranjal's frown was not encouraging. 'I tried a special concoction, a kind of magical equivalent to broad-spectrum antibiotics. It required a special strain of *Stellaria media* – magical chickweed – that doesn't grow in Northern California.'

'It grows here now,' Meg announced.

'Yes,' Pranjal agreed with a smile. 'I may have to keep Meg around. She's pretty handy for growing medicinal plants.'

Meg blushed.

Buster still hadn't moved or blinked. I hoped Pranjal occasionally put a spoon under the unicorn's nostrils to make sure he was breathing.

'At any rate,' Pranjal continued, 'the salve I used wasn't a cure. It will only slow down your . . . your condition.'

My *condition*. What a wonderful euphemism for turning into a walking corpse.

'And if I do want a cure?' I asked. 'Which, by the way, I do.'

'That's going to take more powerful healing than I'm capable of,' he confessed. '*God*-level healing.'

I felt like crying. I decided Pranjal needed to work on his bedside manner, perhaps by having a better collection of miraculous over-the-counter cures that did not require divine intervention.

'We could try more horn shavings,' Meg suggested. 'That's fun. I mean, that might work.'

Between Meg's anxiousness to use the cheese grater and Buster's hungry stare, I was starting to feel like a plate of pasta. 'I don't suppose you have any leads on available healing gods?'

'Actually,' Pranjal said, 'if you're feeling up to it, you should get dressed and have Meg walk you to the principia. Reyna and Frank are anxious to talk to you.'

Meg took pity on me.

Before meeting the praetors, she took me back to Bombilo's so I could wash and change my clothes. Afterwards, we stopped by the legion mess hall for food. Judging from the angle of the sun and the near-empty dining room, I guessed it was late afternoon, between lunch and dinner, which meant I'd been unconscious for almost a full day.

The day after tomorrow, then, would be 8 April – the blood moon, Lester's birthday, the day two evil emperors and an undead king attacked Camp Jupiter. On the bright side, the mess hall was serving fish fingers.

When I was done with my meal (here's a culinary secret I discovered: ketchup really enhances fries and fish fingers), Meg escorted me down the Via Praetoria to legion headquarters.

Most of the Romans seemed to be off doing whatever

Romans did in the late afternoon: marching, digging trenches, playing *Fortiusnitius* . . . I wasn't really sure. The few legionnaires we passed stared at me as we walked by, their conversations sputtering to a stop. I guessed word had spread about our adventure in Tarquin's tomb. Perhaps they'd heard that I had a slight turning-into-a-zombie problem and they were waiting for me to scream for brains.

The thought made me shudder. My gut wound felt so much better at the moment. I could walk without cringing. The sun was shining. I'd eaten a good meal. How could I still be poisoned?

Denial is a powerful thing.

Unfortunately, I suspected Pranjal was right. He had only slowed down the infection. My condition was beyond anything that camp healers, Greek or Roman, could solve. I needed godly help – which was something Zeus had expressly forbidden the other gods to give me.

The guards at the *praetorium* let us through immediately. Inside, Reyna and Frank sat behind a long table laden with maps, books, daggers and a large jar of jelly beans. Against the back wall, in front of a purple curtain, stood the legion's golden eagle, humming with energy. Being so near to it made the hairs on my arms stand up. I didn't know how the praetors could tolerate working here with that thing right behind them. Hadn't they read the medical journal articles about the effects of long-term exposure to electromagnetic Roman standards?

Frank appeared ready for battle in his full armour. Reyna looked like *she* was the one who'd just woken up. She wore her purple cloak hastily pulled over a too-large PUERTO RICO

FUERTE T-shirt, which I wondered if she'd slept in – but that was none of my business. The left side of her hair was an adorable fuzzy black mess of cowlicks that made me wonder if she slept on that side – and, again, that was none of my business.

Curled on the carpet at her feet were two automatons I hadn't seen before – a pair of greyhounds, one gold and one silver. They both raised their heads when they saw me, then sniffed the air and growled as if to say, *Hey, Mom, this guy smells like zombie. Can we kill him?*

Reyna hushed them. She dug some jelly beans out of the jar and tossed them to the dogs. I wasn't sure why metallic greyhounds would like candy, but they snapped up the morsels, then settled their heads back on the carpet.

'Er, nice dogs,' I said. 'Why haven't I seen them before?'

'Aurum and Argentum have been out searching,' Reyna said, in a tone that discouraged follow-up questions. 'How is your wound?'

'My wound is thriving,' I said. 'Me, not so much.'

'He's better than before,' Meg insisted. 'I grated some unicorn-horn shavings on his cut. It was fun.'

'Pranjal helped, too,' I said.

Frank gestured at the two visitors' seats. 'You guys make yourselves comfortable.'

Comfortable was a relative term. The three-legged foldable stools did not look as comfy as the praetors' chairs. They also reminded me of the Oracle's tripod seat in Delphi, which reminded me of Rachel Elizabeth Dare back at Camp Half-Blood, who was not-so-patiently waiting for me to restore her powers of prophecy. Thinking about her reminded me of the Delphic cave, which reminded me of Python, which reminded me of my nightmare and how scared I was of dying. I hate streams of consciousness.

Once we were seated, Reyna spread a parchment scroll across the table. 'So, we've been working with Ella and Tyson since yesterday, trying to decipher some more lines of prophecy.'

'We've made progress,' Frank added. 'We *think* we've found the recipe you were talking about at the senate meeting – the ritual that could summon divine aid to save the camp.'

'That's great, right?' Meg reached for the jar of jelly beans but retracted her hand when Aurum and Argentum began growling.

'Maybe.' Reyna exchanged a worried look with Frank. 'The thing is, if we're reading the lines correctly . . . the ritual requires a death sacrifice.'

The fish fingers began sword-fighting with the french fries in my stomach.

'That can't be right,' I said. 'We gods would never ask you mortals to sacrifice one of your own. We gave that up centuries ago! Or millennia ago, I can't remember. But I'm *sure* we gave it up!'

Frank gripped his armrests. 'Yeah, that's the thing. It's not a mortal who's supposed to die.'

'No.' Reyna locked eyes with me. 'It seems this ritual requires the death of a god.'

19

O book, what's my fate?
What is the secret of life?
See appendix F

WHY WAS EVERYBODY LOOKING AT ME?

I couldn't help it if I was the only (ex-)god in the room.

Reyna leaned over the scroll, tracing her finger across the parchment. 'Frank copied these lines from Tyson's back. As you can probably guess, they read more like an instruction manual than a prophecy . . .'

I was about to crawl out of my skin. I wanted to rip the scroll away from Reyna and read the bad news myself. Was my name mentioned? Sacrificing *me* couldn't possibly please the gods, could it? If we Olympians started sacrificing one another, that would set a terrible precedent.

Meg eyed the jar of jelly beans, while the greyhounds eyed her. 'Which god dies?'

'Well, that particular line . . .' Reyna squinted, then pushed the parchment over to Frank. 'What is that word?'

Frank looked sheepish. '*Shattered.* Sorry, I was writing fast.'

'No, no. It's fine. Your handwriting is better than mine.'

'Can you please just tell me what it says?' I begged.

'Right, sorry,' Reyna said. 'Well, it's not exactly poetry, like the sonnet you got in Indianapolis –'

'Reyna!'

'Okay, okay. It says: *All to be done on the day of greatest need: gather the ingredients for a type-six burnt offering (see appendix B)* –'

'We're doomed,' I wailed. 'We'll never be able to collect those . . . whatever they are.'

'That part's easy,' Frank assured me. 'Ella has the list of ingredients. She says it's all ordinary stuff.' He gestured for Reyna to continue.

'*Add the last breath of the god who speaks not, once his soul is cut free,*' Reyna read aloud, '*together with the shattered glass. Then the single-deity summoning prayer (see appendix C) must be uttered through the rainbow.*' She took a breath. 'We don't have the actual text of that prayer yet, but Ella is confident she can transcribe it before the battle starts, now that she knows what to look for in appendix C.'

Frank glanced at me for a reaction. 'Does the rest of it make any sense to you?'

I was so relieved I almost slumped off my three-legged stool. 'You got me all worked up. I thought . . . Well, I've been called a lot of things, but never *the god who speaks not*. It sounds like we must find the soundless god, whom we've discussed before, and, er –'

'Kill him?' Reyna asked. 'How would killing a god please the gods?'

I didn't have an answer to that. Then again, many prophecies seemed illogical until they played out. Only in retrospect did they appear obvious.

'Perhaps if I knew which god we're talking about . . .' I pounded my fist on my knee. 'I feel like I should know, but it's buried deep. An obscure memory. I don't suppose you've checked your libraries or run a Google search or something?'

'Of course we looked,' Frank said. 'There's no listing for a Roman or Greek god of silence.'

Roman or Greek. I felt sure I was missing something – like part of my brain, for instance. *Last breath. His soul is cut free.* It definitely sounded like instructions for a sacrifice.

'I have to think on it,' I decided. 'As for the rest of the instructions: *shattered glass* seems like an odd request, but I suppose we can find some easily enough.'

'We could break the jelly-bean jar,' Meg suggested.

Reyna and Frank politely ignored her.

'And the *single-deity summoning* thing?' Frank asked. 'I guess that means we won't be getting a host of gods charging down in their chariots?'

'Probably not,' I agreed.

But my pulse quickened. The possibility of being able to speak to even *one* fellow Olympian after all this time – to summon actual grade-AA-quality, jumbo, cage-free, locally sourced divine help . . . I found the idea both exhilarating and terrifying. Would I get to choose which god I called, or was it predetermined by the prayer? 'Nevertheless, even one god can make all the difference.'

Meg shrugged. 'Depends on the god.'

'That hurt,' I said.

'What about the last line?' Reyna asked. 'The prayer *must be uttered through the rainbow.*'

'An Iris-message,' I said, happy I could answer one question at least. 'It's a Greek thing, a way of beseeching Iris, goddess of the rainbow, to carry a message – in this case, a prayer to Mount Olympus. The formula is quite simple.'

'But . . .' Frank frowned. 'Percy told me about Iris-messages. They don't work any more, do they? Not since all our communications went silent.'

Communications, I thought. *Silent. The soundless god.*

I felt as if I'd fallen into the deep end of a very cold pool. 'Oh. I am so stupid.'

Meg giggled, but she resisted the many sarcastic comments that were no doubt filling her mind.

I, in turn, resisted the urge to push her off her stool. 'This soundless god, whoever he is . . . What if he's the *reason* our communications don't work? What if the Triumvirate has somehow been harnessing his power to prevent us all from talking to one another, and to keep us from beseeching the gods for help?'

Reyna crossed her arms, blocking out the word FUERTE on her T-shirt. 'You're saying what – this soundless god is in cahoots with the Triumvirate? We have to kill him to open our means of communication? Then we could send an Iris-message, do the ritual and get divine help? I'm still stuck on the whole *killing a god* thing.'

I considered the Erythraean Sibyl, whom we'd rescued from her prison in the Burning Maze. 'Perhaps this god isn't a willing participant. He might have been trapped, or . . . I don't know, coerced somehow.'

'So we free him by killing him?' Frank asked. 'Gotta agree with Reyna. That sounds harsh.'

'One way to find out,' Meg said. 'We go to this Sutro place. Can I feed your dogs?'

Without waiting for permission, she grabbed the jelly-bean jar and popped it open.

Aurum and Argentum, having heard the magic words *feed* and *dogs*, did not growl or tear Meg apart. They got up, moved to her side and sat watching her, their jewelled eyes sending the message, *Please, please, please.*

Meg doled out a jelly bean to each dog, then ate two herself. Two for the dogs, two for herself. Meg had achieved a major diplomatic breakthrough.

'Meg's right. Sutro is the place Tarquin's minion mentioned,' I recalled. 'Presumably we'll find the soundless god there.'

'Mount Sutro?' Reyna asked. 'Or Sutro Tower? Did he say which?'

Frank raised an eyebrow. 'Isn't it the same place? I always just call that area Sutro Hill.'

'Actually, the biggest hill is Mount Sutro,' said Reyna. 'The giant antenna is on a different hill right next to it. That's Sutro Tower. I only know this because Aurum and Argentum like to go hiking over there.'

The greyhounds turned their heads at the word *hiking*, then went back to studying Meg's hand in the jelly-bean jar. I tried to imagine Reyna hiking with her dogs just for fun. I wondered if Lavinia knew that was her pastime. Maybe Lavinia was such a dedicated hiker because she was trying to outdo the praetor, the same way she had her thinking spot high above Reyna's.

Then I decided that trying to psychoanalyse my

pink-haired, tap-dancing, manubalista-wielding friend was probably a losing proposition.

'Is this Sutro place close?' Meg was slowly depleting all the green jelly beans, which was giving her a different sort of green thumb.

'It's across the bay in San Francisco,' Reyna said. 'The tower is massive. You can see it from all over the Bay Area.'

'Weird place to keep someone,' Frank said. 'But I guess no weirder than under a carousel.'

I tried to remember if I'd ever been to Sutro Tower, or any of the other various Sutro-labelled places in that vicinity. Nothing came to mind, but the instructions from the Sibylline Books had left me deeply unsettled. The last breath of a god was not an ingredient most Ancient Roman temples kept in their pantries. And cutting a god's soul free *really* was not something Romans were supposed to try without adult supervision.

If the soundless god was part of the Triumvirate's scheme for control, why would Tarquin have access to him? What had Tarquin meant by 'doubling the flock' to guard the god's location? And what he'd said about the Sibyl – *I hope the Sibyl lasts long enough to see you humbled. That may be what finally breaks her.* Had he just been messing with my mind? If the Sibyl of Cumae was truly still alive, a captive of Tarquin, I was obliged to help her.

Help her, the cynical part of my mind responded. *Like you helped her before?*

'Wherever the soundless god is,' I said, 'he'll be heavily protected, especially now. Tarquin must know we'll try to locate the hiding place.'

'And we have to do so on April the eighth,' said Reyna. *'The day of greatest need.'*

Frank grunted. 'Good thing we don't have anything else scheduled that day. Like getting invaded on two fronts, for instance.'

'My gods, Meg,' Reyna said, 'you're going to make yourself sick. I'll never get all the sugar out of Aurum and Argentum's gear works.'

'Fine.' Meg put the jelly-bean jar back on the table, but not before grabbing one last fistful for herself and her canine accomplices. 'So we have to wait until the day after tomorrow? What'll we do until then?'

'Oh, we've got plenty to do,' Frank promised. 'Planning. Constructing defences. War games all day tomorrow. We have to run the legion through every possible scenario. Besides . . .'

His voice faltered, as if he'd realized he was about to say something aloud that was best left in his head. His hand drifted towards the pouch where he held his firewood.

I wondered if he'd taken any additional notes from Ella and Tyson – perhaps more harpy ramblings about bridges, fires and something, something, something. If so, Frank apparently didn't want to share.

'Besides,' he started again, 'you guys should rest up for the quest. You'll have to leave for Sutro early on Lester's birthday.'

'Can we please not call it that?' I pleaded.

'Also, who is "you guys"?' Reyna asked. 'We may need another senate vote to decide who goes on the quest.'

'Nah,' Frank said. 'I mean, we can check with the

senators, but this is clearly an extension of the original mission, right? Besides, when we're at war, you and I have full executive power.'

Reyna regarded her colleague. 'Why, Frank Zhang. You've been studying the praetors' handbook.'

'Maybe a little.' Frank cleared his throat. 'Anyway, we know who needs to go: Apollo, Meg and you. The doorway to the soundless god has to be opened by Bellona's daughter, right?'

'But . . .' Reyna looked back and forth between us. 'I can't just leave on the day of a major battle. Bellona's power is all about strength in numbers. I need to lead the troops.'

'And you will,' Frank promised. 'As soon as you get back from San Francisco. In the meantime, I'll hold the fort. I've got this.'

Reyna hesitated, but I thought I detected a gleam in her eye. 'Are you sure, Frank? I mean, yeah, of course you can do it. I know you can, but –'

'I'll be fine.' Frank smiled like he meant it. 'Apollo and Meg need you on this quest. Go.'

Why did Reyna look so excited? How crushing her work must have been, if, after carrying the burden of leadership for so long, she was looking forward to going on an adventure across the bay to kill a god.

'I suppose,' she said with obviously feigned reluctance.

'It's settled, then.' Frank turned to Meg and me. 'You guys rest up. Big day tomorrow. We'll need your help with the war games. I've got a special job in mind for each of you.'

20

Hamster ball of death
Spare me your fiery doom
I'm not feeling it

OH, BOY, A SPECIAL JOB!

The anticipation was killing me. Or maybe that was the poison in my veins.

As soon as I returned to the coffee shop's attic, I crashed on my bed.

Meg huffed, 'It's still light outside. You slept all day.'

'Not turning into a zombie is hard work.'

'I know!' she snapped. 'I'm sorry!'

I looked up, surprised by her tone. Meg kicked an old paper latte cup across the room. She plopped onto her bed and glared at the floor.

'Meg?'

In her windowbox, irises grew with such speed that their flowers crackled open like corn kernels. Just a few minutes ago, Meg had been happily insulting me and gorging on jelly beans. Now . . . Was she *crying*?

'Meg.' I sat up, trying not to wince. 'Meg, you're not responsible for me getting hurt.'

She twisted the ring on her right hand, then the one on her left, as if they'd become too small for her fingers. 'I just thought . . . if I could kill him . . .' She wiped her nose. 'Like in some stories. You kill the master, and you can free the people he's turned.'

It took a moment for her words to sink in. I was pretty sure the dynamic she was describing applied to vampires, not zombies, but I understood what she meant.

'You're talking about Tarquin,' I said. 'You jumped into the throne room because . . . you wanted to save me?'

'Duh,' she muttered, without any heat.

I put my hand over my bandaged abdomen. I'd been so angry with Meg for her recklessness in the tomb. I'd assumed she was just being impulsive, reacting to Tarquin's plans to let the Bay Area burn. But she'd leaped into battle for *me* – in the hope that she could kill Tarquin and erase my curse. That was even *before* I'd realized how bad my condition was. Meg must have been more worried, or more intuitive, than she'd let on.

Which certainly took all the fun out of criticizing her.

'Oh, Meg.' I shook my head. 'That was a crazy, senseless stunt, and I love you for it. But don't beat yourself up. Pranjal's medicine bought me some extra time. And you did, too, of course, with your cheese-grating skills and your magical chickweed. You've done everything you could. When we summon godly help, I can ask for complete healing. I'm sure I'll be as good as new. Or at least as good as a Lester can be.'

Meg tilted her head, making her crooked glasses just about horizontal. 'How can you know? Is this god going to give us three wishes or something?'

I considered that. When my followers called, had I ever

shown up and granted them three wishes? LOL, nope. Maybe *one* wish, if that wish was something I wanted to happen anyway. And if this ritual only allowed me to call one god, who would it be – assuming I could even choose? Perhaps my son Asclepius would be able to heal me, but he couldn't very well fight the Roman emperors' forces and the hordes of undead. Mars might grant us success on the battlefield, but he'd look at my wound and say something like, *Yeah, rough break. Die bravely!*

Here I was with purple lines of infection snaking down my arms, telling Meg not to worry.

'I don't know, Meg,' I confessed. 'You're right. I can't be sure everything will be okay. But I *can* promise you I'm not giving up. We've come this far. I'm not going to let a belly scratch stop us from defeating the Triumvirate.'

She had so much mucus dripping from her nostrils, she would've made Buster the unicorn proud. She sniffled, wiping her upper lip with her knuckle. 'I don't want to lose somebody else.'

My mental gears weren't turning at full speed. I had trouble wrapping my mind around the fact that by 'somebody else', Meg meant *me*.

I recalled one of her early memories, which I'd witnessed in my dreams: she'd been forced to gaze upon her father's lifeless body on the steps of Grand Central Station while Nero, his murderer, hugged her and promised to take care of her.

I remembered how she'd betrayed me to Nero in the Grove of Dodona out of fear of the Beast, Nero's dark side, and how horrible she'd felt afterwards, when we were reunited in Indianapolis. Then she'd taken all her displaced anger and guilt and frustration and projected it onto Caligula (which, to be honest, was a pretty good place to put it). Meg, being unable to lash out at Nero, had wanted so badly to kill Caligula. When Jason died instead, she was devastated.

Now, aside from all the bad memories the Roman trappings of Camp Jupiter might have triggered for her, she was faced with the prospect of losing me. In a moment of shock, like a unicorn staring me right in the face, I realized that despite all the grief Meg gave me, and the way she ordered me around, she cared for me. For the past three months, I had been her one constant friend, just as she had been mine.

The only other person who might have come close was Peaches, Meg's fruit-tree spirit minion, and we hadn't seen him since Indianapolis. At first, I'd assumed Peaches was just being temperamental about when he decided to appear, like most supernatural creatures. But if he *had* tried to follow us to Palm Springs, where even the cacti struggled to survive . . . I didn't relish a peach tree's odds of survival there, much less in the Burning Maze.

Meg hadn't mentioned Peaches to me once since we were in the Labyrinth. Now I realized his absence must have been weighing on her, along with all her other worries.

What a horribly insufficient friend I had been.

'Come here.' I held out my arms. 'Please?'

Meg hesitated. Still sniffling, she rose from her bed and trudged towards me. She fell into my hug like I was a comfy mattress. I grunted, surprised by how solid and heavy she was. She smelled of apple peel and mud, but I didn't mind. I didn't even mind the mucus and tears soaking my shoulder.

I'd always wondered what it would be like to have a younger sibling. Sometimes I'd treated Artemis as my baby sister, since I'd been born a few minutes earlier, but that had mostly been to annoy her. With Meg, I felt as if it were actually true. I had someone who depended on me, who needed me around no matter how much we irritated each other. I thought about Hazel and Frank and the washing away of curses. I supposed that kind of love could come from many different types of relationships.

'Okay.' Meg pushed herself away, wiping her cheeks furiously. 'Enough of that. You sleep. I'm – I'm going to get dinner or whatever.'

For a long time after she left, I lay in my bed staring at the ceiling.

Music floated up from the café: the soothing sounds of Horace Silver's piano, punctuated by the hiss of the espresso machine, accompanying Bombilo singing in two-headed harmony. After spending a few days with these noises, I found them soothing, even homely. I drifted off to sleep, hoping to have warm, fuzzy dreams about Meg and me skipping through sunlit fields with our elephant, unicorn and metal greyhound friends.

Instead, I found myself back with the emperors.

On my list of places I least wanted to be, Caligula's yacht ranked right up there with Tarquin's tomb, the eternal abyss of Chaos and the Limburger cheese factory in Liège, Belgium, where stinking gym socks went to feel better about themselves.

Commodus lounged in a deckchair, an aluminium

tanning bib around his neck reflecting the afternoon sun directly onto his face. Sunglasses covered his scarred eyes. He wore only pink swimming trunks and pink Crocs. I took absolutely no notice of the way the tanning oil glistened on his muscular bronzed body.

Caligula stood nearby in his captain's uniform: white coat, dark slacks and striped shirt, all crisply pressed. His cruel face looked almost angelic as he marvelled at the contraption that now took up the entire aft deck. The artillery mortar was the size of an aboveground swimming pool, with a two-foot-thick rim of dark iron and a diameter wide enough to drive a car through. Nestled in the barrel, a massive green sphere glowed like a giant radioactive hamster ball.

Pandai rushed around the deck, blanket ears flopping, their furry hands moving at preternatural speeds as they plugged in cables and oiled gears at the base of the weapon. Some of the pandai were young enough to have pure white fur, which made my heart hurt, reminding me of my brief friendship with Crest, the youthful aspiring musician who'd lost his life in the Burning Maze.

'It's wonderful!' Caligula beamed, circling the mortar. 'Is it ready for test-firing?'

'Yes, lord!' said the pandos Boost. 'Of course, every sphere of Greek fire is very, very expensive, so –'

'DO IT!' Caligula yelled.

Boost yelped and scrambled to the control panel.

Greek fire. I hated the stuff, and I was a sun god who rode a fiery chariot. Viscous, green and impossible to extinguish, Greek fire was just plain nasty. A cupful could burn down an entire building, and that single glowing sphere held more than I'd ever seen in one place.

'Oh, Commodus?' Caligula called. 'You might want to pay attention to this.'

'I am fully attentive,' Commodus said, turning his face to better catch the sun.

Caligula sighed. 'Boost, you may proceed.'

Boost called out instructions in his own language. His fellow pandai turned cranks and spun dials, slowly swivelling the mortar until it pointed out to sea. Boost double-checked his readings on the control panel, then shouted, '*Ūnus, duo, trēs!*'

With a mighty *boom*, the mortar fired. The entire boat shuddered from the recoil. The giant hamster ball rocketed upward until it was a green marble in the sky, then plummeted towards the western horizon. The sky blazed emerald. A moment later, hot winds buffeted the ship with the smell of burning salt and cooked fish. In the distance, a geyser of green fire churned on the boiling sea.

'Ooh, pretty.' Caligula grinned at Boost. 'And you have one missile for each ship?'

'Yes, lord. As instructed.'

'The range?'

'Once we clear Treasure Island, we'll be able to bring all weapons to bear on Camp Jupiter, my lord. No magical defences can stop such a massive volley. Total annihilation!'

'Good,' Caligula said. 'That's my favourite kind.'

'But remember,' Commodus called from his deckchair, having not even turned to watch the explosion, 'first we try a ground assault. Maybe they'll be wise and surrender! We want New Rome intact, and the harpy and Cyclops taken alive, if possible.'

'Yes, yes,' Caligula said. 'If possible.'

He seemed to savour those words like a beautiful lie. His eyes glittered in the green artificial sunset. 'Either way, this will be fun.'

I woke up alone, the sun baking my face. For a second I thought I might be in a deckchair next to Commodus, a tanning bib around my neck. But no. The days when Commodus and I hung out together were long gone.

I sat up, groggy, disorientated and dehydrated. Why was it still light outside?

Then I realized, judging from the angle of the sun coming into the room, that it must have been about noon. Once again, I'd slept through the night and half a day. I still felt exhausted.

I pressed gently on my bandaged gut. I was horrified to find the wound tender again. The purple lines of infection had darkened. This could only mean one thing: it was time for a long-sleeved shirt. No matter what happened over the next twenty-four hours, I would not add to Meg's worries. I would tough it out until the moment I keeled over.

Wow. Who even was I?

By the time I'd changed my clothes and hobbled out of Bombilo's coffee shop, most of the legion had gathered at the mess hall for lunch. As usual, the dining room bustled with activity. Demigods, grouped by cohort, reclined on couches around low tables while aurae whisked overhead with platters of food and pitchers of drink. Hanging from the cedar rafters, war-game pennants and cohort standards rippled in the constant breeze. When they'd finished eating, diners rose cautiously and walked away hunched over, lest they get decapitated by a flying plate of cold cuts. Except for the Lares, of course. They didn't care what sort of delicacies flew through their ectoplasmic noggins.

I spotted Frank at the officers' table, deep in conversation with Hazel and the rest of the centurions. Reyna was nowhere in sight – perhaps she was taking a nap or preparing for the afternoon's war drills. Given what we were facing tomorrow, Frank looked remarkably relaxed. As he chatted with his officers, he even cracked a smile, which seemed to put the others at ease.

How simple it would be to destroy their fragile confidence, I thought, just by describing the flotilla of artillery yachts I'd seen in my dream. Not yet, I decided. No sense in spoiling their meal.

'Hey, Lester!' Lavinia yelled from across the room, waving me over as if I were her waiter.

I joined her and Meg at the Fifth Cohort table. An aura deposited a goblet of water in my hand, then left a whole pitcher on the table. Apparently, my dehydration was that obvious.

Lavinia leaned forward, her eyebrows arched like pink-and-chestnut rainbows. 'So, is it true?'

I frowned at Meg, wondering which of the many embarrassing stories about me she might have shared. She was too busy ploughing through a row of hot dogs to pay me any mind.

'Is what true?' I asked.

'The shoes.'

'Shoes?'

Lavinia threw her hands in the air. 'The dancing shoes of Terpsichore! Meg was telling us what happened on Caligula's yachts. She said you and that Piper girl saw a pair of Terpsichore's shoes!'

'Oh.' I had completely forgotten about those, or the fact that I'd told Meg about them. Strange, but the other events aboard Caligula's ships – getting captured, seeing Jason killed before our eyes, barely escaping with our lives – had eclipsed my memories of the emperor's footwear collection.

'Meg,' I said, 'of all the things you could have chosen to tell them, you told them about *that*?'

'Wasn't my idea.' Meg somehow managed to enunciate with half a hot dog in her mouth. 'Lavinia likes shoes.'

'Well, what did you think I was going to ask about?' Lavinia demanded. 'You tell me the emperor has an entire boatload of shoes, of course I'm going to wonder if you saw any dancing ones! So it's true, then, Lester?'

'I mean . . . yes. We saw a pair of –'

'Wow.' Lavinia sat back, crossed her arms and glared at me. 'Just *wow*. You wait until now to tell me this? Do you know how rare those shoes are? How important . . .' She seemed to choke on her own indignation. 'Wow.'

Around the table, Lavinia's comrades showed a mixture of reactions. Some rolled their eyes, some smirked, some kept eating as if nothing Lavinia did could surprise them any more.

An older boy with shaggy brown hair dared to stick up

for me. 'Lavinia, Apollo has had a few other things going on.'

'Oh my gods, Thomas!' Lavinia shot back. 'Naturally, you wouldn't understand! You never take off those boots!'

Thomas frowned at his standard-issue combat stompers. 'What? They've got good arch support.'

'Yeesh.' Lavinia turned to Meg. 'We have to figure out a way to get aboard that ship and rescue those shoes.'

'Nah.' Meg sucked a glob of relish off her thumb. 'Way too dangerous.'

'But –'

'Lavinia,' I interrupted, 'you *can't*.'

She must have heard the fear and urgency in my voice. Over the past few days, I had developed a strange fondness for Lavinia. I didn't want to see her charge into a slaughter, especially after my dream about those mortars primed with Greek fire.

She ran her Star of David pendant back and forth on its chain. 'You've got new information? Dish.'

Before I could reply, a plate of food flew into my hands. The aurae had decided I needed chicken nuggets and fries. Lots of them. Either that or they'd heard the word *dish* and taken it as an order.

A moment later, Hazel and the other Fifth Cohort centurion joined us – a dark-haired young man with strange red stains around his mouth. Ah, yes. Dakota, child of Bacchus.

'What's going on?' Dakota asked.

'Lester has news.' Lavinia stared at me expectantly, as if I might be withholding the location of Terpsichore's magical tutu (which, for the record, I hadn't seen in centuries).

I took a deep breath. I wasn't sure if this was the right forum for sharing my dream. I should probably report it to the praetors first. But Hazel nodded at me as if to say, *Go on.* I decided that was good enough.

I described what I'd seen – a top-of-the-range IKEA heavy mortar, fully assembled, shooting a giant hamster ball of green flaming death that blew up the Pacific Ocean. I explained that, apparently, the emperors had fifty such mortars, one on each ship, which would be ready to obliterate Camp Jupiter as soon as they took up positions in the bay.

Dakota's face turned as red as his mouth. 'I need more fruit punch.'

The fact that no goblets flew into his hand told me the aurae disagreed.

Lavinia looked like she'd been slapped with one of her mother's ballet slippers. Meg kept eating hot dogs as if they might be the last ones she would ever get.

Hazel chewed her bottom lip in concentration, perhaps trying to extract any good news from what I'd said. She seemed to find this harder than pulling diamonds out of the ground.

'Okay, look, guys, we knew the emperors were assembling secret weapons. At least now we know what those weapons are. I'll convey this information to the praetors, but it doesn't change anything. You all did a great job in the morning drills –' she hesitated, then generously decided not to add *except for Apollo, who slept through it all* – 'and this afternoon, one of our war games will be about boarding enemy ships. We can get prepared.'

From the expressions around the table, I gathered the Fifth Cohort was not reassured. The Romans had never been known for their naval prowess. Last I'd checked, the Camp Jupiter 'navy' consisted of some old *triremes* they only used for mock naval battles in the Colosseum, and one rowing boat they kept docked in Alameda. Drilling to board enemy ships would be less about practising a workable battle plan and more about keeping the legionnaires busy so they wouldn't think about their impending doom.

Thomas rubbed his forehead. 'I hate my life.'

'Keep it together, legionnaire,' Hazel said. 'This is what we signed up for. Defending the legacy of Rome.'

'From its own emperors,' Thomas said miserably.

'I'm sorry to tell you,' I put in, 'but the biggest threat to the empire was often its own emperors.'

Nobody argued.

At the officers' table, Frank Zhang stood. All around the room, flying pitchers and platters froze in mid-air, waiting respectfully.

'Legionnaires!' Frank announced, managing a confident smile. 'Relay activities will recommence on the Field of Mars in twenty minutes. Drill like your lives depend on it, because they do!'

21

See this right here, kids?
This is how you don't do it.
Questions? Class dismissed.

'HOW'S THE WOUND?' HAZEL ASKED.

I knew she meant well, but I was getting very tired of that question, and even more tired of the wound.

We walked side by side out of the main gates, heading for the Field of Mars. Just ahead of us, Meg cartwheeled down the road, though how she did this without regurgitating the four hot dogs she'd eaten, I had no idea.

'Oh, you know,' I said, in a terrible attempt to sound upbeat, 'all things considered, I'm okay.'

My old immortal self would have laughed at that. *Okay? Are you joking?*

Over the last few months, I had drastically scaled back my expectations. At this point, *okay* meant *still able to walk and breathe.*

'I should have realized earlier,' Hazel said. 'Your death aura is getting stronger by the hour –'

'Can we not talk about my death aura?'

'Sorry, it's just . . . I wish Nico were here. He might know how to fix you.'

I wouldn't have minded seeing Hazel's half-brother. Nico di Angelo, son of Hades, had been quite valuable when we fought Nero at Camp Half-Blood. And of course his boyfriend, my son Will Solace, was an excellent healer. Yet I suspected they wouldn't be able to help me any more than Pranjal had. If Will and Nico were here, they would just be two more people for me to worry about – two more loved ones watching me with concern, wondering how long until I went full-on zombie.

'I appreciate the sentiment,' I said, 'but . . . What is Lavinia doing?'

About a hundred yards away, Lavinia and Don the faun stood on a bridge across the Little Tiber – which was very much *not* on the way to the Field of Mars – having what looked like a serious argument. Perhaps I shouldn't have brought this to Hazel's attention. Then again, if Lavinia wanted to go unnoticed, she should have chosen a different hair colour – like camouflage, for instance – and not waved her arms around so much.

'I don't know.' Hazel's expression reminded me of a tired mother who had found her toddler trying to climb into the monkey enclosure for the dozenth time. 'Lavinia!'

Lavinia looked over. She patted the air as if to say, *Just give me a minute*, then went back to arguing with Don.

'Am I too young to get ulcers?' Hazel wondered aloud.

I had little occasion for humour, given all that was happening, but that comment made me laugh.

As we got closer to the Field of Mars, I saw legionnaires breaking into cohorts, moving to different activities spread across the wasteland. One group was digging defensive trenches. Another had gathered on the shore of an artificial lake that hadn't been there yesterday, waiting to board two makeshift boats that looked nothing like Caligula's yachts. A third group sledged down a dirt hill on their shields.

Hazel sighed. 'That would be my group of delinquents. If you'll excuse me, I'm off to teach them how to slay ghouls.'

She jogged away, leaving me alone with my cartwheeling sidekick.

'So where do we go?' I asked Meg. 'Frank said we had, er, special jobs?'

'Yep.' Meg pointed to the far end of the field, where the Fifth Cohort was waiting at a target range. 'You're teaching archery.'

I stared at her. 'I'm doing *what* now?'

'Frank taught the morning class, since you slept *forever*. Now it's your turn.'

'But – I can't teach as Lester, especially in my condition! Besides, Romans never rely on archery in combat. They think projectile weapons are beneath them!'

'Gotta think in new ways if you want to beat the emperors,' Meg said. 'Like me. I'm weaponizing the unicorns.'

'You're – Wait, what?'

'Later.' Meg skipped across the field towards a large riding ring, where the First Cohort and a herd of unicorns were staring suspiciously at one another. I couldn't imagine how Meg planned to weaponize the non-violent creatures, or who had given her permission to try, but I had a sudden horrible image of Romans and unicorns assaulting one another with large cheese graters. I decided to mind my own business.

With a sigh, I turned towards the firing range and went to meet my new pupils.

The only thing scarier than being bad at archery was discovering that I was suddenly good at it again. That may not sound like a problem, but since becoming mortal I'd experienced a few random bursts of godly skill. Each time, my powers had quickly evaporated again, leaving me more bitter and disillusioned than ever.

Sure, I may have fired a quiverful of amazing shots in Tarquin's tomb. That didn't mean I could do it again. If I tried to demonstrate proper shooting techniques in front of a whole cohort and ended up hitting one of Meg's unicorns in the butt, I would die of embarrassment long before the zombie poison got me.

'Okay, everyone,' I said. 'I suppose we can start.'

Dakota was rummaging through his water-stained quiver, trying to find an arrow that wasn't warped. Apparently, he thought it was a great idea to store his archery supplies in the sauna. Thomas and another legionnaire (Marcus?) were sword-fighting with their bows. The legion's standard-bearer, Jacob, was drawing his bow with the butt of the arrow directly at eye level, which explained why his left eye was covered in a patch from the morning's lessons. He now seemed eager to blind himself completely.

'C'mon, guys!' said Lavinia. She had sneaked in late without being noticed (one of her superpowers) and took it upon herself to help me call the troops to order. 'Apollo might know stuff!'

This was how I knew I had hit rock bottom: the highest praise I could receive from a mortal was that I 'might know stuff'.

I cleared my throat. I'd faced much bigger audiences. Why was I so nervous? Oh, right. Because I was a horribly incompetent sixteen-year-old.

'So . . . let's talk about how to aim.' My voice cracked, naturally. 'Wide stance. Full draw. Then find your target with your dominant eye. Or, in Jacob's case, with your one working eye. Aim along your sight pin, if you have one.'

'I don't have a sight pin,' said Marcus.

'It's the little circle thingie right there.' Lavinia showed him.

'I have a sight pin,' Marcus corrected himself.

'Then you let fly,' I said. 'Like this.'

I shot at the nearest target – then at the target next furthest out, then at the next – firing again and again in a kind of trance.

Only after my twentieth shot did I realize I'd hit every bullseye, two in each target, the furthest about two hundred yards away. Child's play for Apollo. For Lester, quite impossible.

The legionnaires stared at me, their mouths hanging open.

'We're supposed to do *that*?' Dakota demanded.

Lavinia punched my forearm. 'See, you guys? I told you Apollo doesn't suck that much!'

I had to agree with her. I felt oddly *not* suckish.

The display of marksmanship hadn't drained my energy. Nor did it feel like the temporary bursts of godly power I'd experienced before. I was tempted to ask for another quiver to see if I could keep shooting at the same skill level, but I was afraid to press my luck.

'So . . .' I faltered. 'I, uh, don't expect you to be that good right away. I was only demonstrating what's possible with a lot of practice. Let's give it a try, shall we?'

I was relieved to take the focus off myself. I organized the cohort into a firing line and made my way down the ranks, offering advice. Despite his warped arrows, Dakota was not terrible. He actually hit the target a few times. Jacob managed not to blind himself in the other eye. Thomas and Marcus sent most of their arrows skittering across the earth, ricocheting off rocks and into the trenches, which elicited shouts of 'Hey, watch it!' from the ditch-digging Fourth Cohort.

After an hour of frustration with a regular bow, Lavinia gave up and pulled out her manubalista. Her first bolt knocked down the fifty-yard target.

'Why do you insist on using that slow-loading monstrosity?' I asked. 'If you're so ADHD, wouldn't a regular bow give you more instant satisfaction?'

Lavinia shrugged. 'Maybe, but the manubalista makes a statement. Speaking of which –' she leaned towards me, her expression turning serious – 'I need to talk to you.'

'That doesn't sound good.'

'No, it's not. I –'

In the distance, a horn blew.

'Okay, guys!' Dakota called. 'Time to rotate activities! Good team effort!'

Lavinia punched me in the arm again. 'Later, Lester.'

The Fifth Cohort dropped their weapons and ran towards the next activity, leaving me to retrieve all their arrows. Cretins.

The rest of the afternoon, I stayed at the firing range, working with each cohort in turn. As the hours wore on, both the shooting and the teaching became less intimidating for me. By the time I was wrapping up work with my last group, the First Cohort, I was convinced that my improved archery skills were here to stay.

I didn't know why. I still couldn't shoot at my old godly level, but I was definitely better now than the average demigod archer or Olympic gold medallist. I had started to 'jive'. I considered pulling out the Arrow of Dodona to brag, *See what I can do?* But I didn't want to jinx myself. Besides, knowing that I was dying of zombie poison on the eve of a major battle took some of the thrill out of being able to shoot bullseyes again.

The Romans were duly impressed. Some of them even learned a little, like how to fire an arrow without blinding yourself or killing the guy next to you. Still, I could tell they were more excited about the other activities they'd done. I overheard a lot of whispering about unicorns and Hazel's super-secret ghoul-fighting techniques. Larry from the Third Cohort had enjoyed boarding ships so much he declared that he wanted to be a pirate when he grew up. I suspected most of the legionnaires had even enjoyed ditch-digging more than my class.

It was late evening when the final horn blew and the cohorts tromped back to camp. I was hungry and exhausted. I wondered if this was how mortal teachers felt after a full day of classes. If so, I didn't see how they managed. I hoped they were richly compensated with gold, diamonds and rare spices.

At least the cohorts seemed to be in an upbeat mood. If the praetors' goal had been to take the troops' minds off their fears and raise morale on the eve of battle, then our afternoon had been a success. If the goal had been to train the legion to successfully repel our enemies . . . then I was less than hopeful. Also, all day long, everyone had carefully avoided addressing the worst thing about tomorrow's attack. The Romans would have to face their former comrades, returned as zombies under Tarquin's control. I remembered how hard it had been for Lavinia to shoot down Bobby with her crossbow in the tomb. I wondered how the legion's morale would hold up once they faced the same ethical dilemma times fifty or sixty.

I was turning onto the Via Principalis, on my way to the mess hall, when a voice said, 'Pssst.'

Lurking in the alley between Bombilo's café and the chariot repair shop were Lavinia and Don. The faun was wearing an honest-to-gods trenchcoat over his tie-dyed T-shirt, as if that made him look inconspicuous. Lavinia wore a black cap over her pink hair.

'C'mere!' she hissed.

'But dinner –'

'We need you.'

'Is this a mugging?'

She marched over, grabbed my arm and pulled me into the shadows.

'Don't worry, dude,' Don told me. 'It's not a mugging! But, like, if you *do* have any spare change –'

'Shut up, Don,' said Lavinia.

'I'll shut up,' Don agreed.

'Lester,' Lavinia said, 'you need to come with us.'

'Lavinia, I'm tired. I'm hungry. And I have no spare change. Can't it please wait –?'

'No. Because tomorrow we might all die, and this is important. We're sneaking out.'

'Sneaking out?'

'Yeah,' Don said. 'It's when you're sneaking. And you go out.'

'Why?' I demanded.

'You'll see.' Lavinia's tone was ominous, as if she couldn't explain what my coffin looked like. I had to admire it with my own eyes.

'What if we get caught?'

'Oh!' Don perked up. 'I know this one! For a first offence, it's latrine duty for a month. But, see, if we all die tomorrow, it won't matter!'

With that happy news, Lavinia and Don grabbed my hands and dragged me further into the darkness.

22

I sing of dead plants
And heroic shrubberies
Inspiring stuff

SNEAKING OUT of a Roman military camp should not have been so easy.

Once we were safely through a hole in the fence, down a trench, through a tunnel, past the pickets and out of sight of the camp's sentry towers, Don was happy to explain how he'd arranged it all. 'Dude, the place is designed to keep out armies. It's not meant to keep in individual legionnaires, or keep out, you know, the occasional well-meaning faun who's just looking for a hot meal. If you know the patrol schedule and are willing to keep swapping your entry points, it's easy.'

'That seems remarkably industrious for a faun,' I noted.

Don grinned. 'Hey, man. Slacking is hard work.'

'We've got a long walk,' Lavinia said. 'Best keep moving.'

I tried not to groan. Another night-time hike with Lavinia had not been on my evening's agenda. But I had to admit I was curious. What had she and Don been arguing about before? Why had she wanted to talk to me earlier? And where were we going? With her stormy eyes and the black cap over her hair, Lavinia looked troubled and determined, less like a gawky giraffe, more like a tense gazelle. I'd seen her father, Sergei Asimov, perform once with the Moscow Ballet. He'd had that exact expression on his face before launching into a grand jeté.

I wanted to ask Lavinia what was going on, but her posture made it clear she was not in the mood for conversation. Not yet, anyway. We hiked in silence out of the valley and down into the streets of Berkeley.

It must have been about midnight by the time we got to People's Park.

I had not been there since 1969, when I'd stopped by to experience some groovy hippie music and flower power and instead found myself in the middle of a riot. The police officers' tear gas, shotguns and batons had definitely *not* been groovy. It had taken all my godly restraint not to reveal my divine form and blast everyone within a six-mile radius to cinders.

Now, decades later, the scruffy park looked like it was still suffering from the aftermath. The worn brown lawn was strewn with piles of discarded clothing and cardboard signs bearing hand-painted slogans like GREEN SPACE NOT DORM SPACE and SAVE OUR PARK. Several tree stumps held potted plants and beaded necklaces, like shrines to the fallen. Trash cans overflowed. Homeless people slept on benches or fussed over shopping trolleys full of their worldly belongings.

At the far end of the square, occupying a raised plywood stage, was the largest sit-in of dryads and fauns I'd ever seen. It made total sense to me that fauns would inhabit People's Park. They could laze around, beg, eat leftover food out of the garbage bins, and no one would bat an eye. The dryads were more of a surprise. At least two dozen of them were present. Some, I guessed, were the spirits of local eucalyptus and redwood trees, but most, given their sickly appearances, must have been dryads of the park's long-suffering shrubs, grasses and weeds. (Not that I am judging weed dryads. I've known some very fine crabgrasses.)

The fauns and dryads sat in a wide circle as if preparing for a sing-along around an invisible campfire. I got the feeling they were waiting for us – for *me* – to start the music.

I was already nervous enough. Then I spotted a familiar face and nearly jumped out of my zombie-infected skin. '*Peaches?*'

Meg's demon-baby *karpos* bared his fangs and responded, 'Peaches!'

His tree-branch wings had lost a few leaves. His curly green hair was dead brown at the tips, and his lamplike eyes didn't shine as brightly as I remembered. He must've undergone quite an ordeal tracking us to Northern California, but his growl was still intimidating enough to make me fear for my bladder control.

'Where have you *been?*' I demanded.

'Peaches!'

I felt foolish for asking. Of course he had been *peaches*, probably because *peaches*, *peaches* and *peaches*. 'Does Meg know you're here? How did you –?'

Lavinia gripped my shoulder. 'Hey, Apollo. Time is short. Peaches filled us in on what he saw in Southern California, but he arrived there too late to help. He busted his wings to get up here as fast as he could. He wants you to tell the group first-hand what happened in SoCal.'

I scanned the faces in the crowd. The nature spirits looked scared, apprehensive and angry – but mostly tired of being angry. I'd seen that look a lot among dryads in these latter days of human civilization. There was only so much pollution your average plant can breathe, drink and get tangled in her branches before starting to lose all hope.

Now Lavinia wanted me to break their spirits completely by relating what had happened to their brethren in Los Angeles, and what fiery destruction was coming their way tomorrow. In other words, she wanted to get me killed by a mob of angry shrubs.

I gulped. 'Um . . .'

'Here. This might help.' Lavinia slung her backpack off her shoulder. I hadn't paid much attention to how bulky it looked, since she was always tromping around with lots of gear. When she opened it, the last thing I expected her to pull out was my ukulele – newly polished and restrung.

'How . . . ?' I asked, as she placed it in my hands.

'I stole it from your room,' she said, as if this was obviously what friends did for each other. 'You were asleep forever. I took it to a buddy of mine who repairs instruments – Marilyn, daughter of Euterpe. You know, the Muse of Music.'

'I – I know Euterpe. Of course. Her speciality is flutes, not ukuleles. But the action on this fret board is perfect now. Marilyn must be . . . I'm so . . .' I realized I was rambling. 'Thank you.'

Lavinia fixed me with her stare, silently commanding

me to make her effort worthwhile. She stepped back and joined the circle of nature spirits.

I strummed. Lavinia was right. The instrument helped. Not to hide behind – as I'd discovered, one cannot hide behind a ukulele. But it lent confidence to my voice. After a few mournful minor chords, I began to sing 'The Fall of Jason Grace', as I had when we first arrived at Camp Jupiter. The song quickly morphed, however. Like all good performers, I adapted the material to my audience.

I sang of the wildfires and droughts that had scorched Southern California. I sang of the brave cacti and satyrs from the Cistern in Palm Springs, who had struggled valiantly to find the source of the destruction. I sang of the dryads Agave and Money Maker, both gravely injured in the Burning Maze, and how Money Maker had died in the arms of Aloe Vera. I added some hopeful stanzas about Meg and the rebirth of the warrior dryad Meliai – how we'd destroyed the Burning Maze and given SoCal's environment at least a fighting chance to heal. But I couldn't hide the dangers that faced us. I described what I had seen in my dreams: the yachts approaching with their fiery mortars, the hellish devastation they would rain upon the entire Bay Area.

After strumming my final chord, I looked up. Green tears glistened in the dryads' eyes. Fauns wept openly.

Peaches turned to the crowd and growled, 'Peaches!'

This time, I was fairly sure I understood his meaning: *See? I told you so!*

Don sniffled, wiping his eyes with what looked like a used burrito wrapper. 'It's true, then. It's happening. Faunus protect us . . .'

Lavinia dabbed away her own tears. 'Thanks, Apollo.'

As if I'd done her a favour. Why, then, did I feel like I'd just kicked each and every one of these nature spirits right in the taproots? I'd spent a lot of time worrying about the fate of New Rome and Camp Jupiter, the Oracles, my friends and myself. But these hackberries and crabgrasses deserved to live just as much. They, too, were facing death. They were terrified. If the emperors launched their weapons, they stood no chance. The homeless mortals with their shopping trolleys in People's Park would also burn, right along with the legionnaires. Their lives were worth no less.

The mortals might not understand the disaster. They'd attribute it to runaway wildfires or whatever other causes their brains could comprehend. But I would know the truth. If this vast, weird, beautiful expanse of the California coast burned, it would be because I had failed to stop my enemies.

'Okay, guys,' Lavinia continued, after taking a moment to compose herself. 'You heard him. The emperors will be here by tomorrow evening.'

'But that gives us no time,' said a redwood dryad. 'If they do to the Bay Area what they did to LA . . .'

I could feel the fear ripple through the crowd like a cold wind.

'The legion will fight them, though, right?' a faun asked nervously. 'I mean, they might win.'

'C'mon, Reginald,' a dryad chided. 'You want to depend on mortals to protect us? When has *that* ever worked out?'

The others muttered assent.

'To be fair,' Lavinia cut in, 'Frank and Reyna are trying. They're sending a small team of commandos out to intercept the ships. Michael Kahale, and a few other hand-picked demigods. But I'm not optimistic.'

'I hadn't heard anything about that,' I said. 'How did you find out?'

She raised her pink eyebrows like, *Please*. 'And of course Lester here will try to summon godly help with some super-secret ritual, but . . .'

She didn't need to say the rest. She wasn't optimistic about that, either.

'So what will you do?' I asked. 'What *can* you do?'

I didn't mean to sound critical. I just couldn't imagine any options.

The fauns' panicky expressions seemed to hint at their game plan: get bus tickets to Portland, Oregon, immediately. But that wouldn't help the dryads. They were literally rooted to their native soil. Perhaps they could go into deep hibernation, the way the dryads in the south had. But would that be enough to enable them to weather a firestorm? I'd heard stories about certain species of plant that germinated and thrived after devastating fires swept across the landscape, but I doubted most had that ability.

Honestly, I didn't know much about dryad life cycles, or how they protected themselves from climate disasters. Perhaps if I'd spent more time over the centuries talking to them and less time chasing them . . .

Wow. I *really* didn't even know myself any more.

'We have a lot to discuss,' said one of the dryads.

'Peaches,' agreed Peaches. He looked at me with a clear message: *Go away now*.

I had so many questions for him: Why had he been absent so long? Why was he here and not with Meg?

I suspected I wouldn't get any answers tonight. At least nothing beyond snarls, bites and the word *peaches*. I thought about what the dryad had said about not trusting mortals to solve nature-spirit problems. Apparently, that included me. I had delivered my message. Now I was dismissed.

My heart was already heavy, and Meg's state of mind was so fragile . . . I didn't know how I could break the news to her that her diapered little peach demon had become a rogue fruit.

'Let's get you back to camp,' Lavinia said to me. 'You've got a big day tomorrow.'

We left Don behind with the other nature spirits, all deep in crisis-mode conversation, and retraced our steps down Telegraph Avenue.

After a few blocks, I got up the courage to ask, 'What will they do?'

Lavinia stirred as if she'd forgotten I was there. 'You mean what will *we* do. 'Cause I'm with them.'

A lump formed in my throat. 'Lavinia, you're scaring me. What are you planning?'

'I tried to leave it alone,' she muttered. In the glow of the streetlamps, the wisps of pink hair that had escaped her cap seemed to float around her head like candy floss. 'After what we saw in the tomb – Bobby and the others, after you described what we're facing tomorrow –'

'Lavinia, please –'

'I can't fall into line like a good soldier. Me locking

shields and marching off to die with everybody else? That's not going to help anybody.'

'But –'

'It's best you don't ask.' Her growl was almost as intimidating as Peaches'. 'And it's *definitely* best that you not say anything to anybody about tonight. Now, c'mon.'

The rest of the way back, she ignored my questions. She seemed to have a dark bubble-gum-scented cloud hanging over her head. She got me safely past the sentries, under the wall and back to the coffee shop before she slipped away into the dark without even a goodbye.

Perhaps I should have stopped her. Raised the alarm. Got her arrested. But what good would that have done? It seemed to me Lavinia had never been comfortable in the legion. After all, she spent much of her time looking for secret exits and hidden trails out of the valley. Now she'd finally snapped.

I had a sinking feeling that I would never see her again. She'd be on the next bus to Portland with a few dozen fauns, and as much as I wanted to be angry about that, I could only feel sad. In her place, would I have done any different?

When I got back to our guest room, Meg had passed out, snoring, her glasses dangling from her fingers, bedsheets wadded around her feet. I tucked her in as best I could. If she was having any bad dreams about her peach spirit friend plotting with the local dryads only a few miles away, I couldn't tell. Tomorrow I'd have to decide what to say to her. Tonight, I'd let her sleep.

I crawled into my own bed, sure that I'd be tossing and turning until morning.

Instead, I passed out immediately.

When I woke, the early morning sunlight was in my face. Meg's bed was empty. I realized I'd slept like the dead – no dreams, no visions. That did not comfort me. When the nightmares go silent, that usually means something else is coming – something even worse.

I dressed and gathered my supplies, trying not to think about how tired I was, or how much my gut hurt. Then I grabbed a muffin and a coffee from Bombilo and went out to find my friends. Today, one way or another, the fate of New Rome would be decided.

23

In my pickup truck
With my dogs and my weapons
And this fool, Lester

REYNA AND MEG WERE WAITING for me at the camp's front gates, though I barely recognized the former. In place of her praetor's regalia, she wore blue running shoes and skinny jeans, a long-sleeved copper tee and a maroon cardigan. With her hair pulled back in a braided whip and her face lightly brushed with make-up, she could've passed for one of the many thousands of Bay Area college students that nobody would think twice about. I supposed that was the point.

'What?' she asked me.

I realized I'd been staring. 'Nothing.'

Meg snorted. She was dressed in her usual green dress, yellow leggings and red high-tops, so she could blend in with the many thousands of Bay Area first graders – except for her twelve-year-old's height, her gardening belt, and the pink badge pinned to her collar that displayed a stylized unicorn's head with a crossbones underneath. I wondered if she'd bought it in a New Rome gift shop or somehow got it specially made. Either possibility was unsettling.

Reyna spread her hands. 'I *do* have civilian clothes,

Apollo. Even with the Mist helping to obscure things, walking through San Francisco in full legionnaire armour can attract some funny looks.'

'No. Yeah. You look great. I mean good.' Why were my palms sweating? 'I mean, can we go now?'

Reyna put two fingers in her mouth and let loose a taxi-cab whistle so shrill it cleared out my eustachian tubes. From inside the fort, her two metal greyhounds came running, barking like small-weapons fire.

'Oh, good,' I said, trying to suppress my panic-and-run instinct. 'Your dogs are coming.'

Reyna smirked. 'Well, they'd get upset if I drove to San Francisco without them.'

'Drove?' I was about to say, *In what?* when I heard a honk from the direction of the city. A battered bright red Chevy four-by-four rumbled down a road usually reserved for marching legionnaires and elephants.

At the wheel was Hazel Levesque, with Frank Zhang riding shotgun.

They pulled up next to us. The vehicle had barely stopped moving when Aurum and Argentum leaped into the back of the truck, their metal tongues lolling and tails wagging.

Hazel climbed out of the cab. 'All filled up, Praetor.'

'Thank you, Centurion.' Reyna smiled. 'How are the driving lessons coming along?'

'Good! I didn't even run into Terminus this time.'

'Progress,' Reyna agreed.

Frank came around from the passenger's side. 'Yep, Hazel will be ready for public roads in no time.'

I had many things to ask: Where did they keep this

truck? Was there a petrol station in New Rome? Why had I been walking so much if it was possible to drive?

Meg beat me to the real question: 'Do I get to ride in the back with the dogs?'

'No, ma'am,' said Reyna. 'You'll sit in the cab with your seat belt on.'

'Aw.' Meg ran off to pet the dogs.

Frank gave Reyna a bear hug (without turning into a bear). 'Be careful out there, all right?'

Reyna didn't seem to know what to do with this show of affection. Her arms went stiff. Then she awkwardly patted her fellow praetor on the back.

'You too,' she said. 'Any word on the strike force?'

'They left before dawn,' Frank said. 'Kahale felt good about it, but . . .' He shrugged, as if to say their anti-yacht commando mission was now in the hands of the gods. Which, as a former god, I can tell you was *not* reassuring.

Reyna turned to Hazel. 'And the zombie pickets?'

'Ready,' Hazel said. 'If Tarquin's hordes come from the same direction as before, they're in for some nasty surprises. I also set traps along the other approaches to the city. Hopefully we can stop them before they're in hand-to-hand range so . . .'

She hesitated, apparently unwilling to finish her sentence. I thought I understood. *So we don't have to see their faces.* If the legion *had* to confront a wave of undead comrades, it would be much better to destroy them at a distance, without the anguish of having to recognize former friends.

'I just wish . . .' Hazel shook her head. 'Well, I still worry Tarquin has something else planned. I should be able to figure it out, but . . .' She tapped her forehead as if she wanted to reset her brain. I could sympathize.

'You've done plenty,' Frank assured her. 'If they throw surprises at us, we'll adapt.'

Reyna nodded. 'Okay, then, we're off. Don't forget to stock the catapults.'

'Of course,' Frank said.

'And double-check with the quartermaster about those flaming barricades.'

'Of course.'

'And –' Reyna stopped herself. 'You know what you're doing. Sorry.'

Frank grinned. 'Just bring us whatever we need to summon that godly help. We'll keep the camp in one piece until you get back.'

Hazel studied Reyna's outfit with concern. 'Your sword's in the truck. Don't you want to take a shield or something?'

'Nah. I've got my cloak. It'll turn aside most weapons.' Reyna brushed the collar of her cardigan. Instantly it unfurled into her usual purple cape.

Frank's smile faded. 'Does *my* cloak do that?'

'See you, guys!' Reyna climbed behind the wheel.

'Wait, does *my* cloak deflect weapons?' Frank called after us. 'Does mine turn into a cardigan?'

As we pulled away, I could see Frank Zhang in the rear-view mirror, intently studying the stitching of his cape.

Our first challenge of the morning: merging onto the Bay Bridge.

Getting out of Camp Jupiter had been no problem. A

well-hidden dirt road led from the valley up into the hills, eventually depositing us on the residential streets of East Oakland. From there we took Highway 24 until it merged with Interstate 580. Then the real fun began.

The morning commuters had apparently not got word that we were on a vital mission to save the greater metropolitan area. They stubbornly refused to get out of our way. Perhaps we should have taken public transport, but I doubted they let killer dog automatons ride the BART trains.

Reyna tapped her fingers on the wheel, mumbling along to Tego Calderón lyrics on the truck's ancient CD player. I enjoyed reggaeton as much as the next Greek god, but it was perhaps not the music I would've chosen to soothe my nerves on the morning of a quest. I found it a bit too peppy for my pre-combat jitters.

Sitting between us, Meg rummaged through the seeds in her gardener's belt. During our battle in the tomb, she'd told us, lots of packages had opened and got mixed up. Now she was trying to figure out which seeds were which. This meant she would occasionally hold up a seed and stare at it until it burst into its mature form – dandelion, tomato, aubergine, sunflower. Soon the cab smelled like a garden centre.

I had not told Meg about seeing Peaches. I wasn't even sure how to start the conversation. *Hey, did you know your karpos is holding clandestine meetings with the fauns and crabgrasses in People's Park?*

The longer I waited to say something, the harder it became. I told myself it wasn't a good idea to distract Meg during an important quest. I wanted to honour Lavinia's wishes that I not blab. True, I hadn't seen Lavinia that morning before we left, but maybe her plans weren't as nefarious as I thought. Maybe she wasn't actually halfway to Oregon by now.

In reality, I didn't speak because I was a coward. I was afraid to enrage the two dangerous young women I rode with, one of whom could have me ripped apart by a pair of metal greyhounds, while the other could cause cabbages to grow out of my nose.

We inched our way across the bridge, Reyna finger-tapping to the beat of 'El Que Sabe, Sabe'. *He who knows, knows.* I was seventy-five percent sure there was no hidden message in Reyna's choice of songs.

'When we get there,' she said, 'we'll have to park at the base of the hill and hike up. The area around Sutro Tower is restricted.'

'You've decided the tower itself is our target,' I said, 'not Mount Sutro behind it?'

'Can't be sure, obviously. But I double-checked Thalia's list of trouble spots. The tower was on there.'

I waited for her to elaborate. 'Thalia's *what?*'

Reyna blinked. 'Didn't I tell you about that? So, Thalia and the Hunters of Artemis, you know, they keep a running list of places where they've seen unusual monstrous activity, stuff they can't quite explain. Sutro Tower is one of them. Thalia sent me her list of locations for the Bay Area so Camp Jupiter can keep an eye on them.'

'How many trouble spots?' Meg asked. 'Can we visit all of them?'

Reyna nudged her playfully. 'I like your spirit, Killer, but there are dozens in San Francisco alone. We – I mean the legion – we try to keep an eye on them all, but it's a lot. Especially recently . . .'

With the battles, I thought. *And the deaths.*

I wondered about the small hesitation in Reyna's voice when she said *we* and then clarified that she meant *the legion*. I wondered what other '*we*'s Reyna Avila Ramírez-Arellano felt part of. Certainly I had never imagined her in civilian clothes, driving a battered pickup truck, taking her metal greyhounds for a hike. And she'd been in touch with Thalia Grace, my sister's lieutenant, leader of the Hunters of Artemis.

I hated the way that made me feel jealous.

'How do you know Thalia?' I tried to sound nonchalant. Judging from Meg's cross-eyed look, I failed miserably.

Reyna didn't seem to notice. She changed lanes, trying to make headway through the traffic. In the back, Aurum and Argentum barked with joy, thrilling in the adventure.

'Thalia and I fought Orion together in Puerto Rico,' she said. 'The Amazons and Hunters both lost a lot of good women. That sort of thing . . . shared experience . . . Anyway, yeah, we've kept in touch.'

'How? The communication lines are all down.'

'Letters,' she said.

'Letters . . .' I seemed to remember those, back from around the days of vellum and wax seals. 'You mean when you write something by hand on paper, put it in an envelope, stick a stamp on it –'

'And mail it. Right. I mean, it can be weeks or months between letters, but Thalia's a good pen pal.'

I tried to fathom that. Many descriptions came to mind when I thought about Thalia Grace. *Pen pal* was not one of them.

'Where do you even mail the letters *to?*' I asked. 'The Hunters are constantly on the move.'

'They have a PO box in Wyoming and – Why are we talking about this?'

Meg pinched a seed between her fingers. A geranium exploded into bloom. 'Is that where your dogs went? Searching for Thalia?'

I didn't see how she'd made that connection, but Reyna nodded.

'Just after you arrived,' Reyna said, 'I wrote to Thalia about . . . you know, Jason. I knew it was a long shot that she'd get the message in time, so I sent Aurum and Argentum out looking for her, too, in case the Hunters were in the area. No luck.'

I imagined what could happen if Thalia received Reyna's letter. Would she come charging into Camp Jupiter at the head of the Hunters, ready to help us fight the emperors and Tarquin's undead hordes? Or would she turn her wrath on me? Thalia had already bailed me out of trouble once, in Indianapolis. By way of thanks, I'd got her brother killed in Santa Barbara. I doubted anyone would object if a stray Hunter's arrow found me as its target during the fighting. I shivered, thankful for the slowness of the US Postal Service.

We made our way past Treasure Island, the anchor of the Bay Bridge midway between Oakland and San Francisco. I thought about Caligula's fleet, which would be passing this island later tonight, ready to unload its troops and, if necessary, its arsenal of Greek fire bombs on the unsuspecting East Bay. I cursed the slowness of the US Postal Service.

'So,' I said, making a second attempt at nonchalance, 'are you and Thalia, er . . . ?'

Reyna raised an eyebrow. 'Involved *romantically?*'

'Well, I just . . . I mean . . . Um . . .'

Oh, very smooth, Apollo. Have I mentioned I was once the god of poetry?

Reyna rolled her eyes. 'If I had a denarius for every time I got asked that question . . . Aside from the fact that Thalia is in the Hunters, and thus sworn to celibacy . . . Why does a strong friendship always have to progress to romance? Thalia's an excellent friend. Why would I risk messing that up?'

'Uh –'

'That was a rhetorical question,' Reyna added. 'I do not need a response.'

'I know what *rhetorical* means.' I made a mental note to double-check the word's definition with Socrates the next time I was in Greece. Then I remembered Socrates was dead. 'I only thought –'

'I love this song,' Meg interrupted. 'Turn it up!'

I doubted Meg had the slightest interest in Tego Calderón, but her intervention may have saved my life. Reyna cranked up the volume, thus ending my attempt at death by casual conversation.

We stayed silent the rest of the way into the city, listening to Tego Calderón singing 'Punto y Aparte' and Reyna's greyhounds jubilantly barking like semi-automatic clips discharged on New Year's Eve.

24

Stick my godly face
Where it doesn't belong and –
Venus, I hate you

FOR SUCH A POPULATED AREA, San Francisco had a surprising number of wilderness pockets. We parked on a dead-end road at the base of the tower's hill. To our right, a field of rocks and weeds offered a multimillion-dollar view of the city. To our left, the incline was so heavily forested you could almost use the eucalyptus trunks as climbing rungs.

From the hill's summit, perhaps a quarter of a mile above us, Sutro Tower soared into the fog, its red-and-white pylons and crossbeams forming a giant tripod that reminded me uncomfortably of the Delphic Oracle's seat. Or the scaffolding for a funeral pyre.

'There's a relay station at the base.' Reyna pointed towards the hilltop. 'We may have to deal with mortal guards, fences, barbed wire, that kind of thing. Plus whatever Tarquin might have waiting for us.'

'Neat,' Meg said. 'Let's go!'

The greyhounds needed no encouragement. They charged uphill, ploughing through the undergrowth. Meg followed, clearly determined to rip her clothes on as many brambles and thorn bushes as possible.

Reyna must have noticed my pained expression as I contemplated the climb.

'Don't worry,' she said. 'We can take it slow. Aurum and Argentum know to wait for me at the top.'

'But does Meg?' I imagined my young friend charging alone into a relay station filled with guards, zombies and other 'neat' surprises.

'Good point,' Reyna said. 'Let's take it medium, then.'

I did my best, which entailed lots of wheezing, sweating and leaning against trees to rest. My archery skills may have improved. My music was getting better. But my stamina was still one hundred percent Lester.

At least Reyna didn't ask me how my wound felt. The answer was *Somewhere south of horrible.*

When I'd got dressed that morning, I had avoided looking at my gut, but I couldn't ignore the throbbing pain, or the deep purple tendrils of infection now licking at the bases of my wrists and my neck, which not even my long-sleeved hoodie could hide. Occasionally, my vision blurred, turning the world a sickly shade of aubergine. I would hear a distant whisper in my head . . . the voice of Tarquin, beckoning me to return to his tomb. So far, the voice was just an annoyance, but I had the feeling it would get stronger until I could no longer ignore it . . . or fail to obey it.

I told myself I just needed to hang in there until tonight. Then I could summon godly help and get myself cured. Or I'd die in battle. At this point, either option was preferable to a painful, lingering slide into undeath.

Reyna walked alongside me, using her sheathed sword to poke the ground as if she expected to find land mines. Ahead of us, through the dense foliage, I saw no sign of Meg or the greyhounds, but I could hear them rustling through leaves and stepping on twigs. If any sentries waited for us at the summit, we would not be taking them by surprise.

'So,' Reyna said, apparently satisfied that Meg was out of earshot, 'are you going to tell me?'

My pulse accelerated to a tempo suitable for a parade march. 'Tell you what?'

She raised her eyebrows like, *Really?* 'Ever since you showed up at camp, you've been acting jumpy. You stare at me like *I'm* the one who got infected. Then you won't make eye contact. You stammer. You fidget. I do notice these things.'

'Ah.'

I climbed a few more steps. Perhaps if I concentrated on the hike, Reyna would let the matter drop.

'Look,' she said, 'I'm not going to bite you. Whatever is going on, I'd rather not have it hanging over your head, or mine, when we go into battle.'

I swallowed, wishing I had some of Lavinia's bubblegum to cut the taste of poison and fear.

Reyna made a good point. Whether I died today, or turned into a zombie, or somehow managed to live, I would rather face my fate with my conscience clear and no secrets. For one thing, I should tell Meg about my encounter with Peaches. I should also tell her I didn't hate her. In fact, I liked her pretty well. All right, I loved her. She was the bratty little sister I'd never had.

As for Reyna – I didn't know whether I was or wasn't the answer to her destiny. Venus might curse me for levelling with the praetor, but I had to tell Reyna what was bothering me. I was unlikely to get another chance.

'It's about Venus,' I said.

Reyna's expression hardened. It was her turn to stare at the hillside and hope the conversation went away. 'I see.'

'She told me –'

'Her little prediction.' Reyna spat out the words like inedible seeds. 'No mortal or demigod will ever heal my heart.'

'I didn't mean to pry,' I promised. 'It's just –'

'Oh, I believe you. Venus loves her gossip. I doubt there's anyone at Camp Jupiter who doesn't know what she told me in Charleston.'

'I – Really?'

Reyna broke a dry branch off a shrub and flicked it into the undergrowth. 'I went on that quest with Jason, what, two years ago? Venus took one look at me and decided . . . I don't know. I was broken. I needed romantic healing. Whatever. I wasn't back at camp a full day before the whispering started. Nobody would admit that they knew, but they knew. The looks I got: *Oh, poor Reyna.* The innocent suggestions about who I should date.'

She didn't sound angry. It was more like weighed down and weary. I remembered Frank Zhang's concern about how long Reyna had shouldered the burdens of leadership, how he wished he could do more to relieve her. Apparently, a lot of legionnaires wanted to help Reyna. Not all of that help had been welcome or useful.

'The thing is,' she continued, 'I'm *not* broken.'

'Of course not.'

'So why have you been acting nervous? What does Venus have to do with it? Please don't tell me it's pity.'

'N-no. Nothing like that.'

Up ahead, I heard Meg romping through the brush. Occasionally she would say, 'Hey, how's it going?' in a conversational tone, as if passing an acquaintance on the street. I supposed she was talking to the local dryads. Either that or the theoretical guards we were looking out for were very bad at their jobs.

'You see . . .' I fumbled for words. 'Back when I was a god, Venus gave me a warning. About you.'

Aurum and Argentum burst through the bushes to check on Mom, their toothy smiles gleaming like freshly polished bear traps. Oh, good. I had an audience.

Reyna patted Aurum absently on the head. 'Go on, Lester.'

'Um . . .' The marching band in my bloodstream was now doing double-time manoeuvres. 'Well, I walked into the throne room one day, and Venus was studying this hologram of you, and I asked – just completely casually, mind you – "Who's that?" And she told me your . . . your fate, I guess. The thing about healing your heart. Then she just . . . tore into me. She forbade me to approach you. She said if I ever tried to woo you she would curse me forever. It was totally unnecessary. And also embarrassing.'

Reyna's expression remained as smooth and hard as marble. 'Woo? Is that even a thing any more? Do people still woo?'

'I – I don't know. But I stayed away from you. You'll

notice I stayed away. Not that I would've done otherwise without the warning. I didn't even know who you were.'

She stepped over a fallen log and offered me a hand, which I declined. I didn't like the way her greyhounds were grinning at me.

'So, in other words,' she said, 'what? You're worried Venus will strike you dead because you're invading my personal space? I really wouldn't worry about that, Lester. You're not a god any more. You're obviously not trying to woo me. We're comrades on a quest.'

She had to hit me where it hurt – right in the truth.

'Yes,' I said. 'But I was thinking . . .'

Why was this so hard? I had spoken of love to women before. And men. And gods. And nymphs. And the occasional attractive statue before I realized it was a statue. Why, then, were the veins in my neck threatening to explode?

'I thought if – if it would help,' I continued, 'perhaps it was destiny that . . . Well, you see, I'm not a god any more, as you said. And Venus was quite specific that I shouldn't stick my *godly face* anywhere near you. But Venus . . . I mean, her plans are always twisting and turning. She may have been practising reverse psychology, so to speak. If we were meant to . . . Um, I could help you.'

Reyna stopped. Her dogs tilted their metal heads towards her, perhaps trying to gauge their master's mood. Then they regarded me, their jewelled eyes cold and accusatory.

'Lester.' Reyna sighed. 'What in Tartarus are you saying? I'm not in the mood for riddles.'

'That maybe I'm the answer,' I blurted. 'To healing your

heart. I could . . . you know, be your boyfriend. As Lester. If you wanted. You and me. You know, like . . . yeah.'

I was absolutely certain that up on Mount Olympus, the other Olympians all had their phones out and were filming me to post on Euterpe-Tube.

Reyna stared at me long enough for the marching band in my circulatory system to play a complete stanza of 'You're a Grand Old Flag'. Her eyes were dark and dangerous. Her expression was unreadable, like the outer surface of an explosive device.

She was going to murder me.

No. She would order her *dogs* to murder me. By the time Meg rushed to my aid, it would be too late. Or worse – Meg would help Reyna bury my remains, and no one would be the wiser.

When they returned to camp, the Romans would ask, *What happened to Apollo?*

Who? Reyna would say. *Oh, that guy? Dunno, we lost him.*

Oh, well! the Romans would reply, and that would be that.

Reyna's mouth tightened into a grimace. She bent over, gripping her knees. Her body began to shake. Oh, gods, what had I done?

Perhaps I should comfort her, hold her in my arms. Perhaps I should run for my life. Why was I so bad at romance?

Reyna made a squeaking sound, then a sort of sustained whimper. I really *had* hurt her!

Then she straightened, tears streaming down her face, and burst into laughter. The sound reminded me of water rushing over a riverbed that had been dry for ages. Once she started, she couldn't seem to stop. She doubled over, stood upright again, leaned against a tree and looked at her dogs as if to share the joke.

'Oh . . . my . . . gods,' she wheezed. She managed to restrain her mirth long enough to blink at me through the tears, as if to make sure I was really there and she'd heard me correctly. 'You. Me? HA-HA-HA-HA-HA-HA-HA.'

Aurum and Argentum seemed just as confused as I was. They glanced at each other, then at me, as if to say, *What have you done to our mom? If you broke her, we will kill you.*

Reyna's laughter rolled across the hillside.

Once I got over my initial shock, my ears began to burn. Over the last few months I had experienced quite a few humiliations. But being laughed at . . . to my face . . . when I wasn't trying to be funny . . . that was a new low.

'I don't see why –'

'HA-HA-HA-HA-HA-HA!'

'I wasn't saying that –'

'HA-HA-HA-HA-HA-HA! Stop, please. You're killing me.'

'She doesn't mean that literally!' I yelped for the dogs' benefit.

'And you thought . . .' Reyna didn't seem to know where to point – at me, herself, the sky. 'Seriously? Wait. My dogs would have attacked if you were lying. Oh. Wow. HA-HA-HA-HA-HA-HA-HA!'

'So that's a *no*, then,' I huffed. 'Fine. I get it. You can stop –'

Her laughter turned to asthmatic squeaking as she wiped her eyes. 'Apollo. When you were a god . . .' She struggled for breath. 'Like, with your powers and good looks and whatever –'

'Say no more. Naturally, you would have –'

'That would have been a solid, absolute, hard-pass NO.'

I gaped. 'I am *astonished*!'

'And as Lester . . . I mean, you're sweet and kind of adorkable at times.'

'Adorkable? At *times*?'

'But wow. Still a big-time NO. Ha-ha-ha-ha-ha-ha!'

A lesser mortal would have crumbled to dust on the spot, their self-esteem imploding.

In that moment, as she rejected me utterly, Reyna had never seemed more beautiful and desirable. Funny how that works.

Meg emerged from the hackberry bushes. 'Guys, there's nobody up there, but –' She froze, taking in the scene, then glanced at the greyhounds for explanation.

Don't ask us, their metal faces seemed to say. *Mom is never like this*.

'What's so funny?' Meg asked. A smile tugged at her mouth, as if she wanted to join in the joke. Which was, of course, me.

'Nothing.' Reyna held her breath for a moment, then lost it again in a fit of giggles. Reyna Avila Ramírez-Arellano, daughter of Bellona, feared praetor of the Twelfth Legion, giggling.

At last she seemed to regain some of her self-control. Her eyes danced with humour. Her cheeks glowed beet-red. Her smile made her seem like a different person – a *happy* different person.

'Thanks, Lester,' she said. 'I needed that. Now let's go find the soundless god, shall we?'

She led the way up the hill, holding her ribs as if her chest still hurt from too much hilarity.

Then and there, I decided that if I ever became a god again, I would rearrange the order of my vengeance list. Venus had just moved up to the top spot.

25

Frozen in terror
Like a god in the headlights
Why U speeding up?

MORTAL SECURITY WAS NOT A PROBLEM.

There wasn't any.

Across a flat expanse of rocks and weeds, the relay station sat nestled at the base of Sutro Tower. The blocky brown building had clusters of white satellite dishes dotting its roof like toadstools after a rain shower. The door stood wide open. The windows were dark. The parking area at the front was empty.

'This isn't right,' Reyna murmured. 'Didn't Tarquin say they were doubling security?'

'Doubling *the flock*,' Meg corrected. 'But I don't see any sheep or anything.'

That idea made me shudder. Over the millennia, I'd seen quite a few flocks of guardian sheep. They tended to be poisonous and/or carnivorous, and they smelled like mildewed sweaters.

'Apollo, any thoughts?' Reyna asked.

At least she could look at me now without bursting into laughter, but I didn't trust myself to speak. I just shook my head helplessly. I was good at that.

'Maybe we're in the wrong place?' Meg asked.

Reyna bit her lower lip. 'Something's definitely *off* here. Let me check inside the station. Aurum and Argentum can make a quick search. If we encounter any mortals, I'll just say I was hiking and got lost. You guys wait here. Guard my exit. If you hear barking, that means trouble.'

She jogged across the field, Aurum and Argentum at her heels, and disappeared inside the building.

Meg peered at me over the top of her cat-eye glasses. 'How come you made her laugh?'

'That wasn't my intention. Besides, it isn't illegal to make someone laugh.'

'You asked her to be your girlfriend, didn't you?'

'I – What? No. Sort of. Yes.'

'That was stupid.'

I found it humiliating to have my love life criticized by a little girl wearing a unicorn-and-crossbones badge. 'You wouldn't understand.'

Meg snorted.

I seemed to be everyone's source of amusement today.

I studied the tower that loomed above us. Up the side of the nearest support column, a steel-ribbed chute enclosed a row of rungs, forming a tunnel that one could climb through – if one were crazy enough – to reach the first set of crossbeams, which bristled with more satellite dishes and cellular-antenna fungi. From there, the rungs continued upward into a low-lying blanket of fog that swallowed the tower's top half. In the white mist, a hazy black V floated in and out of sight – a bird of some sort.

I shivered, thinking of the *strixes* that had attacked us in the Burning Maze, but strixes only hunted at night-time. That dark shape had to be something else, maybe a hawk looking for mice. The law of averages dictated that once in a while I'd have to come across a creature that didn't want to kill me, right?

Nevertheless, the fleeting shape filled me with dread. It reminded me of the many near-death experiences I'd shared with Meg McCaffrey, and of the promise I'd made to myself to be honest with her, back in the good old days of ten minutes ago, before Reyna had nuked my self-esteem.

'Meg,' I said. 'Last night –'

'You saw Peaches. I know.'

She might have been talking about the weather. Her gaze stayed fixed on the doorway of the relay station.

'You know,' I repeated.

'He's been around for a couple of days.'

'You've seen him?'

'Just sensed him. He's got his reasons for staying away. Doesn't like the Romans. He's working on a plan to help the local nature spirits.'

'And . . . if that plan is to help them run away?'

In the diffused grey light of the fog bank, Meg's glasses looked like her own tiny satellite dishes. 'You think that's what he wants? Or what the nature spirits want?'

I remembered the fauns' fearful expressions at People's Park, the dryads' weary anger. 'I don't know. But Lavinia –'

'Yeah. She's with them.' Meg shrugged one shoulder. 'The centurions noticed her missing at morning roll call. They're trying to downplay it. Bad for morale.'

I stared at my young companion, who had apparently

been taking lessons from Lavinia in Advanced Camp Gossip. 'Does Reyna know?'

'That Lavinia is gone? Sure. Where Lavinia went? Nah. I don't either, really. Whatever she and Peaches and the rest are planning, there's not much we can do about it now. We've got other stuff to worry about.'

I crossed my arms. 'Well, I'm glad we had this talk, so I could unburden myself of all the things you already knew. I was also going to say that you're important to me and I might even love you like a sister, but –'

'I already know that, too.' She gave me a crooked grin, offering proof that Nero really should have taken her to the orthodontist when she was younger. ''S okay. You've got less annoying, too.'

'Hmph.'

'Look, here comes Reyna.'

And so ended our warm family moment, as the praetor reemerged from the station, her expression unsettled, her greyhounds happily circling her legs as if waiting for jelly beans.

'The place is empty,' Reyna announced. 'Looks like everybody left in a hurry. I'd say something cleared them out – like a bomb threat, maybe.'

I frowned. 'In that case, wouldn't there be emergency vehicles here?'

'The Mist,' Meg guessed. 'Could've made the mortals see anything to get them out of here. Clearing the scene before . . .'

I was about to ask, *Before what?* But I didn't want the answer.

Meg was right, of course. The Mist was a strange force. Sometimes it manipulated mortal minds after a supernatural event, like damage control. Other times, it operated in advance of a catastrophe, pushing away mortals who might otherwise wind up as collateral damage – like ripples in a local pond warning of a dragon's first footstep.

'Well,' Reyna said, 'if that's true, it means we're in the right place. And I can only think of one other direction to explore.' Her eyes followed the pylons of Sutro Tower until they disappeared into the fog. 'Who wants to climb first?'

Want had nothing to do with it. I was drafted.

The ostensible reason was so Reyna could steady me if I started feeling shaky on the ladder. The real reason was probably so I couldn't back out if I got scared. Meg went last, I suppose because that would give her time to select the proper gardening seeds to throw at our enemies while they were mauling my face and Reyna was pushing me forward.

Aurum and Argentum, not being able to climb, stayed on the ground to guard our exit like the opposable-thumb-lacking slackers they were. If we ended up plummeting to our deaths, the dogs would be right there to bark excitedly at our corpses. That gave me great comfort.

The rungs were slippery and cold. The chute's metal ribs made me feel like I was crawling through a giant Slinky. I imagined they were meant as some kind of safety feature, but they did nothing to reassure me. If I slipped, they would just be more painful things for me to hit on my way down.

After a few minutes, my limbs were shaking. My fingers trembled. The first set of crossbeams seemed to be getting no closer. I looked down and saw we had barely cleared the radar dishes on the station's rooftop.

The cold wind buffeted me around the cage, ripping through my hoodie, rattling the arrows in my quiver. Whatever Tarquin's guards were, if they caught me on this ladder, my bow and my ukulele would do me no good. At least a flock of killer sheep couldn't climb ladders.

Meanwhile, in the fog high above us, more dark shapes swirled – definitely birds of some kind. I reminded myself that they couldn't be strixes. Still, a queasy sense of danger gnawed at my stomach.

What if –?

Stop it, Apollo, I chided myself. *There's nothing you can do now but keep climbing.*

I concentrated on one perilous slippery rung at a time. The soles of my shoes squeaked against the metal.

Below me, Meg asked, 'Do you guys smell roses?'

I wondered if she was trying to make me laugh. 'Roses? Why in the name of the twelve gods would I smell *roses* up here?'

Reyna said, 'All I smell is Lester's shoes. I think he stepped in something.'

'A large puddle of shame,' I muttered.

'I smell roses,' Meg insisted. 'Whatever. Keep moving.'

I did, since I had no choice.

At last we reached the first set of crossbeams. A catwalk ran the length of the girders, allowing us to stand and rest for a few minutes. We were only about sixty feet above the relay station, but it felt much higher. Below us spread an endless grid of city blocks, rumbling and twisting across the hills whenever necessary, the streets making designs that reminded me of the Thai alphabet. (The goddess Nang Kwak had tried to teach me their language once, over a lovely dinner of spicy noodles, but I was hopeless at it.)

Down in the parking lot, Aurum and Argentum looked up at us and wagged their tails. They seemed to be waiting for us to do something. The mean-spirited part of me wanted to shoot an arrow to the top of the next hill and yell, FETCH! but I doubted Reyna would appreciate that.

'It's fun up here,' Meg decided. She did a cartwheel, because she enjoyed giving me heart palpitations.

I scanned the triangle of catwalks, hoping to see something besides cables, circuit boxes and satellite equipment – preferably something labelled: PUSH THIS BUTTON TO COMPLETE QUEST AND COLLECT REWARD.

Of course not, I grumbled to myself. *Tarquin wouldn't be so kind as to put whatever we needed on the lowest level.*

'Definitely no silent gods here,' Reyna said.

'Thanks a lot.'

She smiled, clearly still in a good mood from my earlier misstep into the puddle of shame. 'I also don't see any doors. Didn't the prophecy say I'm supposed to open a door?'

'Could be a metaphorical one,' I speculated. 'But you're right, there's nothing here for us.'

Meg pointed to the next level of crossbeams – another sixty feet up, barely visible in the belly of the fog bank. 'The smell of roses is stronger from up there,' she said. 'We should keep climbing.'

I sniffed the air. I smelled only the faint scent of

eucalyptus from the woods below us, my own sweat cooling against my skin, and the sour whiff of antiseptic and infection rising from my bandaged abdomen.

'Hooray,' I said. 'More climbing.'

This time, Reyna took the lead. There was no climbing cage going to the second level – just bare metal rungs against the side of the girder, as if the builders had decided, *Welp, if you made it this far, you must be crazy, so no more safety features!* Now that the metal-ribbed chute was gone, I realized it *had* given me some psychological comfort. At least I could pretend I was inside a safe structure, not free-climbing a giant tower like a lunatic.

It made no sense to me that Tarquin would put something as important as his silent god at the top of a radio tower, or that he had allied himself with the emperors in the first place, or that the smell of roses might signal that we were getting closer to our goal, or that those dark birds kept circling above us in the fog. Weren't they cold? Didn't they have jobs?

Still, I had no doubt we were meant to climb this monstrous tripod. It felt right, by which I mean it felt terrifying and wrong. I had a premonition that everything *would* make sense to me soon enough and, when it did, I wouldn't like it.

It was as if I were standing in the dark, staring at small disconnected lights in the distance, wondering what they might be. By the time I realized, *Oh, hey, those are the head-lights of a large truck barrelling towards me!* it would be too late.

We were halfway to the second set of crossbeams when

an angry shadow dived out of the fog, plummeting past my shoulder. The gust from its wings nearly knocked me off the ladder.

'Whoa!' Meg grabbed my left ankle, though that did nothing to steady me. 'What was that?'

I caught a glimpse of the bird as it disappeared back into the fog: oily black wings, black beak, black eyes.

A sob built in my throat, as one of the proverbial truck's headlights became very clear to me. 'A raven.'

'A *raven?*' Reyna frowned down at me. 'That thing was *huge!*'

True, the creature that buzzed me must've had a wingspan of at least twenty feet, but then several angry croaks sounded from somewhere in the mist, leaving me in no doubt.

'Ravens, plural,' I corrected. '*Giant* ravens.'

Half a dozen spiralled into view, their hungry black eyes dancing over us like targeting lasers, assessing our soft-and-tasty weak spots.

'A flock of ravens.' Meg sounded half incredulous, half fascinated. 'Those are the guards? They're pretty.'

I groaned, wishing I could be anywhere else – like in bed, under a thick layer of warm Kevlar quilts. I was tempted to protest that a group of ravens was actually called an *unkindness* or a *conspiracy*. I wanted to shout that Tarquin's guards should be disqualified on that technicality. But I doubted Tarquin cared about such niceties. I knew the ravens didn't. They would kill us either way, no matter how pretty Meg thought they were. Besides, calling ravens unkind and conspiratorial had always seemed redundant to me.

'They're here because of Koronis,' I said miserably. 'This is my fault.'

'Who's Koronis?' Reyna demanded.

'Long story.' I yelled at the birds, 'Guys, I've apologized a million times!'

The ravens croaked back angrily. A dozen more dropped out of the fog and began to circle us.

'They'll tear us apart,' I said. 'We have to retreat – back to the first platform.'

'The second platform is closer,' Reyna said. 'Keep climbing!'

'Maybe they're just checking us out,' Meg said. 'Maybe they won't attack.'

She shouldn't have said that.

Ravens are contrary creatures. I should know – I shaped them into what they are. As soon as Meg expressed the hope that they wouldn't attack, they did.

26

I'd like to sing a
Classic for you now. Thank you.
Please stop stabbing me.

IN RETROSPECT, I should have given ravens sponges for beaks – nice, soft, squishy sponges that weren't capable of stabbing. While I was at it, I should've thrown in some Nerf claws.

But nooo. I let them have beaks like serrated knives and claws like meat hooks. What had I been thinking?

Meg yelled as one of the birds dived by her, raking her arm.

Another flew at Reyna's legs. The praetor levelled a kick at it, but her heel missed the bird and connected with my nose.

'OWEEEEE!' I yelled, my whole face throbbing.

'My bad!' Reyna tried to climb, but the birds swirled around us, stabbing and clawing and tearing away bits of our clothes. The frenzy reminded me of my farewell concert in Thessalonika back in 235 BCE. (I liked to do a farewell tour every ten years or so, just to keep the fans guessing.) Dionysus had shown up with his entire horde of souvenir-hunting *maenads. Not* a good memory.

'Lester, who is Koronis?' Reyna shouted, drawing her

sword. 'Why were you apologizing to the birds?'

'I created them!' My busted nose made me sound like I was gargling syrup.

The ravens cawed in outrage. One swooped, its claws narrowly missing my left eye. Reyna swung her sword wildly, trying to keep the flock at bay.

'Well, can you *un*-create them?' Meg asked.

The ravens didn't like that idea. One dived at Meg. She tossed it a seed – which, being a raven, it instinctively snapped out of the air. A pumpkin exploded to full growth in its beak. The raven, suddenly top-heavy with a mouth full of Halloween, plummeted towards the ground.

'Okay, I didn't exactly *create* them,' I confessed. 'I just changed them into what they are now. And, no, I can't undo it.'

More angry cries from the birds, though for the moment they stayed away, wary of the girl with the sword and the other one with the tasty exploding seeds.

Tarquin had chosen the perfect guards to keep me from his silent god. Ravens *hated* me. They probably worked for free, without even a health plan, just hoping to have the chance to bring me down.

I suspected the only reason we were still alive was that the birds were trying to decide who got the honour of the kill.

Each angry croak was a claim to my tasty bits: *I get his liver!*

No, I get his liver!

Well, I get his kidneys, then!

Ravens are as greedy as they are contrary. Alas, we

couldn't count on them arguing with one another for long. We'd be dead as soon as they figured out their proper pecking order. (Oh, maybe *that's* why they call it a *pecking order!*)

Reyna took a swipe at one that was getting too close. She glanced at the catwalk on the crossbeam above us, perhaps calculating whether she'd have time to reach it if she sheathed her sword. Judging from her frustrated expression, her conclusion was *no*.

'Lester, I need intel,' she said. 'Tell me how we defeat these things.'

'I don't know!' I wailed. 'Look, back in the old days, ravens used to be gentle and white, like doves, okay? But they were *terrible* gossips. One time I was dating this girl, Koronis. The ravens found out she was cheating on me, and they told me about it. I was so angry, I got Artemis to kill Koronis for me. Then I punished the ravens for being tattletales by turning them black.'

Reyna stared at me like she was contemplating another kick to my nose. 'That story is messed up on so many levels.'

'Just wrong,' Meg agreed. 'You had your sister kill a girl who was cheating on you?'

'Well, I –'

'Then you punished the birds that told you about it,' Reyna added, 'by turning them black, as if black was bad and white was good?'

'When you put it that way, it doesn't sound right,' I protested. 'It's just what happened when my curse scorched them. It also made them nasty-tempered flesh-eaters.'

'Oh, that's much better,' Reyna snarled.

'If we let the birds eat you,' Meg asked, 'will they leave Reyna and me alone?'

'I – *What?*' I worried that Meg might not be kidding. Her facial expression did not say *kidding*. It said *serious about the birds eating you*. 'Listen, I was angry! Yes, I took it out on the birds, but after a few centuries I cooled down. I apologized. By then, they kind of *liked* being nasty-tempered flesh-eaters. As for Koronis – I mean, at least I saved the child she was pregnant with when Artemis killed her. He became Asclepius, god of medicine!'

'Your girlfriend was *pregnant* when you had her killed?' Reyna launched another kick at my face. I managed to dodge it, since I'd had a lot of practice cowering, but it hurt to know that this time she hadn't been aiming at an incoming raven. Oh, no. She *wanted* to knock my teeth in.

'You suck,' Meg agreed.

'Can we talk about this later?' I pleaded. 'Or perhaps never? I was a *god* then! I didn't know what I was doing!'

A few months ago, a statement like that would have made no sense to me. Now, it seemed true. I felt as if Meg had given me her thick-lensed rhinestone-studded glasses and, to my horror, they corrected my eyesight. I didn't like how small and tawdry and petty everything looked, rendered in perfect ugly clarity through the magic of Meg-o-Vision. Most of all, I didn't like the way *I* looked – not just present-day Lester, but the god formerly known as Apollo.

Reyna exchanged glances with Meg. They seemed to reach a silent agreement that the most practical course of action would be to survive the ravens now so they could kill me themselves later.

'We're dead if we stay here.' Reyna swung her sword at another enthusiastic flesh-eater. 'We can't fend them off and climb at the same time. Ideas?'

The ravens had one. It was called *all-out attack*.

They swarmed – pecking, scratching, croaking with rage.

'I'm sorry!' I screamed, swatting futilely at the birds. 'I'm sorry!'

The ravens did not accept my apology. Claws ripped my trouser legs. A beak clamped on to my quiver and almost pulled me off the ladder, leaving my feet dangling for a terrifying moment.

Reyna continued to slash away. Meg cursed and threw seeds like party favours from the worst parade float ever. A giant raven spiralled out of control, covered in daffodils. Another fell like a stone, its stomach bulging in the shape of a butternut squash.

My grip weakened on the rungs. Blood dripped from my nose, but I couldn't spare a moment to wipe it away.

Reyna was right. If we didn't move, we were dead. And we couldn't move.

I scanned the crossbeam above us. If we could just reach it, we'd be able to stand and use our arms. We'd have a fighting chance to . . . well, *fight*.

At the far end of the catwalk, abutting the next support pylon, stood a large rectangular box like a shipping container. I was surprised I hadn't noticed it sooner, but compared to the scale of the tower, the container seemed small and insignificant, just another wedge of red metal. I had no idea what such a box was doing up here (a maintenance depot? A storage shed?) but if we could find a way inside, it might offer us shelter.

'Over there!' I yelled.

Reyna followed my gaze. 'If we can reach it . . . We need to buy time. Apollo, what repels ravens? Isn't there something they hate?'

'Worse than *me*?'

'They don't like daffodils much,' Meg observed, as another flower-festooned bird went into a tailspin.

'We need something to drive them *all* away,' Reyna said, swinging her sword again. 'Something they'll hate worse than Apollo.' Her eyes lit up. 'Apollo, sing for them!'

She might as well have kicked me in the face again. 'My voice isn't *that* bad!'

'But you're the – You *used* to be the god of music, right? If you can charm a crowd, you should be able to repulse one. Pick a song these birds will hate!'

Great. Not only had Reyna laughed in my face and busted my nose, now I was her go-to guy for repulsiveness.

Still . . . I was struck by the way she said I *used to be* a god. She didn't seem to mean it as an insult. She said it almost like a concession – like she knew what a horrible deity I had been, but held out hope that I might be capable of being someone better, more helpful, maybe even worthy of forgiveness.

'Okay,' I said. 'Okay, let me think.'

The ravens had no intention of letting me do that. They cawed and swarmed in a flurry of black feathers and pointy talons. Reyna and Meg tried their best to drive them back, but they couldn't cover me completely. A beak stabbed me in the neck, narrowly missing my carotid artery. Claws raked the side of my face, no doubt giving me some bloody new racing stripes.

I couldn't think about the pain.

I wanted to sing for Reyna, to prove that I had indeed changed. I was no longer the god who'd had Koronis killed and created ravens, or cursed the Cumaean Sibyl, or done any of the other selfish things that had once given me no more pause than choosing what dessert toppings I wanted on my ambrosia.

It was time to be helpful. I needed to be repulsive for my friends!

I rifled through millennia of performance memories, trying to recall any of my musical numbers that had totally bombed. Nope. I couldn't think of any. And the birds kept attacking . . .

Birds attacking.

An idea sparked at the base of my skull.

I remembered a story my children Austin and Kayla had told me, back when I was at Camp Half-Blood. We were sitting at the campfire, and they'd been joking about Chiron's bad taste in music. They said that several years earlier, Percy Jackson had managed to drive off a flock of killer Stymphalian birds simply by playing what Chiron had on his boom box.

What had he played? What was Chiron's favourite –?

'"VOLARE"!' I screamed.

Meg looked up at me, a random geranium stuck in her hair. 'Who?'

'It's a song Dean Martin covered,' I said. 'It – it might be unacceptable to birds. I'm not sure.'

'Well, *be* sure!' Reyna yelled. Ravens furiously scratched and pecked at her cloak, unable to tear the magical fabric, but her front side was unprotected. Every time she swung her sword, a bird swooped in, stabbing at her exposed chest and arms. Her long-sleeved tee was quickly turning into a short-sleeved tee.

I channelled my worst King of Cool. I imagined I was on a Las Vegas stage, a line of empty Martini glasses on the piano behind me. I was wearing a velvet tuxedo. I had just smoked a pack of cigarettes. In front of me sat a crowd full of adoring, tone-deaf fans.

'VOOO-LAR-RAAAAY!' I cried, modulating my voice to add about twenty syllables to the word. 'WHOA! OH!'

The response from the ravens was immediate. They recoiled as if we'd suddenly become vegetarian entrées. Some threw themselves bodily against the metal girders, making the whole tower shudder.

'Keep going!' Meg yelled.

Phrased as an order, her words forced me to comply. With apologies to Domenico Modugno, who wrote the song, I gave 'Volare' the full Dean Martin treatment.

It had once been such a lovely, obscure little tune. Originally, Modugno called it 'Nel blu, dipinto di blu', which, granted, was a bad title. I don't know why artists insist on doing that. Like the Wallflowers' 'One Headlight' obviously should have been titled 'Me and Cinderella'. And Ed Sheeran's 'The A-Team' should clearly have been called

'Too Cold for Angels to Fly'. I mean, come on, guys, you're burying the lede.

At any rate, 'Nel blu, dipinto di blu' might have faded into obscurity had Dean Martin not got hold of it, repackaged it as 'Volare', added seven thousand violins and backup singers, and turned it into a sleazy lounge-singer classic.

I didn't have backup singers. All I had was my voice, but I did my best to be terrible. Even when I was a god and could speak any language I wanted, I'd never sung well in Italian. I kept mixing it up with Latin, so I came off sounding like Julius Caesar with a head cold. My newly busted nose just added to the awfulness.

I bellowed and warbled, screwing my eyes shut and clinging to the ladder as ravens flapped around me, croaking in horror at my travesty of a performance. Far below, Reyna's greyhounds bayed as if they'd lost their mother.

I became so engrossed in murdering 'Volare' that I didn't notice that the ravens had gone silent until Meg shouted, 'APOLLO, ENOUGH!'

I faltered halfway through a chorus. When I opened my eyes, the ravens were nowhere in sight. From somewhere in the fog, their indignant caws grew fainter and fainter as the flock moved off in search of quieter, less revolting prey.

'My ears,' Reyna complained. 'Oh, gods, my ears will never heal.'

'The ravens will be back,' I warned. My throat felt like the chute of a cement mixer. 'As soon as they manage to purchase enough raven-size noise-cancelling headphones, they'll be back. Now climb! I don't have another Dean Martin song in me.'

27

Let's play guess the god.
Starts with H. Wants to kill me.
(Besides my stepmom.)

AS SOON AS I REACHED THE CATWALK, I
gripped the rail. I wasn't sure if my legs were wobbly or if
the entire tower was swaying. I felt like I was back on
Poseidon's pleasure trireme – the one pulled by blue whales.
Oh, it's a smooth ride, he'd promised. *You'll love it.*

Below, San Francisco stretched out in a rumpled quilt of
green and grey, the edges frayed with fog. I felt a twinge of
nostalgia for my days on the sun chariot. Oh, San Francisco!
Whenever I saw that beautiful city below, I knew my day's
journey was almost done. I could finally park my chariot at
the Palace of the Sun, relax for the night, and let whatever
other forces that controlled night and day take over for me.
(Sorry, Hawaii. I love you, but I wasn't about to work
overtime to give you a sunrise.)

The ravens were nowhere in sight. That didn't mean
anything. A blanket of fog still obscured the top of the
tower. The killers might swoop out of it at any minute. It
wasn't fair that birds with twenty-foot wingspans could
sneak up on us so easily.

At the far end of the catwalk sat the shipping container.

The scent of roses was so strong now that even I could smell it, and it seemed to be coming from the box. I took a step towards it and immediately stumbled.

'Careful.' Reyna grabbed my arm.

A jolt of energy went through me, steadying my legs. Perhaps I imagined it. Or maybe I was just shocked that she had made physical contact with me and it hadn't involved placing her boot in my face.

'I'm okay,' I said. One godly skill had not abandoned me: lying.

'You need medical attention,' Reyna said. 'Your face is a horror show.'

'Thanks.'

'I've got supplies,' Meg announced.

She rummaged through the pouches of her gardening belt. I was terrified she might try to patch my face with flowering bougainvillea, but instead she pulled out tape, gauze and alcohol wipes. I supposed her time with Pranjal had taught her more than just how to use a cheese grater.

She fussed over my face, then checked me and Reyna for any especially deep cuts and punctures. We had plenty. Soon all three of us looked like refugees from George Washington's camp at Valley Forge. We could have spent the whole afternoon bandaging each other, but we didn't have that much time.

Meg turned to regard the shipping container. She still had a stubborn geranium stuck in her hair. Her tattered dress rippled around her like shreds of seaweed.

'What is that thing?' she wondered. 'What's it doing up here, and why does it smell like roses?'

Good questions.

Judging scale and distance on the tower was difficult. Tucked against the girders, the shipping container looked close and small, but it was probably a full city block away from us, and larger than Marlon Brando's personal trailer on the set of *The Godfather*. (Wow, where did that memory come from? Crazy times.) Installing that huge red box on Sutro Tower would have been a massive undertaking. Then again, the Triumvirate had enough cash to purchase fifty luxury yachts, so they could probably afford a few cargo helicopters.

The bigger question was *why?*

From the sides of the container, glimmering bronze and gold cables snaked outward, weaving around the pylon and crossbeams like grounding wires, connecting to satellite dishes, cellular arrays and power boxes. Was there some sort of monitoring station inside? The world's most expensive greenhouse for roses? Or perhaps the most elaborate scheme ever to steal premium cable-TV channels.

The closest end of the box was fitted with cargo doors, the vertical locking rods laced with rows of heavy chains. Whatever was inside was meant to stay there.

'Any ideas?' Reyna asked.

'Try to get inside that container,' I said. 'It's a terrible idea. But it's the only one I have.'

'Yeah.' Reyna scanned the fog over our heads. 'Let's move before the ravens come back for an encore.'

Meg summoned her swords. She led the way across the catwalk, but after twenty feet or so she stopped abruptly, as if she'd run into an invisible wall.

She turned to face us. 'Guys, is . . . me or . . . feel weird?'

I thought the kick to my face might have short-circuited my brain. 'What, Meg?'

'I said . . . wrong, like . . . cold and . . .'

I glanced at Reyna. 'Did you hear that?'

'Only half of her words are coming through. Why aren't *our* voices affected?'

I studied the short expanse of catwalk separating us from Meg. An unpleasant suspicion wriggled in my head. 'Meg, take a step back towards me, please.'

'Why . . . want . . . ?'

'Just humour me.'

She did. 'So are you guys feeling weird, too? Like, kinda cold?' She frowned. 'Wait . . . it's better now.'

'You were dropping words,' Reyna said.

'I was?'

The girls looked at me for an explanation. Sadly, I thought I might have one – or at least the beginnings of one. The metaphorical truck with the metaphorical headlights was getting closer to metaphorically running me over.

'You two wait here for a second,' I said. 'I want to try something.'

I took a few steps towards the shipping container. When I reached the spot where Meg had been standing, I felt the difference – as if I'd stepped across the threshold of a walk-in freezer.

Another ten feet and I couldn't hear the wind any more, or the pinging of metal cables against the sides of the tower, or the blood rushing in my ears. I snapped my fingers. No sound.

Panic rose in my chest. Complete silence – a music god's worst nightmare.

I faced Reyna and Meg. I tried to shout, 'Can you hear me now?'

Nothing. My vocal cords vibrated, but the sound waves seemed to die before they left my mouth.

Meg said something I couldn't hear. Reyna spread her arms.

I gestured for them to wait. Then I took a deep breath and forced myself to keep going towards the box. I stopped within an arm's length of the cargo doors.

The rose-bouquet smell was definitely coming from inside. The chains across the locking rods were heavy Imperial gold – enough rare magical metal to buy a decent-size palace on Mount Olympus. Even in my mortal form, I could feel the power radiating from the container – not just the heavy silence, but the cold, needling aura of wards and curses placed on the metal doors and walls. To keep us out. To keep something in.

On the left-hand door, stencilled in white paint, was a single word in Arabic:

الإسكندرية

My Arabic was even rustier than my Dean Martin Italian, but I was fairly sure it was the name of a city. ALEXANDRIA. As in Alexandria, Egypt.

My knees almost buckled. My vision swam. I might have sobbed, though I couldn't hear it.

Slowly, gripping the rail for support, I staggered back to my friends. I only knew I'd left the zone of silence when I could hear myself muttering, 'No, no, no, no.'

Meg caught me before I could fall over. 'What's wrong? What happened?'

'I think I understand,' I said. 'The soundless god.'

'Who is it?' Reyna asked.

'I don't know.'

Reyna blinked. 'But you just said –'

'I think I *understand*. Remembering who it is exactly – that's harder. I'm pretty sure we're dealing with a Ptolemaic god, from back in the days when the Greeks ruled Egypt.'

Meg looked past me at the container. 'So there's a god in the box.'

I shuddered, remembering the short-lived fast food franchise Hermes had once tried to open on Mount Olympus. Thankfully, God-in-the-Box never took off. 'Yes, Meg. A very minor Egyptian–Greek hybrid god, I think, which is most likely why he couldn't be found in the Camp Jupiter archives.'

'If he's so minor,' Reyna said, 'why do you look so scared?'

A bit of my old Olympian haughtiness surged through me. *Mortals*. They could never understand.

'Ptolemaic gods are *awful*,' I said. 'They're unpredictable, temperamental, dangerous, insecure –'

'Like a normal god, then,' Meg said.

'I hate you,' I said.

'I thought you loved me.'

'I'm multitasking. Roses were this god's symbol. I – I don't remember why. A connection to Venus? He was in charge of secrets. In the old days, if leaders hung a rose from the ceiling of a conference room, it meant everybody in that conversation was sworn to secrecy. They called it *sub rosa*, under the rose.'

'So you know all that,' Reyna said, 'but you don't know the god's name?'

'I – He's –' A frustrated growl rose from my throat. 'I *almost* have it. I *should* have it. But I haven't thought about this god in millennia. He's *very* obscure. It's like asking me to remember the name of a particular backup singer I worked with during the Renaissance. Perhaps if you hadn't kicked me in the head –'

'After that story about Koronis?' Reyna said. 'You deserved it.'

'You did,' Meg agreed.

I sighed. 'You two are horrible influences on each other.'

Without taking their eyes off me, Reyna and Meg gave each other a silent high five.

'Fine,' I grumbled. 'Maybe the Arrow of Dodona can help jog my memory. At least he insults me in flowery Shakespearean language.'

I drew the arrow from my quiver. 'O prophetic missile, I need your guidance!'

There was no answer.

I wondered if the arrow had been lulled to sleep by the magic surrounding the storage container. Then I realized there was a simpler explanation. I returned the arrow to my quiver and pulled out a different one.

'You chose the wrong arrow, didn't you?' Meg guessed.

'No!' I snapped. 'You just don't understand my process. I'm going back into the sphere of silence now.'

'But –'

I marched away before Meg could finish.

Only when I was surrounded by cold silence again did it occur to me that it might be hard to carry on a conversation with the arrow if I couldn't talk.

No matter. I was too proud to retreat. If the arrow and I couldn't communicate telepathically, I would just pretend to have an intelligent conversation while Reyna and Meg looked on.

'O prophetic missile!' I tried again. My vocal cords vibrated, though no sound came out – a disturbing sensation I can only compare to drowning. 'I need your guidance!'

CONGRATULATIONS, said the arrow. Its voice resonated in my head – more tactile than audible – rattling my eyeballs.

'Thanks,' I said. 'Wait. Congratulations for what?'

THOU HAST FOUND THY GROOVE. AT LEAST THE BEGINNINGS OF THY GROOVE. I SUSPECTED THIS WOULD BE SO, GIVEN TIME. CONGRAT-ULATIONS ARE MERITED.

'Oh.' I stared at the arrow's point, waiting for a *but*. None came. I was so surprised that I could only stutter, 'Th-thanks.'

THOU ART MOST WELCOME.

'Did we just have a polite exchange?'

AYE, the arrow mused. *MOST TROUBLING. BY THE BY, WHAT 'PROCESS' WERT THOU SPEAKING OF TO YON MAIDENS? THOU HAST NO PROCESS SAVE FUMBLING.*

'Here we go,' I muttered. 'Please, my memory needs a jump start. This soundless god . . . he's that guy from Egypt, isn't he?'

WELL REASONED, SIRRAH, the arrow said. *THOU HAST NARROWED IT DOWN TO ALL THE GUYS IN EGYPT.*

'You know what I mean. There was that – that one

Ptolemaic god. The strange dude. He was a god of silence and secrets. But he wasn't, exactly. If you can just give me his name, I think the rest of my memories will shake loose.'

IS MY WISDOM SO CHEAPLY BOUGHT? DOST THOU EXPECT TO WIN HIS NAME WITH NO EFFORT?

'What do you call climbing Sutro Tower?' I demanded. 'Getting slashed to pieces by ravens, kicked in the face and forced to sing like Dean Martin?'

AMUSING.

I may have yelled a few choice words, but the sphere of silence censored them, so you will have to use your imagination.

'Fine,' I said. 'Can you at least give me a hint?'

VERILY, THE NAME DOTH BEGIN WITH AN H.

'Hephaestus . . . Hermes . . . Hera . . . A lot of gods' names begin with H!'

HERA? ART THOU SERIOUS?

'I'm just brainstorming. H, you say . . .'

THINK OF THY FAVOURITE PHYSICIAN.

'Me. Wait. My son Asclepius.'

The arrow's sigh rattled my entire skeleton. YOUR FAVOURITE MORTAL PHYSICIAN.

'Doctor Kildare. Doctor Doom. Doctor House. Doctor – Oh! You mean Hippocrates. But he's not a Ptolemaic god.'

THOU ART KILLING ME, the arrow complained. 'HIPPOCRATES' IS THY HINT. THE NAME THOU SEEKEST IS MOST LIKE IT. THOU NEEDEST CHANGE BUT TWO LETTERS.

'Which two?' I felt petulant, but I'd never enjoyed word puzzles, even before my horrific experience in the Burning Maze.

I SHALL GIVE THEE ONE LAST HINT, said the arrow. *THINK OF THY FAVOURITE MARX BROTHER.*

'The Marx Brothers? How do you even *know* about them? They were from the 1930s! I mean, yes, of course, I loved them. They brightened a dreary decade, but . . . Wait. The one who played the harp. Harpo. I always found his music sweet and sad and . . .'

The silence turned colder and heavier around me.

Harpo, I thought. *Hippocrates. Put the names together and you got . . .*

'Harpocrates,' I said. 'Arrow, please tell me that's not the answer. Please tell me he's not waiting in that box.'

The arrow did not reply, which I took as confirmation of my worst fears.

I returned my Shakespearean friend to his quiver and trudged back to Reyna and Meg.

Meg frowned. 'I don't like that look on your face.'

'Me neither,' Reyna said. 'What did you learn?'

I gazed out at the fog, wishing we could deal with something as easy as killer giant ravens. As I suspected, the name of the god had shaken loose my memories – bad, unwelcome memories.

'I know which god we face,' I said. 'The good news is he's not very powerful, as gods go. About as obscure as you can imagine. A real D-lister.'

Reyna folded her arms. 'What's the catch?'

'Ah . . . well.' I cleared my throat. 'Harpocrates and I didn't exactly get along. He might have . . . er, sworn that someday he'd see me vaporized.'

28

We all need a hand
On our shoulder sometimes so
We can chew through steel

'VAPORIZED,' SAID REYNA.

'Yes.'

'What did you do to him?' Meg asked.

I tried to look offended. 'Nothing! I may have teased him a bit, but he was a very *minor* god. Rather silly-looking. I may have made some jokes at his expense in front of the other Olympians.'

Reyna knitted her eyebrows. 'So you bullied him.'

'No! I mean . . . I did write ZAP ME in glowing letters on the back of his toga. And I suppose I might have been a bit harsh when I tied him up and locked him in the stalls with my fiery horses overnight –'

'Oh my gods!' Meg said. 'You're awful!'

I fought down the urge to defend myself. I wanted to shout, *Well, at least I didn't kill him like I did my pregnant girlfriend Koronis!* But that wasn't much of a gotcha.

Looking back on my encounters with Harpocrates, I realized I *had* been awful. If somebody had treated me, Lester, the way I had treated that puny Ptolemaic god, I would have wanted to crawl into a hole and die. And if I were honest, even back when I was a god, I had been bullied – only the bully had been my father. I should have known better than to share the pain.

I hadn't thought about Harpocrates in aeons. Teasing him had seemed like no big deal. I suppose that's what made it even worse. I had shrugged off our encounters. I doubted he had.

Koronis's ravens . . . Harpocrates . . .

It was no coincidence they were both haunting me today like the Ghosts of Saturnalias Past. Tarquin had orchestrated all this with *me* in mind. He was forcing me to confront some of my greatest hits of dreadfulness. Even if I survived the challenges, my friends would see exactly what kind of dirtbag I was. The shame would weigh me down and make me ineffective – the same way Tarquin used to add rocks to a cage around his enemy's head, until eventually, the burden was too much. The prisoner would collapse and drown in a shallow pool, and Tarquin could claim, *I didn't kill him. He just wasn't strong enough.*

I took a deep breath. 'All right, I was a bully. I see that now. I will march right into that box and apologize. And then hope Harpocrates doesn't vaporize me.'

Reyna did not look thrilled. She pushed up her sleeve, revealing a simple black watch on her wrist. She checked the time, perhaps wondering how long it would take to get me vaporized and then get back to camp.

'Assuming we can get through those doors,' she said, 'what are we up against? Tell me about Harpocrates.'

I tried to summon a mental image of the god. 'He usually looks like a child. Perhaps ten years old?'

'You bullied a ten-year-old,' Meg grumbled.

'He *looks* ten. I didn't say he *was* ten. He has a shaved head except for a ponytail on one side.'

'Is that an Egyptian thing?' Reyna asked.

'Yes, for children. Harpocrates was originally an incarnation of the god Horus – Harpa-Khruti, Horus the Child. Anyway, when Alexander the Great invaded Egypt, the Greeks found all these statues of the god and didn't know what to make of him. He was usually depicted with his finger to his lips.' I demonstrated.

'Like *be quiet*,' Meg said.

'That's exactly what the Greeks thought. The gesture had nothing to do with *shh*. It symbolized the hieroglyph for *child*. Nevertheless, the Greeks decided he must be the god of silence and secrets. They changed his name to Harpocrates. They built some shrines, started worshipping him, and boom, he's a Greek–Egyptian hybrid god.'

Meg snorted. 'It can't be that easy to make a new god.'

'Never underestimate the power of thousands of human minds all believing the same thing. They can remake reality. Sometimes for the better, sometimes not.'

Reyna peered at the doors. 'And now Harpocrates is in there. You think he's powerful enough to cause all our communications failures?'

'He shouldn't be. I don't understand how –'

'Those cables.' Meg pointed. 'They're connecting the

box to the tower. Could they be boosting his signal somehow? Maybe that's why he's up here.'

Reyna nodded appreciatively. 'Meg, next time I need to set up a gaming console, I'm calling you. Maybe we could just cut the cables and not open the box.'

I loved that idea, which was a pretty good indication it wouldn't work.

'It won't be enough,' I decided. 'The daughter of Bellona has to open the door to the soundless god, right? And for our ritual summoning to work we need the last breath of the god after his . . . um, soul is cut free.'

Talking about the Sibylline recipe in the safety of the praetors' office had been one thing. Talking about it on Sutro Tower, facing the god's big red shipping container, was quite another.

I felt a deep sense of unease that had nothing to do with the cold, or the proximity to the sphere of silence, or even the zombie poison circulating in my blood. A few moments ago, I had admitted to bullying Harpocrates. I had decided to apologize. Then what? I would kill him for the sake of a prophecy? Another rock plopped into the invisible cage around my head.

Meg must have felt the same. She made her best *I-don't-wanna* scowl and started fidgeting with the tatters of her dress. 'We don't really have to . . . you know, do we? I mean even if this Harpo guy is working for the emperors . . .'

'I don't think he is.' Reyna nodded towards the chains on the locking rods. 'It looks like he's being kept *in*. He's a prisoner.'

'That's even worse,' Meg said.

From where I stood, I could just make out the white stencilled Arabic for *Alexandria* on the door of the container. I imagined the Triumvirate digging up Harpocrates from some buried temple in the Egyptian desert, wrestling him into that box, then shipping him off to America like third-class freight. The emperors would've considered Harpocrates just another dangerous, amusing plaything, like their trained monsters and humanoid lackeys.

And why not let King Tarquin be his custodian? The emperors could ally themselves with the undead tyrant, at least temporarily, to make their invasion of Camp Jupiter a little easier. They could let Tarquin arrange his cruellest trap for me. Whether I killed Harpocrates or he killed me, what did it matter to the Triumvirate in the end? Either way, they would find it entertaining – one more gladiator match to break the monotony of their immortal lives.

Pain flared from the stab wound in my neck. I realized I'd been clenching my jaw in anger.

'There has to be another way,' I said. 'The prophecy *can't* mean for us to kill Harpocrates. Let's talk to him. Figure something out.'

'How can we,' Reyna asked, 'if he radiates silence?'

'That . . . that's a good question,' I admitted. 'First things first. We have to get those doors open. Can you two cut the chains?'

Meg looked scandalized. 'With my *swords*?'

'Well, I thought they would work better than your teeth, but you tell me.'

'Guys,' said Reyna. 'Imperial gold blades hacking away at Imperial gold chains? Maybe we could cut through, but we'd be here until nightfall. We don't have that kind of time. I've got another idea. Godly strength.'

She looked at me.

'But I don't have any!' I protested.

'You got your archery skills back,' she said. 'You got your musical skills back.'

'That Valerie song didn't count,' Meg said.

'"*Volare*",' I corrected.

'The point is,' Reyna continued, 'I may be able to boost your strength. I think that might be why I'm here.'

I thought about the jolt of energy I'd felt when Reyna touched my arm. It hadn't been physical attraction, or a warning buzz from Venus. I recalled something she had told Frank before we left camp. 'Bellona's power,' I said. 'It has something to do with strength in numbers?'

Reyna nodded. 'I can amplify other people's abilities. The bigger the group, the better it works, but even with three people . . . it might be sufficient to enhance your power enough to rip open those doors.'

'Would that count?' Meg asked. 'I mean, if Reyna doesn't open the door herself, isn't that cheating the prophecy?'

Reyna shrugged. 'Prophecies never mean what you think, right? If Apollo is able to open the door thanks to my help, I'm still responsible, wouldn't you say?'

'Besides . . .' I pointed to the horizon. Hours of daylight remained, but the full moon was rising, enormous and white, over the hills of Marin County. Soon enough, it would turn blood-red – and so, I feared, would a whole lot of our friends. 'We're running out of time. If we can cheat, let's cheat.'

I realized those would make terrible final words. Nevertheless, Reyna and Meg followed me into the cold silence.

When we reached the doors, Reyna took Meg's hand. She turned to me: *Ready?* Then she planted her other hand on my shoulder.

Strength surged through me. I laughed with soundless joy. I felt as potent as I had in the woods at Camp Half-Blood, when I'd tossed one of Nero's barbarian bodyguards into low earth orbit. Reyna's power was awesome! If I could just get her to follow me around the whole time I was mortal, her hand on my shoulder, a chain of twenty or thirty other demigods behind her, I bet there was nothing I couldn't accomplish!

I grabbed the uppermost chains and tore them like crepe paper. Then the next set, and the next. The Imperial gold broke and crumpled noiselessly in my fists. The steel locking rods felt as soft as breadsticks as I pulled them out of their fittings.

That left only the door handles.

The power may have gone to my head. I glanced back at Reyna and Meg with a self-satisfied smirk, ready to accept their silent adulation.

Instead, they looked as if I'd bent *them* in half, too.

Meg swayed, her complexion lima-bean green. The skin around Reyna's eyes was tight with pain. The veins on her temples stood out like lightning bolts. My energy surge was frying them.

Finish it, Reyna mouthed. Her eyes added a silent plea: *Before we pass out.*

Humbled and ashamed, I grabbed the door handles. My friends had got me this far. If Harpocrates was indeed waiting inside this shipping box, I would make sure the full force of his anger fell on me, not Reyna or Meg.

I yanked open the doors and stepped inside.

29

Ever heard the phrase
'The silence is deafening'?
Yeah, that's a real thing

IMMEDIATELY, I crumpled to my hands and knees under the weight of the other god's power.

Silence enfolded me like liquid titanium. The cloying smell of roses was overwhelming.

I'd forgotten how Harpocrates communicated – with blasts of mental images, oppressive and devoid of sound. Back when I was a god, I'd found this annoying. Now, as a human, I realized it could pulp my brain. At the moment, he was sending me one continuous message: *YOU? HATE!*

Behind me, Reyna was on her knees, cupping her ears and screaming mutely. Meg was curled on her side, kicking her legs as if trying to throw off the heaviest of blankets.

A moment before, I'd been tearing through metal like it was paper. Now, I could barely lift my head to meet Harpocrates's gaze.

The god floated cross-legged at the far end of the room.

He was still the size of a ten-year-old child, still wearing his ridiculous toga and pharaonic bowling-pin crown combo, like so many confused Ptolemaic gods who couldn't decide if they were Egyptian or Greco-Roman. His braided ponytail snaked down one side of his shaved head. And, of course, he still held one finger to his mouth like the most frustrated, burned-out librarian in the world: *SSSHHH!*

He could not do otherwise. I recalled that Harpocrates required all his willpower to lower his finger from his mouth. As soon as he stopped concentrating, his hand would pop right back into position. In the old days, I had found that hilarious. Now, not so much.

The centuries had not been kind to him. His skin was wrinkled and saggy. His once-bronze complexion was an unhealthy porcelain colour. His sunken eyes smouldered with anger and self-pity.

Imperial gold fetters were clamped around Harpocrates's wrists and ankles, connecting him to a web of chains, cords and cables – some hooked up to elaborate control panels, others channelled through holes in the walls of the container, leading out to the tower's superstructure. The set-up seemed designed to siphon Harpocrates's power and then amplify it – to broadcast his magical silence across the world. This was the source of all our communications troubles – one sad, angry, forgotten little god.

It took me a moment to understand why he remained imprisoned. Even drained of his power, a minor deity should have been able to break a few chains. Harpocrates seemed to be alone and unguarded.

Then I noticed them. Floating on either side of the god, so entangled in chains that they were hard to distinguish from the general chaos of machinery and wires, were two objects I hadn't seen in centuries: identical ceremonial axes, each about four feet tall, with a crescent blade and a thick bundle of wooden rods fastened around the shaft.

Fasces. The ultimate symbol of Roman might.

Looking at them made my ribs twist into bows. In the old days, powerful Roman officials never left home without a procession of *lictor* bodyguards, each carrying one of those bundled axes to let the commoners know somebody important was coming through. The more fasces, the more important the official.

In the twentieth century, Benito Mussolini revived the symbol when he became Italy's dictator. His ruling philosophy was named after those bundled axes: *Fascism.*

But the fasces in front of me were no ordinary standards. These blades were Imperial gold. Wrapped around the bundles of rods were silken banners embroidered with the names of their owners. Enough of the letters were visible that I could guess what they said. On the left: CAESAR MARCUS AURELIUS COMMODUS ANTONINUS AUGUSTUS. On the right: GAIUS JULIUS CAESAR AUGUSTUS GERMANICUS, otherwise known as Caligula.

These were the personal fasces of the two emperors, being used to drain Harpocrates's power and keep him enslaved.

The god glared at me. He forced painful images into my mind: me stuffing his head into a toilet on Mount Olympus; me howling with amusement as I tied his wrists and ankles and shut him in the stables with my fire-breathing horses. Dozens of other encounters I'd completely forgotten about, and in all of them I was as golden, handsome and powerful as any Triumvirate emperor – and just as cruel.

My skull throbbed from the pressure of Harpocrates's

assault. I felt capillaries bursting in my busted nose, my forehead, my ears. Behind me, Reyna and Meg writhed in agony. Reyna locked eyes with me, blood trickling from her nostrils. She seemed to ask, *Well, genius? What now?*

I crawled closer to Harpocrates.

Tentatively, using a series of mental pictures, I tried to convey a question: *How did you get here?*

I imagined Caligula and Commodus overpowering him, binding him, forcing him to do their bidding. I imagined Harpocrates floating alone in this dark box for months, years, unable to break free from the power of the fasces, growing weaker and weaker as the emperors used his silence to keep the demigod camps in the dark, cut off from one another, while the Triumvirate divided and conquered.

Harpocrates was their prisoner, not their ally.

Was I right?

Harpocrates replied with a withering gust of resentment.

I took that to mean both *Yes* and *You suck, Apollo*.

He forced more visions into my mind. I saw Commodus and Caligula standing where I now was, smiling cruelly, taunting him.

You should be on our side, Caligula told him telepathically. *You should want to help us!*

Harpocrates had refused. Perhaps he couldn't overpower his bullies, but he intended to fight them with every last bit of his soul. That's why he now looked so withered.

I sent out a pulse of sympathy and regret. Harpocrates blasted it away with scorn.

Just because we both hated the Triumvirate did not make us friends. Harpocrates had never forgotten my cruelty. If he hadn't been constrained by the fasces, he would have already blasted me and my friends into a fine mist of atoms.

He showed me that image in vivid colour. I could tell he relished thinking about it.

Meg tried to join our telepathic argument. At first, all she could send was a garbled sense of pain and confusion. Then she managed to focus. I saw her father smiling down at her, handing her a rose. For her, the rose was a symbol of love, not secrets. Then I saw her father dead on the steps of Grand Central Station, murdered by Nero. She sent Harpocrates her life story, captured in a few painful snapshots. She knew about monsters. She had been raised by the Beast. No matter how much Harpocrates hated me – and Meg agreed that I could be pretty stupid sometimes – we had to work together to stop the Triumvirate.

Harpocrates shredded her thoughts with rage. How dare she presume to understand his misery?

Reyna tried a different approach. She shared her memories of Tarquin's last attack on Camp Jupiter: so many wounded and killed, their bodies dragged off by ghouls to be reanimated as vrykolakai. She showed Harpocrates her greatest fear: that after all their battles, after centuries of upholding the best traditions of Rome, the Twelfth Legion might face their end tonight.

Harpocrates was unmoved. He bent his will towards me, burying me in hatred.

All right! I pleaded. *Kill me if you must. But I am sorry! I have changed!*

I sent him a flurry of the most horrible, embarrassing failures I'd suffered since becoming mortal: grieving over the body of Heloise the griffin at the Waystation, holding the dying pandos Crest in my arms in the Burning Maze, and, of course, watching helplessly as Caligula murdered Jason Grace.

Just for a moment, Harpocrates's wrath wavered.

At the very least, I had managed to surprise him. He had not been expecting regret or shame from me. Those weren't my trademark emotions.

If you let us destroy the fasces, I thought, *that will free you. It will also hurt the emperors, yes?*

I showed him a vision of Reyna and Meg cutting through the fasces with their swords, the ceremonial axes exploding.

Yes, Harpocrates thought back, adding a brilliant red tint to the vision.

I had offered him something he wanted.

Reyna chimed in. She pictured Commodus and Caligula on their knees, groaning in pain. The fasces were connected to them. They'd taken a great risk leaving their axes here. If the fasces were destroyed, the emperors might be weakened and vulnerable before the battle.

Yes, Harpocrates replied. The pressure of the silence eased. I could almost breathe without agony again. Reyna staggered to her feet. She helped Meg and me to stand.

Unfortunately, we were not out of danger. I imagined any number of terrible things Harpocrates could do to us if we freed him. And since I'd been talking with my mind I couldn't help but broadcast those fears.

Harpocrates's glare did nothing to reassure me.

The emperors must have anticipated this. They were smart, cynical, horribly logical. They knew that, if I did release Harpocrates, the god's first act would probably be to kill me. For the emperors, the potential loss of their fasces apparently didn't outweigh the potential benefit of having me destroyed . . . or the entertainment value of knowing I'd done it to myself.

Reyna touched my shoulder, making me flinch involuntarily. She and Meg had drawn their weapons. They were waiting for me to decide. Did I really want to risk this?

I studied the soundless god.

Do what you want with me, I thought to him. *Just spare my friends. Please.*

His eyes burned with malice, but also a hint of glee. He seemed to be waiting for me to realize something, as if he'd written ZAP ME on my backpack when I wasn't looking.

Then I saw what he was holding in his lap. I hadn't noticed it while I was down on my hands and knees but, now that I was standing, it was hard to miss: a glass jar, apparently empty, sealed with a metal lid.

I felt as if Tarquin had just dropped the final rock into the drowning cage around my head. I imagined the emperors howling with delight on the deck of Caligula's yacht.

Rumours from centuries before swirled in my head: *The Sibyl's body had crumbled away . . . She could not die . . . Her attendants kept her life force . . . her voice . . . in a glass jar.*

Harpocrates cradled all that remained of the Sibyl of Cumae – another person who had every reason to hate me; a person the emperors and Tarquin knew I would feel obliged to help.

They had left me the starkest of choices: run away, let the Triumvirate win, and watch my mortal friends be destroyed, or free two bitter enemies and face the same fate as Jason Grace.

It was an easy decision.

I turned to Reyna and Meg and thought as clearly as I could: *Destroy the fasces. Cut him free.*

30

A voice and a shh.
I have seen stranger couples.
Wait. No, I haven't.

TURNS OUT THAT WAS A BAD IDEA.

Reyna and Meg moved cautiously – as one does when approaching a cornered wild animal or an angry immortal. They took up positions on either side of Harpocrates, raised their blades above the fasces and mouthed in unison: *One, two, three!*

It was almost like the fasces had been waiting to explode. Despite Reyna's earlier protestations that Imperial gold blades might take forever to hack through Imperial gold chains, her sword and Meg's cut through the cords and cables as if they were nothing but illusions themselves.

Their blades hit the fasces and shattered them – sending bundles of rods blasting into splinters, shafts breaking, golden crescents toppling to the floor.

The girls stepped back, clearly surprised by their own success.

Harpocrates gave me a thin, cruel smile.

Without a sound, the fetters on his hands and feet cracked and fell away like spring ice. The remaining cables and chains shrivelled and blackened, curling against the walls. Harpocrates stretched out his free hand – the one that was not gesturing, *Shh, I'm about to kill you* – and the two golden axe blades from the broken fasces flew into his grip. His fingers turned white hot. The blades melted, gold dribbling through his fingers and pooling beneath him.

A small, terrified voice in my head said, *Well, this is going great.*

The god plucked the glass jar from his lap. He raised it on his fingertips like a crystal ball. For a moment, I was afraid he would give it the gold-axe treatment, melting whatever remained of the Sibyl just to spite me.

Instead, he assaulted my mind with new images.

I saw a eurynomos lope into Harpocrates's prison, the glass jar tucked under one arm. The ghoul's mouth slavered. Its eyes glowed purple.

Harpocrates thrashed in his chains. It seemed he had not been in the box very long at that point. He wanted to crush the eurynomos with silence, but the ghoul seemed unaffected. Its body was being driven by another mind, far away in the tyrant's tomb.

Even through telepathy, it was clear the voice was Tarquin's – heavy and brutal as chariot wheels over flesh.

I brought you a friend, he said. *Try not to break her.*

He tossed the jar to Harpocrates, who caught it out of surprise. Tarquin's possessed ghoul limped away, chuckling evilly, and chained the doors behind it.

Alone in the dark, Harpocrates's first thought was to smash the jar. Anything from Tarquin had to be a trap, or poison, or something worse. But he was curious. *A friend?*

Harpocrates had never had one of those. He wasn't sure he understood the concept.

He could sense a living force inside the jar: weak, sad, fading, but alive, and possibly more ancient than he was. He opened the lid. The faintest voice began to speak to him, cutting straight through his silence as if it didn't exist.

After so many millennia, Harpocrates, the silent god who was never supposed to exist, had almost forgotten *sound*. He wept with joy. The god and the Sibyl began to converse.

They both knew they were pawns, prisoners. They were only here because they served some purpose for the emperors and their new ally, Tarquin. Like Harpocrates, the Sibyl had refused to cooperate with her captors. She would tell them nothing of the future. Why should she? She was beyond pain and suffering. She had literally nothing left to lose and longed only to die.

Harpocrates shared the feeling. He was tired of spending millennia slowly wasting away, waiting until he was obscure enough, forgotten by all humankind, so he could cease to exist altogether. His life had always been bitter – a never-ending parade of disappointments, bullying and ridicule. Now he wanted sleep. The eternal sleep of extinct gods.

They shared stories. They bonded over their hatred of me. They realized that Tarquin wanted this to happen. He had thrown them together, hoping they'd become friends, so he could use them as leverage against each other. But they couldn't help their feelings.

Wait. I interrupted Harpocrates's story. *Are you two . . .* together?

I shouldn't have asked. I didn't mean to send such an incredulous thought, like how does a *shh* god fall in love with a voice in a glass jar?

Harpocrates's rage pressed down on me, making my knees buckle. The air pressure increased, as if I'd plummeted a thousand feet. I almost blacked out, but I guessed Harpocrates wouldn't let that happen. He wanted me conscious, able to suffer.

He flooded me with bitterness and hate. My joints began to unknit, my vocal cords dissolving. Harpocrates might have been ready to die, but that didn't mean he wouldn't kill me first. That would bring him great satisfaction.

I bowed my head, gritting my teeth against the inevitable.

Fine, I thought. *I deserve it. Just spare my friends. Please.*

The pressure eased.

I glanced up through a haze of pain.

In front of me, Reyna and Meg stood shoulder to shoulder, facing down the god.

They sent him their own flurry of images. Reyna pictured me singing 'The Fall of Jason Grace' to the legion, officiating at Jason's funeral pyre with tears in my eyes, then looking goofy and awkward and clueless as I offered to be her boyfriend, giving her the best, most cleansing laugh she'd had in years. (Thanks, Reyna.)

Meg pictured the way I'd saved her in the *myrmekes'* lair at Camp Half-Blood, singing about my romantic failures with such honesty it rendered giant ants catatonic with depression. She envisioned my kindness to Livia the elephant, to Crest, and especially to her, when I'd given her a hug in our room at the café and told her I would never give up trying.

In all their memories, I looked so *human* . . . but in the best possible ways. Without words, my friends asked Harpocrates if I was still the person he hated so much.

The god scowled, considering the two young women.

Then a small voice spoke – actually *spoke* – from inside the sealed glass jar. 'Enough.'

As faint and muffled as her voice was, I should not have been able to hear it. Only the utter silence of the shipping container made her audible, though how she cut through Harpocrates's dampening field I had no idea. It was definitely the Sibyl. I recognized her defiant tone, the same way she'd sounded centuries before, when she vowed never to love me until every grain of sand ran out: *Come back to me at the end of that time. Then, if you still want me, I'm yours.*

Now, here we were, at the wrong end of forever, neither of us in the right form to choose the other.

Harpocrates regarded the jar, his expression turning sad and plaintive. He seemed to ask, *Are you sure?*

'This is what I have foreseen,' whispered the Sibyl. 'At last, we will rest.'

A new image appeared in my mind – verses from the Sibylline Books, purple letters against white skin, so bright it made me squint. The words smoked as if fresh from a harpy tattoo-artist's needle: *Add the last breath of the god who speaks not, once his soul is cut free, together with the shattered glass.*

Harpocrates must have seen the words, too, judging from the way he winced. I waited for him to process their meaning, to get angry again, to decide that if anyone's soul should be cut free it should be mine.

When I was a god, I rarely thought about the passage of time. A few centuries here or there, what did it matter? Now I considered just how long ago the Sibyl had written those lines. They had been scribbled into the original Sibylline Books back when Rome was still a puny kingdom. Had the Sibyl known even then what they meant? Had she realized she would end up as nothing but a voice in a jar, stuck in this dark metal box with her boyfriend who smelled like roses and looked like a withered ten-year-old in a toga and a bowling-pin crown? If so, how could she not want to kill me even more than Harpocrates did?

The god peered into the container, maybe having a private telepathic conversation with his beloved Sibyl.

Reyna and Meg shifted, doing their best to block me from the god's line of sight. Perhaps they thought that, if he couldn't see me, he might forget I was there. I felt awkward peeking around their legs, but I was so drained and light-headed I doubted I could stand.

No matter what images Harpocrates had shown me, or how weary he was of life, I couldn't imagine he would just roll over and surrender. *Oh, you need to kill me for your prophecy thingie? Okay, sure! Stab me right here!*

I definitely couldn't imagine him letting us take the Sibyl's jar and shattering it for our summoning ritual. They had found love. Why would they want to die?

Finally, Harpocrates nodded, as if they'd come to an agreement. His face tightening with concentration, he pulled his index finger from his mouth, lifted the jar to his lips and gave it a gentle kiss. Normally, I would not have been moved by a man caressing a jar, but the gesture was so sad and heartfelt that a lump formed in my throat.

He twisted off the lid.

'Goodbye, Apollo,' said the Sibyl's voice, clearer now. 'I forgive you. Not because you deserve it. Not for your sake at all. But because I will not go into oblivion carrying hate when I can carry love.'

Even if I could've spoken, I wouldn't have known what to say. I was in shock. Her tone asked for no reply, no apology. She didn't need or want anything from me. It was almost as if I were the one being erased.

Harpocrates met my gaze. Resentment still smouldered in his eyes, but I could tell he was trying to let it go. The effort seemed even harder for him than keeping his hand from his mouth.

Without meaning to, I asked, *Why are you doing this? How can you just agree to die?*

It was in my interest that he did so, sure. But it made no sense. He had found another soul to *live* for. Besides, too many other people had already sacrificed themselves for my quests.

I understood now, better than I ever had, why dying was sometimes necessary. As a mortal, I had made that choice just a few minutes ago in order to save my friends. But a *god* agreeing to cease his existence, especially when he was free and in love? No. I couldn't comprehend that.

Harpocrates gave me a dry smirk. My confusion, my sense of near panic must have given him what he needed to finally stop being angry at me. Of the two of us, he was the wiser god. He understood something I did not. He certainly wasn't going to give me any answers.

The soundless god sent me one last image: me at an altar, making a sacrifice to the heavens. I interpreted that as an order: *Make this worth it. Don't fail.*

Then he exhaled deeply. We watched, stunned, as he began to crumble, his face cracking, his crown collapsing like a sandcastle turret. His last breath, a silver glimmer of fading life force, swirled into the glass jar to be with the Sibyl. He had just enough time to twist the lid closed before his arms and chest turned to chunks of dust, and then Harpocrates was gone.

Reyna lunged forward, catching the jar before it could hit the floor.

'That was close,' she said, which was how I realized the god's silence had been broken.

Everything seemed too loud: my own breathing, the sizzle of severed electrical wires, the creaking of the container's walls in the wind.

Meg still had the skin tone of a legume. She stared at the jar in Reyna's hand as if worried it might explode. 'Are they . . . ?'

'I think –' I choked on my words. I dabbed my face and found my cheeks were wet. 'I think they're gone. Permanently. Harpocrates's last breath is all that remains in the jar now.'

Reyna peered through the glass. 'But the Sibyl . . . ?' She turned to face me and almost dropped the jar. 'My gods, Apollo. You look terrible.'

'A horror show. Yes, I remember.'

'No. I mean it's worse now. The infection. When did *that* happen?'

Meg squinted at my face. 'Oh, yuck. We gotta get you healed, quick.'

I was glad I didn't have a mirror or a phone camera to see how I looked. I could only assume the lines of purple infection had made their way up my neck and were now drawing fun new patterns on my cheeks. I didn't feel any more zombie-ish. My stomach wound didn't throb any worse than before. But that could've simply meant my nervous system was shutting down.

'Help me up, please,' I said.

It took both of them to do so. In the process, I put one hand on the floor to brace myself, amid the shattered fasces rods, and got a splinter in my palm. Of course I did.

I wobbled on spongy legs, leaning on Reyna, then on Meg, trying to remember how to stand. I didn't want to look at the glass jar, but I couldn't help it. There was no sign of Harpocrates's silvery life force inside. I had to have faith that his last breath was still there. Either that, or when we tried to do our summoning I would discover that he had played a terrible final joke on me.

As for the Sibyl, I couldn't sense her presence. I was sure her final grain of sand had slipped away. She had chosen to exit the universe with Harpocrates – one last shared experience between two unlikely lovers.

On the outside of the jar, the gluey remains of a paper label clung to the glass. I could just make out the faded words SMUCKER'S GRAPE. Tarquin and the emperors had much to answer for.

'How could they . . . ?' Reyna shivered. 'Can a god do that? Just . . . choose to stop existing?'

I wanted to say *Gods can do anything*, but the truth was, I didn't know. The bigger question was, why would a god even want to try?

When Harpocrates had given me that last dry smile, had he been hinting that someday I might understand? Someday, would even the Olympians be forgotten relics, yearning for non-existence?

I used my nails to pull the splinter from my palm. Blood pooled – regular red human blood. It ran down the groove of my lifeline, which was not a great omen. Good thing I didn't believe in such things . . .

'We need to get back,' Reyna said. 'Can you move –?'

'Shh,' Meg interrupted, putting a finger to her lips.

I feared she was doing the most inappropriate Harpocrates impersonation ever. Then I realized she was quite serious. My newly sensitive ears picked up on what she was hearing – the faint, distant cries of angry birds. The ravens were returning.

31

O blood moon rising
Take a rain check on doomsday
I'm stuck in traffic

WE EMERGED from the shipping container just in time to get dive-bombed.

A raven swooped past Reyna and bit a chunk out of her hair.

'OW!' she yelled. 'All right, that's it. Hold this.'

She shoved the glass jar into my hands, then readied her sword.

A second raven came within range and she slashed it out of the sky. Meg's twin blades whirled, Magimixing another bird into a black cloud. That left only thirty or forty more bloodthirsty hang-gliders of doom swarming the tower.

Anger swelled in me. I decided I was done with the ravens' bitterness. Plenty of folks had valid reasons to hate me: Harpocrates, the Sibyl, Koronis, Daphne . . . maybe a few dozen others. Okay, maybe a few *hundred* others. But the ravens? They were thriving! They'd grown gigantic! They *loved* their new job as flesh-eating killers. Enough with the blame.

I secured the glass jar in my backpack. Then I unslung the bow from my shoulder.

'Scram or die!' I yelled at the birds. 'You get one warning!'

The ravens cawed and croaked with derision. One dived at me and got an arrow between the eyes. It spiralled downward, shedding a funnel cloud of feathers.

I picked another target and shot it down. Then a third. And a fourth.

The ravens' caws became cries of alarm. They widened their circle, probably thinking they could get out of range. I proved them wrong. I kept shooting until ten were dead. Then a dozen.

'I brought extra arrows today!' I shouted. 'Who wants the next one?'

At last, the birds got the message. With a few parting screeches – probably unprintable comments about my parentage – they broke off their assault and flew north towards Marin County.

'Nice work,' Meg told me, retracting her blades.

The best I could manage was a nod and some wheezing. Beads of sweat froze on my forehead. My legs felt like soggy french fries. I didn't see how I could climb back down the ladder, much less race off for a fun-filled evening of god-summoning, combat to the death, and possibly turning into a zombie.

'Oh, gods.' Reyna stared in the direction the flock had gone, her fingers absently exploring her scalp where the raven had ripped off a hank of her hair.

'It'll grow back,' I said.

'What? No, not my hair. Look!'

She pointed to the Golden Gate Bridge.

We must have been inside the shipping container much longer than I'd realized. The sun sat low in the western sky. The daytime full moon had risen above Mount Tamalpais. The afternoon heat had burned away all the fog, giving us a perfect view of the white fleet – fifty beautiful yachts in V formation – gliding leisurely past Point Bonita Lighthouse at the edge of the Marin Headlands, making their way towards the bridge. Once past it, they would have smooth sailing into the San Francisco Bay.

My mouth tasted like god dust. 'How long do we have?'

Reyna checked her watch. 'The *vappae* are taking their time, but even at the rate they're sailing they'll be in position to fire on the camp by sunset. Maybe two hours?'

Under different circumstances, I might have enjoyed her use of the term *vappae*. It had been a long time since I'd heard someone call their enemies *spoiled wines*. In modern parlance, the closest meaning would've been *scumbags*.

'How long will it take for us to reach camp?' I asked.

'In Friday afternoon traffic?' Reyna calculated. 'A little more than two hours.'

From one of her gardening-belt pouches, Meg pulled a fistful of seeds. 'I guess we'd better hurry, then.'

I was not familiar with *Jack and the Beanstalk*.

It didn't sound like a proper Greek myth.

When Meg said we'd have to use a *Jack-and-the-Beanstalk* exit, I didn't have a clue what she meant, even as she scattered handfuls of seeds down the nearest pylon, causing them to explode into bloom until she'd formed a latticework of plant matter all the way to the ground.

'Over you go,' she ordered.

'But –'

'You're in no shape to climb the ladder,' she said. 'This'll be faster. Like falling. Only with plants.'

I hated that description.

Reyna just shrugged. 'What the heck.'

She kicked one leg over the railing and jumped. The plants grabbed her, passing her down the leafy latticework a few feet at a time like a bucket brigade. At first she yelped and flailed her arms, but about halfway to the ground, she shouted up to us, 'NOT – THAT – BAD!'

I went next. It was bad. I screamed. I got flipped upside down. I floundered for something to hold on to, but I was completely at the mercy of creepers and ferns. It was like free-falling through a skyscraper-size bag of leaves, if those leaves were still alive and very touchy-feely.

At the bottom, the plants set me down gently on the grass next to Reyna, who looked like she'd been tarred and flowered. Meg landed beside us and immediately crumpled into my arms.

'Lotta plants,' she muttered.

Her eyes rolled up in her head. She began to snore. I guessed she would not be Jacking any more beanstalks today.

Aurum and Argentum bounded over, wagging their tails and yapping. The hundreds of black feathers strewn around the parking lot told me the greyhounds had been having fun with the birds I'd shot out of the sky.

I was in no condition to walk, much less carry Meg, but somehow, dragging her between us, Reyna and I managed to stumble back down the hillside to the truck. I suspected

Reyna was using her Bellona-mazing skills to lend me some of her strength, though I doubted she had much left to spare.

When we reached the Chevy, Reyna whistled. Her dogs jumped into the back. We wrestled our unconscious beanstalk master into the middle of the bench seat. I collapsed next to her. Reyna cranked the ignition, and we tore off down the hill.

Our progress was great for about ninety seconds. Then we hit the Castro District and got stuck in Friday traffic funnelling towards the highway. It was almost enough to make me wish for another bucket brigade of plants that could toss us back to Oakland.

After our time with Harpocrates, everything seemed obscenely loud: the Chevy's engine, the chatter of passing pedestrians, the thrum of subwoofers from other cars. I cradled my backpack, trying to take comfort in the fact that the glass jar was intact. We had got what we came for, though I could hardly believe the Sibyl and Harpocrates were gone.

I would have to process my shock and grief later, assuming I lived. I needed to figure out a way to properly honour their passing. How did one commemorate the death of a god of silence? A moment of silence seemed superfluous. Perhaps a moment of screaming?

First things first: survive tonight's battle. Then I would figure out the screaming.

Reyna must have noticed my worried expression.

'You did good back there,' she said. 'You stepped up.'

Reyna sounded sincere. But her praise just made me feel more ashamed.

'I'm holding the last breath of a god I bullied,' I said miserably, 'in the jar of a Sibyl I cursed, who were protected by birds I turned into killing machines after they tattled about my cheating girlfriend, whom I subsequently had assassinated.'

'All true,' Reyna said. 'But the thing is, you recognize it now.'

'It feels horrible.'

She gave me a thin smile. 'That's kind of the point. You do something evil, you feel bad about it, you do better. That's a sign you might be developing a conscience.'

I tried to remember which of the gods had created the human conscience. *Had* we created it, or had humans just developed it on their own? Giving mortals a sense of decency didn't seem like the sort of thing a god would brag about on their profile page.

'I – I appreciate what you're saying,' I managed. 'But my past mistakes almost got you and Meg killed. If Harpocrates had destroyed you when you were trying to protect me . . .'

The idea was too awful to contemplate. My shiny new conscience would have blown up inside me like a grenade.

Reyna gave me a brief pat on the shoulder. 'All we did was show Harpocrates how much you've changed. He recognized it. Have you completely made up for all the bad things you've done? No. But you keep adding to the "good things" column. That's all any of us can do.'

Adding to the 'good things' column. Reyna spoke of this superpower as if it were one I could actually possess.

'Thank you,' I said.

She studied my face with concern, probably noting how

far the purple vines of infection had wriggled their way across my cheeks. 'You can thank me by staying alive, okay? We need you for that summoning ritual.'

As we climbed the entrance ramp to Interstate 80, I caught glimpses of the bay beyond the downtown skyline. The yachts had now slipped under the Golden Gate Bridge. Apparently, the cutting of Harpocrates's cords and the destruction of the fasces hadn't deterred the emperors at all.

Stretching out in front of the big vessels were silver wake lines from dozens of smaller boats making their way towards the East Bay shoreline. Landing parties, I guessed. And those boats were moving a whole lot faster than we were.

Over Mount Tam, the full moon rose, slowly turning the colour of Dakota's fruit punch.

Meanwhile, Aurum and Argentum barked cheerfully in the back of the truck. Reyna drummed her fingers on the steering wheel and murmured, '*Vamonos. Vamonos.*' Meg leaned against me, snoring and drooling on my shirt. Because she loved me so much.

We were inching our way onto the Bay Bridge when Reyna finally said, 'I can't stand this. The ships shouldn't have made it past the Golden Gate.'

'What do you mean?' I asked.

'Open the glove compartment, please. Should be a scroll inside.'

I hesitated. Who knew what sort of dangers might lurk in the glove compartment of a praetor's pickup truck? Cautiously, I rummaged past her insurance documents, a few packages of tissues, some bags of dog treats . . .

'This?' I held up a floppy cylinder of vellum.

'Yeah. Unroll it and see if it works.'

'You mean it's a communication scroll?'

She nodded. 'I'd do it myself, but it's dangerous to drive and scroll.'

'Um, okay.' I spread the vellum across my lap.

Its surface appeared blank. Nothing happened.

I wondered if I was supposed to say some magic words or give it a credit card number or something. Then, above the scroll, a faint ball of light flickered, slowly resolving into a miniature holographic Frank Zhang.

'Whoa!' Tiny Frank nearly jumped out of his tiny armour. 'Apollo?'

'Hi,' I said. Then to Reyna, 'It works.'

'I see that,' she said. 'Frank, can you hear me?'

Frank squinted. We must have looked tiny and fuzzy to him, too. 'Is that . . . ? Can barely . . . Reyna?'

'Yes!' she said. 'We're on our way back. The ships are incoming!'

'I know . . . Scout's report . . .' Frank's voice crackled. He seemed to be in some sort of large cave, legionnaires hustling behind him, digging holes and carrying large urns of some kind.

'What are you doing?' Reyna asked. 'Where are you?'

'Caldecott . . .' Frank said. 'Just . . . defensive stuff.'

I wasn't sure if his voice fuzzed out that time because of static, or if he was being evasive. Judging from his expression, we'd caught him at an awkward moment.

'Any word . . . Michael?' he asked. (Definitely changing the subject.) 'Should've . . . by now.'

'What?' Reyna asked, loud enough to make Meg snort in her sleep. 'No, I was going to ask if *you'd* heard anything. They were supposed to stop the yachts at the Golden Gate. Since the ships got through . . .' Her voice faltered.

There could have been a dozen reasons why Michael Kahale and his commando team had failed to stop the emperors' yachts. None of them were good, and none of them could change what would happen next. The only things now standing between Camp Jupiter and fiery annihilation were the emperors' pride, which made them insist on making a ground assault first, and an empty Smucker's jam jar that might or might not allow us to summon godly help.

'Just hang on!' Reyna said. 'Tell Ella to get things ready for the ritual!'

'Can't . . . What?' Frank's face melted to a smudge of coloured light. His voice sounded like gravel shaking in an aluminium can. 'I . . . Hazel . . . Need to –'

The scroll burst into flames, which was not what my crotch needed at that particular moment.

I swatted the cinders off my trousers as Meg woke, yawning and blinking.

'What'd you do?' she demanded.

'Nothing! I didn't know the message would self-destruct!'

'Bad connection,' Reyna guessed. 'The silence must be breaking up slowly – like, working its way outward from the epicentre at Sutro Tower. We overheated the scroll.'

'That's possible.' I stomped out the last bits of smouldering vellum. 'Hopefully we'll be able to send an Iris-message once we reach camp.'

'*If* we reach camp,' Reyna grumbled. 'This traffic . . . Oh.'

She pointed to a blinking road sign ahead of us: HWY 24E CLOSED AT CALDECOTT TUNL FOR EMERG MAINTENANCE. SEEK ALT ROUTES.

'Emergency maintenance?' said Meg. 'You think it's the Mist again, clearing people out?'

'Maybe.' Reyna frowned at the lines of cars in front of us. 'No wonder everything's backed up. What was Frank doing in the tunnel? We didn't discuss any . . .' She knitted her eyebrows, as if an unpleasant thought had occurred to her. 'We have to get back. Fast.'

'The emperors will need time to organize their ground assault,' I said. 'They won't launch their *ballistae* until after they've tried to take the camp intact. Maybe . . . maybe the traffic will slow them down, too. They'll have to seek alternative routes.'

'They're on boats, dummy,' said Meg.

She was right. And once the assault forces landed they'd be marching on foot, not driving. Still, I liked the image of the emperors and their army approaching the Caldecott Tunnel, seeing a bunch of flashing signs and orange cones, and deciding, *Well, darn. We'll have to come back tomorrow.*

'We could ditch the truck,' Reyna mused. Then she glanced at us and clearly dismissed the idea. None of us was in any shape to run a half marathon from the middle of the Bay Bridge to Camp Jupiter.

She muttered a curse. 'We need . . . Ah!'

Just ahead, a maintenance truck was trundling along, a worker on the tailgate picking up cones that had been blocking the left lane for some unknown reason. Typical.

Friday at rush hour, with the Caldecott Tunnel shut down, obviously what you wanted to do was close one lane of traffic on the area's busiest bridge. This meant, however, that ahead of the maintenance truck there was an empty, extremely illegal-to-drive-in lane that stretched as far as the Lester could see.

'Hold on,' Reyna warned. And as soon as we edged past the maintenance truck she swerved in front of it, ploughing down a half-dozen cones, and gunned the engine.

The maintenance truck blared its horn and flashed its headlights. Reyna's greyhounds barked and wagged their tails in reply like, *See ya!*

I imagined we would have a few California Highway Patrol vehicles ready to chase us at the bottom of the bridge but, for the time being, we blasted past traffic at speeds that would have been creditable even for my sun chariot.

We reached the Oakland side. Still no sign of pursuit. Reyna veered onto the 580, smashing through a line of orange delineator posts and rocketing up the merge ramp for Highway 24. She politely ignored the guys in hard hats who waved their orange DANGER signs and screamed things at us.

We had found our alternative route. It was the regular route we weren't supposed to take.

I glanced behind us. No cops yet. Out on the water, the emperors' yachts had passed Treasure Island and were leisurely taking up positions, forming a necklace of billion-dollar luxury death machines across the bay. I saw no trace of the smaller landing craft, which meant they must have reached the shore. That wasn't good.

On the bright side, we were making great time. We

soared along the overpass all by ourselves, our destination only a few miles away.

'We're going to make it,' I said, like a fool.

Once again, I had broken the First Law of Percy Jackson: Never say something is going to work out, because, as soon as you do, it won't.

KALUMP!

Above our heads, foot-shaped indentations appeared in the truck's ceiling. The vehicle lurched under the extra weight. It was déjà ghoul all over again.

Aurum and Argentum barked wildly.

'Eurynomos!' Meg yelled.

'Where do they *come* from?' I complained. 'Do they just hang around on highway signs all day, waiting to drop?'

Claws punctured the metal and upholstery. I knew what would happen next: skylight installation.

Reyna shouted, 'Apollo, take the wheel! Meg, accelerator!'

For a heartbeat, I thought she meant that as some kind of prayer. In moments of personal crisis, my followers often used to implore me: *Apollo, take the wheel*, hoping I would guide them through their problems. Most of the time, though, they didn't mean it *literally*, nor was I physically sitting in the passenger's seat, nor did they add anything about Meg and accelerators.

Reyna didn't wait for me to figure it out. She released her grip and reached behind her seat, groping for a weapon. I lunged across and grabbed the wheel. Meg put her foot on the accelerator.

Quarters were much too close for Reyna to use her

sword, but that didn't bother her. Reyna had daggers. She unsheathed one, glared at the roof bending and breaking above us, and muttered, 'Nobody messes with my truck.'

A lot happened in the next two seconds.

The roof ripped open, revealing the familiar, disgusting sight of a fly-coloured eurynomos, its white eyes bulging, its fangs dripping with saliva, its vulture-feather loincloth fluttering in the wind.

The smell of rancid meat wafted into the truck, making my stomach turn. All the zombie poison in my system seemed to ignite at once.

The eurynomos screamed, 'FOOOOOOO–'

Its battle cry was cut short, however, when Reyna launched herself upward and impaled her dagger straight up its vulture diaper.

She had apparently been studying the weak spots of the ghouls. She had found one. The eurynomos toppled off the truck, which would have been wonderful, except that I, too, felt like I had been stabbed in the diaper.

I said, 'Glurg.'

My hand slipped off the wheel. Meg hit the accelerator in alarm. With Reyna still half out of the cab, her greyhounds howling furiously, our Chevy veered across the ramp and crashed straight through the guardrail. Lucky me. Once again, I went flying off an East Bay highway in a car that couldn't fly.

32

We have a special
Today on slightly used trucks
Thanks, Target shoppers

MY SON ASCLEPIUS once explained the purpose of physical shock to me.

He said it's a safety mechanism for coping with trauma. When the human brain experiences something too violent and frightening to process, it just stops recording. Minutes, hours, even days can be a complete blank in the victim's memory.

Perhaps this explained why I had no recollection of the Chevy crashing. After hurtling through the guardrail, the next thing I remembered was stumbling around the parking lot of a Target store, pushing a three-wheeled shopping trolley filled with Meg. I was muttering the lyrics to '(Sittin' on) The Dock of the Bay'; Meg, semiconscious, was listlessly waving one hand, trying to conduct.

My cart bumped into a steaming crumpled heap of metal – a red Chevy Silverado with its tyres popped, its windshield broken and its airbags deployed. Some inconsiderate driver had plummeted from the heavens and landed right on top of the trolley park, smashing a dozen shopping trolleys beneath the weight of the pickup.

Who would do such a thing?

Wait . . .

I heard growling. A few car-lengths away, two metal greyhounds stood protectively over their wounded master, keeping a small crowd of spectators at bay. A young woman in maroon and gold (Right, I remembered her! She liked to laugh at me!) was propped on her elbows, grimacing mightily, her left leg bent at an unnatural angle. Her face was the same colour as the tarmac.

'Reyna!' I wedged Meg's shopping trolley against the truck and ran to help the praetor. Aurum and Argentum let me through.

'Oh. Oh. Oh.' I couldn't seem to say anything else. I should've known what to do. I was a healer. But that break in the leg – yikes.

'I'm alive,' Reyna said through gritted teeth. 'Meg?'

'She's conducting,' I said.

One of the Target shoppers inched forward, braving the fury of the dogs. 'I called nine-one-one. Is there anything else I can do?'

'She'll be fine!' I yelped. 'Thank you! I – I'm a doctor?'

The mortal woman blinked. 'Are you asking me?'

'No. I'm a doctor!'

'Hey,' said a second shopper. 'Your other friend is rolling away.'

'ACK!' I ran after Meg, who was muttering '*Whee*' as she picked up steam in her red plastic trolley. I grabbed the handles and navigated her back to Reyna's side.

The praetor tried to move but choked on the pain. 'I might . . . black out.'

'No, no, no.' *Think, Apollo, think.* Should I wait for the mortal paramedics, who knew nothing of ambrosia and nectar? Should I check for more first-aid supplies in Meg's gardening belt?

A familiar voice from across the parking lot yelled, 'Thank you, everybody! We'll take it from here!'

Lavinia Asimov jogged towards us, a dozen naiads and fauns in her wake, many of whom I recognized from People's Park. Most were dressed in camouflage, covered with vines and branches like they had just arrived via beanstalk. Lavinia wore pink camo pants and a green tank top, her manubalista clanking against her shoulder. With her spiky pink hair and pink eyebrows, her jaw working furiously on a wad of bubblegum, she just radiated *authority figure.*

'This is now an active investigation scene!' she announced to the mortals. 'Thank you, Target shoppers. Please move along!'

Either the tone of her voice or the barking of the greyhounds finally convinced the onlookers to disperse. Nevertheless, sirens were blaring in the distance. Soon we'd be surrounded by paramedics, or the highway patrol, or both. Mortals weren't nearly as used to vehicles hurtling off highway overpasses as I was.

I stared at our pink-haired friend. 'Lavinia, what are you *doing* here?'

'Secret mission,' she announced.

'That's *cacaseca,*' Reyna grumbled. 'You *left* your post. You're in *so* much trouble.'

Lavinia's nature-spirit friends looked jumpy, like they were on the verge of scattering, but their pink-frosted leader calmed them with a glance. Reyna's greyhounds didn't snarl or attack, which I guessed meant they'd detected no lies from Lavinia.

'All due respect, Praetor,' she said, 'but it looks like you're in more trouble than I am at the moment. Harold, Felipe – stabilize her leg and let's get her out of this parking lot before more mortals arrive. Reginald, push Meg's trolley. Lotoya, retrieve whatever supplies they have in the truck, please. I'll help Apollo. We make for those woods. Now!'

Lavinia's definition of *woods* was generous. I would've called it a gully where shopping trolleys went to die. Still, her People's Park platoon worked with surprising efficiency. In a matter of minutes, they had us all safely hidden in the ditch among the broken trolleys and trash-festooned trees, just as emergency vehicles came wailing into the parking lot.

Harold and Felipe splinted Reyna's leg – which only caused her to scream and throw up a little. Two other fauns constructed a stretcher for her out of branches and old clothing while Aurum and Argentum tried to help by bringing them sticks . . . or perhaps they just wanted to play fetch. Reginald extricated Meg from her shopping trolley and revived her with hand-fed bits of ambrosia.

A couple of dryads checked me for injuries – meaning even *more* injuries than I'd had before – but there wasn't much they could do. They didn't like the look of my zombie-infected face, or the way the undead infection made me smell. Unfortunately, my condition was beyond any nature-spirit healing.

As they moved off, one muttered to her friend, 'Once it gets fully dark . . .'

'I know,' said her friend. 'With a blood moon tonight? Poor guy . . .'

I decided to ignore them. It seemed the best way to avoid bursting into tears.

Lotoya – who must have been a redwood dryad, judging from her burgundy complexion and impressive size – crouched next to me and deposited all the supplies she'd retrieved from the truck. I grabbed frantically – not for my bow and quiver, or even for my ukulele, but for my backpack. I almost fainted with relief when I found the Smucker's jar inside, still intact.

'Thank you,' I told her.

She nodded sombrely. 'A good jar is hard to find.'

Reyna struggled to sit up among the fauns fussing over her. 'We're wasting time. We have to get back to camp!'

Lavinia arched her pink eyebrows. 'You're not going anywhere with that leg, Praetor. Even if you could, you wouldn't be much help. We can heal you faster if you just relax –'

'Relax? The legion *needs* me! It needs you too, Lavinia! How could you desert?'

'Okay, first, I *didn't* desert. You don't know all the facts.'

'You left camp without leave. You –' Reyna leaned forward too fast and gasped in agony. The fauns took her shoulders. They helped her to sit back, easing her onto the new stretcher with its lovely padding of moss, trash and old tie-dyed T-shirts.

'You left your comrades,' Reyna croaked. 'Your friends.'

'I'm right here,' Lavinia said. 'I'm going to ask Felipe to lull you to sleep now so you can rest and heal.'

'No! You . . . you can't run away.'

Lavinia snorted. 'Who said anything about running away? Remember, Reyna, this was *your* backup plan. Plan L for *Lavinia*! When we all get back to camp, you're going to thank me. You'll tell everybody this was your idea.'

'What? I would never . . . I didn't give you any such . . . This is mutiny!'

I glanced at the greyhounds, waiting for them to rise to their master's defence and tear Lavinia apart. Strangely, they just kept circling Reyna, occasionally licking her face or sniffing her broken leg. They seemed concerned about her condition, but not at all about Lavinia's rebellious lies.

'Lavinia,' Reyna pleaded, 'I'll have to bring you up on desertion charges. Don't do this. Don't make me –'

'Now, Felipe,' Lavinia ordered.

The faun raised his panpipes and played a lullaby, soft and low, right next to Reyna's head.

'Can't!' Reyna struggled to keep her eyes open. 'Won't. Ahhggghh.'

She went limp and began to snore.

'That's better.' Lavinia turned to me. 'Don't worry, I'll leave her someplace safe with a couple of fauns, and of course Aurum and Argentum. She'll be taken care of while she heals. You and Meg, do what you need to do.'

Her confident stance and her take-charge tone made her almost unrecognizable as the gawky, nervous legionnaire we'd met at Lake Temescal. She reminded me more of Reyna now, and of Meg. Mostly, though, she seemed like a stronger version of herself – a Lavinia who had decided what she needed to do and would not rest until she did it.

'Where are you going?' I asked, still utterly confused. 'Why won't you come back to camp with us?'

Meg stumbled over, ambrosia crumbles stuck around her mouth. 'Don't pester her,' she told me. Then to Lavinia: 'Is Peaches . . . ?'

Lavinia shook her head. 'He and Don are with the advance group, making contact with the Nereids.'

Meg pouted. 'Yeah. Okay. The emperors' ground forces?'

Lavinia's expression turned sombre. 'They already passed by. We hid and watched. Yeah . . . It's not good. I'm sure they'll be in combat with the legion by the time you get there. You remember the path I told you about?'

'Yeah,' Meg agreed. 'Okay, good luck.'

'Whoa, whoa, whoa.' I tried to make a time-out sign, though my uncoordinated hands made it look more like a tent. 'What are you talking about? What path? Why would you come out here just to hide as the enemy army passes by? Why are Peaches and Don talking to . . . Wait. Nereids?'

Nereids are spirits of the sea. The nearest ones would be . . . Oh.

I couldn't see much from our trash-filled gully. I definitely couldn't see the San Francisco Bay, or the string of yachts taking up position to fire on the camp. But I knew we were close.

I looked at Lavinia with newfound respect. Or disrespect. Which is it when you realize that someone you knew was crazy is actually even crazier than you suspected?

'Lavinia, you are *not* planning –'

'Stop right there,' she warned, 'or I'll have Felipe put you down for a nap, too.'

'But Michael Kahale –'

'Yeah, we know. He failed. The emperors' troops were bragging about it as they marched past. It's one more thing they have to pay for.'

Brave words, but her eyes betrayed a flicker of worry, telling me she was more terrified than she let on. She was having trouble keeping up her own courage and preventing her makeshift troops from losing their nerve. She did *not* need me reminding her how insane her plan was.

'We've all got a lot to do,' she said. 'Good luck.' She ruffled Meg's hair, which did not need any more ruffling. 'Dryads and fauns, let's move!'

Harold and Felipe picked up Reyna's makeshift stretcher and jogged off down the gully, Aurum and Argentum bounding around them like, *Oh, boy, another hike!* Lavinia and the others followed. Soon they were lost in the undergrowth, vanishing into the terrain as only nature spirits and girls with bright pink hair can do.

Meg studied my face. 'You whole?'

I almost wanted to laugh. Where had she picked up *that* expression? I had zombie poison coursing through my body and up into my face. The dryads thought I would turn into a shambling undead minion of Tarquin as soon as it got fully dark. I was shaking from exhaustion and fear. We apparently had an enemy army between us and camp, and Lavinia was leading a suicide attack on the imperial fleet with inexperienced nature spirits, when an *actual* elite commando force had already failed.

When had I last felt 'whole'? I wanted to believe it was back when I was a god, but that wasn't true. I hadn't been completely myself for centuries. Maybe millennia.

At the moment, I felt more like a *hole* – a void in the cosmos through which Harpocrates, the Sibyl and a lot of people I cared about had vanished.

'I'll manage,' I said.

'Good, because look.' Meg pointed towards the Oakland Hills. I thought I was seeing fog, but fog didn't rise vertically from hillsides. Close to the perimeter of Camp Jupiter, fires were burning.

'We need wheels,' said Meg.

33

Welcome to the war
We hope you enjoy your death
Please come again soon!

OKAY, but why did it have to be *bicycles*?

I understood that cars were a deal-breaker. We had crashed enough vehicles for one week. I understood that jogging to camp was out of the question, given the fact that we could barely stand.

But why didn't demigods have some sort of ride-share app for summoning giant eagles? I decided I would create one as soon as I became a god again. Right after I figured out a way to let demigods use smartphones safely.

Across the street from Target stood a rack of canary-yellow Go-Glo bikes. Meg inserted a credit card into the kiosk (where she got the card, I had no idea), freed two bicycles from the rack and offered one to me.

Joy and happiness. Now we could pedal into battle like the neon-yellow warriors of old.

We took the side streets and pavements, using the columns of smoke in the hills to guide our way. With Highway 24 closed, traffic was snarled everywhere, angry drivers honking and yelling and threatening violence. I was tempted to tell them that if they really wanted a fight they could just follow us. We could use a few thousand angry commuters on our side.

As we passed the Rockridge BART station, we spotted the first enemy troops. Pandai patrolled the elevated platform, with furry black ears folded around themselves like firefighter turnout coats, and flat-head axes in their hands. Fire engines were parked along College Avenue, their lights strobing in the underpass. More faux-firefighter pandai guarded the station doors, turning away mortals. I hoped the real firefighters were okay, because firefighters are important and also because they are hot, and no, that wasn't relevant right then.

'This way!' Meg veered up the steepest hill she could find, just to annoy me. I was forced to stand as I pedalled, pushing with all my weight to make progress against the incline.

At the summit, more bad news.

In front of us, arrayed across the higher hills, troops marched doggedly towards Camp Jupiter. There were squads of blemmyae, pandai, and even some six-armed Earthborn who had served Gaia in the Recent Unpleasantness, all fighting their way through flaming trenches, staked barricades, and Roman skirmishers trying to put my archery lessons to good use. In the early evening gloom, I could only see bits and pieces of the battle. Judging from the mass of glittering armour and the forest of battle pennants, the main part of the emperors' army was concentrated on Highway 24, forcing its way towards the Caldecott Tunnel. Enemy catapults hurled projectiles towards the legion's positions, but most disappeared in bursts of purple light as soon as they got close. I assumed that was the work of Terminus, doing his part to defend the camp's borders.

Meanwhile, at the base of the tunnel, flashes of lightning pinpointed the location of the legion's standard. Tendrils of electricity zigzagged down the hillsides, arcing through enemy lines and frying them to dust. Camp Jupiter's ballistae launched giant flaming spears at the invaders, raking through their lines and starting more forest fires. The emperors' troops kept coming.

The ones making the best progress were huddled behind large armoured vehicles that crawled on eight legs and . . . Oh, gods. My guts felt like they'd got tangled in my bike chain. Those weren't vehicles.

'Myrmekes,' I said. 'Meg, those are myr–'

'I see them.' She didn't even slow down. 'It doesn't change anything. Come on!'

How could it *not* change anything? We'd faced a nest of those giant ants at Camp Half-Blood and barely survived. Meg had nearly been pulped into Gerber's larva purée.

Now we were confronting myrmekes trained for war, snapping trees in half with their pincers and spraying acid to melt through the camp's defensive pickets.

This was a brand-new flavour of horrible.

'We'll never get through their lines!' I protested.

'Lavinia's secret tunnel.'

'It collapsed!'

'Not *that* tunnel. A different secret tunnel.'

'How many does she *have*?'

'Dunno. A lot? C'mon.'

With that rousing oratory complete, Meg pedalled onward. I followed, having nothing better to do.

She led me up a dead-end street to a generator station at the base of an electrical tower. The area was ringed in barbed-wire fencing, but the gate stood wide open. If Meg had told me to climb the tower, I would have given up and made my peace with zombie eternity. Instead, she pointed to the side of the generator, where metal doors were set into the concrete like the entrance to a storm cellar or a bomb shelter.

'Hold my bike,' she said.

She jumped off and summoned one of her swords. With a single strike, she slashed through the padlocked chains, then pulled open the doors, revealing a dark shaft slanting downward at a precarious angle.

'Perfect,' she said. 'It's big enough to ride through.'

'*What?*'

She hopped back on her Go-Glo and plunged into the tunnel, the *click, click, click* of her bike chain echoing off the concrete walls.

'You have a very *broad* definition of perfect,' I muttered. Then I coasted in after her.

Much to my surprise, in the total darkness of the tunnel, the Go-Glo bike actually, well, *glowed*. I suppose I should have expected that. Ahead of me, I could see the faint, fuzzy apparition of Meg's neon war machine. When I looked down, the yellow aura of my own bike was almost blinding. It did little to help me navigate down the steep shaft, but it would make me a much easier target for enemies to pick out in the gloom. Hooray!

Against all odds, I did not wipe out and break my neck. The tunnel levelled, then began to climb again. I wondered who had excavated this passageway and why they hadn't installed a convenient lift system so I didn't have to expend so much energy pedalling.

Somewhere overhead, an explosion shook the tunnel, which was excellent motivation to keep moving. After a bit more sweating and gasping, I realized I could discern a dim square of light ahead of us – an exit covered in branches.

Meg burst straight through it. I wobbled after her, emerging in a landscape lit by fire and lightning and ringing with the sounds of chaos.

We had arrived in the middle of the war zone.

I will give you free advice.

If you plan to pop into a battle, the place you do *not* want to be is in the middle of it. I recommend the very back, where the general often has a comfortable tent with hors d'oeuvres and beverages.

But the middle? No. *Always* bad, especially if you arrive on canary-yellow glow-in-the-dark bikes.

As soon as Meg and I emerged, we were spotted by a dozen large humanoids covered in shaggy blond hair. They pointed at us and began to scream.

Khromandae. Wow. I hadn't seen any of their kind since Dionysus's drunken invasion of India back in the BCE. Their species has gorgeous grey eyes, but that's about the only flattering thing I can say about them. Their dirty, shaggy blond pelts make them look like Muppets who have been used as dust rags. Their doglike teeth clearly never get a proper flossing. They are strong, aggressive, and can only communicate in earsplitting shrieks. I once asked Ares and Aphrodite if the Khromandae were their secret love children from their longstanding affair, because they were such a perfect mix of the two Olympians. Ares and Aphrodite did not find that funny.

Meg, like any reasonable child when confronted with a dozen hairy giants, hopped off her bike, summoned her swords and charged. I yelped in alarm and drew my bow. I was low on arrows after playing catch with the ravens, but I managed to slay six of the Khromandae before Meg reached them. Despite how exhausted she must've been, she handily dispatched the remaining six with a blur of her golden blades.

I laughed – actually *laughed* – with satisfaction. It felt so good to be a decent archer again, and to watch Meg at her swordplay. What a team we made!

That's one of the dangers of being in a battle. (Along with getting killed.) When things are going well, you tend to get tunnel vision. You zero in on your little area and forget the big picture. As Meg gave the last Khromanda a haircut straight through the chest, I allowed myself to think that we were winning!

Then I scanned our surroundings, and I realized we were surrounded by a whole lot of *not winning*. Gargantuan ants trampled their way towards us, spewing acid to clear the hillside of skirmishers. Several steaming bodies in Roman armour sprawled in the undergrowth, and I did not want to think about who they might have been or how they had died.

Pandai in black Kevlar and helmets, almost invisible in the dusk, glided around on their huge parasail ears, dropping onto any unsuspecting demigod they could find. Higher up, giant eagles fought with giant ravens, their wingtips glinting in the blood-red moonlight. Just a hundred yards to my left, wolf-headed cynocephali howled as they bounded into battle, crashing into the shields of the nearest cohort (the Third?), which looked small and alone and critically undermanned in a sea of bad guys.

That was only on *our* hill. I could see fires burning across the whole western front along the valley's borders – maybe half a mile of patchwork battles. Ballistae launched glowing spears from the summits. Catapults hurled boulders that shattered on impact, spraying shards of Imperial gold into the enemy lines. Flaming logs – always a fun Roman party game – rolled down the hillsides, smashing through packs of Earthborn.

For all the legion's efforts, the enemy kept advancing. On the empty eastbound lanes of Highway 24, the emperors' main columns marched towards the Caldecott Tunnel, their gold-and-purple banners raised high. Roman colours. Roman emperors bent on destroying the last true Roman legion. This was how it ended, I thought bitterly. Not fighting threats from the outside, but fighting against the ugliest side of our own history.

'*TESTUDO!*' A centurion's shout brought my attention back to the Third Cohort. They were struggling to form a protective turtle formation with their shields as the cynocephali swarmed over them in a snarling wave of fur and claws.

'Meg!' I yelled, pointing to the imperilled cohort.

She ran towards them, me at her heels. As we closed in, I scooped up an abandoned quiver from the ground, trying not to think about why it had been dropped there, and sent a fresh volley of arrows into the pack. Six fell dead. Seven. Eight. But there were still too many. Meg screamed in fury and launched herself at the nearest wolf-headed men. She was quickly surrounded, but our advance had distracted the pack, giving the Third Cohort a few precious seconds to regroup.

'Offence ROMULUS!' shouted the centurion.

If you have ever seen a woodlouse uncurl, revealing its hundreds of legs, you can imagine what the Third Cohort looked like as it broke testudo and formed a bristling forest of spears, skewering the cynocephali.

I was so impressed I almost got my face chewed off by a stray charging wolf-man. Just before it reached me, Centurion Larry hurled his javelin. The monster fell at my feet, impaled in the middle of his incredibly un-manscaped back.

'You made it!' Larry grinned at us. 'Where's Reyna?'

'She's okay,' I said. 'Er, she's alive.'

'Cool! Frank wants to see you, ASAP!'

Meg stumbled to my side, breathing hard, her swords glistening with monster goo. 'Hey, Larry. How's it going?'

'Terrible!' Larry sounded delighted. 'Carl, Reza – escort these two to Praetor Zhang immediately.'

'YESSIR!' Our escorts hustled us off towards the Caldecott Tunnel, while behind us Larry called his troops back to action: 'Come on, legionnaires! We've drilled for this. We've got this!'

After a few more terrible minutes of dodging pandai, jumping fiery craters and skirting mobs of monsters, Carl and Reza brought us safely to Frank Zhang's command post at the mouth of the Caldecott Tunnel. Much to my disappointment, there were no hors d'oeuvres or beverages. There wasn't even a tent – just a bunch of stressed-out Romans in full battle gear, rushing around carrying orders and shoring up defences. Above us, on the concrete terrace that stretched over the tunnel's mouth, Jacob the standard-bearer stood with the legion's eagle and a couple of spotters, keeping watch on all the approaches. Whenever an enemy got too close, Jacob would zap them like the Oprah Winfrey version of Jupiter: *And YOU get a lightning bolt! And YOU get a lightning bolt!* Unfortunately, he'd been using the eagle so much that it was beginning to smoke. Even super-powerful magic items have their limits. The legion's standard was close to total overload.

When Frank Zhang saw us, a whole *g* of weight seemed to lift from his shoulders. 'Thank the gods! Apollo, your face looks terrible. Where's Reyna?'

'Long story.' I was about to launch into the short version of that long story when Hazel Levesque materialized on a horse right next to me, which was an excellent way of testing whether my heart still worked properly.

'What's going on?' Hazel asked. 'Apollo, your face –'

'I know.' I sighed.

Her immortal steed, the lightning-fast Arion, gave me the side-eye and nickered as if to say, *This fool ain't no Apollo*.

'Good to see you too, cuz,' I grumbled.

I told them all in brief what had happened, with Meg occasionally adding helpful comments like, 'He was stupid,' and, 'He was more stupid,' and, 'He did good; then he got stupid again.'

When Hazel heard about our encounter in the Target parking lot, she gritted her teeth. 'Lavinia. That girl, I swear. If anything happens to Reyna –'

'Let's focus on what we can control,' Frank said, though he looked shaken that Reyna wouldn't be coming back to help. 'Apollo, we'll buy you as much time as possible for your summoning. Terminus is doing what he can to slow the emperors down. Right now, I've got ballistae and catapults targeting the myrmekes. If we can't bring them down, we'll never stop the advance.'

Hazel grimaced. 'The First to Fourth Cohorts are spread pretty thin across these hills. Arion and I have been zipping back and forth between them as needed, but –' She stopped herself from stating the obvious: *We're losing ground.* 'Frank, if you can spare me for a minute, I'll get Apollo and Meg to Temple Hill. Ella and Tyson are waiting.'

'Go.'

'Wait,' I said – not that I wasn't super anxious to summon a god with a jam jar, but something Hazel said had made me uneasy. 'If the First to Fourth Cohorts are here, where's the Fifth?'

'Guarding New Rome,' said Hazel. 'Dakota's with them. At the moment, thank the gods, the city is secure. No sign of Tarquin.'

POP. Right next to me appeared a marble bust of Terminus, dressed in a First World War British Army cap and khaki greatcoat that covered him to the foot of his pedestal. With his loose sleeves, he might have been a double amputee from the trenches of the Somme. Unfortunately, I'd met more than a few of those in the Great War.

'The city is *not* secure!' he announced. 'Tarquin is attacking!'

'What?' Hazel looked personally offended. 'From where?'

'Underneath!'

'The sewers.' Hazel cursed. 'But how –?'

'Tarquin built the original *cloaca maxima* of Rome,' I reminded her. 'He knows sewers.'

'I remembered that! I sealed the exits myself!'

'Well, somehow he unsealed them!' Terminus said. 'The Fifth Cohort needs help. Immediately!'

Hazel wavered, clearly rattled by Tarquin outfoxing her.

'Go,' Frank told her. 'I'll send the Fourth Cohort to reinforce you.'

Hazel laughed nervously. 'And leave you here with only three? No.'

'It's fine,' Frank said. 'Terminus, can you open our defensive barriers here at the main gate?'

'Why would I do that?'

'We'll try the Wakanda thing.'

'The what?'

'You know,' Frank said. 'We'll funnel the enemy into one location.'

Terminus glowered. 'I do not recall any "Wakanda thing" in the Roman military manuals. But very well.'

Hazel frowned. 'Frank, you're not going to do anything stupid –'

'We'll concentrate our people here and hold the tunnel. I can do this.' He mustered another confident smile. 'Good luck, guys. See you on the other side!'

Or not, I thought.

Frank didn't wait for more protests. He marched off, shouting orders to form up the troops and send the Fourth Cohort into New Rome. I remembered the hazy images I'd seen from the holographic scroll – Frank ordering his workers around in the Caldecott Tunnel, digging and toting urns. I recalled Ella's cryptic words about bridges and fires . . . I didn't like where those thoughts led me.

'Saddle up, kids,' Hazel said, offering me a hand.

Arion whinnied indignantly.

'Yes, I know,' Hazel said. 'You don't like carrying three. We'll just drop these two off at Temple Hill and then head straight for the city. There'll be plenty of undead for you to trample, I promise.'

That seemed to mollify the horse.

I climbed on behind Hazel. Meg took the rumble seat on the horse's rear.

I barely had time to hug Hazel's waist before Arion zoomed off, leaving my stomach on the Oakland side of the hills.

34

O insert name here
Please hear us and fill in blank
What is this, Mad Libs?

TYSON AND ELLA were not good at waiting.

We found them at the steps of Jupiter's temple, Ella pacing and wringing her hands, Tyson bouncing up and down in excitement like a boxer ready for round one.

The heavy hessian bags hanging from a belt around Ella's waist swung and clunked together, reminding me of Hephaestus's office desk toy – the one with the ball bearings that bounced against each other. (I hated visiting Hephaestus's office. His desk toys were so mesmerizing I found myself staring at them for hours, sometimes decades. I missed the entire 1480s that way.)

Tyson's bare chest was now completely covered with tattooed lines of prophecy. When he saw us, he broke into a grin.

'Yay!' he exclaimed. 'Zoom Pony!'

I was not surprised Tyson had dubbed Arion 'Zoom Pony' or that he seemed happier to see the horse than me. I *was* surprised that Arion, despite some resentful snorting, allowed the Cyclops to pet his snout. Arion had never struck me as the cuddly type. Then again, Tyson and Arion were both related through Poseidon, which made them brothers of a sort, and . . . You know what? I'm going to stop thinking about this before my brain melts.

Ella scuttled over. 'Late. Very late. Come on, Apollo. You're late.'

I bit back the urge to tell her that we'd had a few things going on. I climbed off Arion's back and waited for Meg, but she stayed on with Hazel.

'You don't need me for the summoning thing,' Meg said. 'I'm gonna help Hazel and unleash the unicorns.'

'But –'

'Gods' speed,' Hazel told me.

Arion vanished, leaving a trail of smoke down the hillside and Tyson patting empty air.

'Aww.' The Cyclops pouted. 'Zoom Pony left.'

'Yes, he does that.' I tried to convince myself Meg would be fine. I'd see her soon. The last words I ever heard from her would not be *unleash the unicorns*. 'Now, if we're ready –?'

'Late. Later than ready,' Ella complained. 'Pick a temple. Yes. Need to pick.'

'I need to –'

'Single-god summoning!' Tyson did his best to roll up his trouser leg while hopping over to me on one foot. 'Here, I will show you again. It is on my thigh.'

'That's okay!' I told him. 'I remember. It's just . . .'

I scanned the hill. So many temples and shrines – even more now that the legion had completed its Jason-inspired building spree. So many statues of gods staring at me.

As a member of a pantheon, I had an aversion to picking only one god. That was like picking your favourite child or your favourite musician. If you were *capable* of picking only one, you were doing something wrong.

Also, picking one god meant all the other gods would be mad at me. It didn't matter if they wouldn't have wanted to help me or would've laughed in my face if I'd asked. They would still be offended that I hadn't put them at the top of my list. I knew how they thought. I used to be one of them.

Sure, there were some obvious *nos*. I would not be summoning Juno. I would not bother with Venus, especially since Friday night was her spa night with the Three Graces. Somnus was a nonstarter. He'd answer my call, promise to be right over, and then fall asleep again.

I gazed at the giant statue of Jupiter Optimus Maximus, his purple toga rippling like a matador's cape.

C'mon, he seemed to be telling me. *You know you want to.*

The most powerful of the Olympians. It was well within his power to smite the emperors' armies, heal my zombie wound and set everything right at Camp Jupiter (which, after all, was named in his honour). He might even notice all the heroic things I'd done, decide I'd suffered enough and free me from the punishment of my mortal form.

Then again . . . he might not. Could be that he was *expecting* me to call on him for help. Once I did, he might make the heavens rumble with his laughter and a deep, divine *Nope!*

To my surprise, I realized I did not want my godhood back *that* badly. I didn't even want to *live* that badly. If

Jupiter expected me to crawl to him for help, begging for mercy, he could stick his lightning bolt right up his cloaca maxima.

There had only ever been one choice. Deep down, I'd always known which god I had to call.

'Follow me,' I told Ella and Tyson.

I ran for the temple of Diana.

Now, I'll admit I've never been a huge fan of Artemis's Roman persona. As I've said before, I never felt like I personally changed that much during Roman times. I just stayed Apollo. Artemis, though . . .

You know how it is when your sister goes through her moody teenage years? She changes her name to Diana, cuts her hair, hangs out with a different, more hostile set of maiden hunters, starts associating with Hecate and the moon, and basically acts weird? When we first relocated to Rome, the two of us were worshipped together like in the old days – twin gods with our own temple – but soon Diana went off and did her own thing. We just didn't talk like we used to when we were young and Greek, you know?

I was apprehensive about summoning her Roman incarnation, but I needed help, and Artemis – sorry, *Diana* – was the most likely to respond, even if she would never let me hear the end of it afterwards. Besides, I missed her terribly. Yes, I said it. If I was going to die tonight, which seemed increasingly likely, first I wanted to see my sister one last time.

Her temple was an outdoor garden, as one might expect from a goddess of the wild. Inside a ring of mature oak trees gleamed a silver pool with a single perpetual geyser burbling in the centre. I imagined the place was meant to evoke Diana's old oak-grove sanctuary at Lake Nemi, one of the first places where the Romans had worshipped her. At the edge of the pool stood a fire pit stacked with wood, ready for lighting. I wondered if the legion kept every shrine and temple in such good maintenance, just in case someone got a craving for a last-minute middle-of-the-night burnt offering.

'Apollo should light the fire,' Ella said. 'I will mix ingredients.'

'I will dance!' Tyson announced.

I didn't know whether that was part of the ritual or if he just felt like it, but when a tattooed Cyclops decides to launch into an interpretive dance routine it's best not to ask questions.

Ella rummaged in her supply pouches, pulling out herbs, spices and vials of oil, which made me realize how long it had been since I'd eaten. Why wasn't my stomach growling? I glanced at the blood moon rising over the hilltops. I hoped my next meal would not be braaaaaains.

I looked around for a torch or a box of matches. Nothing. Then I thought: *Of course not.* I could have the wood pre-stacked for me, but Diana, always the wilderness expert, would expect me to create my own fire.

I unslung my bow and pulled out an arrow. I gathered the lightest, driest kindling into a small pile. It had been a long time since I'd made a fire the old mortal way – spinning an arrow in a bowstring to create friction – but I gave it a go. I fumbled half a dozen times, nearly poking my eye out. My archery student Jacob would've been proud.

I tried to ignore the sound of explosions in the distance. I spun the arrow until my gut wound felt like it was opening up. My hands became slick with popped blisters. The god of the sun struggling to make fire . . . The ironies would never cease.

Finally, I succeeded in creating the tiniest of flames. After some desperate cupping, puffing and praying, the fire was lit.

I stood, trembling from exhaustion. Tyson kept dancing to his own internal music, flinging out his arms and spinning like a three-hundred-pound, heavily tattooed Julie Andrews in the *Sound of Music* remake Quentin Tarantino always wanted to do. (I convinced him it was a bad idea. You can thank me later.)

Ella began sprinkling her proprietary blend of oils, spices and herbs into the pit. The smoke smelled like a Mediterranean summer feast. It filled me with a sense of peace – reminding me of happier times when we gods were adored by millions of worshippers. You never appreciate a simple pleasure like that until it is taken away.

The valley turned quiet, as if I'd stepped back into Harpocrates's sphere of silence. Perhaps it was just a lull in the fighting, but I felt as if all of Camp Jupiter were holding its breath, waiting for me to complete the ritual. With trembling hands, I pulled the Sibyl's glass jar from my backpack.

'What now?' I asked Ella.

'Tyson,' Ella said, waving him over, 'that was good dancing. Now show Apollo your armpit.'

Tyson lumbered over, grinning and sweaty. He lifted his

left arm much closer to my face than I would have liked. 'See?'

'Oh, gods.' I recoiled. 'Ella, why would you write the summoning ritual in his *armpit?*'

'That's where it goes,' she said.

'It *really* tickled!' Tyson laughed.

'I – I will begin.' I tried to focus on the words and not the hairy armpit that they encircled. I tried not to breathe any more than necessary. I will say this, however: Tyson had excellent personal hygiene. Whenever I was forced to inhale, I did not pass out from his body odour, despite his exuberant sweaty dancing. The only smell I detected was a hint of peanut butter. Why? I did not want to know.

'*O protector of Rome!*' I read aloud. '*O insert name here!*'

'Uh,' Ella said, 'that's where you –'

'I will start again. *O protector of Rome! O Diana, goddess of the hunt! Hear our plea and accept our offering!*'

I do not remember all the lines. If I did, I would not record them here for just anyone to use. Summoning Diana with burnt offerings is the very definition of *Do Not Try This at Home, Kids*. Several times, I choked up. I was tempted to add personal bits, to let Diana know it wasn't just *anyone* making a request. This was *me!* I was *special!* But I stuck to the armpit script. At the appropriate moment (insert sacrifice here), I dropped the Sibyl's jam jar into the fire. I was afraid it might just sit there heating up, but the glass shattered immediately, releasing a sigh of silver fumes. I hoped I hadn't squandered the soundless god's final breath.

I finished the incantation. Tyson mercifully lowered his

arm. Ella stared at the fire, then at the sky, her nose twitching anxiously. 'Apollo hesitated,' she said. 'He didn't read the third line right. He probably messed up. I hope he didn't mess it up.'

'Your confidence is heartwarming,' I said.

But I shared her concern. I saw no signs of divine help in the night sky. The red full moon continued to leer at me, bathing the landscape in bloody light. No hunting horns trumpeted in the distance – just a fresh round of explosions from the Oakland Hills, and cries of battle from New Rome.

'You messed up,' Ella decided.

'Give it time!' I said. 'Gods don't always show up immediately. Once it took me ten years to answer some prayers from the city of Pompeii, and by the time I got there . . . Maybe that's not a good example.'

Ella wrung her hands. 'Tyson and Ella will wait here in case the goddess shows up. Apollo should go fight stuff.'

'Aww.' Tyson pouted. 'But *I* wanna fight stuff!'

'Tyson will wait here with Ella,' Ella insisted. 'Apollo, go fight.'

I scanned the valley. Several rooftops in New Rome were now on fire. Meg would be fighting in the streets, doing gods-knew-what with her weaponized unicorns. Hazel would be desperately shoring up the defences as zombies and ghouls boiled up from the sewers, attacking civilians. They needed help, and it would take me less time to reach New Rome than to get to the Caldecott Tunnel.

But just thinking about joining the battle made my stomach flare with pain. I remembered how I'd collapsed in the tyrant's tomb. I would be of little use against Tarquin.

Being near him would just accelerate my promotion to Zombie of the Month.

I gazed at the Oakland Hills, their silhouettes lit by flickering explosions. The emperors must be battling Frank's defenders at the Caldecott Tunnel by now. Without Arion or a Go-Glo bike, I wasn't sure I could make it there in time to do any good, but it seemed like my least horrible option.

'Charge,' I said miserably.

I jogged off across the valley.

35

Such a deal for you
Two-for-one single combat
Kill us both for free!

THE MOST EMBARRASSING THING? As I wheezed and huffed up the hill, I found myself humming 'Ride of the Valkyries'. Curse you, Richard Wagner. Curse you, *Apocalypse Now*.

By the time I reached the summit, I was dizzy and drenched in sweat. I took in the scene below and decided my presence would mean nothing. I was too late.

The hills were a scarred wasteland of trenches, shattered armour and broken war machines. A hundred yards down Highway 24, the emperors' troops had formed in columns. Instead of thousands, there were now a few hundred: a combination of Germanus bodyguards, Khromandae, pandai and other humanoid tribes. One small mercy: no myrmekes remained. Frank's strategy of targeting the giant ants had apparently worked.

At the entrance to the Caldecott Tunnel, directly beneath me, waited the remnants of the Twelfth Legion. A dozen ragged demigods formed a shield wall across the inbound lanes. A young woman I didn't recognize held the legion standard, which could only mean that Jacob had either been killed or gravely wounded. The overheated gold eagle smoked so badly I couldn't make out its form. It wouldn't be zapping any more enemies today.

Hannibal the elephant stood with the troops in his Kevlar armour, his trunk and legs bleeding from dozens of cuts. In front of the line towered an eight-foot-tall Kodiak bear – Frank Zhang, I assumed. Three arrows bristled in his shoulder, but his claws were out and ready for more battle.

My heart twisted. Perhaps, as a large bear, Frank could survive with a few arrows stuck in him. But what would happen when he tried to turn human again?

As for the other survivors . . . I simply couldn't believe they were all that remained of three cohorts. Maybe the missing ones were wounded rather than dead. Perhaps I should've taken comfort in the possibility that, for every legionnaire who had fallen, hundreds of enemies had been destroyed. But they looked so tragic, so hopelessly outnumbered guarding the entrance to Camp Jupiter . . .

I lifted my gaze beyond the highway, out to the bay, and lost all hope. The emperors' fleet was still in position – a string of floating white palaces ready to rain destruction upon us, then host a massive victory celebration.

Even if we somehow managed to destroy all the enemies remaining on Highway 24, those yachts were beyond our reach. Whatever Lavinia had been planning, she had apparently failed. With a single order, the emperors could lay waste to the entire camp.

The clop of hooves and rattle of wheels drew my

attention back to the enemy lines. Their columns parted. The emperors themselves came out to parley, standing side-by-side in a golden chariot.

Commodus and Caligula looked like they'd had a competition to pick the gaudiest armour, and both of them had lost. They were clad head to toe in Imperial gold: greaves, kilts, breastplates, gloves, helmets, all with elaborate gorgon and Fury designs, encrusted with precious gems. Their faceplates were fashioned like grimacing demons. I could only tell the two emperors apart because Commodus was taller and broader in the shoulders.

Pulling the chariot were two white horses . . . No. Not horses. Their backs carried long, ugly scars on either side of their spines. Their withers were scored with lash marks. Their handlers/torturers walked beside them, gripping their reins and keeping cattle prods ready in case the beasts got any ideas.

Oh, gods . . .

I fell to my knees and retched. Of all the horrors I had seen, this struck me as the worst of all. Those once-beautiful steeds were pegasi. What kind of monster would cut off the wings of a pegasus?

The emperors obviously wanted to send a message: they intended to dominate the world at any cost. They would stop at nothing. They would mutilate and maim. They would waste and destroy. Nothing was sacred except their own power.

I rose unsteadily. My hopelessness turned into boiling anger.

I howled, 'NO!'

My cry echoed through the ravine. The emperors' retinue clattered to a stop. Hundreds of faces turned upward, trying to pinpoint the source of the noise. I clambered down the hill, lost my footing, somersaulted, banged into a tree, staggered to my feet and kept going.

No one tried to shoot me. No one yelled, *Hooray, we're saved!* Frank's defenders and the emperors' troops simply watched, dumbstruck, as I made my way downhill – a single beat-up teenager in tattered clothes and mud-caked shoes, with a ukulele and a bow on my back. It was, I suspected, the least impressive arrival of reinforcements in history.

At last I reached the legionnaires on the highway.

Caligula studied me from across fifty feet of tarmac. He burst out laughing.

Hesitantly, his troops followed his example – except for the Germani, who rarely laughed.

Commodus shifted in his golden armour. 'Excuse me, could someone caption this scene for me? What's going on?'

Only then did I realize Commodus's eyesight had not recovered as well as he'd hoped. Probably, I thought with bitter satisfaction, my blinding flash of divine radiance at the Waystation had left him able to see a little bit in full daylight, but not at all at night. A small blessing, if I could figure out how to use it.

'I wish I could describe it,' Caligula said dryly. 'The mighty god Apollo has come to the rescue, and he's never looked better.'

'That was sarcasm?' Commodus asked. 'Does he look horrible?'

'Yes,' Caligula said.

'HA!' Commodus forced a laugh. 'Ha! Apollo, you look horrible!'

My hands trembling, I nocked an arrow and fired it at Caligula's face. My aim was true, but Caligula swatted aside the projectile like it was a sleepy horsefly.

'Don't embarrass yourself, Lester,' he said. 'Let the leaders talk.'

He turned his grimacing face mask towards the Kodiak bear. 'Well, Frank Zhang? You have a chance to surrender with honour. Bow to your emperor!'

'Emperors,' Commodus corrected.

'Yes, of course,' Caligula said smoothly. 'Praetor Zhang, you are duty-bound to recognize Roman authority, and we are it! Together, we can rebuild this camp and raise your legion to glory! No more hiding. No more cowering behind Terminus's weak boundaries. It is time to be true Romans and conquer the world. Join us. Learn from Jason Grace's mistake.'

I howled again. This time, I launched an arrow at Commodus. Yes, it was petty. I thought I could hit a blind emperor more easily, but he, too, swatted the arrow away.

'Cheap shot, Apollo!' he yelled. 'There's nothing wrong with my hearing or my reflexes.'

The Kodiak bear bellowed. With one claw, he broke the arrow shafts in his shoulder. He shrank, changing into Frank Zhang. The arrow stubs pierced his breastplate at the shoulder. He'd lost his helmet. The side of his body was soaked in blood, but his expression was pure determination.

Next to him, Hannibal trumpeted and pawed the ground, ready to charge.

'No, buddy.' Frank glanced at his last dozen comrades, weary and wounded but still ready to follow him to the death. 'Enough blood has been shed.'

Caligula inclined his head in agreement. 'So, you yield, then?'

'Oh, no.' Frank straightened, though the effort made him wince. 'I have an alternative solution. *Spolia opima.*'

Nervous murmurs rippled through the emperors' columns. Some of the Germani raised their bushy eyebrows. A few of Frank's legionnaires looked like they wanted to say something – *Are you crazy?*, for instance – but they held their tongues.

Commodus laughed. He pulled off his helmet, revealing his shaggy curls and beard, his cruel, handsome face. His gaze was milky and unfocused, the skin around his eyes still pitted as if he'd been splashed with acid.

'Single combat?' He grinned. 'I *love* this idea!'

'I'll take you both,' Frank offered. 'You and Caligula against me. You win and make it through the tunnel, the camp is yours.'

Commodus rubbed his hands. 'Glorious!'

'Wait,' Caligula snapped. He removed his own helmet. He did not look delighted. His eyes glittered, his mind no doubt racing as he thought over all the angles. 'This is too good to be true. What are you playing at, Zhang?'

'Either I kill you, or I die,' Frank said. 'That's all. Get through me, and you can march right into camp. I'll order my remaining troops to stand down. You can have your triumphal parade through New Rome like you've always wanted.' Frank turned to one of his comrades. 'You hear that, Colum? Those are my orders. If I die, you will make sure they are honoured.'

Colum opened his mouth but apparently didn't trust himself to speak. He just nodded dourly.

Caligula frowned. 'Spolia opima. It's so primitive. It hasn't been done since –'

He stopped himself, perhaps remembering the kind of troops he had at his back: 'primitive' Germani, who viewed single combat as the most honourable way for a leader to win a battle. In earlier times, Romans had felt the same way. The first king, Romulus, had personally defeated an enemy king, Acron, stripping him of his armour and weapons. For centuries after, Roman generals tried to emulate Romulus, going out of their way to find enemy leaders on the battlefield for single combat, so they could claim spolia opima. It was the ultimate display of courage for any true Roman.

Frank's ploy was clever. The emperors couldn't refuse his challenge without losing face in front of their troops. On the other hand, Frank was badly wounded. He couldn't possibly win without help.

'Two against two!' I yelped, surprising even myself. 'I'll fight!'

That got another round of laughter from the emperors' troops. Commodus said, 'Even better!'

Frank looked horror-stricken, which wasn't the sort of thank-you I'd been hoping for.

'Apollo, no,' he said. 'I can handle this. Clear off!'

A few months ago, I would have been happy to let Frank take this hopeless fight on his own while I sat back, ate chilled grapes and checked my messages. Not now, not after Jason Grace. I glanced at the poor maimed pegasi chained to the emperors' chariot, and I decided I couldn't live in a world where cruelty like that went unchallenged.

'Sorry, Frank,' I said. 'You won't face this alone.' I looked at Caligula. 'Well, Baby Booties? Your colleague emperor has already agreed. Are you in, or do we terrify you too much?'

Caligula's nostrils flared. 'We have lived for thousands of years,' he said, as if explaining a simple fact to a slow student. 'We are gods.'

'And I'm the son of Mars,' Frank countered, 'praetor of the Twelfth Legion Fulminata. I'm not afraid to die. Are you?'

The emperors stayed silent for a count of five.

Finally, Caligula called over his shoulder, 'Gregorix!'

One of the Germani jogged forward. With his massive height and weight, his shaggy hair and beard and his thick hide armour, he looked like Frank in Kodiak bear form, only with an uglier face.

'Lord?' he grunted.

'The troops are to stay where they are,' Caligula ordered. 'No interference while Commodus and I kill Praetor Zhang and his pet god. Understood?'

Gregorix studied me. I could imagine him silently wrestling with his ideas of honour. Single combat was good. Single combat against a wounded warrior and a zombie-infected weakling, however, was not much of a victory. The smart thing would be to slaughter all of us and march on into the camp. But a challenge had been issued. Challenges had to be accepted. But his job was to protect the emperors, and if this was some sort of trap . . .

I bet Gregorix was wishing he'd pursued that business degree his mom always wanted him to get. Being a barbarian bodyguard was mentally exhausting.

'Very well, my lord,' he said.

Frank faced his remaining troops. 'Get out of here. Find Hazel. Defend the city from Tarquin.'

Hannibal trumpeted in protest.

'You too, buddy,' Frank said. 'No elephants are going to die today.'

Hannibal huffed. The demigods obviously didn't like it either, but they were Roman legionnaires, too well trained to disobey a direct order. They retreated into the tunnel with the elephant and the legion's standard, leaving only Frank Zhang and me on Team Camp Jupiter.

While the emperors climbed down from their chariot, Frank turned to me and wrapped me in a sweaty, bloody embrace. I'd always figured him for a hugger, so this didn't surprise me, until he whispered in my ear, 'You're interfering with my plan. When I say, "Time's up," I don't care where you are or how the fight is going, I want you to run away from me as fast as you can. That's an order.'

He clapped me on my back and let me go.

I wanted to protest, *You're not the boss of me!* I hadn't come here to run away on command. I could do that quite well on my own. I certainly wasn't going to allow another friend to sacrifice himself for my sake.

On the other hand, I didn't know Frank's plan. I'd have to wait and see what he had in mind. Then I could decide what to do. Besides, if we stood any chance of winning a death match against Commodus and Caligula, it wouldn't be on account of our superior strength and charming personalities. We needed some serious, industrial-strength cheating.

The emperors strode towards us across the scorched and buckled tarmac.

Up close, their armour was even more hideous. Caligula's breastplate looked like it had been coated with glue, then rolled through the display cases at Tiffany & Co.

'Well.' He gave us a smile as bright and cold as his jewel collection. 'Shall we?'

Commodus took off his gauntlets. His hands were huge and rough, calloused as if he'd been punching brick walls in his spare time. It was hard to believe I had ever held those hands with affection.

'Caligula, you take Zhang,' he said. 'I'll take Apollo. I don't need my eyesight to find him. I'll just follow my ears. He'll be the one whimpering.'

I hated that he knew me so well.

Frank drew his sword. Blood still oozed from his shoulder wounds. I wasn't sure how he planned to remain standing, much less do battle. His other hand brushed the cloth pouch that held his piece of firewood.

'So we're clear on the rules,' he said. 'There aren't any. We kill you, you die.'

Then he gestured at the emperors: *Come and get it.*

36

Not again. My heart.
How many syllables is
'Total hopelessness'?

EVEN IN MY WEAKENED CONDITION, you'd think I would be able to stay out of reach of a blind opponent.

You'd be wrong.

Commodus was only ten yards away when I shot my next arrow at him. Somehow he dodged it, rushed in, and yanked the bow out of my hands. He broke the weapon over his knee.

'RUDE!' I yelled.

In retrospect, that was not the way I should have spent that millisecond. Commodus punched me square in the chest. I staggered backwards and collapsed on my butt, my lungs on fire, my sternum throbbing. A hit like that should have killed me. I wondered if my godly strength had decided to make a cameo appearance. If so, I squandered the opportunity to strike back. I was too busy crawling away, crying in pain.

Commodus laughed, turning to his troops. 'You see? He's always the one whimpering!'

His followers cheered. Commodus wasted valuable time basking in their adulation. He couldn't help being a showman. He also must've known I wasn't going anywhere.

I glanced at Frank. He and Caligula circled each other, occasionally trading blows, testing each other's defences. With the arrowheads in his shoulder, Frank had no choice but to favour his left side. He moved stiffly, leaving a trail of bloody footprints on the tarmac that reminded me – quite inappropriately – of a ballroom-dancing diagram Fred Astaire had once given me.

Caligula prowled around him, supremely confident. He wore the same self-satisfied smile he'd had when he impaled Jason Grace in the back. For weeks I'd had nightmares about that smile.

I shook myself out of my stupor. I was supposed to be doing something. Not dying. Yes. That was at the top of my *to-do* list.

I managed to get up. I fumbled for my sword, then remembered I didn't have one. My only weapon now was my ukulele. Playing a song for an enemy who was hunting me by sound did not seem like the wisest move, but I grabbed the uke by the fret board.

Commodus must have heard the strings twang. He turned and drew his sword.

For a big man in blinged-out armour, he moved much too fast. Before I could even decide which Dean Martin number to play for him, he jabbed at me, nearly opening up my belly. The point of his blade sparked against the bronze body of the ukulele.

With both hands, he raised his sword overhead to cleave me in two.

I lunged forward and poked him in the gut with my instrument. 'Ha-ha!'

There were two problems with this: 1) his gut was covered in armour, and 2) the ukulele had a rounded bottom. I made a mental note that if I survived this battle I would design a version with spikes at the base, and perhaps a flamethrower – the Gene Simmons ukulele.

Commodus's counterstrike would've killed me if he hadn't been laughing so hard. I leaped aside as his sword hurtled down, sinking into the spot where I'd been standing. One good thing about battling on a highway – all those explosions and lightning strikes had made the tarmac soft. While Commodus tried to tug his sword free, I charged and slammed into him.

To my surprise, I actually managed to shove him off-balance. He stumbled and landed on his armour-plated rear, leaving his sword quivering in the ground.

Nobody in the emperors' army cheered for me. Tough crowd.

I took a step back, trying to catch my breath. Someone pressed against my back. I yelped, terrified that Caligula was about to spear me, but it was only Frank. Caligula stood about twenty feet away from him, cursing as he wiped bits of gravel from his eyes.

'Remember what I said,' Frank told me.

'Why are you doing this?' I wheezed.

'It's the only way. If we're lucky, we're buying time.'

'Buying time?'

'For godly help to arrive. That's still happening, right?'

I gulped. 'Maybe?'

'Apollo, please tell me you did the summoning ritual.'

'I did!'

'Then we're buying time,' Frank insisted.

'And if help doesn't arrive?'

'Then you'll have to trust me. Do what I told you. On my cue, get out of the tunnel.'

I wasn't sure what he meant. We weren't *in* the tunnel, but our chat time had ended. Commodus and Caligula closed in on us simultaneously.

'Gravel in the eyes, Zhang?' Caligula snarled. 'Really?'

Their blades crossed as Caligula pushed Frank towards the mouth of the Caldecott Tunnel . . . or was Frank letting himself be pushed? The clang of metal against metal echoed through the empty passageway.

Commodus tugged his own sword free of the tarmac. 'All right, Apollo. This has been fun. But you need to die now.'

He howled and charged, his voice booming back at him from the depths of the tunnel.

Echoes, I thought.

I ran for the Caldecott.

Echoes can be confusing for people who depend on their hearing. Inside the shaft, I might have more luck avoiding Commodus. Yes . . . that was my strategy. I wasn't simply panicking and running for my life. Entering the tunnel was a perfectly level-headed, well-reasoned plan that just happened to involve me screaming and fleeing.

I turned before Commodus overtook me. I swung my ukulele, intending to imprint its soundboard on his face, but Commodus anticipated my move. He yanked the instrument out of my hands.

I stumbled away from him, and Commodus committed

the most heinous of crimes: with one huge fist, he crumpled my ukulele like an aluminium can and tossed it aside.

'Heresy!' I roared.

A reckless, terrible anger possessed me. I challenge you to feel differently when you've just watched someone destroy your ukulele. It would render any person insensible with rage.

My first punch left a fist-size crater in the emperor's gold breastplate. *Oh*, I thought in some distant corner of my mind. *Hello, godly strength!*

Off-balance, Commodus slashed wildly. I blocked his arm and punched him in the nose, causing a brittle *squish* that I found delightfully disgusting.

He yowled, blood streaming through his moustache. 'U duhh stike bee? I kilb u!'

'You won't kilb me!' I shouted back. 'I have my strength back!'

'HA!' Commodus cried. 'I nebbeh lost mine! An I'm stih bigguh!'

I hate it when megalomaniac villains make valid points.

He barrelled towards me. I ducked underneath his arm and kicked him in the back, propelling him into a guardrail on the side of the tunnel. His forehead hit the metal with a dainty sound like a triangle: *DING!*

That should have made me feel quite satisfied, except my ruined-ukulele-inspired rage was ebbing, and with it my burst of divine strength. I could feel the zombie poison creeping through my capillaries, wriggling and burning its way into every part of my body. My gut wound seemed to be unravelling, about to spill my stuffing everywhere like a raggedy Olympian Pooh Bear.

Also, I was suddenly aware of the many large, unmarked crates stacked along one side of the tunnel, taking up the entire length of the raised pedestrian walkway. Along the other side of the tunnel, the shoulder of the road was torn up and lined with orange traffic barrels . . . Not unusual in themselves, but it struck me that they were just about the right size to contain the urns I'd seen Frank's workers carrying during our holographic scroll call.

In addition, every five feet or so, a thin groove had been cut across the width of the tarmac. Again, not unusual in itself – the highway department could've just been doing some repaving work. But each groove glistened with some kind of liquid . . . Oil?

Taken together, these things made me deeply uncomfortable, and Frank kept retreating further into the tunnel, luring Caligula to follow.

Apparently, Caligula's lieutenant, Gregorix, was also getting worried. The Germanus shouted from the front lines, 'My emperor! You're getting too far –'

'Shut up, GREG!' Caligula yelled. 'If you want to keep your tongue, don't tell me how to fight!'

Commodus was still struggling to get up.

Caligula stabbed at Frank's chest, but the praetor wasn't there. Instead, a small bird – a common swift, judging from its boomerang-shaped tail – shot straight towards the emperor's face.

Frank knew his birds. Swifts aren't large or impressive.

They aren't obvious threats like falcons or eagles, but they are incredibly fast and manoeuvrable.

He drove his beak into Caligula's left eye and zoomed away, leaving the emperor shrieking and swatting at the air.

Frank materialized in human form right next to me. His eyes looked sunken and glazed. His bad arm hung limp at his side.

'If you really want to help,' he said in a low voice, 'hobble Commodus. I don't think I can hold them both.'

'What –?'

He transformed back into a swift and was gone – darting at Caligula, who cursed and slashed at the tiny bird.

Commodus charged me once more. This time he was smart enough not to announce himself by howling. By the time I noticed him bearing down on me – blood bubbling from his nostrils, a deep guardrail-shaped groove in his forehead – it was too late.

He slammed his fist into my gut, the *exact* spot I didn't want to be hit. I collapsed in a moaning, boneless heap.

Outside, the enemy troops erupted in a fresh round of cheering. Commodus again turned to accept their adulation. I'm ashamed to admit that instead of feeling relieved to have a few extra seconds of life I was annoyed that he wasn't executing me faster.

Every cell in my miserable mortal body screamed, *Just finish it!* Getting killed could *not* hurt any worse than the way I already felt. If I died, maybe I'd at least come back as a zombie and get to bite off Commodus's nose.

I was now certain Diana wasn't coming to the rescue. Maybe I had messed up the ritual, as Ella feared. Maybe my sister hadn't received the call. Or maybe Jupiter had forbidden her from helping on pain of sharing my mortal punishment.

Whatever the case, Frank, too, must have known our situation was hopeless. We were well past the 'buying time' phase. We were now into the 'dying as a futile gesture sure is painful' phase.

My line of vision was reduced to a blurry red cone, but I focused on Commodus's calves as he paced in front of me, thanking his adoring fans.

Strapped to the inside of his calf was a sheathed dagger.

He had always carried one of those back in the old days. When you're an emperor, the paranoia never stops. You could be assassinated by your housekeeper, your waiter, your launderer, your best friend. And then, despite all your precautions, your godly ex-lover disguised as your wrestling trainer ends up drowning you in your bathtub. Surprise!

Hobble Commodus, Frank had told me.

I had no energy left, but I owed Frank a last request.

My body screamed in protest as I stretched out my hand and grabbed the dagger. It slipped easily from its sheath – kept well oiled for a quick draw. Commodus didn't even notice. I stabbed him in the back of the left knee, then the right before he had even registered the pain. He screamed and toppled forward, spewing Latin obscenities I hadn't heard since the reign of Vespasian.

Hobbling accomplished. I dropped the knife, all my willpower gone. I waited to see what would kill me. The emperors? The zombie poison? The suspense?

I craned my neck to see how my friend the common

swift was doing. Not well, it turned out. Caligula scored a lucky hit with the flat of his blade, smacking Frank into the wall. The little bird tumbled limply, and Frank shifted back into human form just in time for his face to hit the ground.

Caligula grinned at me, his wounded eye closed tight, his voice filled with hideous glee. 'Are you watching, Apollo? You remember what happens next?'

He raised his sword over Frank's back.

'NO!' I screamed.

I could not witness another friend's death. Somehow, I got to my feet, but I was much too slow. Caligula brought down his blade . . . which bent in half like a pipe cleaner against Frank's cloak. Thank the gods of military fashion statements! Frank's praetor's cape *could* turn back weapons, even as its ability to transform into a sweater wrap remained unknown.

Caligula snarled in frustration. He drew his dagger, but Frank had recovered enough strength to stand. He slammed Caligula against the wall and wrapped his good hand around the emperor's throat.

'Time's up!' he roared.

Time's up. Wait . . . that was my cue. I was supposed to run. But I couldn't. I stared, frozen in horror, as Caligula buried his dagger in Frank's belly.

'Yes, it is,' Caligula croaked. 'For you.'

Frank squeezed harder, crushing the emperor's throat, making Caligula's face turn a bloated purple. Using his wounded arm, which must have been excruciating, Frank pulled the piece of firewood from his pouch.

'Frank!' I sobbed.

He glanced over, silently ordering me: GO.

I could not bear it. Not again. Not like Jason. I was dimly aware of Commodus struggling to crawl towards me, to grab my ankles.

Frank raised his piece of firewood to Caligula's face. The emperor fought and thrashed, but Frank was stronger – drawing, I suspected, on everything that remained of his mortal life.

'If I'm going to burn,' he said, 'I might as well burn bright. This is for Jason.'

The firewood spontaneously combusted, as if it had been waiting years for this chance. Caligula's eyes widened with panic, perhaps just now beginning to understand. Flames roared around Frank's body, sparking the oil in one of the grooves on the tarmac – a liquid fuse, racing in both directions to the crates and traffic barrels that packed the tunnel. The emperors weren't the only ones who kept a supply of Greek fire.

I am not proud of what happened next. As Frank became a column of flame, and the emperor Caligula disintegrated into white-hot embers, I followed Frank's last order. I leaped over Commodus and ran for open air. At my back, the Caldecott Tunnel erupted like a volcano.

37

I didn't do it.
Explosion? I don't know her.
Probably Greg's fault.

A THIRD-DEGREE BURN was the least painful thing
I carried from that tunnel.

I staggered into the open, my back sizzling, my hands
steaming, every muscle in my body feeling like it had been
scored with razorblades. Before me spread the remaining
forces of the emperors: hundreds of battle-ready warriors. In
the distance, stretched across the bay, fifty yachts waited,
primed to fire their doomsday artillery.

None of that hurt as much as knowing I had left Frank
Zhang in the flames.

Caligula was gone. I could feel it – like the earth heaved
a sigh of relief as his consciousness disintegrated in a blast
of superheated plasma. But, oh, the cost. Frank. Beautiful,
awkward, lumbering, brave, strong, sweet, noble Frank.

I would have sobbed, but my tear ducts were as dry as
Mojave gulches.

The enemy forces looked as stunned as I was. Even the
Germani were slack-jawed. It takes a lot to shock an
imperial bodyguard. Watching your bosses get blown up in

a massive fiery belch from the side of a mountain – that will do it.

Behind me, a barely human voice gurgled, 'URGSSHHH.'

I turned.

I was too dead inside to feel fear or disgust. Of *course* Commodus was still alive. He crawled out of the smoke-filled cavern on his elbows, his armour half-melted, his skin coated with ash. His once-beautiful face looked like a burnt loaf of tomato bread.

I hadn't hobbled him well enough. Somehow, I'd missed his ligaments. I'd messed up everything, even Frank's last request.

None of the troops rushed to the emperor's aid. They remained frozen in disbelief. Perhaps they didn't recognize this wrecked creature as Commodus. Perhaps they thought he was doing another one of his spectacles and they were waiting for the right moment to applaud.

Incredibly, Commodus struggled to his feet. He wobbled like a 1975 Elvis.

'SHIPS!' he croaked. He slurred the word so badly, for a moment I thought he'd yelled something else. I suppose his troops thought the same thing, since they did nothing.

'FIRE!' Commodus groaned, which again could have simply meant *HEY, LOOK, I'M ON FIRE*.

I only understood his order a heartbeat later, when Gregorix yelled, 'SIGNAL THE YACHTS!'

I choked on my tongue.

Commodus gave me a ghastly smile. His eyes glittered with hatred.

I don't know where I found the strength, but I charged and tackled him. We hit the tarmac, my legs straddling his chest, my hands wrapped around his throat as they had been thousands of years before, the first time I killed him. This time, I felt no bittersweet regret, no lingering sense of love. Commodus fought, but his fists were like paper. I let loose a guttural roar – a song with only one note: pure rage, and only one volume: maximum.

Under the onslaught of sound, Commodus crumbled to ash.

My voice faltered. I stared at my empty palms. I stood and backed away, horrified. The charred outline of the emperor's body remained on the tarmac. I could still feel the pulse of his carotid arteries under my fingers. What had I done? In my thousands of years of life, I'd never destroyed someone with my voice. When I sang, people would often say I 'killed it', but they never meant that *literally*.

The emperors' troops stared at me in astonishment. Given another moment, they surely would have attacked, but their attention was diverted by a flare gun going off nearby. A tennis-ball-size globe of orange fire arced into the sky, trailing Tango-coloured smoke.

The troops turned towards the bay, waiting for the fireworks show that would destroy Camp Jupiter. I'll admit – as tired and helpless and emotionally shattered as I was, all I could do was watch, too.

On fifty aft decks, green dots flickered as the Greek fire

charges were uncovered in their mortars. I imagined pandos technicians scrambling about, inputting their final coordinates.

PLEASE, ARTEMIS, I prayed. NOW WOULD BE A GREAT TIME TO SHOW UP.

The weapons fired. Fifty green fireballs rose into the sky, like emeralds on a floating necklace, illuminating the entire bay. They rose straight upward, struggling to gain altitude.

My fear turned to confusion. I knew a few things about flying. You couldn't take off at a ninety-degree angle. If I tried that in the sun chariot . . . well, first of all, I would've fallen off and looked really stupid. But also, the horses could never have made such a steep climb. They would have toppled into each other and crashed back into the gates of the Sun Palace. You'd have an eastern sunrise, followed immediately by an eastern sunset and lots of angry whinnying.

Why would the mortars be aimed like that?

The green fireballs climbed another fifty feet. A hundred feet. Slowed. On Highway 24, the entire enemy army mimicked their movements, standing up straighter and straighter as the projectiles rose, until all the Germani, Khromandae and other assorted baddies were on their tiptoes, poised as if levitating. The fireballs stopped and hovered in mid-air.

Then the emeralds fell straight down, right onto the yachts from which they had come.

The display of mayhem was worthy of the emperors themselves. Fifty yachts exploded in green mushroom clouds, sending confetti of shattered wood, metal and tiny little flaming monster bodies into the air. Caligula's multi-billion-dollar fleet was reduced to a string of burning oil slicks on the surface of the bay.

I may have laughed. I know that was quite insensitive, considering the environmental impact of the disaster. Also terribly inappropriate, given how heartbroken I felt about Frank. But I couldn't help it.

The enemy troops turned as one to stare at me.

Oh, right, I reminded myself. *I am still facing hundreds of hostiles.*

But they didn't look very hostile. Their expressions were stunned and unsure.

I had destroyed Commodus with a shout. I had helped burn Caligula to cinders. Despite my humble appearance, the troops had probably heard rumours that I was once a god. Was it possible, they'd be wondering, that I had somehow caused the fleet's destruction?

In point of fact, I had no idea what had gone wrong with the fleet's weapons. I doubted it was Artemis. It just didn't *feel* like something she would do. As for Lavinia . . . I didn't see how she could've pulled off a trick like that with just some fauns, a few dryads and some chewing gum.

I knew it wasn't me.

But the army didn't know that.

I cobbled together the last shreds of my courage. I channelled my old sense of arrogance, from back in the days when I loved to take credit for things I didn't do (as long as they were good and impressive). I gave Gregorix and his army a cruel, emperor-like smile.

'BOO!' I shouted.

The troops broke and ran. They scattered down the highway in a panic, some leaping straight over the guardrails and into the void just to get away from me faster. Only the poor tortured pegasi stayed put, since they had no choice. They were still fastened in their harnesses, the chariot wheels staked to the tarmac to keep the animals from bolting. In any case, I doubted they would have wanted to follow their tormentors.

I fell to my knees. My gut wound throbbed. My charred back had gone numb. My heart seemed to be pumping cold, liquid lead. I would be dead soon. Or undead. It hardly mattered. The two emperors were gone. Their fleet was destroyed. Frank was no more.

On the bay, the burning oil pools belched columns of smoke that turned orange in the light of the blood moon. It was without a doubt the loveliest trash fire I'd ever beheld.

After a moment of shocked silence, the Bay Area emergency services seemed to register the new problem. The East Bay had already been deemed a disaster area. With the tunnel closure and the mysterious string of wildfires and explosions in the hills, sirens had been wailing across the flatlands. Emergency lights flickered everywhere on the jammed streets.

Now Coast Guard vessels joined the party, cutting across the water to reach the burning oil spills. Police and news helicopters veered towards the scene from a dozen different directions as if being pulled by a magnet. The Mist would be working overtime tonight.

I was tempted to just lie down on the road and go to sleep. I knew if I did that, I would die, but at least there would be no more pain. Oh, Frank.

And why hadn't Artemis come to help me? I wasn't mad at her. I understood all too well how gods could be, all the different reasons they might not show up when you called. Still, it hurt, being ignored by my own sister.

An indignant huff jarred me from my thoughts. The pegasi were glaring at me. The one on the left had a blind eye, poor thing, but he shook his bridle and made a raspberry kind of sound as if to say, *GET OVER YOURSELF, DUDE*.

The pegasus was correct. Other people were hurting. Some of them needed my help. Tarquin was still alive – I could feel it in my zombie-infected blood. Hazel and Meg might well be fighting undead in the streets of New Rome.

I wouldn't be much good to them, but I had to try. Either I could die with my friends, or they could cut off my head after I turned into a brain-eater, which was what friends were for.

I rose and staggered towards the pegasi.

'I'm so sorry this happened to you,' I told them. 'You are beautiful animals and you deserve better.'

One Eye grunted as if to say, *YA THINK?*

'I'll free you now, if you'll let me.'

I fumbled with their tack and harness. I found an abandoned dagger on the tarmac and cut away the barbed wire and spiked cuffs that had been digging into the animals' flesh. I carefully avoided their hooves in case they decided I was worth a kick in the head.

Then I started humming Dean Martin's 'Ain't That a Kick in the Head', because that's just the kind of awful week I was having.

'There,' I said when the pegasi were free. 'I have no right to ask anything of you, but if you could see your way to giving me a ride over the hills, my friends are in danger.'

The pegasus on the right, who still had both eyes but whose ears had been cruelly snipped, whinnied an emphatic *NO!* He trotted towards the College Avenue exit, then stopped halfway and looked back at his friend.

One Eye grunted and tossed his mane. I imagined his silent exchange with Short Ears went something like this.

One Eye: *I'm gonna give this pathetic loser a ride. You go ahead. I'll catch up.*

Short Ears: *You're crazy, man. If he gives you any trouble, kick him in the head.*

One Eye: *You know I will.*

Short Ears trotted off into the night. I couldn't blame him for leaving. I hoped he would find a safe place to rest and heal.

One Eye nickered at me. *Well?*

I took one last look at the Caldecott Tunnel, the interior still a maelstrom of green flames. Even without fuel, Greek fire would just keep burning and burning, and that conflagration had been started with Frank's life force – a final, thermal burst of heroism that had vaporized Caligula. I didn't pretend to understand what Frank had done, or why he had made that choice, but I understood he'd felt it was the only way. He'd burned brightly, all right.

The last word Caligula had heard as he got blasted into tiny particles of soot was *Jason*.

I stepped closer to the tunnel. I could barely get within fifty feet without the breath being sucked out of my lungs.

'FRANK!' I yelled. 'FRANK?'

It was hopeless, I knew. There was no way Frank could have survived that. Caligula's immortal body had disintegrated instantly. Frank couldn't have lasted more than a few seconds longer, held together by sheer courage and force of will, just to be sure he took Caligula down with him.

I wished I could cry. I vaguely recalled having tear ducts, once upon a time.

Now all I had was despair, and the knowledge that as long as I wasn't dead I had to try to help my remaining friends, no matter how much I hurt.

'I'm so sorry,' I said to the flames.

The flames didn't answer. They didn't care who or what they destroyed.

I fixed my gaze on the crest of the hill. Hazel, Meg and the last of the Twelfth Legion were on the other side, fighting off the undead. That's where I needed to be.

'Okay,' I told One Eye. 'I'm ready.'

38

Got two words for you:
Swiss Army unicorns, man!
Okay, that's four words.

IF YOU EVER GET THE CHANCE to see weaponized
unicorns in action, *don't*. It's something you can't unsee.

As we got closer to the city, I detected signs of
continuing battle: columns of smoke, flames licking the
tops of buildings, screams, shouts, explosions. You know,
the usual.

One Eye dropped me at the Pomerian Line. He snorted
in a tone that said, *Yeah, good luck with that*, then galloped
away. Pegasi are intelligent creatures.

I glanced at Temple Hill, hoping to see storm clouds
gathering, or a divine aura of silver light bathing the hillside,
or an army of my sister's Hunters charging to the rescue. I
saw nothing. I wondered if Ella and Tyson were still pacing
around the shrine of Diana, checking the fire pit every thirty
seconds to see if the Sibyl's jam-jar shards were cooked yet.

Once again, I had to be a cavalry of one. Sorry, New
Rome. I jogged towards the Forum, which was where I
caught my first glimpse of the unicorns. Definitely *not* the
usual.

Meg herself led the charge. She was not riding a unicorn.

No one who values their life (or their crotch) would ever dare ride one. But she did run alongside them, exhorting them to greatness as they galloped into battle. The beasts were outfitted in Kevlar with their names printed in white block letters along their ribs: MUFFIN, BUSTER, WHANGDOODLE, SHIRLEY and HORATIO, the Five Unicorns of the Apocalypse. Their leather helmets reminded me of those worn by football players in the 1920s. The steeds' horns were fitted with specially designed . . . What would you call them? Attachments? Imagine, if you will, massive conical Swiss Army knives, with various slots from which sprang a convenient array of destructive implements.

Meg and her friends slammed into a horde of vrykolakai – former legionnaires killed in Tarquin's previous assault, judging from their grungy bits of armour. A member of Camp Jupiter might have had trouble attacking old comrades, but Meg had no such qualms. Her swords whirled, slicing and dicing and making mounds and mounds of julienned zombies.

With a flick of their snouts, her equine friends activated their favourite accessories: a sword blade, a giant razor, a corkscrew, a fork and a nail file. (Buster chose the nail file, which did not surprise me.) They ploughed through the undead, forking them, corkscrewing them, stabbing them and nail-filing them into oblivion.

You may wonder why I did not find it horrifying that Meg would use unicorns for war while I *had* found it horrifying that the emperors had used pegasi for their chariot. Setting aside the obvious difference – that the unicorns weren't tortured or maimed – it was clear the one-horned steeds were enjoying themselves immensely. After centuries of being treated as delightful, fanciful creatures who frolicked in meadows and danced through rainbows, these unicorns finally felt *seen* and appreciated. Meg had recognized their natural talent for kicking undead posterior.

'Hey!' Meg grinned when she saw me, like I'd just come back from the bathroom instead of the brink of doomsday. 'It's working great. Unicorns are immune to undead scratches and bites!'

Shirley huffed, clearly pleased with herself. She showed me her corkscrew attachment as if to say, *Yeah, that's right. I ain't your Rainbow Pony.*

'The emperors?' Meg asked me.

'Dead. But . . .' My voice cracked.

Meg studied my face. She knew me well enough. She had been at my side in moments of tragedy.

Her expression darkened. 'Okay. Grieve later. Right now, we should find Hazel. She's –' Meg waved vaguely towards the middle of the town – 'somewhere. So is Tarquin.'

Just hearing his name made my gut contort. Why, oh, why couldn't I be a unicorn?

We ran with our Swiss Army herd up the narrow, winding streets. The battle was mostly pockets of house-to-house combat. Families had barricaded their homes. Shops were boarded up. Archers lurked in upper-storey windows on the lookout for zombies. Roving bands of eurynomoi attacked any living thing they could find.

As horrible as the scene was, something about it seemed oddly *subdued*. Yes, Tarquin had flooded the city with undead. Every sewer grate and manhole cover was open. But he wasn't attacking in force, sweeping systematically through the city to take control. Instead, small groups of undead were popping up everywhere at once, forcing the Romans to scramble and defend the citizenry. It felt less like an invasion and more like a diversion, as if Tarquin himself were after something specific and didn't want to be bothered.

Something specific . . . like a set of Sibylline Books he'd paid good money for back in 530 BCE.

My heart pumped more cold lead. 'The bookshop. Meg, the bookshop!'

She frowned, perhaps wondering why I wanted to shop for books at a time like this. Then realization dawned in her eyes. 'Oh.'

She picked up speed, running so fast the unicorns had to break into a trot. How I managed to keep up, I don't know. I suppose, at that point, my body was so far beyond help it just said, *Run to death? Yeah, okay. Whatever.*

The fighting intensified as we climbed the hill. We passed part of the Fourth Cohort battling a dozen slavering ghouls outside a pavement café. From the windows above, small children and their parents were tossing things at the eurynomoi – rocks, pots, pans, bottles – while the legionnaires jabbed their spears over the tops of their locked shields.

A few blocks further on, we found Terminus, his World War I greatcoat peppered with shrapnel holes, his nose broken clean off his marble face. Crouching behind his pedestal was a little girl – his helper, Julia, I presumed – clutching a steak knife.

Terminus turned on us with such fury I feared he would zap us into stacks of customs declaration forms.

'Oh, it's you,' he grumbled. 'My borders have failed. I hope you've brought help.'

I looked at the terrified girl behind him, feral and fierce and ready to spring. I wondered who was protecting whom. 'Ah . . . maybe?'

The old god's face hardened a bit more, which shouldn't have been possible for stone. 'I see. Well. I've concentrated the last bits of my power here, around Julia. They may destroy New Rome, but they will *not* harm this girl!'

'Or this statue!' said Julia.

My heart turned to Smucker's jam. 'We'll win today, I promise.' Somehow I made it sound like I actually believed that statement. 'Where's Hazel?'

'Over there!' Terminus pointed with his nonexistent arms. Based on his glance (I couldn't go by his nose any more), I assumed he meant to the left. We ran in that direction until we found another cluster of legionnaires.

'Where's Hazel?' Meg yelled.

'That way!' shouted Leila. 'Two blocks maybe!'

'Thanks!' Meg sprinted on with her unicorn honour guard, their nail file and corkscrew attachments at the ready.

We found Hazel just where Leila had predicted – two blocks down, where the street widened into a neighbourhood piazza. She and Arion were surrounded by zombies in the middle of the square, outnumbered by about twenty to one. Arion didn't look particularly alarmed, but he grunted and whinnied in frustration, unable to use his speed in such close quarters. Hazel slashed away with her spatha while Arion kicked at the mob to keep them back.

No doubt Hazel could've handled the situation without help, but our unicorns couldn't resist the opportunity for more zombie-posterior-kicking. They crashed into the fray, slicing and bottle-opening and tweezing the undead in an awesome display of multifunction carnage.

Meg leaped into battle, her twin blades spinning. I scanned the street for abandoned projectile weapons. Sadly, they were easy to find. I scooped up a bow and quiver and went to work, giving the zombies some very fashionable skull-piercings.

When Hazel realized it was us, she laughed with relief, then scanned the area behind me, probably looking for Frank. I met her eyes. I'm afraid my expression told her everything she didn't want to hear.

Emotions rippled across her face: utter disbelief, desolation, then anger. She yelled in rage, spurring Arion, and ploughed through the last of the zombie mob. They never had a chance.

Once the piazza was secure, Hazel cantered up to me. 'What happened?'

'I . . . Frank . . . The emperors . . .'

That's all I could manage. It wasn't much of a narrative, but she seemed to get the gist.

She doubled over until her forehead touched Arion's mane. She rocked and murmured, clutching her wrist like a baseball player who had just broken her hand and was trying to fight the pain. At last she straightened. She took a shaky breath. She dismounted, wrapped her arms around Arion's neck, and whispered something in his ear.

The horse nodded. Hazel stepped back and he raced away – a streak of white heading west towards the Caldecott Tunnel. I wanted to warn Hazel there was nothing to find there, but I didn't. I understood heartache a little better now. Each person's grief has its own life span; it needs to follow its own path.

'Where can we find Tarquin?' she demanded. What she meant was: *Who can I kill to make myself feel better?*

I knew the answer was *No one.* But again I didn't argue with her. Like a fool, I led the way to the bookshop to confront the undead king.

Two eurynomoi stood guard at the entrance, which I assumed meant Tarquin was already inside. I prayed Tyson and Ella were still on Temple Hill.

With a flick of her hand, Hazel summoned two precious stones from the ground: Rubies? Fire opals? They shot past me so fast I couldn't be sure. They hit the ghouls right between the eyes, reducing each guard to a pile of dust. The unicorns looked disappointed – both because they couldn't use their combat utensils, and because they realized we were going through a doorway too small for them to follow.

'Go find other enemies,' Meg told them. 'Enjoy!'

The Five Unicorns of the Apocalypse happily bucked, then galloped off to do Meg's bidding.

I barged into the bookshop, Hazel and Meg at my heels, and waded straight into a crowd of undead. Vrykolakai shuffled through the new-release aisle, perhaps looking for the latest in zombie fiction. Others bonked against the shelves of the history section, as if they knew they belonged in the past. One ghoul squatted on a comfy reading chair, drooling as he perused *The Illustrated Book of Vultures*. Another crouched on the balcony above, happily chewing a leather-bound edition of *Great Expectations*.

Tarquin himself was too busy to notice our entrance. He stood with his back to us, at the information desk, yelling at the bookshop cat.

'Answer me, beast!' the king screamed. 'Where are the Books?'

Aristophanes sat on the desk, one leg straight up in the air, calmly licking his nether regions – which, last I checked, was considered impolite in the presence of royalty.

'I will destroy you!' Tarquin said.

The cat looked up briefly, hissed, then returned to his personal grooming.

'Tarquin, leave him alone!' I shouted, though the cat seemed to need no help from me.

The king turned, and I immediately remembered why I shouldn't be near him. A tidal wave of nausea crashed over me, pushing me to my knees. My veins burned with poison. My flesh seemed to be turning inside out. None of the zombies attacked. They just stared at me with their flat dead eyes as if waiting for me to put on my HELLO, MY NAME USED TO BE name tag and start mingling.

Tarquin had accessorized for his big night out. He wore a mouldy red cloak over his corroded armour. Gold rings adorned his skeletal fingers. His golden circlet crown looked newly polished, making it clash nicely with his rotten cranium. Tendrils of oily purple neon slithered around his limbs, writhing in and out of his ribcage and circling his neck bones. Since his face was a skull, I couldn't tell if he was smiling, but when he spoke he sounded pleased to see me.

'Well, good! Killed the emperors, did you, my faithful servant? Speak!'

I had no desire to tell him anything, but a giant invisible hand squeezed my diaphragm, forcing out the words. 'Dead. They're dead.' I had to bite my tongue to keep from adding *lord*.

'Excellent!' Tarquin said. 'So many lovely deaths tonight. And the praetor, Frank –?'

'Don't.' Hazel shouldered past me. 'Tarquin, don't you dare say his name.'

'Ha! Dead, then. Excellent.' Tarquin sniffed the air, purple gas scrolling through his skeletal nose slits. 'The city is ripe with fear. Agony. Loss. Wonderful! Apollo, you're mine now, of course. I can feel your heart pumping its last few beats. And, Hazel Levesque . . . I'm afraid you'll have to die for collapsing my throne room on top of me. *Very* naughty trick. But this McCaffrey child . . . I'm in such a good mood that I might let her flee for her life and spread word of my great victory! That is, of course, if you cooperate and explain –' he pointed at the cat – 'the meaning of this.'

'It's a cat,' I said.

So much for Tarquin's good mood. He snarled, and another wave of pain turned my spine to putty. Meg grabbed my arm before my face could hit the carpet.

'Leave him alone!' she yelled at the king. 'There's no way I'm fleeing anywhere.'

'Where are the Sibylline Books?' Tarquin demanded. 'They are none of these!' He gestured dismissively at the shelves, then glared at Aristophanes. 'And this *creature* will not speak! The harpy and the Cyclops who were rewriting the prophecies – I can *smell* that they were here, but they are gone. Where *are* they?'

I said a silent prayer of thanks for stubborn harpies. Ella and Tyson must've still been waiting at Temple Hill for divine help that wasn't coming.

Meg snorted. 'You're stupid for a king. The Books aren't here. They're not even books.'

Tarquin regarded my small master, then turned to his zombies. 'What language is she speaking? Did that make sense to anyone?'

The zombies stared at him unhelpfully. The ghouls were too busy reading about vultures and eating *Great Expectations*.

Tarquin faced me again. 'What does the girl mean? Where are the Books, and how are they not books?'

Again, my chest constricted. The words burst out of me: 'Tyson. Cyclops. Prophecies tattooed on his skin. He's on Temple Hill with –'

'Quiet!' Meg ordered. My mouth clamped shut, but it was too late. The words were out of the barn. Was that the right expression?

Tarquin tilted his skull. 'The chair in the back room . . . Yes. Yes, I see now. Ingenious! I will have to keep this harpy alive and watch her practise her art. Prophecies on flesh? Oh, I can work with that!'

'You'll never leave this place,' Hazel growled. 'My troops are cleaning up the last of your invaders. It's just us now. And you're about to rest in pieces.'

Tarquin hissed a laugh. 'Oh, my dear. Did you think *that* was the invasion? Those troops were just my skirmishers, tasked with keeping you all divided and confused while I came here to secure the Books. Now I know where they are, which means the city can be properly pillaged! The rest of my army should be coming through your sewers right about –' he snapped his bone fingers – 'now.'

39

Captain Underpants
Does not appear in this book
Copyright issues

I WAITED FOR THE SOUNDS of renewed combat outside. The bookshop was so quiet I could almost hear the zombies breathing.

The city remained silent.

'Right about now,' Tarquin repeated, snapping his finger bones again.

'Having communications issues?' Hazel asked.

Tarquin hissed. 'What have you done?'

'Me? Nothing yet.' Hazel drew her spatha. 'That's about to change.'

Aristophanes struck first. Of course the cat would make the fight all about him. With an outraged *mewl* and no apparent provocation, the giant orange tub of fur launched himself at Tarquin's face, fastening his foreclaws to the skull's eye sockets and kicking his back feet against Tarquin's rotten teeth. The king staggered under this surprise assault, screaming in Latin, his words garbled because of the cat paws in his mouth. And so the Battle of the Bookshop began.

Hazel launched herself at Tarquin. Meg seemed to

accept that Hazel had first dibs on the big baddie, considering what had happened to Frank, so she concentrated on the zombies instead, using her double blades to stab and hack and push them towards the non-fiction section.

I drew an arrow, intending to shoot the ghoul on the balcony, but my hands trembled too badly. I couldn't get to my feet. My eyesight was dim and red. On top of all that, I realized I'd drawn the only arrow remaining in my original quiver: the Arrow of Dodona.

HOLDEST THOU ON, APOLLO! the arrow said in my mind. YIELDETH THYSELF NOT TO THE UNDEAD KING!

Through my fog of pain, I wondered if I was going crazy.

'Are you giving me a pep talk?' The idea made me giggle. 'Whew, I'm tired.'

I collapsed on my butt.

Meg stepped over me and slashed a zombie who had been about to eat my face.

'Thank you,' I muttered, but she'd already moved on. The ghouls had reluctantly put down their books and were now closing in on her.

Hazel stabbed at Tarquin, who had just flung Aristophanes off his face. The cat yowled as he flew across the room. He managed to catch the edge of a bookshelf and scramble to the top. He glared down at me with his green eyes, his expression implying I meant to do that.

The Arrow of Dodona kept talking in my head: THOU HAST DONE WELL, APOLLO! THOU HAST ONLY ONE JOB NOW: LIVE!

'That's a really hard job,' I muttered. 'I hate my job.'

THOU HAST ONLY TO WAIT! HOLD ON!

'Wait for what?' I murmured. 'Hold on to what? Oh . . . I guess I'm holding on to you.'

YES! the arrow said. *YES, DOEST THOU THAT! STAYEST THOU WITH ME, APOLLO. DAREST THOU NOT DIE UPON ME, MAN!*

'Isn't that from a movie?' I asked. 'Like . . . every movie? Wait, you actually care if I die?'

'Apollo!' yelled Meg, slashing at Great Expectations. 'If you're not going to help, could you at least crawl someplace safer?'

I wanted to oblige. I really did. But my legs wouldn't work.

'Oh, look,' I muttered to no one in particular. 'My ankles are turning grey. Oh, wow. My hands are, too.'

NO! said the arrow. *HOLD ON!*

'For what?'

CONCENTRATE UPON MY VOICE. LET US SING A SONG! THOU LIKEST SONGS, DOST THOU NOT?

'Sweet Caroline!' I warbled.

PERHAPS A DIFFERENT SONG?

'BAHM! BAHM! BAHM!' I continued.

The arrow relented and began singing along with me, though he lagged behind, since he had to translate all the lyrics into Shakespearean language.

This was how I would die: sitting on the floor of a bookshop, turning into a zombie while holding a talking arrow and singing Neil Diamond's greatest hit. Even the Fates cannot foresee all the wonders the universe has in store for us.

At last my voice dried up. My vision tunnelled. The sounds of combat seemed to reach my ears from the ends of long metal tubes.

Meg slashed through the last of Tarquin's minions. That was a good thing, I thought distantly. I didn't want her to die, too. Hazel stabbed Tarquin in the chest. The Roman king fell, howling in pain, ripping the sword hilt from Hazel's grip. He collapsed against the information desk, clutching the blade with his skeletal hands.

Hazel stepped back, waiting for the zombie king to dissolve. Instead, Tarquin struggled to his feet, purple gas flickering weakly in his eye sockets.

'I have lived for millennia,' he snarled. 'You could not kill me with a thousand tons of stone, Hazel Levesque. You will not kill me with a sword.'

I thought Hazel might fly at him and rip his skull off with her bare hands. Her rage was so palpable I could smell it like an approaching storm. Wait . . . I *did* smell an approaching storm, along with other forest scents: pine needles, morning dew on wildflowers, the breath of hunting dogs.

A large silver wolf licked my face. Lupa? A hallucination? No . . . a whole pack of the beasts had trotted into the store and were now sniffing the bookshelves and the piles of zombie dust.

Behind them, in the doorway, stood a girl who looked about twelve, her eyes silver-yellow, her auburn hair pulled back in a ponytail. She was dressed for the hunt in a shimmering grey frock and leggings, a white bow in her hand. Her face was beautiful, serene and as cold as the winter moon.

She nocked a silver arrow and met Hazel's eyes, asking permission to finish her kill. Hazel nodded and stepped aside. The young girl aimed at Tarquin.

'Foul undead thing,' she said, her voice hard and bright with power. 'When a good woman puts you down, you had best stay down.'

Her arrow lodged in the centre of Tarquin's forehead, splitting his frontal bone. The king stiffened. The tendrils of purple gas sputtered and dissipated. From the arrow's point of entry, a ripple of fire the colour of Christmas tinsel spread across Tarquin's skull and down his body, disintegrating him utterly. His gold crown, the silver arrow and Hazel's sword all dropped to the floor.

I grinned at the newcomer. 'Hey, Sis.'

Then I keeled over sideways.

The world turned fluffy, bleached of all colour. Nothing hurt any more.

I was dimly aware of Diana's face hovering over me, Meg and Hazel peering over the goddess's shoulders.

'He's almost gone,' Diana said.

Then I *was* gone. My mind slipped into a pool of cold, slimy darkness.

'Oh, no, you don't.' My sister's voice woke me rudely.

I'd been so comfortable, so nonexistent.

Life surged back into me – cold, sharp, and unfairly painful. Diana's face came into focus. She looked annoyed, which seemed on-brand for her.

As for me, I felt surprisingly good. The pain in my gut

was gone. My muscles didn't burn. I could breathe without difficulty. I must have slept for decades.

'H-how long was I out?' I croaked.

'Roughly three seconds,' she said. 'Now, get up, drama queen.'

She helped me to my feet. I felt a bit unsteady, but I was delighted to find that my legs had any strength at all. My skin was no longer grey. The lines of infection were gone. The Arrow of Dodona was still in my hand, though he had gone silent, perhaps in awe of the goddess's presence. Or perhaps he was still trying to get the taste of 'Sweet Caroline' out of his imaginary mouth.

Meg and Hazel stood nearby, bedraggled but unharmed. Friendly grey wolves milled around them, bumping against their legs and sniffing their shoes, which had obviously been to many interesting places over the course of the day. Aristophanes regarded us all from his perch atop the bookshelf, decided he didn't care, then went back to cleaning himself.

I beamed at my sister. It was so good to see her disapproving *I-can't-believe-you're-my-brother* frown again. 'I love you,' I said, my voice hoarse with emotion.

She blinked, clearly unsure what to do with this information. 'You really *have* changed.'

'I missed you!'

'Y-yes, well. I'm here now. Even Dad couldn't argue with a Sibylline invocation from Temple Hill.'

'It worked, then!' I grinned at Hazel and Meg. 'It worked!'

'Yeah,' Meg said wearily. 'Hi, Artemis.'

'Diana,' my sister corrected. 'But hello, Meg.' For her, my sister had a smile. 'You've done well, young warrior.'

Meg blushed. She kicked at the scattered zombie dust on the floor and shrugged. 'Eh.'

I checked my stomach, which was easy, since my shirt was in tatters. The bandages had vanished, along with the festering wound. Only a thin white scar remained. 'So . . . I'm healed?' My flab told me she hadn't restored me to my godly self. Nah, that would have been too much to expect.

Diana raised an eyebrow. 'Well, I'm not the goddess of healing, but I'm still a goddess. I think I can take care of my little brother's boo-boos.'

'*Little* brother?'

She smirked, then turned to Hazel. 'And you, Centurion. How have you been?'

Hazel was no doubt sore and stiff, but she knelt and bowed her head like a good Roman. 'I'm . . .' She hesitated. Her world had just been shattered. She'd lost Frank. She apparently decided not to lie to the goddess. 'I'm heartbroken and exhausted, my lady. But thank you for coming to our aid.'

Diana's expression softened. 'Yes. I know it has been a difficult night. Come, let's go outside. It's rather stuffy in here, and it smells like burnt Cyclops.'

The survivors were slowly gathering on the street. Perhaps some instinct had drawn them there, to the place of Tarquin's defeat. Or perhaps they'd simply come to gawk at the glowing silver chariot with its team of four golden reindeer now parallel-parked in front of the bookshop.

Giant eagles and hunting falcons shared the rooftops. Wolves hobnobbed with Hannibal the elephant and the weaponized unicorns. Legionnaires and citizens of New Rome milled about in shock.

At the end of the street, huddled with a group of survivors, was Thalia Grace, her hand on the shoulder of the legion's new standard-bearer, comforting the young woman as she cried. Thalia was dressed in her usual black denim, various punk-band badges gleaming on the lapel of her leather jacket. A silver circlet, the symbol of Artemis's lieutenant, glinted in her spiky dark hair. Her sunken eyes and slumped shoulders made me suspect that she already knew about Jason's death – perhaps had known for a while and had gone through the first hard wave of grieving.

I winced with guilt. I should have been the one to deliver the news about Jason. The cowardly part of me felt relieved that I didn't have to bear the initial brunt of Thalia's anger. The rest of me felt horrible that I felt relieved.

I needed to go talk to her. Then something caught my eye in the crowd checking out Diana's chariot. People were packed into its carriage tighter than New Year's Eve revellers in a stretch limo's sunroof. Among them was a lanky young woman with pink hair.

From my mouth escaped another completely inappropriate, delighted laugh. 'Lavinia?'

She looked over and grinned. 'This ride is *so* cool! I never want to get out.'

Diana smiled. 'Well, Lavinia Asimov, if you want to stay on board, you'd have to become a Hunter.'

'Nope!' Lavinia hopped off as if the chariot's floorboards had become lava. 'No offence, my lady, but I like girls too much to take that vow. Like . . . *like* them. Not just *like* them. Like –'

'I understand.' Diana sighed. 'Romantic love. It's a plague.'

'Lavinia, h-how did you . . .' I stammered. 'Where did you –?'

'This young woman,' said Diana, 'was responsible for the destruction of the Triumvirate's fleet.'

'Well, I had a lot of help,' Lavinia said.

'PEACHES!' said a muffled voice from somewhere in the chariot.

He was so short that I hadn't noticed him before, hidden as he was behind the carriage's sideboard and the crowd of big folk, but now Peaches squirmed and climbed his way to the top of the railing. He grinned his wicked grin. His diaper sagged. His leafy wings rustled. He beat his chest with his minuscule fists and looked very pleased with himself.

'Peaches!' Meg cried.

'PEACHES!' Peaches agreed, and he flew into Meg's arms. Never had there been such a bittersweet reunion between a girl and her deciduous fruit spirit. There were tears and laughter, hugs and scratches, and cries of 'Peaches!' in every tone from scolding to apologetic to jubilant.

'I don't understand,' I said, turning to Lavinia. 'You made all those mortars malfunction?'

Lavinia looked offended. 'Well, yeah. Somebody had to

stop the fleet. I *did* pay attention during siege-weapon class and ship-boarding class. It wasn't that hard. All it took was a little fancy footwork.'

Hazel finally managed to pick her jaw up off the pavement. 'Wasn't that *hard?*'

'We were motivated! The fauns and dryads did great.' Lavinia paused, her expression momentarily clouding, as if she remembered something unpleasant. 'Um . . . besides, the Nereids helped a lot. There was only a skeleton crew aboard each yacht. Not, like, actual skeletons, but – you know what I mean. Also, look!'

She pointed proudly at her feet, which were now adorned with the shoes of Terpsichore from Caligula's private collection.

'You mounted an amphibious assault on an enemy fleet,' I said, 'for a pair of shoes.'

Lavinia huffed. 'Not just for the shoes, obviously.' She tap-danced a routine that would've made Savion Glover proud. 'Also to save the camp, and the nature spirits and Michael Kahale's commandos.'

Hazel held up her hands to stop the overflow of information. 'Wait. Not to be a killjoy – I mean, you did an amazing thing! – but you still deserted your post, Lavinia. I certainly didn't give you permission –'

'I was acting on praetor's orders,' Lavinia said haughtily. 'In fact, Reyna helped. She was knocked out for a while, healing, but she woke up in time to instill in us the power of Bellona, right before we boarded those ships. Made us all strong and stealthy and stuff.'

'Reyna?' I yelped. 'Where is she?'

'Right here,' called the praetor.

I didn't know how I'd missed seeing her. She'd been hiding in plain sight among the group of survivors talking with Thalia. I suppose I'd been too focused on Thalia, wondering whether or not she was going to kill me and whether or not I deserved it.

Reyna limped over on crutches, her broken leg now in a full cast covered with signatures like *Felipe*, *Lotoya* and *Sneezewart*. Considering all she'd been through, Reyna looked great, though she still had a hank of hair missing from the raven attack, and her maroon cardigan was going to need a few days at the magical dry cleaner.

Thalia smiled, watching her friend come towards us. Then Thalia met my eyes, and her smile wavered. Her expression turned bleak. She gave me a curt nod – not hostile, just sad, acknowledging that we had things to talk about later.

Hazel exhaled. 'Thank the gods.' She gave Reyna a delicate hug, careful not to unbalance her. 'Is it true about Lavinia acting on your orders?'

Reyna glanced at our pink-haired friend. The praetor's pained expression said something like, *I respect you a lot, but I also hate you for being right.*

'Yes,' Reyna managed to say. 'Plan L was my idea. Lavinia and her friends acted on my orders. They performed heroically.'

Lavinia beamed. 'See? I told you.'

The assembled crowd murmured in amazement, as if, after a day full of wonders, they had finally witnessed something that could not be explained.

'There were many heroes today,' Diana said. 'And many losses. I'm only sorry that Thalia and I couldn't get here sooner. We were only able to rendezvous with Lavinia and Reyna's forces after their raid, then destroy the second wave of undead, who were waiting in the sewers.' She waved dismissively, as if annihilating Tarquin's main force of ghouls and zombies had been an afterthought.

Gods, I missed being a god.

'You also saved me,' I said. 'You're here. You're actually *here.*'

She took my hand and squeezed it. Her flesh felt warm and human. I couldn't remember the last time my sister had shown me such open affection.

'Let's not celebrate quite yet,' she warned. 'You have many wounded to attend to. The camp's medics have set up tents outside the city. They will need every healer, including you, brother.'

Lavinia grimaced. 'And we'll have to have more funerals. Gods. I wish –'

'Look!' Hazel shrieked, her voice an octave higher than usual.

Arion came trotting up the hill, a hulking human form draped over his back.

'Oh, no.' My heart wilted. I had flashbacks of Tempest, the *ventus* horse, depositing Jason's body on the beach in Santa Monica. No, I couldn't watch. Yet I couldn't look away.

The body on Arion's back was unmoving and steaming. Arion stopped and the form slipped off one side. But it did not fall.

Frank Zhang landed on his feet. He turned towards us. His hair was singed to a fine black stubble. His eyebrows were gone. His clothes had completely burned away except for his briefs and his praetor's cape, giving him a disturbing resemblance to Captain Underpants.

He looked around, his eyes glazed and unfocused.

'Hey, everybody,' he croaked. Then he fell on his face.

40

Stop making me cry
Or buy me some new tear ducts
My old ones broke down

PRIORITIES CHANGE when you're rushing a friend to emergency medical care.

It no longer seemed important that we had won a major battle, or that I could finally take *BECOME A ZOMBIE* off my alert calendar. Lavinia's heroism and her new dancing shoes were momentarily forgotten. My guilt about Thalia's presence was also pushed aside. She and I didn't exchange so much as a word as she rushed in to help along with the rest of us.

I even failed to register that my sister, who'd been at my side only a moment before, had quietly vanished. I found myself barking orders at legionnaires, directing them to grate some unicorn horn, get me some nectar, stat, and rush, rush, rush Frank Zhang to the medical tent.

Hazel and I stayed at Frank's bedside until well past dawn, long after the other medics assured us he was out of danger. None of them could explain how he had survived, but his pulse was strong, his skin was remarkably unburned and his lungs were clear. The arrow punctures in his shoulder and the dagger wound in his gut had given us some trouble, but they were now stitched up, bandaged and healing well. Frank slept fitfully, muttering and flexing his hands as if he were still reaching for an imperial throat to strangle.

'Where's his firewood?' Hazel fretted. 'Should we look for it? If it's lost in the –'

'I don't think so,' I said. 'I – I saw it burn up. That's what killed Caligula. Frank's sacrifice.'

'Then how . . . ?' Hazel put her fist in her mouth to block a sob. She hardly dared to ask the question. 'Will he be okay?'

I had no answer for her. Years ago, Juno had decreed that Frank's life span was tied to that stick. I wasn't there to hear her exact words – I try not to be around Juno any more than I have to. But she'd said something about Frank being powerful and bringing honour to his family, et cetera, though his life would be short and bright. The Fates had decreed that when that piece of tinder burned up he was destined to die. Yet now the firewood was gone, and Frank still lived. After so many years keeping that piece of wood safe, he had intentionally burned it to . . .

'Maybe that's it,' I muttered.

'What?' Hazel asked.

'He took control of his destiny,' I said. 'The only other person I've ever known to have this, er, firewood problem, back in the old days, was this prince named Meleager. His mom got the same kind of prophecy when he was a baby. But she never even *told* Meleager about the firewood. She just hid it and let him live his life. He grew up to be kind of a privileged, arrogant brat.'

Hazel held Frank's hand with both of hers. 'Frank could never be like that.'

'I know,' I said. 'Anyway, Meleager ended up killing a bunch of his relatives. His mom was horrified. She went and found the piece of firewood and threw it in the fire. Boom. End of story.'

Hazel shuddered. 'That's horrible.'

'The point is, Frank's family was honest with him. His grandmother told him the story of Juno's visit. She let him carry his own lifeline. She didn't try to protect him from the hard truth. That shaped who he is.'

Hazel nodded slowly. 'He knew what his fate would be. What his fate was *supposed* to be, anyway. I still don't understand how –'

'It's just a guess,' I admitted. 'Frank went into that tunnel knowing he might die. He willingly sacrificed himself for a noble cause. In doing so, he broke free of his fate. By burning his own tinder, he kind of . . . I don't know, started a new fire with it. He's in charge of his own destiny now. Well, as much as any of us are. The only other explanation I can think of is that Juno somehow released him from the Fates' decree.'

Hazel frowned. 'Juno, doing someone a favour?'

'Doesn't sound like her, I agree. She does have a soft spot for Frank, though.'

'She had a soft spot for Jason, too.' Hazel's voice turned brittle. 'Not that I'm complaining that Frank is alive, of course. It just seems . . .'

She didn't need to finish. Frank's survival was wonderful. A miracle. But somehow it made losing Jason feel all the more unfair and painful. As a former god, I knew all the usual responses to mortal complaints about the unfairness of dying. *Death is part of life. You have to accept it. Life would be meaningless without death. The deceased will always be alive as long as we remember them.* But as a mortal, as Jason's friend, I didn't find much comfort in those thoughts.

'Umph.' Frank's eyes fluttered open.

'Oh!' Hazel wrapped her arms around his neck, smothering him in a hug. This wasn't the best medical practice for someone just returning to consciousness, but I let it pass. Frank managed to pat Hazel feebly on the back.

'Breathe,' he croaked.

'Oh, sorry!' Hazel pulled away. She brushed a tear from her cheek. 'You're thirsty, I bet.' She rummaged for the canteen at his bedside and tipped it towards his mouth. He took a few painful sips of nectar.

'Ah.' He nodded his thanks. 'So . . . are we . . . good?'

Hazel hiccupped a sob. 'Yes. Yes, we're good. The camp is saved. Tarquin is dead. And you . . . you killed Caligula.'

'Eh.' Frank smiled weakly. 'That was my pleasure.' He turned to me. 'Did I miss the cake?'

I stared at him. 'What?'

'Your birthday. Yesterday.'

'Oh. I . . . I have to admit I completely forgot about that. And the cake.'

'So there might still be cake in our future. Good. Do you feel a year older, at least?'

'That's a definite yes.'

'You scared me, Frank Zhang,' Hazel said. 'You broke my heart when I thought . . .'

Frank's expression turned sheepish (without him actually, you know, turning into a sheep). 'I'm sorry, Hazel. It was just . . .' He curled his fingers, like he was trying to catch an elusive butterfly. 'It was the only way. Ella told me some prophecy lines, just for me . . . Only fire could stop the emperors, kindled by the most precious firewood, on the bridge to camp. I guessed that she meant the Caldecott Tunnel. She said New Rome needed a new Horatius.'

'Horatius Cocles,' I recalled. 'Nice guy. He defended Rome by holding off an entire army single-handedly on the Sublician Bridge.'

Frank nodded. 'I . . . I asked Ella not to tell anyone else. I just . . . I kind of had to process it, carry it around by myself for a while.' His hand went instinctively to his belt, where the cloth pouch no longer was.

'You could've died,' Hazel said.

'Yeah. "Life is only precious because it ends, kid."'

'Is that a quote?' I asked.

'My dad,' Frank said. 'He was right. I just had to be willing to take the risk.'

We remained quiet for a moment, considering the enormity of Frank's risk, or perhaps just marvelling that Mars had actually said something wise.

'How did you survive the fire?' Hazel demanded.

'I don't know. I remember Caligula burning up. I passed out, thought I was dead. Then I woke up on Arion's back. And now I'm here.'

'I'm glad.' Hazel kissed his forehead tenderly. 'But I'm still going to kill you later for scaring me like that.'

He smiled. 'That's fair. Could I have another . . . ?'

Maybe he was going to say *kiss*, or *sip of nectar*, or *moment alone with my best friend, Apollo*. But before he could finish the sentence his eyes rolled up in his head and he started snoring.

Not all my bedside visits were so happy.

As the morning stretched on, I tried to visit as many of the wounded as I could.

Sometimes I could do nothing but watch as the bodies were prepared for an anti-zombie washing and final rites. Tarquin was gone, and his ghouls seemed to have dissolved with him, but no one wanted to take any chances.

Dakota, long-time centurion of the Fifth Legion, had died overnight from wounds he received fighting in the city. We decided by consensus that his funeral pyre would be fruit-punch scented.

Jacob, the legion's former standard-bearer and my former archery student, had died at the Caldecott Tunnel when he took a direct hit from a myrmeke's acidic spray. The magic golden eagle had survived, as magic items tend to do, but not Jacob. Terrel, the young woman who had snatched up the standard before it could hit the ground, had stayed at Jacob's side until he passed.

So many more had perished. I recognized their faces, even if I didn't know their names. I felt responsible for every single one. If I'd just done more, just acted more quickly, just been godlier . . .

My hardest visit was to Don the faun. He'd been brought in by a squad of Nereids who recovered him from the wreckage of the imperial yachts. Despite the danger, Don had stayed behind to make sure the sabotage was done right. Unlike what happened to Frank, the Greek fire explosions had ravaged poor Don. Most of the goat fur had burned off his legs. His skin was charred. Despite the best healing music his fellow fauns could offer, and being covered with glistening healing goo, he must have been in terrible pain. Only his eyes were the same: bright and blue and jumping from spot to spot.

Lavinia knelt next to him, holding his left hand, which for some reason was the only part of him left unscathed. A group of dryads and fauns stood nearby, at a respectful distance, with Pranjal the healer, who had already done everything he could.

When Don saw me, he grimaced, his teeth speckled with bits of ash. 'H-hey, Apollo. Got any . . . spare change?'

I blinked back tears. 'Oh, Don. Oh, my sweet, stupid faun.'

I knelt at his bedside, opposite Lavinia. I scanned the horrors of Don's condition, desperately hoping I could see something to fix, something the other medics had missed, but of course there was nothing. The fact that Don had survived this long was a miracle.

'It's not so bad,' Don rasped. 'Doc gave me some stuff for the pain.'

'Jarritos cherry soda,' said Pranjal.

I nodded. That was powerful pain medicine indeed for satyrs and fauns, only to be used in the most serious of cases, lest the patients become addicted.

'I just . . . I wanted . . .' Don groaned, his eyes becoming brighter.

'Save your strength,' I pleaded.

'For what?' He croaked a grotesque version of a laugh. 'I wanted to ask: Does it hurt? Reincarnation?'

My eyes were too blurry to see properly. 'I – I've never reincarnated, Don. When I became human, that was different, I think. But I hear reincarnation is peaceful. Beautiful.'

The dryads and fauns nodded and murmured in agreement, though their expressions betrayed a mixture of fear, sorrow and desperation, making them not the best sales team for the Great Unknown.

Lavinia cupped her hands around the faun's fingers. 'You're a hero, Don. You're a great friend.'

'Hey . . . cool.' He seemed to have trouble locating Lavinia's face. 'I'm scared, Lavinia.'

'I know, babe.'

'I hope . . . maybe I come back as a hemlock? That would be like . . . an action-hero plant, right?'

Lavinia nodded, her lips quivering. 'Yeah. Yeah, absolutely.'

'Cool . . . Hey, Apollo, you – you know the difference between a faun and a satyr . . . ?'

He smiled a little wider, as if ready to deliver the punchline. His face froze that way. His chest stopped moving. Dryads and fauns began to cry. Lavinia kissed the faun's hand, then pulled a piece of bubblegum from her bag and reverently slipped it into Don's shirt pocket.

A moment later, his body collapsed with a noise like a relieved sigh, crumbling into fresh loam. In the spot where his heart had been, a tiny sapling emerged from the soil. I immediately recognized the shape of those miniature leaves. Not a hemlock. A laurel – the tree I had created from poor Daphne, and whose leaves I had decided to make into wreaths. The laurel, the tree of victory.

One of the dryads glanced at me. 'Did you do that . . . ?'

I shook my head. I swallowed the bitter taste from my mouth.

'The only difference between a satyr and a faun,' I said, 'is what we see in them. And what they see in themselves. Plant this tree somewhere special.' I looked up at the dryads. 'Tend it and make it grow healthy and tall. This was Don the faun, a hero.'

41

If you hate me, fine
Just don't hit me in the gut
Or, well, anywhere

THE NEXT FEW DAYS were almost as hard as the battle itself. War leaves a huge mess that cannot simply be addressed with a mop and a bucket.

We cleared the rubble and shored up the most precarious damaged buildings. We put out fires, both literal and figurative. Terminus had made it through the battle, though he was weak and shaken. His first announcement was that he was formally adopting little Julia. The girl seemed delighted, though I wasn't sure how Roman law would work out adoption-by-statue. Tyson and Ella were safely accounted for. Once Ella learned that I hadn't messed up the summoning after all, she announced that she and Tyson were going back to the bookshop to clean up the mess, finish the Sibylline Books and feed the cat, not necessarily in that order. Oh, and she was also grateful that Frank was alive. As for me . . . I got the feeling she was still making up her mind.

Peaches left us once more to go help the local dryads and fauns, but he promised us, 'Peaches,' which I took to mean that we would see him again soon.

With Thalia's help, Reyna somehow managed to find One Eye and Short Ears, the abused pegasi from the emperors' chariot. She talked to them in soothing tones, promised them healing, and convinced them to come back with her to camp, where she spent most of her time dressing their wounds and providing them with good food and plenty of open air. The animals seemed to recognize that Reyna was a friend of their immortal forefather, the great Pegasus himself. After what they'd been through, I doubted they would have trusted anyone else to care for them.

We didn't count the dead. They weren't numbers. They were people we had known, friends we had fought with.

We lit all the funeral pyres on one night, at the base of Jupiter's temple, and shared the traditional feast for the dead to send our fallen comrades off to the Underworld. The Lares turned out in full force until the hillside was a glowing field of purple, ghosts outnumbering the living.

I noticed that Reyna stood back and let Frank officiate. Praetor Zhang had quickly regained his strength. Dressed in full armour and his maroon cloak, he gave his eulogy while the legionnaires listened with awed reverence, as one does when the speaker has recently sacrificed himself in a fiery explosion and then, somehow, made it out alive with his underwear and cape intact.

Hazel helped, too, going through the ranks and comforting those who were crying or looking shell-shocked. Reyna stayed at the edge of the crowd, leaning on her crutches, gazing wistfully at the legionnaires as if they were loved ones she hadn't seen in a decade and now barely recognized.

As Frank finished his speech, a voice next to me said, 'Hey.'

Thalia Grace wore her usual black and silver. In the light of the funeral pyres, her electric-blue eyes turned piercing violet. Over the past few days, we had spoken a few times, but it had all been surface talk: where to bring supplies, how to help the wounded. We had avoided *the subject*.

'Hey,' I said, my voice hoarse.

She folded her arms and stared at the fire. 'I don't blame you, Apollo. My brother . . .' She hesitated, steadying her breath. 'Jason made his own choices. Heroes have to do that.'

Somehow, having her not blame me only made me feel guiltier and more unworthy. Ugh, human emotions were like barbed wire. There was just no safe way to grab hold of them or get through them.

'I'm so sorry,' I said at last.

'Yeah. I know.' She closed her eyes as if listening for a distant sound – a wolf cry in the forest, perhaps. 'I got Reyna's letter, a few hours before Diana received your summons. An aura – one of the breeze nymphs – she plucked it out of the mail and flew it to me personally. So dangerous for her, but she did it anyway.' Thalia picked at one of the badges on her lapel: Iggy and the Stooges, a band older than she was by several generations. 'We came as fast as we could, but still . . . I had some time to cry and scream and throw things.'

I remained very still. I had vivid memories of Iggy Pop throwing peanut butter, ice cubes, watermelons and other dangerous objects at his fans during his concerts. I found Thalia more intimidating than him by far.

'It seems so cruel,' she continued. 'We lose someone and finally get them back, only to lose them again.'

I wondered why she used the word *we*. She seemed to be saying that she and I shared this experience – the loss of an only sibling. But she had suffered so much worse. My sister couldn't die. I couldn't lose her permanently.

Then, after a moment of disorientation, like I'd been flipped upside down, I realized she wasn't talking about me losing someone. She was talking about Artemis – Diana.

Was she suggesting that my sister missed me, even grieved for me as Thalia grieved for Jason?

Thalia must have read my expression. 'The goddess has been beside herself,' she said. 'I mean that literally. Sometimes she gets so worried she splits into two forms, Roman and Greek, right in front of me. She'll probably get mad at me for telling you this, but she loves you more than anyone else in the world.'

A marble seemed to have lodged in my throat. I couldn't speak, so I just nodded.

'Diana didn't want to leave camp so suddenly like that,' Thalia continued. 'But you know how it is. Gods can't stick around. Once the danger to New Rome had passed, she couldn't risk overstaying her summons. Jupiter . . . Dad wouldn't approve.'

I shivered. How easy it was to forget that this young woman was *also* my sister. And Jason was my brother. At one time, I would have discounted that connection. *They're just demigods*, I would have said. *Not* really *family*.

Now I found the idea hard to accept for a different reason. I didn't feel worthy of that family. Or Thalia's forgiveness.

Gradually, the funeral picnic began to break up. Romans drifted off in twos and threes, heading for New Rome, where a special night-time meeting was being held at the Senate House. Sadly, the valley's population was so reduced that the entire legion and the citizenry of New Rome could now fit inside that one building.

Reyna hobbled over to us.

Thalia gave her a smile. 'So, Praetor Ramírez-Arellano, you ready?'

'Yes.' Reyna answered without hesitation, though I wasn't sure what she was ready for. 'Do you mind if . . .' She nodded at me.

Thalia gripped her friend's shoulder. 'Of course. See you at the Senate House.' She strode away into the darkness.

'Come on, Lester.' Reyna winked. 'Limp with me.'

The limping was easy. Even though I was healed, I tired easily. It was no problem to walk at Reyna's pace. Her dogs, Aurum and Argentum, weren't with her, I noticed, perhaps because Terminus didn't approve of deadly weapons inside the city limits.

We made our way slowly down the road from Temple Hill towards New Rome. Other legionnaires gave us a wide berth, apparently sensing we had private business to discuss.

Reyna kept me in suspense until we reached the bridge spanning the Little Tiber.

'I wanted to thank you,' she said.

Her smile was a ghost of the one she'd had on the hillside of Sutro Tower, when I'd offered to be her boyfriend. That left me in no doubt about what she meant – not *Thank you for helping to save the camp*, but *Thank you for giving me a good laugh*.

'No problem,' I grumbled.

'I don't mean it in a negative way.' Seeing my dubious look, she sighed and stared out at the dark river, its ripples curling silver in the moonlight. 'I don't know if I can explain this. My whole life, I've been living with other people's expectations of what I'm supposed to be. *Be this. Be that.* You know?'

'You're talking to a former god. Dealing with people's expectations is our job description.'

Reyna conceded this with a nod. 'For years, I was supposed to be a good little sister to Hylla in a tough family situation. Then, on Circe's island, I was supposed to be an obedient servant. Then I was a pirate for a while. Then a legionnaire. Then a praetor.'

'You do have an impressive résumé,' I admitted.

'But the whole time I've been a leader here,' she forged on, 'I was looking for a partner. Praetors often partner up. In power. But also romantically, I mean. I thought Jason. Then for a hot minute Percy Jackson. Gods help me, I even considered Octavian.' She shuddered. 'Everybody was always trying to ship me with somebody. Thalia. Jason. Gwen. Even Frank. *Oh, you'd be perfect together! That's who you need!* But I was never really sure if I *wanted* that, or if I just felt like I was *supposed* to want it. People, well-meaning, would be like, *Oh, you poor thing. You deserve somebody in your life. Date him. Date her. Date whoever. Find your soul mate.'*

She looked at me to see if I was following. Her words came out hot and fast, as if she'd been holding them in for a long time. 'And that meeting with Venus. That *really* messed me up. *No demigod will heal your heart.* What was *that* supposed to mean? Then finally you came along.'

'Do we have to review that part again? I am quite embarrassed enough.'

'But you *showed* me. When you proposed dating . . .' She took a deep breath, her body shaking with silent giggles. 'Oh, gods. I saw how ridiculous I'd been. How ridiculous the whole situation was. That's what healed my heart – being able to laugh at myself again, at my stupid ideas about destiny. That allowed me to break free – just like Frank broke free of his firewood. I don't need another person to heal my heart. I don't need a partner . . . at least, not until and unless I'm ready on my own terms. I don't need to be force-shipped with anyone or to wear anybody else's label. For the first time in a long time, I feel like a weight has been lifted from my shoulders. So thank you.'

'You're welcome?'

She laughed. 'Don't you see, though? Venus put you up to the job. She tricked you into it, because she knew you were the only one in the cosmos with an ego big enough to handle the rejection. I could laugh in your face, and you would heal.'

'Hmph.' I suspected she was right about Venus manipulating me. I wasn't so sure the goddess cared whether or not I would heal, though. 'So what does this mean for you, exactly? What's next for Praetor Reyna?'

Even as I asked the question, I realized I knew the answer.

'Come along to the Senate House,' she said. 'We've got a few surprises in store.'

42

Life is uncertain
Accept presents, and always
Eat your birthday cake

MY FIRST SURPRISE: A FRONT-ROW SEAT.

Meg and I were given places of honour next to the senior senators, and the most important citizens of New Rome, and those demigods with accessibility needs. When Meg saw me, she patted the bench next to her, as if there were any other place to sit. The chamber was absolutely packed. Somehow, it was reassuring to see everyone together, even if the populace was much reduced and the sea of white bandages could have caused snow blindness.

Reyna limped into the chamber right behind me. The entire assembly came to its feet. They waited in respectful silence as she made her way to her praetor's seat next to Frank, who nodded at his colleague.

Once she was seated, everyone else followed suit.

Reyna gestured at Frank like, *Let the fun begin*.

'So,' Frank addressed the audience, 'I call to order this extraordinary meeting of the people of New Rome and the Twelfth Legion. First item on the agenda: a formal thank-you to all. We survived through a team effort. We've dealt a huge blow to our enemies. Tarquin is dead – *really* dead at last. Two out of three emperors of the Triumvirate have been destroyed, along with their fleet and their troops. This was done at great cost. But you all acted like true Romans. We live to see another day!'

There was applause, some nods and a few cheers of 'Yes!' and 'Another day!' One guy in the back, who must not have been paying attention for the last week, said, '*Tarquin?*'

'Second,' Frank said, 'I want to reassure you that I'm alive and well.' He patted his chest as if to prove it. 'My fate is no longer tied to a piece of wood, which is nice. And if you would all please forget that you saw me in my underwear, I'd appreciate it.'

That got some laughs. Who knew Frank could be funny on purpose?

'Now . . .' His expression turned serious. 'It's our duty to inform you of some personnel changes. Reyna?'

He watched her quizzically, as if wondering whether she would really go through with it.

'Thank you, Frank.' She pulled herself to her feet. Again, everyone in the assembly who could stand did.

'Guys. Please.' She gestured for us to be seated. 'This is hard enough.'

When we were all settled, she scanned the faces in the crowd: a lot of anxious, sad expressions. I suspected many people knew what was coming.

'I've been praetor for a long time,' Reyna said. 'It's been an honour to serve the legion. We've been through some rough times together. Some . . . interesting years.'

A bit of nervous laughter. *Interesting* was the perfect curse word.

'But it's time for me to step down,' she continued. 'So I am resigning my post as praetor.'

A moan of disbelief filled the chamber, as if homework had just been assigned on a Friday afternoon.

'It's for personal reasons,' Reyna said. 'Like, my sanity, for instance. I need time to just be Reyna Avila Ramírez-Arellano, to find out who I am outside the legion. It may take a few years, or decades, or centuries. And so . . .' She removed her praetor's cloak and badge and handed them to Frank.

'Thalia?' she called.

Thalia Grace made her way down the central aisle. She winked at me as she passed.

She stood before Reyna and said, 'Repeat after me: *I pledge myself to the goddess Diana. I turn my back on the company of men, accept eternal maidenhood and join the hunt.*'

Reyna repeated the words. Nothing magical happened that I could see: no thunder or lightning, no silver glitter falling from the ceiling. But Reyna looked as if she'd been given a new lease on life, which she had – infinity years, with zero interest and no money down.

Thalia clasped her shoulder. 'Welcome to the hunt, sister!'

Reyna grinned. 'Thanks.' She faced the crowd. 'And thank you, all. Long live Rome!'

The crowd rose again and gave Reyna a standing ovation. They cheered and stomped with such jubilation I was afraid the duct-taped dome might collapse on us.

Finally, when Reyna was seated in the front row with her new leader, Thalia (having taken the seats of two senators who were more than happy to move), everyone turned their attention back to Frank.

'Well, guys –' he spread his arms – 'I could thank Reyna all day long. She has given so much to the legion. She's been the best mentor and friend. She can never be replaced. On the other hand, I'm up here all alone now, and we have an empty praetor's chair. So I'd like to take nominations for –'

Lavinia started the chant: 'HA-ZEL! HA-ZEL!'

The crowd quickly joined in. Hazel's eyes widened. She tried to resist when those sitting around her pulled her to her feet, but her Fifth Cohort fan club had evidently been preparing for this possibility. One of them produced a shield, which they hoisted Hazel onto like a saddle. They raised her overhead and marched her to the middle of the senate floor, turning her around and chanting, 'HAZEL! HAZEL!' Reyna clapped and yelled right along with them. Only Frank tried to remain neutral, though he had to hide his smile behind his fist.

'Okay, settle down!' he called at last. 'We have one nomination. Are there any other –?'

'HAZEL! HAZEL!'

'Any objections?'

'HAZEL! HAZEL!'

'Then I recognize the will of the Twelfth Legion. Hazel Levesque, you are hereby promoted to praetor!'

More wild cheering. Hazel looked dazed as she was dressed in Reyna's old cloak and badge of office, then led to her chair.

Seeing Frank and Hazel side by side, I had to smile.

They looked so *right* together – wise and strong and brave. The perfect praetors. Rome's future was in good hands.

'Thank you,' Hazel managed at last. 'I – I'll do everything I can to be worthy of your trust. Here's the thing, though. This leaves the Fifth Cohort without a centurion, so –'

The entire Fifth Cohort started chanting in unison: 'LAVINIA! LAVINIA!'

'What?' Lavinia's face turned pinker than her hair. 'Oh, no. I don't do leadership!'

'LAVINIA! LAVINIA!'

'Is this a joke? Guys, I –'

'Lavinia Asimov!' Hazel said with a smile. 'The Fifth Cohort read my mind. As my first act as praetor, for your unparalleled heroism in the Battle of San Francisco Bay, I hereby promote you to centurion – unless my fellow praetor has any objections?'

'None,' Frank said.

'Then come forward, Lavinia!'

To more applause and whistling, Lavinia approached the rostrum and got her new badge of office. She hugged Frank and Hazel, which wasn't the usual military protocol, but no one seemed to care. Nobody clapped louder or whistled more shrilly than Meg. I know because she left me deaf in one ear.

'Thanks, guys,' Lavinia announced. 'So, Fifth Cohort, first we're going to learn to tap-dance. Then –'

'Thank you, Centurion,' Hazel said. 'You may be seated.'

'What? I'm not kidding –'

'On to our next order of business!' Frank said, as Lavinia skipped grumpily (if that's even possible) back to her seat. 'We realize the legion will need time to heal. There's lots to be done. This summer we will rebuild. We'll speak to Lupa about getting more recruits as quickly as possible, so we can come back from this battle stronger than ever. But for now our fight is won, and we have to honour two people who made that possible: Apollo, otherwise known as Lester Papadopoulos, and his comrade, Meg McCaffrey!'

The crowd applauded so much, I doubt many people heard Meg say, 'Master, not comrade,' which was fine with me.

As we stood to accept the legion's thanks, I felt strangely uncomfortable. Now that I finally had a friendly crowd cheering for me, I just wanted to sit down and cover my head with a toga. I had done so little compared to Hazel or Reyna or Frank, not to mention all those who had died: Jason, Dakota, Don, Jacob, the Sibyl, Harpocrates . . . dozens more.

Frank raised his hand for quiet. 'Now, I know you two have another long, hard quest ahead of you. There's still one emperor who needs his *podex* kicked.'

As the crowd chuckled, I wished our next task would be as easy as Frank made it sound. Nero's podex, yes . . . but there was also the small matter of Python, my old immortal enemy, presently squatting in my old holy place of Delphi.

'And I understand,' Frank continued, 'that you two have decided to leave in the morning.'

'We *have?*' My voice cracked. I'd been imagining a week

or two relaxing in New Rome, enjoying the thermal baths, maybe seeing a chariot race.

'Shh,' Meg told me. 'Yes, we've decided.'

That didn't make me feel any better.

'Also,' Hazel chimed in, 'I know you two are planning to visit Ella and Tyson at dawn to receive prophetic help for the next stage of your quest.'

'We *are*?' I yelped. All I could think of was Aristophanes licking his nether regions.

'But tonight,' Frank said, 'we want to honour what you two have done for this camp. Without your help, Camp Jupiter might not still be here. So we would like to present you with these gifts.'

From the back of the room, Senator Larry came down the aisle carrying a big equipment bag. I wondered if the legion had bought us a ski vacation at Lake Tahoe. Larry reached the rostrum and set down the duffel bag. He rummaged out the first gift and handed it to me with a grin. 'It's a new bow!'

Larry had missed his calling as a game-show announcer.

My first thought: *Oh, cool. I need a new bow.*

Then I looked more carefully at the weapon in my hands, and I squealed in disbelief. 'This is mine!'

Meg snorted. 'Of course it is. They just gave it to you.'

'No, I mean it's *mine* mine! Originally mine, from when I was a god!'

I held up the bow for all to ooh and ahh at: a masterpiece of golden oak, carved with gilded vines that flashed in the light as if on fire. Its taut curve hummed with power. If I remembered correctly, the bowstring was woven from Celestial bronze and threads from the looms of the Fates (which . . . gosh, where did those come from? I certainly didn't steal them). The bow weighed almost nothing.

'That has been in the principia treasure room for centuries,' Frank said. 'No one can wield it. It's too heavy to draw. Believe me, I would have if I could have. Since it was originally a gift from you to the legion, it seemed only right that we give it back. With your godly strength returning, we figured you could put it to good use.'

I didn't know what to say. Usually I was against re-gifting, but in this case I was overwhelmed with gratitude. I couldn't remember when or why I'd given the legion this bow – for centuries, I'd passed them out like party favours – but I was certainly glad to have it back. I drew the string with no trouble at all. Either my strength was godlier than I realized, or the bow recognized me as its rightful owner. Oh, yes. I could do some damage with this beauty.

'Thank you,' I said.

Frank smiled. 'I'm just sorry we didn't have any replacement combat ukuleles in storage.'

From the bleachers, Lavinia grumbled, 'After I went and fixed it for him, too.'

'But,' Hazel said, carefully ignoring her new centurion, 'we do have a gift for Meg.'

Larry rummaged through his Santa bag again. He pulled out a black silk pouch about the size of a deck of playing cards. I resisted the urge to shout, HA! My gift is bigger!

Meg peeked in the pouch and gasped. 'Seeds!'

That would not have been my reaction, but she seemed genuinely delighted.

Leila, daughter of Ceres, called out from the stands, 'Meg, those are very ancient. We all got together, the camp's gardeners, and collected them for you from our greenhouse storage bins. Honestly, I'm not even sure what they'll all grow into, but you should have fun finding out! I hope you can use them against the last emperor.'

Meg was at a loss for words. Her lip quivered. She nodded and blinked her thanks.

'Okay, then!' Frank said. 'I know we ate at the funeral, but we need to celebrate Hazel's and Lavinia's promotions, wish Reyna the best on her new adventures, and wish Apollo and Meg goodbye. And, of course, we've got a belated birthday cake for Lester! Party in the mess hall!'

43

Our great opening!
Win a free Inferno trip!
And take a cupcake!

I DON'T KNOW which goodbye was the hardest.

At first light, Hazel and Frank met us at the coffee shop for one final thank-you. Then they were off to rouse the legion. They intended to get right to work on repairs to the camp to take everyone's minds off the many losses before shock could set in. Watching them walk away together down the Via Praetoria, I felt a warm certainty that the legion was about to see a new golden age. Like Frank, the Twelfth Legion Fulminata would rise from the ashes, though hopefully wearing more than just their undergarments.

Minutes later, Thalia and Reyna came by with their pack of grey wolves, their metal greyhounds and their pair of rescue pegasi. Their departure saddened me as much as my sister's, but I understood their ways, those Hunters. Always on the move.

Reyna gave me one last hug. 'I'm looking forward to a long vacation.'

Thalia laughed. 'Vacation? RARA, I hate to tell you, but we've got hard work ahead! We've been tracking the

Teumessian Fox across the Midwest for months now, and it hasn't been going well.'

'Exactly,' Reyna said. 'A vacation.' She kissed Meg on the top of her head. 'You keep Lester in line, okay? Don't let him get a big head just because he's got a nice new bow.'

'You can count on me,' Meg said.

Sadly, I had no reason to doubt her.

When Meg and I left the café for the last time, Bombilo actually cried. Behind his gruff exterior, the two-headed barista turned out to be a real sentimentalist. He gave us a dozen scones and a bag of coffee beans, and told us to get out of his sight before he started bawling again. I took charge of the scones. Meg, gods help me, took the coffee.

At the camp's gates, Lavinia waited, chewing her bubblegum while she polished her new centurion badge. 'This is the earliest I've been up in years,' she complained. 'I'm going to hate being an officer.'

The sparkle in her eyes told a different story.

'You'll do great,' Meg said.

As Lavinia bent to hug her, I noticed a stippled rash running down Ms Asimov's left cheek and neck, unsuccessfully covered by some foundation.

I cleared my throat. 'Did you perhaps sneak out last night to see Poison Oak?'

Lavinia blushed adorably. 'Well? I'm told that my centurionship makes me *very* attractive.'

Meg looked concerned. 'You're going to have to invest in some calamine lotion if you keep seeing her.'

'Hey, no relationship is perfect,' Lavinia said. 'At least

with her I know the problems right up front! We'll figure it out.'

I had no doubt she would. She hugged me and ruffled my hair. 'You'd better come back and see me. And don't die. I will kick your butt with my new dancing shoes if you die.'

'Understood,' I said.

She did one last soft-shoe routine, gestured to us like, *Over to you*, then raced off to muster the Fifth Cohort for a long day of tap-dancing.

Watching her go, I marvelled at how much had happened to all of us since Lavinia Asimov first escorted us into camp just a few days before. We had defeated two emperors and a king, which would have been a strong hand in even the most cutthroat poker game. We had put to rest the souls of a god and a Sibyl. We had saved a camp, a city and a lovely pair of shoes. Most of all, I had seen my sister, and she had restored me to good health – or what passed for good health for Lester Papadopoulos. As Reyna might say, we had added quite a bit to our 'good things' column. Now Meg and I were embarking on what might be our last quest with good expectations and hopeful spirits . . . or at least a good night's sleep and a dozen scones.

We took one final trip into New Rome, where Tyson and Ella were expecting us. Over the entrance of the book-shop, a newly painted sign proclaimed CYCLOPS BOOKS.

'Yay!' Tyson cried as we came through the doorway. 'Come in! We are having our great opening today!'

'*Grand* opening,' Ella corrected, fussing over a platter of cupcakes and a bunch of balloons at the information desk. 'Welcome to Cyclops Books and Prophecies and Also an Orange Cat.'

'That wouldn't all fit on the sign,' Tyson confided.

'It should have fitted on the sign,' Ella said. 'We need a bigger sign.'

On top of the old-fashioned cash register, Aristophanes yawned as if it was all the same to him. He was wearing a tiny party hat and an expression that said, *I am only wearing this because demigods don't have phone cameras or Instagram.*

'Customers can get prophecies for their quests!' Tyson explained, pointing at his chest, which was covered even more densely with Sibylline verse. 'They can pick up the latest books, too!'

'I recommend the 1924 *Farmer's Almanac*,' Ella told us. 'Would you like a copy?'

'Ah . . . maybe next time,' I said. 'We were told you had a prophecy for us?'

'Yep, yep.' Ella ran her finger down Tyson's ribs, scanning for the correct lines.

The Cyclops squirmed and giggled.

'Here,' Ella said. 'Over his spleen.'

Wonderful, I thought. *The Prophecy of Tyson's Spleen.*

Ella read aloud:

'*O son of Zeus the final challenge face*
The tow'r of Nero two alone ascend
Dislodge the beast that hast usurped thy place.'

I waited.

Ella nodded. 'Yep, yep, yep. That's it.' She went back to her cupcakes and balloons.

'That can't be it,' I complained. 'That makes no poetic sense. It's not a haiku. It's not a sonnet. It's not . . . Oh.'

Meg squinted at me. 'Oh, what?'

'Oh, as in *Oh, no*.' I remembered a dour young man I'd met in medieval Florence. It had been a long time ago, but I never forgot someone who invented a new type of poetry. 'It's terza rima.'

'Who?' Meg asked.

'It's a style Dante invented. In *The Inferno*. Three lines. The first and the third line rhyme. The middle line rhymes with the first line of the *next* stanza.'

'I don't get it,' Meg said.

'I want a cupcake,' Tyson announced.

'*Face* and *place* rhyme,' I told Meg. 'The middle line ends with *ascend*. That tells us that when we find the next stanza we'll know it's correct if the first line and third lines rhyme with *ascend*. Terza rima is like an endless paper chain of stanzas, all linked together.'

Meg frowned. 'But there *isn't* a next stanza.'

'Not here,' I agreed. 'Which means it must be somewhere out there . . .' I waved vaguely to the east. 'We're on a scavenger hunt for more stanzas. This is just the starting point.'

'Hmph.'

As always, Meg had summarized our predicament perfectly. It was very much *hmph*. I also did not like the fact that our new prophecy's rhyme scheme had been invented to describe a descent into hell.

'"The tower of Nero",' Ella said, repositioning her balloon display. 'New York, I bet. Yep.'

I suppressed a whimper.

The harpy was right. We would need to return to where my problems began – Manhattan, where the gleaming Triumvirate headquarters rose from downtown. After that, I would have to face the beast who had usurped my place. I suspected that line didn't mean Nero's alter ego, *the Beast*, but the actual beast Python, my ancient enemy. How I could reach him in his lair at Delphi, much less defeat him, I had no idea.

'New York.' Meg clenched her jaw.

I knew this would be the worst of homecomings for her, back to her stepfather's house of horrors, where she'd been emotionally abused for years. I wished I could spare her the pain, but I suspected she'd always known this day would come and, like most of the pain she had gone through, there was no choice but to . . . well, go through it.

'Okay,' she said, her voice resolute. 'How do we get there?'

'Oh! Oh!' Tyson raised his hand. His mouth was coated in cupcake frosting. 'I would take a rocket ship!'

I stared at him. 'Do you *have* a rocket ship?'

His expression deflated. 'No.'

I looked out of the bookshop's picture windows. In the distance, the sun rose over Mount Diablo. Our journey of thousands of miles could not begin with a rocket ship, so we'd have to find another way. Horses? Eagles? A self-driving car that was programmed not to fly off highway overpasses? We'd have to trust in the gods for some good luck. (Insert HA-HA-HA-HA-HA-HA-HA-HA-HA-HA here.) And maybe, if we were very fortunate, we could at least call on our old friends at Camp Half-Blood once we returned to New York. That thought gave me courage.

'Come on, Meg,' I said. 'We've got a lot of miles to cover. We need to find a new ride.'

GUIDE TO APOLLO-SPEAK

ab urbe condita Latin for *from the founding of the city*; for a time, Romans used the acronym AUC to mark the years since the founding of Rome

Achilles a Greek hero of the Trojan War; a nearly invulnerable warrior who slew the Trojan hero Hector outside the walls of Troy and then dragged his corpse behind his chariot

Aphrodite the Greek goddess of love and beauty. Roman form: Venus

Ares the Greek god of war; the son of Zeus and Hera, and half-brother to Athena. Roman form: Mars

Argentum Latin for *silver*; the name of one of Reyna's two automaton greyhounds that can detect lying

Argo II a flying trireme built by the Hephaestus cabin at Camp Half-Blood to take the demigods of the Prophecy of Seven to Greece

Artemis the Greek goddess of the hunt and the moon; the daughter of Zeus and Leto, and the twin of Apollo. Roman form: Diana

Asclepius   the god of medicine; son of Apollo; his temple was the healing centre of Ancient Greece

Athena   the Greek goddess of wisdom. Roman form: Minerva

aura **(*aurae*, pl.)**   wind spirit

Aurum   Latin for *gold*; the name of one of Reyna's two automaton greyhounds that can detect lying

ave   Latin for *hail*; a Roman greeting

Bacchus   the Roman god of wine and revelry; son of Jupiter. Greek form: Dionysus

ballista (ballistae, pl.)   a Roman missile siege weapon that launches a large projectile at a distant target

Bellona   a Roman goddess of war; daughter of Jupiter and Juno

Benito Mussolini   an Italian politician who became the leader of the National Fascist Party, a paramilitary organization; he ruled Italy from 1922 to 1943, first as a prime minister and then as a dictator

blemmyae   a tribe of headless people with faces in their chests

Britomartis   the Greek goddess of hunting and fishing nets; her sacred animal is the griffin

Burning Maze   a magical, puzzle-filled underground labyrinth in Southern California controlled by the Roman emperor Caligula and Medea, a Greek sorceress

cacaseca   dried poop

Caldecott Tunnel   a four-lane highway that cuts through the Berkeley Hills and connects Oakland and Orinda, California; it contains a secret middle tunnel, guarded by Roman soldiers, that leads to Camp Jupiter

Caligula the nickname of the third of Rome's emperors, Gaius Julius Caesar Augustus Germanicus, infamous for his cruelty and carnage during the four years he ruled, from 37 to 41 CE; he was assassinated by his own guard

Camp Half-Blood the training ground for Greek demigods, located in Long Island, New York

Camp Jupiter the training ground for Roman demigods, located in California, between the Oakland Hills and the Berkeley Hills

Celestial bronze a powerful magical metal used to create weapons wielded by Greek gods and their demigod children

centurion an officer in the Roman army

charmspeak a rare type of hypnotism power that chosen children of Aphrodite possess

Cicero a Roman statesman who was renowned for his public speeches

Circe a Greek goddess of magic

Circus Maximus a stadium designed for horse and chariot racing

cloaca maxima Latin for *greatest sewer*

clunis Latin for *buttocks*

cohort groups of legionnaires

Colosseum an elliptical amphitheatre built for gladiator fights, monster simulations and mock naval battles

Commodus Lucius Aurelius Commodus was the son of Roman Emperor Marcus Aurelius; he became co-emperor when he was sixteen and emperor at eighteen, when his father died; he ruled from 177 to

192 CE and was megalomaniacal and corrupt; he considered himself the New Hercules and enjoyed killing animals and fighting gladiators at the Colosseum

Cumaean Sibyl   an Oracle of Apollo from Cumae who collected her prophetic instructions for averting disaster in nine volumes but destroyed six of them when trying to sell them to Tarquinius Superbus of Rome

Cyclops (Cyclopes, pl.)   a member of a primordial race of giants, each with a single eye in the middle of his or her forehead

cynocephalus (cynocephali, pl.)   a being with a human body and a dog's head

Dante   an Italian poet of the late Middle Ages who invented terza rima; author of *The Divine Comedy*, among other works

Daphne   a beautiful naiad who attracted Apollo's attention; she transformed into a laurel tree in order to escape him

decimation   the Ancient Roman punishment for bad legions in which every tenth soldier was killed whether they were guilty or innocent

Delos   a Greek island in the Aegean Sea near Mykonos; birthplace of Apollo

Demeter   the Greek goddess of agriculture; a daughter of the Titans Rhea and Kronos. Roman form: Ceres

denarius (denarii, pl.)   a unit of Roman currency

Diana   the Roman goddess of the hunt and the moon; the daughter of Jupiter and Leto, and the twin of Apollo. Greek form: Artemis

Dionysus   Greek god of wine and revelry; the son of Zeus. Roman form: Bacchus

dryad   a spirit (usually female) associated with a certain tree

Eagle of the Twelfth   the standard of Camp Jupiter, a gold icon of an eagle on top of a pole, symbolizing the god Jupiter

Earthborn   a race of six-armed giants, also called Gegenes

Elysium   the paradise to which Greek heroes are sent when the gods grant them immortality

Erythraean Sibyl   a prophetess who presided over Apollo's Oracle at Erythrae in Ionia

eurynomos (eurynomoi, pl.)   a corpse-eating ghoul that lives in the Underworld and is controlled by Hades; the slightest cut from their claws causes a wasting disease in mortals, and when their victims die they rise again as *vrykolakai*, or zombies. If a eurynomos manages to devour the flesh of a corpse down to the bones, the skeleton will become a fierce undead warrior, many of whom serve as Hades's elite palace guards.

Euterpe   the Greek goddess of lyric poetry; one of the Nine Muses; daughter of Zeus and Mnemosyne

fasces   a ceremonial axe wrapped in a bundle of thick wooden rods with its crescent-shaped blade projecting outward; the ultimate symbol of authority in Ancient Rome; origin of the word *fascism*

Fates   three female personifications of destiny; they control the thread of life for every living thing from birth to death

faun   a Roman forest god, part goat and part man

Faunus   the Roman god of the Wild. Greek form: Pan

Field of Mars   part battlefield, part party zone, the place where drills and war games are held at Camp Jupiter

First Titan War also known as the Titanomachy, the eleven-year conflict between the Titans from Mount Othrys and the younger gods, whose future home would be Mount Olympus

Forum the centre of life in New Rome; a plaza with statues and fountains that is lined with shops and night-time entertainment venues

fuerte Spanish for *strong*

fulminata armed with lightning; a Roman legion under Julius Caesar whose emblem was a lightning bolt (*fulmen*)

Gaia the Greek earth goddess; wife of Ouranos; mother of the Titans, giants, Cyclopes and other monsters

Gamelion the seventh month of the Attic or Athenian calendar that was used in Attica, Greece, at one time; roughly equivalent to January/February on the Gregorian calendar

Germani bodyguards for the Roman Empire from the Gaulish and Germanic tribes

Greek fire a magical, highly explosive, viscous green liquid used as a weapon; one of the most dangerous substances on earth

Grove of Dodona the site of the oldest Greek Oracle, second only to Delphi in importance; the rustling of trees in the grove provided answers to priests and priestesses who journeyed to the site. The grove is located in Camp Half-Blood Forest and accessible only through the myrmekes' lair.

Hades the Greek god of death and riches; ruler of the Underworld. Roman form: Pluto

Harpocrates the Ptolemaic god of silence and secrets, a Greek adaptation of Harpa-Khruti, Horus the Child, who was often depicted in art and statuary with his finger held up to his lips, a gesture symbolizing childhood

harpy a winged female creature that snatches things

Hecate the goddess of magic and crossroads

Hector a Trojan champion who was ultimately slain by the Greek warrior Achilles and then dragged by the heels behind Achilles's chariot

Helios the Titan god of the sun; son of the Titan Hyperion and the Titaness Theia

Hephaestus the Greek god of fire, including volcanic, and of crafts and blacksmithing; the son of Zeus and Hera, and married to Aphrodite. Roman form: Vulcan

Hera the Greek goddess of marriage; Zeus's wife and sister; Apollo's stepmother. Roman form: Juno

Hermes the Greek god of travellers; guide to spirits of the dead; god of communication. Roman form: Mercury

hippocampus a sea creature with a horse's head and a fish's body

Horatius Cocles a Roman officer who, according to legend, single-handedly defended the Sublician Bridge over the Tiber River from the invading Etruscan army

Hyacinthus a Greek hero and Apollo's lover, who died while trying to impress Apollo with his discus skills

immortuos Latin for *undead*

Imperial gold a rare metal deadly to monsters, consecrated at the Pantheon; its existence was a closely guarded secret of the emperors

Iris Greek goddess of the rainbow

jiangshi   Chinese for *zombie*

Julius Caesar   a Roman politician and general whose military accomplishments extended Rome's territory and ultimately led to a civil war that enabled him to assume control of the government in 49 BCE. He was declared 'dictator for life' and went on to institute social reforms that angered some powerful Romans. A group of senators conspired against him and assassinated him on 15 March, 44 BCE.

Juno   the Roman goddess of marriage; Jupiter's wife and sister; Apollo's stepmother. Greek form: Hera

Jupiter   the Roman god of the sky and king of the gods. Greek form: Zeus

Jupiter Optimus Maximus   Latin for *Jupiter, the best and greatest god*

Khromanda (Khromandae, pl.)   a humanoid monster with grey eyes, a shaggy blond pelt and doglike teeth; it can only communicate in loud shrieks

Koronis   daughter of a king; one of Apollo's girlfriends, who fell in love with another man. A white raven Apollo had left to guard her informed him of the affair. Apollo was so angry at the raven for failing to peck out the man's eyes that he cursed the bird, scorching its feathers. Apollo sent his sister, Artemis, to kill Koronis, because he couldn't bring himself to do it.

Kronos   the Titan lord of time, evil and the harvest. He is the youngest but boldest and most devious of Gaia's children; he convinced several of his brothers to aid him in the murder of their father, Ouranos. He was also Percy Jackson's primary opponent. Roman form: Saturn

Labyrinth   an underground maze originally built on the island of Crete by the craftsman Daedalus to hold the Minotaur

lamia   Roman term for *zombie*

Lar (*Lares*, pl.)   Roman house gods

legionnaire   a member of the Roman army

Lemurian   from the ancient continent of Lemuria, now lost, but once thought to be located in the Indian Ocean

Leto   mother of Artemis and Apollo with Zeus; goddess of motherhood

libri   Latin for *books*

lictor   an officer who carried a fasces and acted as a bodyguard for Roman officials

Little Tiber   named after the Tiber River of Rome, the smaller river that forms the barrier of Camp Jupiter

Luna   the moon Titan. Greek form: Selene

Lupa   the wolf goddess, guardian spirit of Rome

maenad   a female follower of Dionysus/Bacchus, often associated with frenzy

manubalista   a Roman heavy crossbow

Mars   the Roman god of war. Greek form: Ares

Medea   a Greek enchantress, daughter of King Aeëtes of Colchis and granddaughter of the Titan sun god, Helios; wife of the hero Jason, whom she helped to obtain the Golden Fleece

Meleager   a prince who the Fates predicted would die when a piece of firewood was consumed; when his mother discovered that Meleager had killed her two brothers, she threw the wood into the fire, bringing about his death

Meliai   Greek nymphs of the ash tree, born of Gaia; they nurtured and raised Zeus in Crete

Mercury   the Roman god of travellers; guide to spirits of the dead; god of communication. Greek form: Hermes

Minerva   the Roman goddess of wisdom. Greek form: Athena

Mist   a magical force that prevents mortals from seeing gods, mythical creatures and supernatural occurrences by replacing them with things the human mind can comprehend

Mount Olympus   home of the Twelve Olympians

Mount Othrys   a mountain in central Greece; the Titans' base during the ten-year war between the Titans and the Olympians; the seat of the Titans in Marin County, California; known by mortals as Mount Tamalpais

Mount Vesuvius   a volcano near the Bay of Naples in Italy that erupted in the year 79 CE, burying the Roman city of Pompeii under ash

muster   a formal assembly of troops

myrmeke   a giant antlike creature the size of a full-grown German shepherd. Myrmekes live in enormous anthills, where they store shiny loot, like gold. They spit poison and have nearly invincible body armour and vicious mandibles.

naiad   a female water spirit

Nereid   a spirit of the sea

Nero   ruled as Roman Emperor from 54 to 58 CE; he had his mother and his first wife put to death; many believe he was responsible for setting a fire that gutted Rome, but he blamed the Christians, whom he burned on crosses; he built an extravagant new palace on the cleared land and lost support when construction expenses forced him to raise taxes; he committed suicide

New Rome both the valley in which Camp Jupiter is located and a city – a smaller, modern version of the imperial city – where Roman demigods can go to live in peace, study and retire

Nine Muses goddesses who grant inspiration for and protect artistic creation and expression; daughters of Zeus and Mnemosyne; as children, they were taught by Apollo. Their names are: Clio, Euterpe, Thalia, Melpomene, Terpsichore, Erato, Polymnia, Ourania and Calliope.

nuntius Latin for *messenger*

nymph a female deity who animates nature

Oliver Cromwell a devout Puritan and influential political figure who led the parliamentary army during the English Civil War (1642–1651)

Oracle of Delphi a speaker of the prophecies of Apollo

Ouranos the Greek personification of the sky; husband of Gaia; father of the Titans

Pan the Greek god of the Wild; the son of Hermes. Roman form: Faunus

pandos (pandai, pl.) a man with gigantic ears, eight fingers and toes, and a body covered with hair that starts out white and turns black with age

People's Park a property located off Telegraph Avenue in Berkeley, California, that was the site of a major confrontation between student protestors and police in May 1969

Phlegethon the River of Fire in the Underworld

Pluto   the Roman god of death and ruler of the Underworld. Greek form: Hades

Pomerian Line   the border of Rome

Pompeii   a Roman city that was destroyed in 79 CE when the volcano Mount Vesuvius erupted and buried it under ash

Poseidon   the Greek god of the sea; son of the Titans Kronos and Rhea, and the brother of Zeus and Hades. Roman form: Neptune

praetor   an elected Roman magistrate and commander of the army

praetorium   the living quarters for the praetors at Camp Jupiter

princeps   Latin for *first citizen* or *first in line*; the early Roman emperors adopted this title for themselves, and it came to mean *prince of Rome*

principia   the military headquarters for the praetors at Camp Jupiter

probatio   the rank assigned to new members of the legion at Camp Jupiter

Ptolemaic   relating to the Greco-Egyptian kings who ruled Egypt from 323 to 30 BCE

Python   a monstrous dragon that Gaia appointed to guard the Oracle at Delphi

River Styx   the river that forms the boundary between Earth and the Underworld

Romulus   a demigod son of Mars, twin brother of Remus; first king of Rome, who founded the city in 753 BCE

Saturnalia   an Ancient Roman festival held in December in honour of the god Saturn, the Roman equivalent of Kronos

satyr   a Greek forest god, part goat and part man

Selene   the moon Titan. Roman form: Luna

Senate   a council of ten representatives elected from the legion at Camp Jupiter

Senate House   the building at Camp Jupiter where the senators meet to discuss such issues as whether a quest should be granted or whether war should be declared

Sibyl   a prophetess

Sibylline Books   the Cumaean Sibyl's prophecies – prescriptions for warding off disasters – dating back to Ancient Roman times, collected in nine volumes, six of which were destroyed by the Sibyl herself. The three remaining books were sold to the last Roman king, Tarquin, and then lost over time. Ella the harpy read a copy of the three Books and is trying to reconstruct all the prophecies with her photographic memory and the help of Tyson the Cyclops.

sica (siccae, pl.)   a short, curved sword

Somme   a battle of World War I fought by the British and French against the Germans by the River Somme in France

Somnus   the Roman god of sleep

spatha   a Roman cavalry sword

spolia opima   one-on-one combat between two opposing leaders in a war, the ultimate display of courage for a Roman; literally, *spoils of war*

strix (strixes, pl.)   a large blood-drinking owl-like bird of ill omen

Stymphalian birds   monstrous man-eating birds with sharp

Celestial bronze beaks that can tear through flesh; they can also shoot their feathers at prey like arrows

Styx   a powerful water nymph; the eldest daughter of the sea Titan, Oceanus; goddess of the Underworld's most important river; goddess of hatred; the River Styx is named after her

sub rosa   Latin for *under the rose*, meaning sworn to secrecy

Subura   a crowded lower-class area of Ancient Rome

Summer of Love   a gathering of more than 100,000 hippies or 'flower children' in the San Francisco neighbourhood of Haight-Ashbury during the summer of 1967 to enjoy art, music and spiritual practices while also protesting the government and materialistic values

Tarquin   Lucius Tarquinius Superbus was the seventh and final king of Rome, reigning from 534 to 509 BCE, when, after a popular uprising, the Roman Republic was established

Temple Hill   the site just outside the city limits of New Rome where the temples to all the gods are located

Terminus   the Roman god of boundaries

Terpsichore   the Greek goddess of dance; one of the Nine Muses

terza rima   a form of verse consisting of three-line stanzas in which the first and third lines rhyme, and the middle line rhymes with the first and third lines of the following stanza

testudo   a tortoise battle formation in which legionnaires put their shields together to form a barrier

Teumessian Fox a gigantic fox sent by the Olympians to prey upon the children of Thebes; it is destined never to be caught

Three Graces the three charities: Beauty, Mirth and Elegance; daughters of Zeus

Tiber River the third-longest river in Italy; Rome was founded on its banks; in Ancient Rome, criminals were thrown into the river

Titans a race of powerful Greek deities, descendants of Gaia and Ouranos, who ruled during the Golden Age and were overthrown by a race of younger gods, the Olympians

trireme a Greek warship, having three tiers of oars on each side

triumvirate a political alliance formed by three parties

Trojan War according to legend, the Trojan War was waged against the city of Troy by the Achaeans (Greeks) after Paris of Troy took Helen from her husband, Menelaus, king of Sparta

Troy a pre-Roman city situated in modern-day Turkey; site of the Trojan War

Underworld the kingdom of the dead, where souls go for eternity; ruled by Hades

Vnicornes Imperant Latin for *Unicorns Rule*

vappae Latin for *spoiled wines*

ventus (venti, pl.) storm spirits

Venus the Roman goddess of love and beauty. Greek form: Aphrodite

Via Praetoria the main road into Camp Jupiter that runs from the barracks to the headquarters

vrykolakas (vrykolakai, pl.)   Greek word for *zombie*

Vulcan   the Roman god of fire, including volcanic, and of crafts and blacksmithing. Greek form: Hephaestus

Waystation   a place of refuge for demigods, peaceful monsters and Hunters of Artemis located above Union Station in Indianapolis, Indiana

Zeus   the Greek god of the sky and the king of the gods. Roman form: Jupiter

FIND OUT WHAT HAPPENS NEXT!

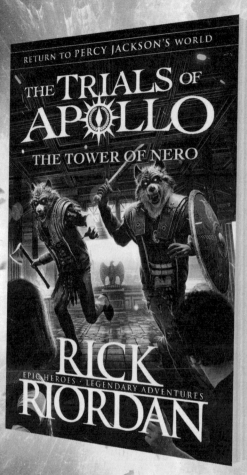

RETURN TO PERCY JACKSON'S WORLD

THE TRIALS OF APOLLO

THE TOWER OF NERO

EPIC HEROES · LEGENDARY ADVENTURES

RICK RIORDAN

Turn over to read the thrilling opening of

THE TRIALS OF APOLLO

THE TOWER OF NERO

1

Two-headed snake dude
Jamming up my quiet ride
Also, Meg's shoes stink

WHEN TRAVELLING THROUGH WASHINGTON,
DC, one expects to see a few snakes in human clothing.
Still, I was concerned when a two-headed boa constrictor
boarded our train at Union Station.

The creature had threaded himself through a blue silk
business suit, looping his body into the sleeves and trouser
legs to approximate human limbs. Two heads protruded from
the collar of his shirt like twin periscopes. He moved with
remarkable grace for what was basically an oversize balloon
animal, taking a seat at the opposite end of the coach, facing
our direction.

The other passengers ignored him. No doubt the Mist
warped their perceptions, making them see just another
commuter. The snake made no threatening moves. He
didn't even glance at us. For all I knew, he was simply a
working-stiff monster on his way home.

And yet I could not assume . . .

I whispered to Meg, 'I don't want to alarm you –'

'Shh,' she said.

Meg took the quiet-car rules seriously. Since we'd boarded,

most of the noise in the coach had consisted of Meg shushing me every time I spoke, sneezed or cleared my throat.

'But there's a monster,' I persisted.

She looked up from her complimentary Amtrak magazine, raising an eyebrow above her rhinestone-studded cat-eye glasses: *Where?*

I chin-pointed towards the creature. As our train pulled away from the station, his left head stared absently out of the window. His right head flicked its forked tongue into a bottle of water held in the loop that passed for his hand.

'It's an *amphisbaena*,' I whispered, then added helpfully, 'a snake with a head at each end.'

Meg frowned, then shrugged, which I took to mean: *Looks peaceful enough.* Then she went back to reading.

I suppressed the urge to argue. Mostly because I didn't want to be shushed again.

I couldn't blame Meg for wanting a quiet ride. In the past week, we had battled our way through a pack of wild centaurs in Kansas, faced an angry famine spirit at the World's Largest Fork in Springfield, Missouri (I did not get a selfie), and outrun a pair of blue Kentucky drakons that had chased us several times around Churchill Downs. After all that, a two-headed snake in a suit was perhaps not cause for alarm. Certainly, he wasn't bothering us at the moment.

I tried to relax.

Meg buried her face in her magazine, enraptured by an article on urban gardening. My young companion had grown taller in the months that I'd known her, but she was still compact enough to prop her red high-tops comfortably on the seatback in front of her. Comfortable for *her*, I mean, not for me or the other passengers. Meg hadn't changed her shoes since our run around the racetrack, and they looked and smelled like the back end of a horse.

At least she had traded her tattered green dress for Dollar General jeans and a green VNICORNES IMPERANT! T-shirt she'd bought at the Camp Jupiter gift shop. With her pageboy haircut beginning to grow out and an angry red zit erupting on her chin, she no longer looked like a kindergartener. She looked almost her age: a sixth-grader entering the circle of hell known as puberty.

I had not shared this observation with Meg. For one thing, I had my own acne to worry about. For another thing, as my master, Meg could literally order me to jump out of the window and I would be forced to obey.

The train rolled through the suburbs of Washington. The late-afternoon sun flickered between the buildings like the lamp of an old movie projector. It was a wonderful time of day, when a sun god should be wrapping up his work, heading to the old stables to park his chariot, then kicking back at his palace with a goblet of nectar, a few dozen adoring nymphs and a new season of *The Real Goddesses of Olympus* to binge-watch.

Not for me, though. I got a creaking seat on an Amtrak train and hours to binge-watch Meg's stinky shoes.

At the opposite end of the car, the amphisbaena still made no threatening moves . . . unless one considered drinking water from a non-reusable bottle an act of aggression.

Why, then, were my neck hairs tingling?

I couldn't regulate my breathing. I felt trapped in my window seat.

Perhaps I was just nervous about what awaited us in New York. After six months in this miserable mortal body, I was approaching my endgame.

Meg and I had blundered our way across the United States and back again. We'd freed ancient Oracles, defeated legions of monsters and suffered the untold horrors of the American public transportation system. Finally, after many tragedies, we had triumphed over two of the Triumvirate's evil emperors, Commodus and Caligula, at Camp Jupiter.

But the worst was yet to come.

We were heading back to where our troubles began – Manhattan, the base of Nero Claudius Caesar, Meg's abusive stepfather and my least favourite fiddle-player. Even if we somehow managed to defeat him, a still more powerful threat lurked in the background: my arch-nemesis, Python, who had taken up residence at my sacred Oracle of Delphi as if it were some cut-price Airbnb.

In the next few days, either I would defeat these enemies and become the god Apollo again (assuming my father Zeus allowed it) or I would die trying. One way or the other, my time as Lester Papadopoulos was coming to an end.

Perhaps it wasn't a mystery why I felt so agitated . . .

I tried to focus on the beautiful sunset. I tried not to obsess about my impossible to-do list or the two-headed snake in row sixteen.

I made it all the way to Philadelphia without having a nervous breakdown. But, as we pulled out of Thirtieth Street Station, two things became clear to me: 1) the amphisbaena wasn't leaving the train, which meant he probably wasn't a daily commuter, and 2) my danger radar was pinging more strongly than ever.

I felt *stalked*. I had the same ants-in-the-pores feeling I used to get when playing hide-and-seek with Artemis and her Hunters in the woods, just before they jumped from the bushes and riddled me with arrows. That was back when my sister and I were younger deities and could still enjoy such simple amusements.

I risked a look at the amphisbaena and nearly jumped out of my jeans. The creature was staring at me now, his four yellow eyes unblinking and . . . were they beginning to glow? Oh, no, no, no. Glowing eyes are never good.

'I need to get out,' I told Meg.

'Shh.'

'But that creature. I want to check on it. His eyes are glowing!'

Meg squinted at Mr Snake. 'No, they're not. They're *gleaming*. Besides, he's just sitting there.'

'He's sitting there suspiciously!'

The passenger behind us whispered, 'Shh!'

Meg raised her eyebrows at me: *Told you so*.

I pointed at the aisle and pouted at Meg.

She rolled her eyes, untangled herself from the hammock-like position she'd taken up and let me out. 'Don't start a fight,' she ordered.

Great. Now I would have to wait for the monster to attack before I could defend myself.

I stood in the aisle, waiting for the blood to return to my numb legs. Whoever invented the human circulatory system had done a lousy job.

The amphisbaena hadn't moved. His eyes were still fixed on me. He appeared to be in some sort of trance. Maybe he was building up his energy for a massive attack. Did amphisbaenae do that?

I scoured my memory for facts about the creature but came up with very little. The Roman writer Pliny claimed that wearing a live baby amphisbaena around your neck could assure you a safe pregnancy. (Not helpful.) Wearing its skin could make you attractive to potential partners. (Hmm. No, also not helpful.) Its heads could spit poison. Aha! That must be it. The monster was powering up for a dual-mouthed poison vomit hose-down of the train car!

What to do . . . ?

Despite my occasional bursts of godly power and skill, I couldn't count on one when I needed it. Most of the time, I was still a pitiful seventeen-year-old boy.

I could retrieve my bow and quiver from the overhead luggage compartment. Being armed would be nice. Then again, that would telegraph my hostile intentions. Meg would probably scold me for overreacting. (I'm sorry, Meg, but those eyes were *glowing*, not gleaming.)

If only I'd kept a smaller weapon, perhaps a dagger, concealed in my shirt. Why wasn't I the god of daggers?

I decided to stroll down the aisle as if I were simply on my way to the restroom. If the amphisbaena attacked, I would scream. Hopefully Meg would put down her magazine long enough to come rescue me. At least I would have forced the inevitable confrontation. If the snake didn't make a move, well, perhaps he really was harmless. Then I *would* go to the restroom, because I actually needed to.

I stumbled on my tingly legs, which didn't help my 'look casual' approach. I considered whistling a carefree tune, then remembered the whole quiet-car thing.

Four rows from the monster. My heart hammered. Those eyes were definitely glowing, definitely fixed on me. The monster sat unnaturally motionless, even for a reptile.

Two rows away. My trembling jaw and sweaty face made it hard to appear nonchalant. The amphisbaena's suit looked expensive and well-tailored. Probably, being a giant snake, he couldn't wear clothes right off the rack. His glistening brown-and-yellow diamond-pattern skin did not seem like the sort of thing one might wear to look more attractive on a dating app, unless one dated boa constrictors.

When the amphisbaena made his move, I thought I was prepared.

I was wrong. The creature lunged with incredible speed, lassoing my wrist with the loop of his false left arm. I was too surprised even to yelp. If he'd meant to kill me, I would have died.

Instead, he simply tightened his grip, stopping me in my tracks, clinging to me as if he were drowning.

He spoke in a low double hiss that resonated in my bone marrow:

> *'The son of Hades, cavern-runners' friend,*
> *Must show the secret way unto the throne.*
> *On Nero's own your lives do now depend.'*

As abruptly as he'd grabbed me, he let me go. Muscles undulated along the length of his body as if he were coming to a slow boil. He sat up straight, elongating his necks until he was almost noses-to-nose with me. The glow faded from his eyes.

'What am I do–?' His left head looked at his right head. 'How . . . ?'

His right head seemed equally mystified. It looked at me. 'Who are –? Wait, did I miss the Baltimore stop? My wife is going to kill me!'

I was too shocked to speak.

Those lines he'd spoken . . . I recognized the poetic metre. This amphisbaena had delivered a prophetic message. It dawned on me that this monster might in fact be a regular commuter who'd been possessed, hijacked by the whims of Fate because . . . Of course. He was a snake. Since ancient times, snakes have channelled the wisdom of the earth, because they live underground. A giant serpent would be especially susceptible to oracular voices.

I wasn't sure what to do. Should I apologize to him for his inconvenience? Should I give him a tip? And if he wasn't the threat that had set off my danger radar, what was?

I was saved from an awkward conversation, and the amphisbaena was saved from his wife killing him, when two crossbow bolts flew across the coach and killed him instead, pinning the poor snake's necks against the back wall.

I shrieked. Several nearby passengers shushed me.

The amphisbaena disintegrated into yellow dust, leaving nothing behind but a well-tailored suit.

I raised my hands slowly and turned as if pivoting on a land mine. I half-expected another crossbow bolt to pierce my chest. There was no way I could dodge an attack from someone with such accuracy. The best I could do was appear non-threatening. I was good at that.

At the opposite end of the coach stood two hulking figures. One was a Germanus, judging from his beard and scraggly beaded hair, his hide armour and his Imperial gold greaves and breastplate. I did not recognize him, but I'd met too many of his kind recently. I had no doubt who he worked for. Nero's people had found us.

Meg was still seated, holding her magical twin golden *sica* blades, but the Germanus had the edge of his broadsword against her neck, encouraging her to stay put.

His companion was the crossbow-shooter. She was even taller and heavier, wearing an Amtrak conductor's uniform that fooled no one – except, apparently, all the mortals on the train, who didn't give the newcomers a second look. Under her conductor's hat, the shooter's scalp was shaved on the sides, leaving a lustrous brown mane down the middle that curled over her shoulder in a braided rope. Her short-sleeved shirt stretched so tight against her muscular shoulders I thought her epaulettes and name tag would pop off. Her arms were covered with interlocking circular tattoos, and around her neck was a thick golden ring – a torque.

I hadn't seen one of those in ages. This woman was a Gaul! The realization made my stomach frost over. In the old days of the Roman Republic, Gauls were feared even more than the Germani.

She had already reloaded her double crossbow and was pointing it at my head. Hanging from her belt was a variety of other weapons: a gladius, a club and a dagger. Oh, sure, *she* got a dagger.

Keeping her eyes on me, she jerked her chin towards her shoulder, the universal sign for *C'mere or I'll shoot you*.

I calculated my odds of charging down the aisle and tackling our enemies before they killed Meg and me. Zero. My odds of cowering in fear behind a chair while Meg took care of both of them? Slightly better, but still not great.

I made my way down the aisle, my knees wobbling. The mortal passengers frowned as I passed. As near as I could figure, they thought my shriek had been a disturbance unworthy of the quiet car, and the conductor was now calling me out. The fact that the conductor wielded a crossbow and had just killed a two-headed serpentine commuter did not seem to register with them.

I reached my row and glanced at Meg, partly to make sure she was all right, partly because I was curious why she hadn't attacked. Just holding a sword to Meg's throat was normally not enough to discourage her.

She was staring in shock at the Gaul. 'Luguselwa?'

The woman nodded curtly, which told me two horrifying things: first, Meg knew her. Second, Luguselwa was her name. As she regarded Meg, the fierceness in the Gaul's eyes dialled back a few notches, from *I am going to kill everyone now* to *I am going to kill everyone soon*.

'Yes, Sapling,' said the Gaul. 'Now put away your weapons before Gunther is obliged to chop off your head.'

2

Pastries for dinner?
Your fave Lester could never.
Got to pee. Later.

THE SWORD-WIELDER LOOKED DELIGHTED.
'Chop off head?'

His name, GUNTHER, was printed on an Amtrak name tag he wore over his armour – his only concession to being in disguise.

'Not yet.' Luguselwa kept her eyes on us. 'As you can see, Gunther loves decapitating people, so let's play nice. Come along –'

'Lu,' Meg said. 'Why?'

When it came to expressing hurt, Meg's voice was a fine-tuned instrument. I'd heard her mourn the deaths of our friends. I'd heard her describe her father's murder. I'd heard her rage against her foster father, Nero, who had killed her dad and twisted her mind with years of emotional abuse.

But, when addressing Luguselwa, Meg's voice played in an entirely different key. She sounded as if her best friend had just dismembered her favourite doll for no reason and without warning. She sounded hurt, confused, incredulous – as if, in a life full of indignities, this was one indignity she never could have anticipated.

Lu's jaw muscles tightened. Veins bulged on her temples. I couldn't tell if she was angry, feeling guilty or showing us her warm-and-fuzzy side.

'Do you remember what I taught you about duty, Sapling?' Meg gulped back a sob.

'Do you?' Lu said, her voice sharper.

'Yes,' Meg whispered.

'Then get your things and come along.' Lu pushed Gunther's sword away from Meg's neck.

The big man grumbled, 'Hmph,' which I assumed was Germanic for *I never get to have any fun*.

Looking bewildered, Meg rose and opened the overhead compartment. I couldn't understand why she was going along so passively with Luguselwa's orders. We'd fought against worse odds. Who *was* this Gaul?

'That's it?' I whispered as Meg passed me my backpack. 'We're giving up?'

'Lester,' Meg muttered, 'just do what I say.'

I shouldered my pack, my bow and quiver. Meg fastened her gardening belt around her waist. Lu and Gunther did not look concerned that I was now armed with arrows and Meg with an ample supply of heirloom-vegetable seeds. As we got our gear in order, the mortal passengers gave us annoyed looks, but no one shushed us, probably because they did not want to anger the two large conductors escorting us out.

'This way.' Lu pointed with her crossbow to the exit behind her. 'The others are waiting.'

The others?

I did not want to meet any more Gauls or Gunthers, but Meg followed Lu meekly through the Plexiglas double doors.

I went next, Gunther breathing down my neck behind me, probably contemplating how easy it would be to separate my head from my body.

A gangway connected our car to the next: a loud, lurching hallway with automatic double doors on either end, a closet-size restroom in one corner, and exterior doors to port and starboard. I considered throwing myself out of one of these exits and hoping for the best, but I feared 'the best' would mean dying on impact with the ground. It was pitch-black outside. Judging from the rumble of the corrugated steel panels beneath my feet, I guessed the train was going well over a hundred miles an hour.

Through the far set of Plexiglas doors, I spied the café car: a grim concession counter, a row of booths and a half-dozen large men milling around – more Germani. Nothing good was going to happen in there. If Meg and I were going to make a break for it, this was our chance.

Before I could make any sort of desperate move, Luguselwa stopped abruptly just before the café-car doors. She turned to face us.

'Gunther,' she snapped, 'check the bathroom for infiltrators.'

This seemed to confuse Gunther as much as it did me, either because he didn't see the point, or he had no idea what an infiltrator was.

I wondered why Luguselwa was acting so paranoid. Did she worry we had a legion of demigods stashed in the restroom, waiting to spring out and rescue us? Or perhaps like me she'd once surprised a Cyclops on the porcelain throne and no longer trusted public toilets.

After a brief stare-down, Gunther muttered, 'Hmph,' and did as he was told.

As soon as he poked his head in the loo, Lu (the other Lu, not *loo*) fixed us with an intent stare. 'When we go through the tunnel to New York,' she said, 'you will both ask to use the toilet.'

I'd taken a lot of silly commands before, mostly from Meg, but this was a new low.

'Actually, I need to go now,' I said.

'Hold it,' she said.

I glanced at Meg to see if this made any sense to her, but she was staring morosely at the floor.

Gunther emerged from potty patrol. 'Nobody.'

Poor guy. If you had to check a train's toilet for infiltrators, the *least* you could hope for was a few infiltrators to kill.

'Right, then,' said Lu. 'Come on.'

She herded us into the café car. Six Germani turned and stared at us, their meaty fists full of Danishes and cups of coffee. Barbarians! Who else would eat breakfast pastries at night? The warriors were dressed like Gunther in hides and gold armour, cleverly disguised behind Amtrak name tags. One of the men, AEDELBEORT (the number-one most popular Germanic baby boy's name in 162 BCE), barked a question at Lu in a language I didn't recognize. Lu responded in the same tongue. Her answer seemed to satisfy the warriors, who went back to their coffee and Danishes. Gunther joined them, grumbling about how hard it was to find good enemies to decapitate.

'Sit there,' Lu told us, pointing to a window booth.

Meg slid in glumly. I settled in across from her, propping my longbow, quiver and backpack next to me. Lu stood within earshot, just in case we tried to discuss an escape plan. She needn't have worried. Meg still wouldn't meet my eyes.

I wondered again who Luguselwa was, and what she meant to Meg. Not once in our months of travel had Meg mentioned her. This fact disturbed me. Rather than indicating that Lu was unimportant, it made me suspect she was very important indeed.

And why a Gaul? Gauls had been unusual in Nero's Rome. By the time he became emperor, most of them had been conquered and forcibly 'civilized'. Those who still wore tattoos and torques and lived according to the old ways had been pushed to the fringes of Brittany or forced over to the British Isles. The name Luguselwa . . . My Gaulish had never been very good, but I thought it meant *beloved of the god Lugus*. I shuddered. Those Celtic deities were a strange, fierce bunch.

My thoughts were too unhinged to solve the puzzle of Lu. I kept thinking back to the poor amphisbaena she'd killed – a harmless monster commuter who would never make it home to his wife, all because a prophecy had made him its pawn.

His message had left me shaken – a verse in terza rima, like the one we'd received at Camp Jupiter:

> *O son of Zeus the final challenge face.*
> *The tow'r of Nero two alone ascend.*
> *Dislodge the beast that hast usurped thy place.*

Yes, I had memorized the cursed thing.

Now we had our second set of instructions, clearly linked to the previous set, because the first and third lines rhymed with *ascend*. Stupid Dante and his stupid idea for a never-ending poem structure:

> *The son of Hades, cavern-runners' friend,*
> *Must show the secret way unto the throne.*
> *On Nero's own your lives do now depend.*

I knew a son of Hades: Nico di Angelo. He was probably still at Camp Half-Blood on Long Island. If he had some secret way to Nero's throne, he'd never get the chance to show us unless we escaped this train. How Nico might be a 'cavern-runners' friend', I had no idea.

The last line of the new verse was just cruel. We were presently surrounded by 'Nero's own', so of course our lives depended on them. I wanted to believe there was more to that line, something positive . . . maybe tied to the fact that Lu had ordered us to go to the bathroom when we entered the tunnel to New York. But, given Lu's hostile expression and the presence of her seven heavily caffeinated and sugar-fuelled Germanus friends, I didn't feel optimistic.

I squirmed in my seat. Oh, *why* had I thought about the bathroom? I *really* needed to go now.

Outside, the illuminated billboards of New Jersey zipped by: ads for auto dealerships where you could buy an impractical race car; injury lawyers you could employ to blame the other drivers once you crashed that race car; casinos where you could gamble away the money you won from the injury lawsuits. The great circle of life.

The station-stop for Newark Airport came and went. Gods help me, I was so desperate I considered making a break for it. In *Newark*.

Meg stayed put, so I did, too.

The tunnel to New York would be coming up soon. Perhaps, instead of asking to use the restroom, we could spring into action against our captors . . .

Lu seemed to read my thoughts. 'It's a good thing you surrendered. Nero has three other teams like mine on this train alone. *Every* passage – every train, bus and flight into Manhattan has been covered. Nero's got the Oracle of Delphi on his side, remember. He knew you were coming tonight. You were never going to get into the city without being caught.'

Way to crush my hopes, Luguselwa. Telling me that Nero had his ally Python peering into the future for him, using *my* sacred Oracle against me . . . Harsh.

Meg, however, suddenly perked up, as if something Lu said gave her hope. 'So how is it *you're* the one who found us, Lu? Just luck?'

Lu's tattoos rippled as she flexed her arms, the swirling Celtic circles making me seasick.

'I *know* you, Sapling,' she said. 'I know how to track you. There is no luck.'

I could think of several gods of luck who would disagree with that statement, but I didn't argue. Being a captive had dampened my desire for small talk.

Lu turned to her companions. 'As soon as we get to

Penn Station, we deliver our captives to the escort team. I want no mistakes. No one kills the girl or the god unless it's absolutely necessary.'

'Is it necessary now?' Gunther asked.

'No,' Lu said. 'The *princeps* has plans for them. He wants them alive.'

The princeps. My mouth tasted bitterer than the bitterest Amtrak coffee. Being marched through Nero's front door was *not* how I'd planned to confront him.

One moment we were rumbling across a wasteland of New Jersey warehouses and dockyards. The next, we plunged into darkness, entering the tunnel that would take us under the Hudson River. On the intercom, a garbled announcement informed us that our next stop would be Penn Station.

'I need to pee,' Meg announced.

I stared at her, dumbfounded. Was she *really* going to follow Lu's strange instructions? The Gaul had captured us and killed an innocent two-headed snake. Why would Meg trust her?

Meg pressed her heel hard on the top of my foot.

'Yes,' I squeaked. 'I also need to pee.' For me, at least, this was painfully true.

'Hold it,' Gunther grumbled.

'I *really* need to pee.' Meg bounced up and down.

Lu heaved a sigh. Her exasperation did not sound faked. 'Fine.' She turned to her squad. 'I'll take them. The rest of you stay here and prepare to disembark.'

None of the Germani objected. They'd probably heard

enough of Gunther's complaints about potty patrol. They began shoving last-minute Danishes into their mouths and gathering up their equipment as Meg and I extracted ourselves from our booth.

'Your gear,' Lu reminded me.

I blinked. Right. Who went to the bathroom without their bow and quiver? That would be stupid. I grabbed my things.

Lu herded us back into the gangway. As soon as the double doors closed behind her, she murmured, '*Now.*'

Meg bolted for the quiet car.

'Hey!' Lu shoved me out of the way, pausing long enough to mutter, 'Block the door. Decouple the coaches,' then raced after Meg.

Do what *now?*

Two scimitars flashed into existence in Lu's hands. Wait – she had Meg's swords? No. Just before the end of the gangway, Meg turned to face her, summoning her own blades, and the two women fought like demons. They were *both dimachaeri*, the rarest form of gladiator? That must mean – I didn't have time to think about what that meant.

Behind me, the Germani were shouting and scrambling. They would be through the doors any second.

I didn't understand exactly what was happening, but it occurred to my stupid slow mortal brain that perhaps, just perhaps, Lu was trying to help us. If I didn't block the doors like she'd asked, we would be overrun by seven angry, sticky-fingered barbarians.

I slammed my foot against the base of the double doors. There were no handles. I had to press my palms against the panels and push them together to keep them shut.

Gunther tackled the doors at full speed, the impact nearly dislocating my jaw. The other Germani piled in behind him. My only advantages were the narrow space they were in, which made it difficult for them to combine their strength, and the Germani's own lack of sense. Instead of working together to prise the doors apart, they simply pushed and shoved against one another, using Gunther's face as a battering ram.

Behind me, Lu and Meg jabbed and slashed, their blades furiously clanging against one another.

'Good, Sapling,' Lu said under her breath. 'You remember your training.' Then louder, for the sake of our audience: 'I'll kill you, foolish girl!'

I imagined how this must look to the Germani on the other side of the Plexiglas: their comrade Lu, trapped in combat with an escaped prisoner, while I attempted to hold them back. My hands were going numb. My arm and chest muscles ached. I glanced around desperately for an emergency door lock, but there was only an emergency OPEN button. What good was that?

The train roared on through the tunnel. I estimated we had only minutes before we pulled into Penn Station, where Nero's 'escort team' would be waiting. I did not wish to be escorted.

Decouple the coaches, Lu had told me.

How was I supposed to do that, especially while holding the gangway doors shut? I was no train engineer! Choo-choos were more Hephaestus's thing.

I looked over my shoulder, scanning the gangway. Shockingly, there was no clearly labelled switch that would allow a passenger to decouple the train. What was wrong with Amtrak?

There! On the floor, a series of hinged metal flaps overlapped, creating a safe surface for passengers to walk across when the train twisted and turned. One of those flaps had been kicked open, perhaps by Lu, exposing the coupling underneath.

Even if I could reach it from where I stood, which I couldn't, I doubted I would have the strength and dexterity to stick my arm down there, cut the cables and prise open the clamp. The gap between the floor panels was too narrow, the coupling too far down. Just to hit it from here, I would have to be the world's greatest archer!

Oh. Wait . . .

Against my chest, the doors were bowing under the weight of seven barbarians. An axe blade jutted through the rubber lining next to my ear. Turning around so I could shoot my bow would be madness.

Yes, I thought hysterically. *Let's do that*.

I bought myself a moment by pulling out an arrow and jabbing it through the gap between the doors. Gunther howled. The pressure eased as the clump of Germani readjusted. I flipped around so my back was to the Plexiglas, one heel wedged against the base of the doors. I fumbled with my bow and managed to nock an arrow.

My new bow was a god-level weapon from the vaults of Camp Jupiter. My archery skills had improved dramatically over the last six months. Still, this was a terrible idea.

It was impossible to shoot properly with one's back against a hard surface. I simply couldn't draw the bowstring far enough.

Nevertheless, I fired. The arrow disappeared into the gap in the floor, completely missing the coupling.

'Penn Station in just a minute,' said a voice on the PA system. 'Doors will open on the left.'

'Running out of time!' Lu shouted. She slashed at Meg's head. Meg jabbed low, nearly impaling the Gaul's thigh.

I shot another arrow. This time the point sparked against the clasp, but the train cars remained stubbornly connected.

The Germani pounded against the doors. A Plexiglas panel popped out of its frame. A fist reached through and grabbed my shirt.

With a desperate shriek, I lurched away from the doors and shot one last time at a full draw. The arrow sliced through the cables and slammed into the clasp. With a shudder and a groan, the coupling broke.

Germani poured into the gangway as I leaped across the widening gap between the coaches. I almost skewered myself on Meg's and Lu's scimitars, but I somehow managed to regain my footing.

I turned as the rest of the train shot into the darkness at seventy miles an hour, seven Germani staring at us in disbelief and yelling insults I will not repeat.

For another fifty feet, our decoupled section of the train rolled forward of its own momentum, then slowed to a stop. Meg and Lu lowered their weapons. A brave passenger from the quiet car dared to stick her head out and ask what was going on.

I shushed her.

Lu glared at me. 'Took you long enough, Lester. Now let's move before my men come back. You two just went from *capture alive* to *proof of death is acceptable*.'

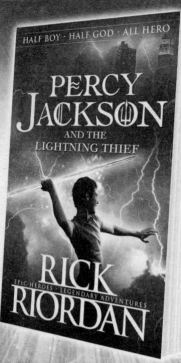

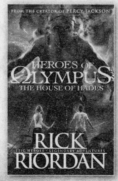

Have you gone on all the quests?

Fought all the monsters?

Done all the world-saving?

Discover the complete collection of adventures
from genius storyteller Rick Riordan . . .

THE WORLD OF PERCY JACKSON

PERCY JACKSON

THE GREEK GODS ARE ALIVE AND KICKING!

Percy is having a pretty ordinary day, until he learns he's the son
of Poseidon, god of the sea. Now he must travel to Camp Half-Blood –
a secret base dedicated to the training of young demigods.

There are missions to complete, monsters to defeat and a whole lot
of universe to save. Welcome to the world of Percy Jackson . . .

1. PERCY JACKSON AND THE LIGHTNING THIEF

2. PERCY JACKSON AND THE SEA OF MONSTERS

3. PERCY JACKSON AND THE TITAN'S CURSE

4. PERCY JACKSON AND THE BATTLE OF THE LABYRINTH

5. PERCY JACKSON AND THE LAST OLYMPIAN

HEROES OF OLYMPUS

THOUGHT THE PERCY JACKSON ADVENTURES WERE OVER? YOU COULDN'T BE MORE WRONG . . .

Sometimes a handful of half-bloods isn't quite enough to save humanity.
Sometimes you need a whole lot more.

Introducing Jason, Piper and Leo.

Along with Percy Jackson and his friends, they must team up to stop
a new and powerful threat from destroying the world.

THE TRIALS OF APOLLO

PERCY JACKSON AND THE DEMIGODS HAVE TRIED SAVING HUMANITY. NOW IT'S TIME FOR A GOD TO HAVE A GO . . .

Bad news for the god Apollo – he's been banished
to Earth, stuck in the body of a teenage boy.

Help from Percy Jackson is at hand, but if Apollo wants to
regain his godly form, there will be harrowing trials to face
and a trio of Roman emperors to defeat.

IT'S NOT JUST PERCY JACKSON AND FRIENDS SAVING THE WORLD.

Discover a whole new host of heroes,
villains and gods . . .

THE GODS OF ANCIENT EGYPT
ARE FAR FROM DEAD AND BURIED . . .

Since their mother's death, siblings Carter and
Sadie Kane have become near strangers.

Until one night their brilliant Egyptologist father unleashes the
Egyptian god Set, who banishes him to oblivion.

Now only Carter and Sadie can save the day, as they travel
the globe and battle the gods of Ancient Egypt.

THE VIKING MYTHS ARE TRUE. THOR IS REAL.
THE GODS OF ASGARD ARE PREPARING FOR WAR . . .

Magnus Chase has been killed in battle with a fire giant, resurrected in Valhalla
and chosen to be a warrior of the Norse god Odin.

He's had better days.

Now the gods of Asgard are readying themselves for Ragnarok –
the Norse doomsday – and Magnus has a leading role . . .

WANT MORE FROM YOUR FAVOURITE HEROES AND GODS?

Discover training manuals, character guides,
short stories and so much more . . .

THE WORLD OF PERCY JACKSON

Diaries of your favourite heroes, files on the scariest monsters, and an in-depth guide to Camp Half-Blood. It's all here.

THE DEMIGOD FILES
THE DEMIGOD DIARIES
CAMP HALF-BLOOD CONFIDENTIAL
PERCY JACKSON AND THE GREEK GODS
PERCY JACKSON AND THE GREEK HEROES

THE TRIALS OF APOLLO

Find out what's really behind all the strange things happening in Camp Jupiter through Claudia's journal entries. Warning: secrets will be uncovered.

CAMP JUPITER CLASSIFIED

THE KANE CHRONICLES

These companion guides and incredible short stories give readers the inside scoop on the Kane Chronicles.

THE KANE CHRONICLES SURVIVAL GUIDE
BROOKLYN HOUSE MAGICIAN'S MANUAL

DEMIGODS AND MAGICIANS: THREE STORIES
FROM THE WORLD OF PERCY JACKSON AND THE KANE
CHRONICLES

MAGNUS CHASE

Travel the Nine Worlds with your favourite characters and enjoy the ultimate companion guide to Magnus Chase and the gods of Asgard.

HOTEL VALHALLA GUIDE TO THE NORSE WORLDS
9 FROM THE NINE WORLDS

RICK RIORDAN, dubbed 'storyteller of the gods' by *Publishers Weekly*, is the author of five *New York Times* number-one bestselling middle-grade series with millions of copies sold throughout the world: Percy Jackson, the Heroes of Olympus and the Trials of Apollo, based on Greek and Roman mythology; the Kane Chronicles, based on Egyptian mythology; and Magnus Chase, based on Norse mythology. His Greek myth collections, *Percy Jackson and the Greek Gods* and *Percy Jackson and the Greek Heroes*, were *New York Times* number-one bestsellers as well.

Rick lives in Boston, Massachusetts, with his wife and two sons.

Follow him on Twitter @camphalfblood.
To learn more about him and his books, visit:

www.rickriordan.co.uk